Heavy

A Dark High School Romance

Sarah JD, Sarah Jane Duncan

For Shane, Renaye, Jordan and Trista
who breathe life into my world!
And for my friends and family who have
supported me, and my book baby.

Content Warning

This book contains adult themes and
scenes which may cause trigger reactions
for some readers, which include, but
aren't limited to:
*Abusive and sexually abusive situations,
non-consensual acts, demeaning acts,
emotional and physical blackmail, drug and
alcohol use, and foul language.*

PLEASE NOTE:
*This book is written in Australian English,
therefore some words will appear slightly
different for my beloved US readers*

HEAVY PLAYLIST

https://open.spotify.com/playlist/0M2Jg5lbhIMSh6p6
wzaOyB?si=616afced760641a6

Heavy (feat. Rain Paris) - Fame on Fire, Rain Paris
idontwannabeyouanymore - Billie Eilish
Take the Bullets Away (feat. Lacey Sturm) - We As Human, Lacey Sturm
King of the Clouds - Panic! At The Disco
Dance With The Devil - Breaking Benjamin
Animal I Have Become - Three Days Grace
Courtesy Call - Thousand Foot Krutch
Fire Uo The Night - New Medicine
Failure - Breaking Benjamin
Pain - Three Days Grace
Please - Staind
Comatose - Skillet
Down with the Sickness - Disturbed
lovely (with Khalid) - Billie Eilish, Khalid
Take This - Staind
when the party's over - Billie Eilish
Monster - Skillet
Never Too Late - Three Days Grace
Vermilion, Pt. 2 - Slipknot
So Far Away - Staind
listen before i go - Billie Eilish
Angels Fall - Breaking Benjamin
Without Me - Fame on Fire
Hero - Skillet
I Am Machine - Three Days Grace
Right Here - Staind
Snuff - Slipknot
Until The End - Breaking Benjamin
Awake and Alive - Skillet
Gone Forever - Three Days Grace

One

My bedroom door rattles on its hinges, threatening to fly open as my good for nothing half brother beats it from the other side. My lungs betray me, seizing up so no air can get in, and I slap my hand to my chest a couple of times, trying to force them to work. A cough escapes me as my body fights to breathe past my fear, and I hurry to my window, my fingers fumbling as I struggle to get it open fast enough.

"Open the fucking door, Ali!" he bellows, and a squeak escapes me as I panic and jump in fright, worried he's about to break through.

"Shit. Shit. Shit." I whisper, feeling hot tears burn my eyes before I finally manage to get the window open.

Hurrying to climb over the sill, I slip out onto the rooftop, desperate to get away before it's too late.

Even though my heart is thrashing against my ribs, being out here in the open helps me to think clearer, knowing he can't trap me. I carefully balance my way across the tiled roof as fast as I can, desperate to escape without notice before I climb down over the edge.

This has been my escape route for a little while now. It used to be my way of sneaking out to go and have fun with my friends. I never imagined I'd have to use it to flee, but that all changed when my half brother moved in unexpectedly, and the strange boy I used to know growing up, is now a sinister man.

As my feet land on solid ground, I can still hear him beating on my door, yelling. It's not as loud out here, but it makes me wonder if our neighbours have heard the noises that come from my house lately. Or perhaps they are none the wiser, thinking us to be the happy family my mum tries to portray.

My phone vibrating in my pocket reminds me that Abbey keeps calling, so I hurry along the side of my house and out onto the path before I call her back.

"Lex. Where are you? I've been trying to get a hold of you for ages."

"Sorry. I must have fallen asleep." I lie as I hurry to the end of my street, checking over my shoulder to see if Mike is coming.

"Only you would fall asleep when everyone else is already half drunk at a party." Abbey laughs, and I laugh too, glad she can't see my face and the lack of smile on it.

"I'm on my way. I'll be there in twenty minutes."

"Okay. You'll find me at the beer pong table. Or by the fire, although that's close to the shed where all the stoners are sucking on bongs which I'd prefer to avoid."

This time, I do smile, although it's only slight. "You already sound drunk Abs. Maybe steer clear of the beer pong?"

"No way. I'm the champion." She sing-songs. "Oh, I have to go. It's my turn. Byyyye."

The call disconnects, and I stop on the path, talking in a deep breath.

Fuck.

How the hell has my life come to this?

Looking down at myself, I shake my head. I'm still wearing my skinny jeans and hoodie from earlier, and I can only imagine my blonde hair is a mess. The dress I was going to wear was in the laundry, but I couldn't get to it. As soon as Mike saw me, he was in my face, too close, behaving too fucking inappropriate that my only other option was to get back into my room and hope he'd go away.

He didn't.

My hands are still trembling even though my heart rate has eased, and all I want to do is go to the party and pretend for the night that I'm just like all the other seventeen-year-olds there. I need to pretend I'm happy. That I'm carefree.

After all, it's what everyone expects from me. Lexi West. The pretty blonde popular girl with a perfect life.

They don't know.

No one knows. Not even my best friend, Abbey.

Needing to keep moving in case Mike discovers me missing and decides to come looking, I press forward, taking the back streets where I can, and make my way to the party.

It's at Tasha's house, one of my friends. And I mean that loosely. Tasha is in our circle of friends, but I endure her more than I like her, which I know is fucked up, but if I want to hang out with my best friend Abbey, I need to learn to deal with Tasha.

The party has been going for hours now, everyone is completely smashed, and I get hugs from people I don't even know as I weave through the crowd in search of my best friend. Unfortunately, when I find her, she's a little preoccupied in a dark corner with Daniel. Her new boyfriend.

Great.

"Lexi!" Allison runs into me, throwing her arms around my neck and sending us both backwards, tumbling to the floor from the force.

"Jesus, Allison. How drunk are you?" I ask, trying to shove her off me, and she rolls off, laughing before Tasha stumbles over and pulls her up off the floor.

"What are you wearing?" Tasha asks, screwing her face up, not at all trying to hide her disgust at my clothing choice. "You've known about my party for months, Lexi. Why the hell are you wearing that?" She points a claw-like finger at me.

"What's wrong with wanting to wear pants and a hoodie?" I ask, standing up after she doesn't even bother to offer me a hand up.

Her brows shoot high, and she cocks her hip, ignoring Allison who runs off to hug-tackle some random guy across the room.

"You look like a homeless person. Jesus, Lexi. My party has standards. If you're going to dress like a pothead, you may as well go and hang out with them."

My cheeks heat at her insult, and my top lip threatens to sneer at her, but I hold it back. Like always, I keep my real feelings in.

"You know what?" I step up into her personal space. "I think I will go and join the potheads."

I want to say that at least they aren't stuck up bitches like you, but I don't. I just turn my back on her exasperated expression and push my way through the crowd, heading to the shed where the stoners hang out.

I don't know why I do it. I don't know why I go inside. Or why I snatch a bong off some guy who starts cackling at me when I press it to my mouth and suck the damp smoke in. And I don't know why I drop my arse onto the old, tattered couch and accept a joint off some other random guy I don't know.

All I know is that I just want all the fucking noise in my head, and in my life, to stop.

Just for a while.

As I sit in the shed, with a haze of smoke hovering in the air, I finally relax and just be. I drag back on the joint, loving the burn as it seeps into my lungs, and the longer I hold it, the lighter I feel.

In fact, everything feels lighter now as I continue to smoke the joint. People talk to me, but I don't acknowledge them, and I don't even care.

Time slows, or maybe it speeds up. Lights are brighter but then they are duller. Sounds are muffled and it all just seems so easy.

It's peaceful. Moving, walking, it feels both harder and easier at the same time. I feel tired, yet wide awake, and the stars in the sky look huge.

Wait? The stars?

When did I come outside?

It doesn't matter. It's nice out here. Less people. No one around.

Where did everyone go? Is the party over?

I glance around, fairly sure the streetlights I'm looking at are lining a different road to where Tasha's house is.

Did I leave the party?

There's someone here. I don't feel alone. I can't really see them, though. He—I'm pretty sure it's a he—is more like a shadow. I can't seem to see his face.

Smashing glass echoes through the silence, forcing me to sharpen my attention. It's a hard task, given the fuzzy feeling in my head and the way my eyes struggle to focus. I blink fiercely, trying to clear my vision, my eyes locking on to the blurry shape of a hand pulling back through the now shattered window. As the scene before me comes into clearer view, the moonlight filtering from above allows me to see tiny droplets of blood splattered across the pale skin of a dainty hand.

Ouch, that has to hurt.

Normally, the sight of blood turns my stomach, especially when it's not mine. Right now, though, I find the way the crimson beads over the ivory skin quite fascinating. I watch, transfixed, as the molten juice starts to ooze and trickle over my hand and down my wrist.

Wait...

My hand?

My wrist?

What?

"You're such a badass!" A deep voice interrupts me. "A sexy badass!"

Forgetting about my hand, I drop it lazily to my side and turn to whoever dared to interrupt me while I examine the nectar seeping from my body. The shadow I saw earlier is here again. Definitely a guy. Why is he here, and where did he come from? Where did we both come from? And where are we exactly?

He's laughing at something he said as he walks away from me, and the view of his broad shoulders gives me no clue as to who he is. I should probably ask him, but the fuzziness in my head is making me too tired, and I just can't be bothered talking.

Through the haze clouding my eyes, I watch as the guy climbs through the smashed window into the building, being careful to avoid the jagged shards of glass protruding from the frame. He disappears into the darkened room, which kind of resembles a classroom. It's hard to tell from outside in the shade of night and my lacking ability to see straight. The room doesn't look as vibrant and as full of life as a classroom normally would, especially with the artworks lining the walls that are now devoid of colour. In this light, everything appears to be monochrome.

My feet shuffle on the concrete path just outside the building and I curiously watch the guy through the shattered windows as he lifts his leg and kicks a few chairs out of his way. Walking up to the wall of art, he laughs and rips piece by piece down, tearing some in the process as they float down to the floor.

I frown.

This isn't funny. I know I should tell him to stop, but I don't have the energy to speak.

Once he finishes destroying the artwork, he turns and stalks towards the chairs he kicked out of his path. I still can't see his face from where I stand outside, and I squint, hoping it will help. I can't tell if the reason why I'm unable to see him is because the night shadows his features from me, or if my head is really just that fucked up. I can, however, make out his form, which is now lifting a chair over his head.

What the hell is he doing now?

I get an answer to my silent question when he hurls the chair towards the bank of windows next to where I'm standing.

Time slows to sloth speed. The moment the chair leaves the guy's grip, and sails across the room seems to take forever. The intense shattering of glass fills the silent night again as the chair explodes through it, coming to a crashing thud as it lands outside on the concrete path below.

The boy jumps and fist-pumps the air, calling out a loud "whoop." He then turns his sights on me, his face shadowed in darkness except for the white of his teeth spreading into a smile.

"Your turn, Lexi," he encourages.

How does he know my name? Do I know him? His voice isn't familiar to me. Surely, I would remember his voice if I knew him. Come to think of it, why am I here again?

I should care about these things, I know, but I don't. My body feels heavy and numb, yet light as a feather, and if a bed were close by, I'm pretty sure I could fall asleep before my head even hit the pillow.

Even as I think this, my mind flutters to what the guy did, and oddly enough, the thought of it makes my heart race a little. Throwing the chair through the window did kind of look like fun. If there's one thing I like, it's fun.

The chair that was hurled through the window only moments before catches my eye, and I find myself approaching it. It's laying on its side on the path surrounded by shards of glass. Reaching down, I clasp the cold metal legs and lift the chair above my head. Turning towards the windows that still remain intact, I toss the chair with a grunt, keeping my eyes on it as it sails through the window, before tumbling to the floor inside the classroom. The sound of the shattering glass sends a spike of adrenaline rushing through my veins while the guy repeats his jumping and fist-pumping as he leaps out through the glassless window.

"Damn, girl, that was sick!" He appears in front of me, and the moonlight touches the side of his face, giving me a better glimpse of dirty blonde hair and brown eyes. He has a faint smattering of freckles across his nose that makes him look more boyish than manly.

Who is this person?

I tilt my head to study his familiar face, but I keep coming up blank. My brain flutters with the knowledge, but it's not playing fair and won't divulge the secret.

"Who are you?" My voice rasps, feeling dry and unused.

Confusion flits across his face briefly. Then he throws his head back as he laughs hysterically. "Oh man, Lex, you're baked as fuck!" His grin is wide and pleased as he places his hands on my shoulders, turning me into the moonlight to examine my eyes.

I shrug him off, not wanting him to touch me. I'm not sure why I don't want him to touch me. He seems to know who I am, and he's decent looking enough, but for some reason, I can't stand the thought of his hands on me.

A loud gurgle rumbles in the silence between us, and then he laughs, throwing his head back again.

"Damn girl, was that your tummy? You hungry?"

I shrug, "Yeah, I could eat."

"Me too. Let's crash the canteen before security turns up." The boy nudges my shoulder, and we quickly lose interest in the classroom we just demolished.

A canteen with food sounds like the best idea, so I nod and follow him as he leads the way. As I stagger slowly behind, I gaze lazily up at the stars, trying to tune out his annoying yapping. After stumbling a few times, I reluctantly draw my eyes away from the twinkling sky and look around at my surroundings.

There's an Australian flag floating in the breeze, and it looks familiar, much like the one we have at school. Come to think of it, this place really does look like a school. I'm sure I'd be able to confirm that if my fuzzy vision wasn't making it so hard to see clearly.

If this is a school, then why am I here at night? And why am I with this weirdo whose incessant yapping is irritating the crap out of me? He won't shut up. I don't know what he's saying, and while I want to tell him to stop, I can't find it in me to bother. My eyes are too tired, and my stomach won't stop growling at me.

Am I getting *hangry*?

The stupid thought makes me giggle as we come to a stop in front of two glass doors with the word 'Canteen' displayed overhead.

Oh good. Food.

"Shit, the glass looks thicker than the classroom windows. I'll break my hand if I try to smash it." The boy, who I shall name Weirdo, has a point, although his head looks thick enough to do the job. I giggle again, and he grins at me like he's the one who just thought that hilarious thought, even though he has no idea what's going on inside my head.

"I love this version of you, Lexi. Who would have known such a bad girl was inside this gorgeous prim and proper body?" He chuckles, giving me a lopsided smirk, which I think is meant to come across as sexy, but it looks the opposite and just makes me laugh again.

Eventually deciding that food is more important than talking to this weird guy, I look around the dark yard to find something to help us break through the doors. Keeping in line with the theme of the night, I spot a chair under the covered eating area and walk lazily over to collect it. Lifting it seems like too much effort, so I drag it, and the normally irritating sound of metal on concrete doesn't bother me in the slightest.

As I approach Weirdo, I witness idiocy at its finest when he tries to take matters into his own hands by repeatedly ramming the glass doors with a flimsy tree branch. Backing up, he charges towards the doors with a grunt and nearly face plants the concrete ground when the branch snaps.

The laugh rips from my mouth before I have time to stop it, and his reddened face turns to me in fury, which only makes me laugh harder. Dusting himself off, he starts towards me, his hands balling into fists at his sides.

I get the impression he thinks he's going to intimidate me.

Huh! Not likely. I have bigger monsters than him in my life.

I repeat my earlier actions and lift the chair above my head. Weirdo, using his brain for once, freezes in place, his heated face turning worried. Ignoring him, I lunge with force, letting the chair fly from my grip. Weirdo's eyes widen right before he drops to the ground to duck out of the way as the chair sails mere inches from his head, before the knowing sound of smashing glass greets us again, and I grin.

Even though I don't seem to feel much at the moment, I feel my grin. That was legit good!

"Fuck, Lexi!" Weirdo hisses as he rises and turns to me. At first, I think he's going to try and act angry and intimidating again, but he surprises me and laughs. "Seriously, can I kiss you?"

I look at him, now advancing on me with a determined look in his eyes. I don't answer, and before I can react, his hands delve into my hair, tugging my head close as his lips close over mine.

I kiss him back... I think. It's hard to tell because I feel nothing. My face is numb, and my mind is fuzzy. I don't typically let random guys kiss me, but then again, I don't typically break into schools and throw chairs through windows, either. I'm not sure why I'm doing any of this. I can't remember how I got here. My memory is nothing but a haze of fog.

"You're a great kisser." Weirdo draws away, his eyes flicking back down to my lips as he licks his own.

I think about his words and realise I must have been kissing him back. It seems strange that I didn't feel it.

I shrug, not caring if I'm a good kisser or not, and step around him to climb through the broken glass doors of the school canteen. My food of choice is chocolate cake and juice boxes. He chooses potato chips and a can of cola. We don't speak now that food is in our hands and filling our mouths, and when we are all stocked up, I follow him out of the canteen.

Walking in silence, we're both too ecstatic with the food we've scored to care much about anything. I probably should care about a lot of things right now.

Like who the hell he is, and if kissing him is something I would normally do. I should probably care that we were just in a school instead of the party. And as we make our way towards the back of the school, where the shadows are at their darkest, I should care more that at any point, I could run into my brother, and if that happens, I should really fucking care about what he will do to me.

Two

My mouth feels like a desert, dry to the bone and gritty. Groaning, I try to force my heavy eyes open, knowing too well that I'm going to regret it. Still, I try. Cracking one eye, the blinding light of day shoots a sharp pain into the side of my head, forcing my lids shut again.

Shit, this is going to be a killer hangover.

I inhale a few deep breaths, willing the pain to ease, and when it does, I try again, this time prying both lids open. The brightness sends more stabbing pain into my skull, but I force myself to keep my eyes open this time. Blinking slowly, my vision begins to clear, and with it, more sharp pain pulses behind my eyes in the form of a throbbing headache.

Today is going to suck big time.

I shrink back a little, noticing a sleeping face partially draped in white blonde hair in front of me. It only takes me a moment to recognise this sleeping beauty, and I grin. My best friend Abbey is snoring quietly next to me.

She doesn't believe she's a snorer. I should get my phone out and record her, and I would but Abbey's payback is a bitch. She'd make it her mission to return the favour, which will only lead to me embarrassing myself.

Taking in her unconscious face, she looks a little flushed but peaceful, and I grin at the trail of drool spilling from her pink lips. If I film this, she will kill me. I know that much, but it's hard to find self-control in this moment. Luckily, Abbey is saved by the pounding in my head. Getting evidence of her sleeping habits will have to wait for another day.

Glancing around, I notice we aren't in Abbey's bed. Like me, she has a double bed, which gives us more personal space when we have sleepovers. This bed, however, is nowhere near big enough to be a double. As close as our friendship is, sleeping practically on top of each other isn't something we tend to do.

Needing more space, I try to roll over and nearly fall out of the narrow bed we occupy. The jarring movement causes a jackhammer to go off in my head, so I suck in slow, deep breaths to try and get the pain under control. When I'm sure my head won't splinter open, I shuffle over onto my side to take in my surroundings.

We are on the bottom of a single bunk, and I can hear faint snoring coming from above. Slowly pushing myself up, I swing my legs over the side of the bed but stop quickly when my feet nearly land on two sleeping bodies on the floor below.

Jesus, how many people are crammed into this tiny bedroom?

Maddie and Kyle are a tangled mess of arms and legs on the floor below me and are barely covered with a fleece blanket. I'm thankful they have clothes on since they typically spend most of their time trying to rip them off each other while playing tonsil hockey.

A glance around the room tells me we are in a child's bedroom. Going by the light blue tone of the walls and the bookshelf lined with Star Wars Lego, I assume this room belongs to a boy.

Confused, I run my hands over my hair, trying to will my brain to remember how I got here. My mind is foggy. Things seem familiar, yet I can't remember how. This room has to be in Tasha's house since that's where the party was last night, but why can't I remember any of it? I don't feel hungover enough to have been blackout drunk, so what's going on with my head?

Searching my body for my phone, I find it in the back pocket of my black skinny jeans. Keying in my passcode, I go straight for the photo app. Taking photos and videos of our shenanigans is a given, and looking back through them can usually tell a detailed story.

What the hell?

Where are all the pictures?

There are only a few pictures, but they are blurry. I can't even make out what they are meant to be of.

Shaking my head in frustration, I pull the blankets back to search for Abbey's phone. She's still wearing her blue jeans and white frilly top, which barely covers her busty chest. Trying not to wake her, I find her phone underneath her sleeping body and slowly ease it out from under her before keying in her passcode.

Yes! There are so many photos of last night on Abbey's phone. She always says every opportunity is a photo opportunity, and right now I'm glad. Surely her camera reel will help me fill in the blanks.

Scrolling through the pictures, I'm left looking at shots I have no memory of. There are a couple of me, looking like a hot mess. I zoom in on one picture of me showing my red rimmed eyes and dazed expression.

Jesus, do I have twigs in my hair?

What the fuck did I do last night?

Looking through the rest of the photos, a frown creases my brow when I realise there are quite a few with everyone in them, except for me.

Why aren't I in them?

Knowing I won't be able to fill in the gaps until Abbey wakes up, I place her phone next to her head before carefully stepping over Maddie's and Kyle's legs to sneak out of the room.

At the door, I turn back to see who's sleeping on the top bunk. Tight dark curls cover the sleeping face, which can only be Daniel, Abbey's new boyfriend. No one has curls like he does.

Abbey and Daniel have the kind of cute new love that is consuming, and they can't keep their hands off each other. Which raises the question. Why is Abbey sharing a bed with me and not him?

The murmur of voices float down the hall, so I duck into the small, cluttered bathroom to freshen up before I face the world.

Glancing in the mirror, my gut twists at what I see. To say I look like shit is an understatement. I regret looking at my reflection, forced to see my bloodshot eyes smudged with black mascara. My skin appears sickly pale instead of my natural sun-kissed tone. And to top it off, I have an extreme case of bed hair.

"Jesus." I whisper to myself, shaking my head at what I see.

How in the hell did I let myself get to whatever is looking back at me?

Shame slams into me.

Why did I let myself lose so much control last night?

Guilt causes my tummy to roll, a feeling that's becoming all too familiar lately. I wish it would just go the fuck away, but I'm constantly anxious. Never really sure if today is the day that my life will change in the worst of ways.

Shaking my head, I assess the rest of me. While my jeans appear to have handled the night, my grey hoodie looks a little worse for wear. It's dirty and stained down the right side. *Seriously, what the fuck Lexi!*

Sighing, I rummage through the bathroom cabinet and find some makeup wipes. In a matter of minutes, I remove the charcoal smears of makeup framing my blue eyes and the invisible grime that feels like it's coating my face. Stealing some toothpaste, I squirt it on my finger and rub it along my teeth before rinsing my mouth. My teeth definitely aren't clean, but the fresh mint flavour helps to mask the weird smoky taste I've woken up with.

Reaching to turn off the tap, my eyes catch on several cuts on my hand and a smear of blood on my sleeve.

How in the hell did I get these?

Once again, my head pounds as I try to remember, but this time, a faint memory of seeing blood trickle down my hand pops into my mind. Running a finger over the grazes, I feel the rough and tender marks, hoping it will spark more memories.

It doesn't.

Fuck. What did I do?

Confusion is making me emotional, and hot tears burn the backs of my eyes, threatening to spill. I hate that I can't remember how I got the scratches or what I did last night. The unknown sends a ripple of fear through me and reminds me of how little control I have of my life lately. Surely Abbey will be able to tell me what happened to my hand, and why I'm in such a mess this morning.

Needing to tackle my matted hair, I use a pink hairbrush I find in the vanity to brush out the long blonde waves. Eventually, I'm able to tame it a little, and my hair finally resembles a smoother texture. I feel dirty and need a shower, but that will have to wait until I get home. Unfortunately, going home is not something I'm looking forward to, but I have no choice. I can't stay away too long, or it will just cause me more problems.

Deciding there's nothing more I can do to make myself look any better, I drag myself out of the bathroom in search of information.

I find my friends sitting around a table in the kitchen, which I'm now certain is Tasha's house. My friends look sleepy with bloodshot eyes, like they haven't even been to bed yet.

"Hey girl," Tasha cheers fakely as I enter the room, and all eyes turn to me.

I give them all what I hope is a warm smile and pretend like I'm comfortable being around them. I'm not. Not in the way that they make me nervous, but in the way that I don't seem to relate much to these girls anymore. While Abbey has been my best friend since we were five years old, Tasha, Allison, Amanda and Sophie have trickled into our circle along the way.

"You guys been up all night?" I ask, spotting a phone charger by the toaster and head over to it.

"Most of us have. Not Allison though, she's been busy cosying up to Travis." Tasha explains, and Allison, with her pink flushed cheeks showing through her dark skin, tosses an empty plastic cup at her, but Tasha dodges it easily.

While we're all in year eleven at Fox Pines Catholic College, Travis comes from the other side of the tracks, so to speak. He's a Fox Pines High brat and is in the year below us. It's funny to think of Allison hooking up with a sixteen-year-old. Yes, he may only be a year younger, but it still seems weird.

Laughter fills the room at Allison's expense, but I don't join in as my mind tries to open up a memory—something to do with Travis. I can't seem to reach it though, and it's starting to piss me off.

"Where did you get to last night anyway, Lexi? You were missing for ages." Allison changes the subject, pulling her raven waves back into a low pony.

I frown, "I went missing?"

The girls stay quiet and look between each other before returning their eyes to me.

"You don't remember?" Tasha asks, a smirk tugging the corner of her lips as she gets up from her chair and walks over to me.

I shake my head, embarrassed and frustrated.

"How much did you drink last night?" she asks, now standing in front of me, her chocolate eyes roaming my face, knowingly.

Normally looking more put together, Tasha's brown ringlets are frizzing at the ends, and her pale skin is peeking through in patches where her too dark foundation has worn off.

"I don't remember," I shrug, "but what I do know is that I don't feel hungover enough to have drunk so much that I can't remember."

"She wasn't feeling well and went for a walk." Abbey takes that moment to walk into the room and smiles at me before coming to my side.

Tasha turns to Abbey and raises a dark brow. "That's bullshit Abbey, and you know it."

"No, it's not." Abbey hisses back.

I am so confused right now.

"It is bullshit, Abbey! You were running around frantically trying to find her when you noticed she'd disappeared, freaking out because she left her phone behind!"

My heart races as I comprehend their words.

I went missing?

And I left my phone behind?

That doesn't sound like me at all.

"Yes, well, she explained everything when she got back. She was embarrassed to have gotten so sick." Abbey defends me, sliding her arm around my shoulders.

Tasha goes quiet while she processes what Abbey said, and then she responds with, "whatever."

The tension in the air is thick, and I feel like I may suffocate from it, but as luck would have it, Maddie and Kyle enter the room, and all the attention falls to them.

Thankful I'm no longer the centre of whatever that was, I take a deep breath, filling my aching lungs when Abbey leans towards my ear and whispers, "We should get going. I'll just go and say bye to Daniel and then meet you out the front."

I nod and watch Abbey exit the room before I unplug my phone from the charger and do the same. Slipping quietly out of Tasha's house, I walk to the end of her drive and sit on the curb in the barely warm Sunday morning sun to wait for Abbey.

Saying goodbye to Daniel will take a few minutes. Even though they'll be in each other's company again later this afternoon, Abbey and Daniel really can't get enough of each other.

"Sexy Lexi," a voice comes from behind me before feet appear at my side.

I look up and watch as Travis takes a seat next to me on the curb.

"Seriously?" The unwanted endearment, if that's what you can even call it, is not new to my ears. Why boys think I like the childish rhyming is beyond me.

"Fun night last night, hey?" Travis nudges my shoulder, his brown eyes looking bloodshot.

I nod, not even knowing if it was a fun night or not. I kind of hope it wasn't, because I'd hate to not remember the fun.

"You wanna know what my favourite part was?" He asks, and I shrug, not caring before Travis leans in to whisper in my ear, "our kiss."

My head snaps in his direction, his face a mask of seriousness before he chuckles.

"Oh, Sexy Lexi, you were so fucking baked. Don't you remember our kiss?"

I gape at him and scan his face to see if he's joking, but even though he's smiling, he exudes certainty.

"Lost for words?" he chuckles again, his eyes flicking to my mouth.

Travis is one of those cocky full of themselves 'footy' boys who's popular with a lot of the girls, just like Allison, who was getting cosy with him last night, apparently.

"When exactly did we share a kiss?" I can't hide the disdain from my voice.

His gaze lingers on my lips before darting back to my eyes. "Right after you threw a chair through the glass doors." He grins, dropping his gaze to my lips again, momentarily, before giving me a wink.

Frowning, I turn away, trying to remember. I can't recollect what happened, but I feel like he's telling the truth, and it makes me shudder.

Did I really kiss him? And why did I throw a chair? Through a fucking door?

"I can't remember what happened, Travis, but whatever happened, you need to keep it to yourself." I snap, shooting him a glare, and he studies my face before nodding.

"Okay."

"As far as you're concerned, there was no kiss." I snap again, needing him to understand.

He grins, "Okay, Sexy Lexi. I'll keep the kiss to myself, but when you come back for more," he leans in close, "and you *will* come back for more," he sits back again, "I won't be keeping *that* to myself."

I'm generally not a nasty person, but I'm in full bitch mode now.

"Like fuck." I hiss, standing from the curb in time to see Abbey walking out of Tasha's front door.

Travis chuckles once again, and I try to ignore it as I put distance between us, shaking my head at Abbey's questioning brow raise. My heart is thudding in my chest, and I'm feeling beyond anxious. Looking from me to Travis, Abbey sighs and reaches out her hand to me. Knowing I need to keep myself grounded, I take it, and we start to walk home.

I'm quiet as we walk, racking my brain for information on last night's events. Abbey ends the silence when we've put good distance between us and Tasha's house.

"Alexis West, what has gotten into you?"

I stop walking, shocked at her tone and the use of my full name.

Sighing again, she looks down at her feet, tucking her dead straight hair behind her ear before looking back at me. "You don't remember, do you?"

I shake my head, feeling ashamed.

Abbey's brown eyes roam my worried face before pulling me in for a hug.

"Sorry, Lex, I don't mean to sound like such a nag, but you scared the crap out of me last night."

Having Abbey's arms around me sends my emotions spiralling, and a tear escapes my eye before I wipe it away quickly, stepping back from Abbey's embrace.

"Can you please tell me what the hell I did last night?" I shake my head again at myself. "I really can't remember a thing."

Grabbing my hand, Abbey tugs me along.

"I can only tell you what you told me last night, but I can't be sure if what you told me was right. You were very... out of it."

"Did I take something?" My whisper is laced with the shame I feel.

"Well, not so much as take, as smoked."

"What?!"

"You smoked weed last night, Lex. It's not like you to do that."

"Fuck." I mutter in disgust.

"Fuck's right. You went into the shed with all the stoners and came out like a frigging zombie. You disappeared for like an hour after that, and I found you wandering back with Travis, of all people."

"Shit."

Abbey nods, "Yep, exactly."

"What did I do with Travis?" I'm reluctant to ask, but I have to know.

"I'm not 100% sure. He was tight-lipped about what you two got up to. Daniel helped me sneak you into the house, and I hopped into bed with you. I felt too scared to leave you alone. You seemed so... reckless."

"I'm so sorry, Abs." A wave of nausea rolls my stomach.

"You had cuts on your hand, and Travis said you fell into a rosebush. Do you remember that?"

I shake my head. "No, but I think I remember seeing blood on my hand."

"Yeah, apparently Travis cleaned your hand up by sneaking into someone's front yard and using their hose."

I sigh. "I can't remember any of it."

Abbey rubs her thumb over my hand as we continue our walk home.

"You told me you think Travis kissed you, but you couldn't really feel it."

"What?!" I screech again, and Abbey laughs.

"Yep, you kept saying your face was numb, and that's why you couldn't feel his kiss."

"Oh my god." I stop walking and bury my head in my hands.

Abbey pries my hands away. "Hey, you told me I should never let you kiss him again if that makes you feel any better?"

"Yes, good. At least I was coming to my senses at some point." A little too late, it seems. I'm such an idiot! How could I think smoking weed was a good idea?

We walk again, and Abbey's tone turns serious again. "I think you should stay away from weed, Lex."

I nod. "Agreed."

Abbey spends the rest of the walk talking about how in love with Daniel she is, and I'm thankful for the distraction, even though I have a hard time focusing on what she is saying. We part ways as we get closer to our houses, Abbey going north and I head south.

As I get nearer to my childhood home, dread starts to fill me. Once, a long time ago, the house I grew up in had been my haven. The place I could go to be myself and feel safe and loved. Now, the thought of stepping foot inside that house makes me sick to my stomach.

The urge to turn around and run in the opposite direction consumes me, but knowing there's nowhere else for me to go unless I want to speak of my shame to someone else, means I have no choice but to go home.

Slowing my steps as I approach my house from across the street, I search for my brother's blue car. When I don't see it, relief sweeps over me. If his car isn't here, it usually means he's not home.

My house, now looking aged and outdated, would have looked classy in its day. The two-story house screams suburban family with the beige render and the terracotta tiles lining the roof. Dead centre of the second story is my bedroom, jutting out as a feature. The white framed windows match the white railing that runs along the front door and portico, and the gardens are neat and well maintained.

I shake my head at this house. It looks like it comes out of a family sitcom, only in truth, the family that lives there is nothing like the families on those TV shows. Looks can be deceiving after all.

Hurrying up the front path, I see the familiar sight of closed curtains, which instantly pisses me off. I glance down at my phone screen. 11:07am. It may be a Sunday when a lot of people like to spend a little extra time in bed, but I know why the curtains are closed, and it's not because my mum slept in.

They are closed because she is sobering up.

Reaching the portico, I get the spare key from under the planter and unlock the front door before returning it. Inside, I head straight for the front windows in the living room and draw the heavy brown curtains open, letting the winter sun filter in. I continue to do this in each room I pass as I make my way through the house.

Just being here has turned my mood sour, which adds to an already pretty shit start to my Sunday.

Going to my parents' bedroom, which is at the back of the house on the ground floor, I crack the door open. Actually, I can't really call it my parents' bedroom because that would imply that I have two parents living here. It's my mum's bedroom. Even though she's not a very present mum, she is a hell of a lot more present than my dad, who claims he is too busy working in the city to come home.

His absence feels like more than work to me. My dad hasn't been back here for a couple of months, and the time when he was here was only for one night before leaving again. It's been like that for the past two years, only each time he comes home, I notice how different he is. He's more of a moody arsehole these days, and resembles less and less the dad that doted on me when I was younger. I don't know what's going on with him, and if I'm being honest, I don't think I want to know. Dread creeps into my heart any time I let myself wonder what he is doing with all his time away from us.

There's no sign of my mum in her bedroom, which means she's either at the doctor's trying to get something to take the edge off, or she's gone to whoever supplies her with the substances she abuses. If she's not at either of those places, then I'd probably find her at the Bottlo buying up their scotch supplies.

This is the way it's always been, and while I didn't seem to care when I was younger, I do now. I'm sick of suffering because of her decisions, or lack of them. I can't remember the last time she even asked me where I've been, or how school is going. I could be running a brothel from my bedroom, and the woman wouldn't even know. I wonder if she'd even care? Unlikely.

The rumble of my tummy distracts my thoughts, and I go to the kitchen to make some breakfast. Even though empty fast-food containers and boxes line the bench, there is no actual food in sight. There's no bread, no milk, no tins of spaghetti, or packets of noodles.

Shit.

The burn of tears threatens again because, well, I'm hungry, damn it!

The sound of a car pulling in the driveway quickly scares away any stupid crying I was about to do and replaces my sadness with fear. My heart rate picks up, and I hold my breath, waiting for the front door to open.

Please let it be mum. Please let it be mum. Please let it be mum.

Still in the kitchen, I stay out of view from the front door but keep my eyes focused on the hall mirror, which gives me a good view of the entrance and anyone walking in.

My heart sinks as dirty blonde hair comes into view. I struggle to breathe as Mike walks through the front door, followed by some guy I don't know. Panic escalates my heart rate when I realise they are heading my way, so I quickly make myself look busy by filling a glass with water from the tap.

Mike walks into the kitchen, spotting me straight away and narrowing his eyes, while I force myself to look calm and unaffected as I take a sip of the water.

"Ali," he says in a growled greeting, using the shortened name for Alexis. I've never liked it. Abbey started calling me Lexi when we were five, and ever since, I've made myself known as that. My parents refer to me as Alexis even after I begged them not to when I was younger, but not Mike. No. That arsehole has his own name for me.

Ali.

I raise my brow to him, not wanting to speak in fear that my voice will give away how scared I am.

The guy with him turns his head towards me and flicks his ratty brown hair off his face, his lifeless brown eyes raking over my body.

"Far out, Mike. This sexy little thing, your sister?"

"Sure fucking is," Mike smiles, as if he's proud to call me sexy.

Sick bastard.

Mike is seven years older than me, now getting close to his mid-twenties. He's the result of my dad's brief first marriage to Suzie, a dark-haired hippy that he married in a drug-induced frenzy during his college days up in Sydney. Their marriage lasted three months, but it was enough time to produce the devil's spawn, Mike.

Growing up, my only interactions with Mike were during school holidays when he would fly down to Victoria to stay with us. To me, he has always been strange. We never got along, and he creeped me out with his odd behaviour and attempts to hurt me when my parents' backs were turned. When I went to them to 'dob' on him, they would always tell me that siblings fight sometimes, and we need to work it out ourselves.

As Mike got older, his interactions with me became even stranger, and I remember feeling scared of him when I was about twelve, after I woke to him watching me sleep one night. After that, he stayed away for a while and didn't come back for visits until a few months ago, when my dad advised me that Mike was moving in.

"She keen?" Mike's ratty haired friend asks him.

Mike sits at the dining table and starts unpacking food from a Maccas paper bag, placing a burger and fries on the table.

"Not yet, but she will be." Mike deliberately licks his lip in a vulgar way.

I nearly gag.

"Where's the old bitch?" Mike mumbles with a mouth full of fries. His stringy hair has grown so long that some strands nearly get caught in his mouth as he speaks and chews at the same time.

The smell of his food reaches me, making my tummy rumble again.

"No idea." I shrug and move to leave the room.

"Where the fuck do you think you're going?" Mike hisses, and I freeze, turning to him with a questioning raised brow, and Mike's mate chuckles to himself, pleased with the way he speaks to me.

Douche!

"Why are there locks on the doors upstairs, Ali?"

I gulp. "Privacy," I say and walk off again.

A loud crack pierces my ears, and I spin, heart in my throat, to see Mike standing with his hands slammed down on the table in anger. As he stares me down, his nostrils flare, and his dull blue eyes burn with disdain.

"Dad gave you permission to get a lock for your room?" Mike's snarling voice makes it hard for me to answer straight away.

"He paid the bill."

It's not a lie. My dad *did* pay the bill. He just didn't question what bill he was paying.

Mike's mate wears a devious grin as he looks between us, all while shovelling fries into his mouth, and Mike continues to glare before hissing as he sits back down to eat his food, "Fuck off, will ya?"

He doesn't have to tell me twice.

Twisting, I race out of the room, and taking two steps at a time, I climb the stairs to the second floor, eager to get to the safety of my bedroom. With shaky hands, I fumble with the key that's on the chain around my neck and unlock my door.

A few days ago, I arranged for locks to be installed on the upstairs rooms. Well, all rooms except for Mike's. I arranged to have traditional internal locks installed for the toilet and bathroom that you flick on when you enter the room to maintain privacy.

On my bedroom door, I had a deadbolt installed in the hope of keeping people out 24/7. I didn't have the money to pay for it, but like with all of our bills, I had it sent to my dad's secretary in the city, and it got paid.

Once I'm inside my room, I make sure to lock my door before I lean back against it and sink to the floor, no longer able to keep myself together. Tears stream down my face while I try to stay silent, but I feel myself breaking because it's all too much. Pulling out my phone, I open Spotify, and Billie Eilish's voice immediately fills my room with *'idontwannabeyouanymore.'*

Throwing myself onto my bed face first, I bury my head in my pillow and scream. I yell and cry and scream some more, letting my shame from last night, and from inside the walls of this house flow out of my body, until I'm left in a trembling mess and cry myself to sleep.

Three

A noise jolts me from sleep, and I instantly panic. My room is dark, with a hint of moonlight filtering through my open curtains. A rattling sound gains my attention, and I comprehend that it's the lock on my bedroom door jiggling.

Bolting upright, I blindly search for my phone, sweeping my hands over my sheets until I find it next to my pillow. The screen reads 10:31pm. My music no longer fills the room, my playlist ending long ago.

From underneath my bedroom door, I can see the hall light seeping through, and the shadow of feet standing just on the other side. As the lock jiggles again, my eyes dart towards my window. Should I make a run for it? Should I sneak out and call Abbey? Maybe I can stay there for the night?

The muffled curse from my brother filters through the silence before the shadow moves away from my door.

"I'm okay. I'm okay." I whisper to myself, trying to calm my nerves.

Moving off my bed, I double-check that my door is still locked, even though I know Mike couldn't open it moments ago. I'm paranoid as hell, and relief washes over me when I confirm the lock has done its job.

Inhaling deep, needing to calm my pounding heart, I remind myself over and over that I'm okay. As risky as it was knowing all too well that my dad would have said no, I'm thankful that I had the lock installed.

My mum doesn't know about the locks. She wasn't home when I had them put in, and she never comes upstairs. I'd asked both my parents repeatedly about having locks put on when I found out Mike was moving in, but it fell on deaf ears. As far as I'm concerned, they can go fuck themselves. It was a necessity.

Not wanting to turn my light on and alert Mike that I'm awake, I use my phone torch to illuminate my white ceiling, which offers a light glow to filter across my boring off-white walls. So many times over the years, I asked my parents to paint my walls pink or purple or yellow, and not once did they say yes. It was always a "don't be ridiculous Alexis," or "it will just be a phase that we will have to paint over again in a year when you change your mind." Ugh. My parents are as boring as bat shit. Just like my bedroom. They never even allowed me to put up a damn poster.

Like, who does that?

The only splash of personality is my hot pink quilt, my black Netflix and Chill cushion, and my charcoal fleece throw blanket. The mirror above my dresser is the only other thing that hints to my life with assorted pictures of me and my friends covering the frame from over the years. Sometimes I sit and stare at them, letting myself remember a time when I was happy.

Two problems present themselves to me right now.

One is that I need to pee, and the other is that I still haven't eaten, and the intense hunger is making me feel sick. Knowing Mike is still out there somewhere in the house means there is no way I'm stepping foot outside my bedroom door. My only other option is sneaking out my bedroom window.

Grabbing a handful of tissues off my bedside table, I move to the window, and like I've done so many times before, climb out onto the roof. Moving slowly, trying to avoid making noise, I shuffle across the roof tiles, ignoring their icy chill. I was twelve when I discovered this escape route, where I found my way down off the roof by swinging my legs over the edge and easing myself down onto the fence below. Back then, I used it to sneak out with Abbey, Marcus, and Jared when we would roam the night streets and dream of a future that seems so out of reach now.

We were so naïve. Even so, growing up with them really was filled with adventure. The four of us would always find ourselves in some sort of trouble but managed to talk our way out of it. My childhood would have been lonely if it weren't for the three of them.

My feet hit solid ground as I make my escape and creep through my backyard to the back corner where an overgrown garden resides. The bushy area provides adequate cover and I undo my jeans, tugging them down and squat, doing my business, before making use of the tissues.

Abbey and I used to play in these bushes with our dolls for hours when we were kids. Now I'm using the spot as a toilet—my how times have changed.

When I finish, I climb over the fence into my neighbour's backyard. Creeping around their shed, I dispose of the tissues in their rubbish bin and check to see if Mr and Mrs Brown are anywhere in sight.

Their large kitchen window overlooks the backyard, so I stick to the shadows, hoping not to get caught.

Making a run for it, I dash across the yard to the small orchard to investigate their fruit trees. These fruit trees are now my fucked up version of takeaway food.

Since it's winter, there's not a lot of options. I bypass the lemons and pick a handful of mandarins, slipping them into the pocket of my hoodie.

Turning to sneak back across the yard, I freeze in place when I see a small dark silhouette standing before me.

"If you're hungry, I can make you a sandwich," the sweet voice of my twelve-year-old neighbour, Valarie, says, watching my every move.

"Ahh... um, no, that's okay, thanks anyway."

"I don't mind," Valarie says, looking genuine with her big sincere eyes that stand out even in the dark.

Glancing towards her house, I shake my head. "I'm sorry for taking the fruit without asking," I laugh nervously. "I just really felt like some fruit, you know?"

I hope she doesn't see through the lie. I hate fruit, but it's what's on the menu for tonight's dinner.

Deciding I should probably just leave, I retreat through Valarie's backyard.

She surprises me by following and rushing to my side, looking up with a big smile. Valarie is a pretty little thing with her jet black hair and ebon eyes to match. Her features appear more Asian, like her mum. I don't know her mum's origins exactly, and I've never asked, not wanting to be rude. It doesn't really matter to me where their bloodlines come from. They have always been friendly to me, unlike some of our other snobby neighbours.

"Why did you climb out of your window?"

Taken back a little by her forward question, I work to keep a straight face. "It seemed like a fun thing to do."

"It's kind of dangerous," she states, and I nod.

"Yes, you're right. It is." I quicken my pace, "I won't do it again."

"You do it all the time," Valarie accuses.

I stop and sigh, looking at her young, innocent face and nod. "Yes, I do. I shouldn't, but I do."

"Why?" she asks curiously, sounding too mature to be wearing pink unicorn pyjamas.

"Shouldn't you be in bed? It's kind of late." I deflect.

"Shouldn't you?" Valarie's quick wit makes me smile. She doesn't miss a thing.

"I'm a fair bit older than you, so no, I'm never in bed this early."

"Why do you climb out of your window?" She's not going to give up, is she?

I sigh, "Different reasons."

"Like?" she asks, testing my patience.

"Sometimes, I meet up with friends. Sometimes I like to go for walks. Tonight, I wanted fruit."

Valarie nods, considering what I said.

"Why don't you just use the front door?"

"Where's the fun in that?" I ask, and she raises a dark brow at me. "Okay, I can see I'm not going to pull the wool over your eyes, am I?"

Valarie shakes her head. "Nope."

"I use my window sometimes because I shouldn't be leaving my house."

"So, you sneak out?" Valarie states more than asks.

I nod, and at that, she nods too.

"I can't sneak out of my window like you do." Valarie turns to look at her house, and my eyes follow.

It's a tall double story house, built like a square box. There is no first story roof or eaves. It's all just one tall block.

"No, I guess you can't," I agree.

"I don't need to climb out a window to sneak out, anyway. I just use the door."

I smile, and Valarie looks at me with a mischievous grin on her face.

"I better go sneak back in," I snicker.

"Okay, Lexi. Come over for fruit any time." And with that, Valarie smiles and skips back towards her house.

I shake my head, smiling genuinely for the first time today. Valarie is a smart kid. I can tell she'll give the boys a run for their money when she's older. She has always been fascinated by me, although I don't know why. I'm no one special. She's an only child, and I rarely see or hear her parents. She's probably very lonely in that big old house. I babysat her a handful of times a few years ago, but there really was no need for me to be there, other than to be company. Valarie may only be twelve, but I swear her soul is older than mine.

I make my way back over my side of the fence and climb back onto the roof, and through my bedroom window. The fruit is devoured in no time, leaving me surprisingly full. Sleeping most of the day has left me wide awake, so I settle back on my bed with my phone, laptop, and earphones needing to keep occupied.

There's a text message from Abbey on my phone. It's a picture of her and Daniel at a Chinese restaurant. I smile and send back a love heart emoji. I haven't seen Abbey this happy or into a boy before. It's nice to see, even though there's a part of me that's envious. It's a part of my cold heart that I'm trying hard to ignore. The part of me that longs for someone to look at me the way Daniel looks at her. To have someone who cares so deeply for me that they want to spend every waking moment with me. I didn't really think that sort of thing existed until I witnessed it with Maddie and Kyle, and now with Abbey and Daniel. I guess it doesn't just happen in the movies and books. I wonder if I'll ever be lucky enough to find that sort of love.

A new SnapChat message pops up on my screen from Marcus. I frown, realising he has sent me a private message. He usually just chats to me along with the other guys from school in the group chat we have.

I'm the only girl left in their group chat. Over the last couple of years they've removed the other girls, but for some reason left me in it. As weird as that sounds, it's not at all that weird to me. I find the idiotic banter between the boys more calming than the persistent bitching from Tasha and some of the girls.

Opening SnapChat, I tap on the message from Marcus.

Marcus-Grady
Hey Lex. I heard Tasha's party was a blast.
Did you have a good time?

Shit. Does he know how wasted I got? Are rumours already spreading?

And why is he sending me this message privately? I know we were close friends growing up, but we haven't been that close for a long time. This seems weird. Not weird enough for me to shut my phone off and ignore though, so I type out my response.

Lexi-West

Hi Marcus. The party was great. Tasha's parties are always fun!
Where were you? It's not like you to miss a party.

Lies! Lies! Lies!
The party was shit as far as I'm concerned.

Marcus-Grady

I'm glad you had a good time. ☺
I couldn't make it because I had to help my aunty and cousin move house. My cousin will be starting school with us tomorrow.

Lexi-West

Nice! Is he in year eleven too? I remember you used to go to Melbourne all the time when we were kids to visit your cousin, but that's all I can remember.

Marcus-Grady

Yep, he's in our year. You have a good memory, Lex. You used to get shitty at me for leaving you with Jared and Abbey for a couple of weeks each summer.

Lexi-West

That's right, I remember that now. It's because Abbey was always so in love with Jared, and she would fall all over him while I just sat around trying to ignore what was going on. When you were with us, it meant I had someone to help distract me from witnessing Jared trying to fight her off all the time.

It's funny, Abbey never did win him over.

Marcus-Grady

Well, there was that one time when we stole the bottle of Jim Beam from your mum and shared it between us. Jared gave in and kissed her that night.

Lexi-West

OMG, I forgot all about that! Jared started barfing after that kiss and didn't stop until the next night. I don't think he even remembered kissing Abbey.

Marcus-Grady

He didn't. Still doesn't believe it when I remind him now. That shit is too funny.

Lexi-West

Yeah!

Our chat goes quiet for a minute. If we were in the same room having this conversation, it would probably be awkward.

Marcus-Grady

Well, I'd better get ready for bed. I'll make sure to introduce you to the guy who used to steal me away from you each summer when I see you at school tomorrow. ☺

Why does his comment sound so personal? Like our friendship is more than it is? Fuck, my head hurts. Why does everything seem so complicated lately?

Lexi-West

Okay. See you tomorrow.

Can my weekend get any stranger? Seriously?

Annoyed with my thoughts and needing to get out of my own head, I spend the next few hours binge-watching Riverdale episodes before sleep pulls me under for a restless night of tossing and turning.

My Monday morning starts with the unwelcome feeling of guilt. I'm not sure what I'm guilty about, but it's there in the back of my mind and gently nudges my already weakened emotions, making itself known.

Mike's re-appearance in my life after being absent for a few years has been extremely unsettling. He may be my half brother, but I don't even know him. I overheard my mum talking on the phone a few weeks back about how he's been in prison and is staying here because he can't leave the state. I have no idea what he did to land himself in prison, and my parents haven't bothered to give me any details. Like, isn't that something I should know? Is he a murderer? A paedophile? A rapist? Those last two seem pretty believable given his behaviour towards me.

A shiver runs up my spine at that thought, and my mind instantly goes to the night I woke to him standing over me, watching me sleep. He wasn't looking at me with brotherly eyes. He was looking at me like I was something he wanted in a way a brother shouldn't want his sister.

It's creeping me the fuck out having him living under the same roof, sleeping down the other end of the hall. Why would my dad allow someone like him to stay here? Why would my mum agree to it? What the hell is wrong with my family?

With reluctance, I roll out of bed early, knowing I need a shower. I didn't have time to have one yesterday after coming home and locking myself away. Mike is never up this early, so I quietly use the toilet before locking myself in the bathroom and shower the weekend away.

My mood is flat. A big dark shadow is circling my heart and filtering into my brain. I can't recall a time when I've ever felt so unsettled. So on edge. My control is waning, tittering on the edge of a steep cliff with nothing but a dark abyss below. I need to take my control back, but the problem is, I don't know how.

Knowing I need to stop overthinking, I focus on the task at hand. I dry my hair when I'm back in my room and put on the usual splash of concealer, blush, and mascara. Studying myself in the dresser mirror, I see someone staring back that looks a little more like the normal me. The dark shadows that were under my eyes are now hidden beneath my makeup. Pink blush helps my skin appear to have more colour, and the black mascara framing my blue eyes makes them more striking.

I usually run the straightener through my hair to trick the world into thinking it's smooth and perfectly straight. Today, however, I've decided the natural blonde waves in my hair will do, and I tie it back into the school regulation ponytail.

I smile at myself. It's not a genuine smile. It's the fake smile I don on my face every day so people can't see the truth. I'm such a liar, and no one knows. Everyone sees my fake identity—the in control, popular, friendly girl who does the right thing without being a pushover. The truth is, I don't have my shit together at all. I'm a mess. I'm hanging by a thread, and my friends have no idea who I really am. I'm sick of doing the right thing when the people in my life do anything but, and I wish I didn't have to act all the time.

"Fake bitch," I mutter to my reflection before turning away and getting dressed in my school uniform.

The winter uniform at Fox Pines Catholic College is snobby and formal. The long-sleeved crisp white shirt is hidden under a navy blazer trimmed with white binding and is finished with a formal navy tie. When winter starts, the uniform regulations change from the navy and white tartan summer skirt to a lengthened winter version. Regulations or not, none of the girls follow that rule and keep wearing their summer skirt. Yes, we choose fashion over comfort where this is concerned, and for a school with so many rules, the Principal doesn't say a thing. The creeper is most likely loving the eyeful of skin that shows between the knee-high navy socks and the shorter kilt.

Keen to get away before Mike rises, I tiptoe downstairs and through the house to check on my mum. Cracking her bedroom door open, a cloud of cigarette smoke wafts out, nearly choking me. My mum is asleep, sitting up in bed with her mouth open and her golden brown hair in a messy ponytail. Next to her on the bed is a burning cigarette in an ashtray. I've found her quite a few times asleep with the cigarette still sitting in her fingers. Even though she managed to get it in the ashtray this time, I fear she'll burn herself alive one day.

Stepping into her room, I butt out the burning cigarette, moving the ashtray to her bedside table. My mum doesn't wake, obviously still affected by whatever substance she managed to get her hands on yesterday. Her phone is lying beside her on the bed next to a pile of scrunched up tissues. It's a telltale sign that she's been fighting with my dad over the phone again. I've heard her multiple times while on the phone, begging him to come home from the city to spend time with her.

I often wonder if dad just gave her the attention she wanted, then maybe she'd be a different person who doesn't have a need for potent drugs. It's hard to say. Perhaps she is the way she is because he's always away working in the city, or maybe he's still living away to work in the city because she is the way she is.

I momentarily feel bad for mum, and whatever internal war goes on in her head. Will I turn out like her when I'm a mum? That's if I ever get the chance to. It's unlikely anyone will want to have kids with someone like me. A fucking headcase.

The negative thoughts come from a dark place within me, and I know I just need to get away from this house and these people to help me feel better.

Since there's still no food, I accept that today will be just another day that I don't get the luxury of breakfast, and I rush out of the house to go and meet Abbey. I'm early to arrive at the corner house on Mill Street, where we meet every day before school.

One morning back in grade five, we made a plan to leave our houses at the same time and make our way to each other. We mapped out the route first and decided that where we met would be halfway between our houses. This corner house on Mill Street was where we met, and it's been our meet up place ever since.

Sitting on the brick fence, I listen to Spotify through my earphones while I wait. Today my dark mood leads me to my playlist called 'Heavy.' I named it that because it's how I feel most of the time these days. I feel heavy, weighed down by the secrets I keep. By the shame I carry.

The sounds of Panic at the Disco, Three Days Grace, and Breaking Benjamin soothe my soul briefly as I let myself feel the music, clearing my thoughts. The anger and pain I feel through the heavy beats and biting lyrics draw me in. Sometimes I feel like these songs were written just for me, and I wonder what unspeakable things happened to whoever wrote them.

My shoulder gets nudged and my lids fly open as a scream rips from my lungs.

Abbey is standing in front of me, buckled over, laughing, and I rip the earphones out of my ears, pushing myself off the fence.

"Oh, you're hilarious, aren't you?"

Abbey can hardly speak. "Y-y-your face." She slaps her leg, continuing to laugh, "L-looked so freaking scared."

If only she knew.

I'd been so consumed by the music that I forgot where I was for a moment. My mind instantly thought it was Mike who nudged me.

Abbey tries to calm herself, sucking in deep breaths through her mouth, wiping the happy tears from her eyes. She has no idea how her attempt to joke around really affects me.

"Are you done?" I'm not impressed, and I work hard to tamp down how upset I really am.

She nods, "Yep."

I start walking in the direction of school, and Abbey falls in beside me.

"Did you have a good night with Daniel last night?" I ask, making the usual small talk.

"Sure did. His family is so nice, Lex. I was so nervous at first, but they all treated me like I was part of the family and made me feel so special." Abbey is visibly swooning.

"So he's not just a nice guy, but also has a nice family? It sounds like you've won the jackpot, Abs."

She does a little jump. "I know, right!"

I laugh. It's nice to see her so happy. She deserves happiness, and Daniel seems to be perfect for her.

"I'm going away with them on the weekend," Abbey reveals, grabbing my hand and squeezing it.

"Really? Where to?"

"To their beach house at Phillip Island." She beams.

Jealousy prickles at me again, and I shove it down, trying to keep it hidden. I'm not jealous because I like Daniel. I'm jealous because of their relationship and where it's heading. Not to mention that Daniel is winning more of Abbey's time these days than me, and quite frankly, I miss her.

"Your parents are cool with that?" I try to sound happy, but I'm not sure it's convincing.

Abbey nods, "Yep. Rose, Daniel's mum, called my mum last night and talked to her about it. They hit it off, and by the end of the phone call, my mum said yes to me going away with them. They even set up a morning tea date to catch up later in the week."

Again, jealousy pricks at me. Why can't my parents be more normal like that?

"That's awesome, Abs." I try to sound genuine.

"Yep," Abbey agrees. "Oh, I have something to tell you."

Curious, I glance Abbey's way and wait for her to continue.

"So, Nathan was texting me last night."

"What?!" I all but shout.

Abbey smiles. "He was asking about you."

Nathan is my on-again-off-again boyfriend that I've had since I was thirteen. At the moment, he is off again. Very off again.

It's out of character for him to be texting Abbey. Maybe he's trying a different angle to get my attention back. At this point, I'm not sure what I ever saw in him. We are such opposites, and I know it will never work. It will never be more than a fling.

He goes to Fox Pines High, and I go to Fox Pines Catholic College.

His dad is in jail, and I have no idea what his mum does. My dad works in a large finance firm in Melbourne, and my mum, well, she's a junky that doesn't have a job.

I mostly get good grades and have a large group of respectable friends, while Nathan is lucky to even turn up to school, has fewer friends, and those he calls friends are lawbreakers.

When we were younger, the bad boy thing was appealing, but I'm not so into it these days. Nathan has never been interested in me. Our conversations have only ever been small talk and typically happen when he's drunk or high. That seems to be the only time I get a half-decent conversation out of him. It's just never been real. I couldn't tell you a real truth about him, and he sure as shit couldn't reveal one about me. Yet I always go back. Not this time, though.

"What about?" I attempt to sound like I don't care.

"Well, he wanted me to ask you to come to a party at his mate's place tomorrow night."

I frown, "On a Tuesday night? Who even has a party on a Tuesday night?" I ask, needing confirmation.

Abbey nods and shrugs at the same time.

"And why couldn't he ask me himself?"

"He's scared you won't respond to him, I guess, after your last breakup," Abbey says.

I sigh, unsure of how to take this information.

"What did you say to him?" I ask, ignoring the huge grin spreading across Abbey's face.

"Well, I told him that if he wants you to go to a party, he needs to grow a pair of big hairy man balls, pick up the phone and call you himself. Not text, but call." She looks happy with herself.

"Oh, you did, did you?" I grin, and she nods enthusiastically.

"He's going to call you tonight." She wags her eyebrows.

I roll my eyes. As if Nathan is going to call me tonight, or ever. He prefers texting or avoidance. The idea of talking to him irks me, so I steer the conversation to our regular small talk for the rest of the walk to school.

When we reach school, Daniel is waiting for Abbey at the front gate, and the moment they spot each other, it's like a magnet draws them together. I silently curse myself at my growing jealousy. Abbey is entitled to this happiness. I just wish I could have that sort of happiness too.

Approaching our group of friends who are huddling in front of the school hall, I pick up on the buzz of excitement stirring the girls. Tasha doesn't even try to be quiet as she speaks about the new guy starting today. Apparently, this new guy who has all the girls frothing at the mouth is Marcus' cousin. The same cousin that Marcus spoke about in his messages last night. All the girls in the crowd are fanning their faces and acting pathetic. I feel like slapping them. God, have I ever been like that?

"Good lord Lex, will you take a look at that fine specimen?" Abbey whisper shouts.

"You know I can hear you, right?" Daniel reminds her, not impressed at Abbey's apparent physical attraction to the newbie.

"Oh Daniel," Abbey forgets all about me and turns in his arms to kiss him, "You know I only have eyes for you."

Rolling my eyes, I step through our group of friends needing to get away from all the lovey-dovey stuff.

"Oh, hey Lexi," Marcus all but jumps in front of me, looking eager.

I stop just in time to avoid crashing into his tall frame and huff, raising an unimpressed brow.

"I just wanted to introduce you to my cousin." Marcus picks up on my mood, speaking warily.

Turning my head, I take in his cousin, who has all the girls practically dropping their panties. He's tall, but so is almost everyone compared to my 5'5" height. I can tell he's related to Marcus as they have a similar strong jawline and the same dark hair. However, this guy looks a little older with the dusting of facial hair shading his jaw and upper lip.

Then he smiles.

Oh man, now I know why the other girls are fanning themselves. He has one of those melting smiles. One that lights up his whole face, framing his straight white teeth and drawing attention to those piercing blue eyes that somehow darken when they look at me.

"Hey," he says, and my feet remain stuck on the spot, not able to move.

Heat ripples over my skin, my body deceiving me by showing the flush on my face. I can feel the way my cheeks burn like they're on fire, and I watch as his smile gets wider, as if he's pleased.

Dammit. I internally do an eye roll at how pathetic I am right now, and force myself to respond, hoping to say something smart and witty.

Instead I say, "hey."

Seriously? Hey?

Naturally, like a coward, I snap my mouth closed and do what any respectable girl would do.

I dash around Marcus to escape, never catching his cousin's name.

Four

Typically, our school day starts with homeroom, however, today, it's cancelled for a whole school assembly. Like sheep, the teachers herd us into the school hall, which isn't even big enough to hold the capacity of students trying to find seats.

Surely this is a fire hazard.

Unscheduled assemblies are rarely the result of something good at FP Catholic. It usually means there's an issue of some kind or something bad has happened. The last unscheduled assembly we were called to was about five weeks ago when the Principal broke the news about the suicide of Carla Wilson. That was a tough day. Even though I didn't know her that well, the heartbreaking truth still affected me. There have been times over the last few months that I've felt so alone that I almost wished my life would end.

It's a cold, desolate place to be. A place I fight hard to avoid going to on a daily basis. Carla's suicide was a shock to everyone. No one knew how much pain she had carried. On the outside, she appeared happy, just like me.

Last year, the Principal called an unscheduled assembly to advise us that the teachers were disgusted with some of the students' behaviour and their treatment of the college veggie patch. So really, who knows what this assembly will be about? Hopefully, nothing too brutal.

I take a seat next to Abbey and Daniel, feeling very much like the third wheel. My mood is plummeting fast. I'm struggling with the need to run out of this claustrophobic hall, feeling like a trapped sardine.

Principal Ryland stands on the stage at the front of the hall, looking like his usual ruffled self, and notifies us that the school has been vandalised over the weekend. He advises us that the arts block and the school canteen are strictly out-of-bounds until further notice, and for the time being, the school canteen will operate out of the cooking rooms.

The more the Principal talks, the more my heart sinks with an unsettled feeling taking root in my chest. My mind flits back to yesterday morning, and Travis' words come back to me, "Right after you threw a chair through the glass doors."

No.

The two situations can't be related.

As if I would be involved in something like that.

Right?

I have no memory of Saturday night, and the little I do know, tells me I'd already done things I wouldn't normally do.

Shit!

The cheers of a group of immature boys ignite a ripple effect across the sea of students. While they think the vandalism is funny, the thought of it only makes me feel sick. I have to stay calm. I shouldn't jump to the conclusion that I was involved, but the more I think about it, the more my gut is screaming at me that I was a part of it.

Holy shit. I think I did this!

I can't let anyone see my truth. Why do I feel like everyone is looking at me?

I suck in slow, deep breaths, trying to push down my paranoia and work hard to keep my face looking neutral, so I don't appear as guilty as sin.

Abbey's attention is too wrapped up in something Daniel is whispering to her, so she doesn't notice my rigid body. Someone does, though. I can feel it. I feel eyes on me, and I'm almost certain that it's not just my imagination. Pretending to look around the hall casually, my eyes are automatically drawn to the wall on the far side, lined with students who couldn't find a seat.

As if my subconscious is seeking him out, my eyes lock with the dark gaze of the new guy.

Shit.

My face heats, having caught him looking at me, but he doesn't look away or even seem to care that I've sprung him. He's studying me curiously, and it makes me squirm.

His face is unreadable, so I can't tell what motivates him to continue staring, but dread fills me, worried he can tell I'm the guilty bitch who trashed the school.

Breaking the stare, I glance down at my hands and make myself look busy with my phone, which is how I stay for the rest of the assembly. When it's finally over, I tell Abbey that I'm not feeling well, and rush out of the hall beelining for the closest toilets.

Shutting myself in a cubicle, I send Travis a message through Instagram.

@lexiwest
What happened on Saturday night?

I'm surprised when I get an immediate response.

@travthe_man
If you want information, it will cost you.

I growl in frustration.

@lexiwest
What do you want?

@travthe_man
Another kiss. X

I roll my eyes. Of course, that's his response.

@lexiwest
It's not going to happen, Travis!

@travthe_man
Oh Lexi, you break my heart!
Fine. If you won't kiss me AGAIN, then I want something else.

@lexiwest
Stop stuffing around and tell me what you want?

@travthe_man
Wow! Someone's a grumpy bitch today!
I would like you to score me a bag of weed off your brother.
If you do that, then I'll tell you everything.

What is he talking about? Weed off my brother?

@lexiwest
What????

@travthe_man

Get me a bag of weed off your brother, and I'll tell you everything. Can you not read? Or do you not know all the juicy details about your brother?

@lexiwest

You know I can read Travis!!!
Tell me about my brother.

@travthe_man

Tell me what happened on Saturday night?
Tell me about my brother?
You are very needy, aren't you, Sexy Lexi!

@lexiwest

God damn it, Travis, don't fuck with me!

@travthe_man

And there she is, the real Lexi West! Nice to have you back. I have to say I feel pretty special knowing you only bring the real Lexi

*out for me. And before you lose your shit,
I will tell you about your brother, but not
about Saturday night until you get me a bag
of weed.*

@lexiwest
Fine.

@travthe_man
*Your brother has quickly become a
well-known local dealer. He has made
himself quite a reputation since he moved
here. He sells the good shit too, but it's
expensive. Get me some, and I'll tell you
whatever you want to know.*

To be honest, this news doesn't surprise me that much. Mike frequently uses drugs in front of me, and he's always got an entourage of different people with him who look more fucked up than he does. I know nothing about buying drugs, but I need to know if I had something to do with the school vandalism, so it looks like I'm going to learn how to score drugs fast.

@lexiwest
Fine. When do you want it?

Knowing I'm late for History, I fly out of the toilets and across the yard. My teacher, Mr Boyer, thankfully doesn't scold me. I'm never late, and he seems to like me, so I count that as a small win.

I'm beyond concerned by this morning's events, and I just want to run away and hide. To do that, though, it would mean going home where Mike is, and there is no way I'm going back there until I have no other choice.

Looking across the classroom to the back table where I usually sit with Abbey, I notice Daniel is sitting in my seat, with his books scattered over the desk I usually occupy. He has made himself at home.

I roll my eyes. I can't even stop myself, but thankfully Abbey and Daniel are so wrapped up in each other that they don't even notice me standing at the front of the room.

Someone else notices me, though.

The new guy.

Great.

Worry overwhelms me again, and I turn, looking longingly at the classroom door, wanting nothing more than to walk back through it.

I can't do this, and I don't want to be here. I should just leave now and stop torturing myself, especially since I'm five seconds away from bursting into tears.

Sucking in a steadying breath, I walk up to Mr Boyer's desk at the front of the room. The new guy is sitting with Mr Boyer going through classwork, but I try to ignore him. My need to get the hell out of here stronger than my need to avoid him.

"Yes, Miss West?" Mr Boyer looks up from the worksheets.

"Can I please have a pass to the library?"

Mr Boyer frowns, "Why?"

I clear my throat, trying hard to avoid eye contact with the new guy. "For, um… personal reasons?"

Mr Boyer seems confused, and he rises from his chair and approaches me.

"Is everything okay, Lexi?" Concern fills his voice. He's a friendly teacher, old but nice, and someone I've always had a good rapport with. He's always dressed sharply like he spends hours pressing his suit just to come to a job to teach arrogant teenagers. His slick salt and pepper hair has started balding in the back, and I wonder if he has a wife at home to tell him about his thinning hair.

Unfortunately, his concern is breaking down the walls I try so hard to keep up. My eyes glass over, ready to leak and destroy the illusion of thick skin I've worked so hard to fool everyone with. Embarrassed, my gaze automatically darts to the new guy. Even though he's been watching me, he looks away just as quickly, either wanting to give me a bit of privacy or in disgust that I'm as weak and pathetic as every other needy girl.

"I'm just having a bad day," I speak so softly it's nearly a whisper, "I'm up to date with my Ancient Pyramid assignment."

Mr Boyer takes a moment to consider my request and then nods, turning to his desk to fill out a library pass.

"Here you go, Miss West. I hope tomorrow is a better day for you." I take the pass from his hand and nod, taking another deep breath.

Standing tall, I lift my chin to leave, throwing on my *'I'm happy and confident, and nothing can get me down'* smile, ignoring the new guy's curious gaze once again.

Unfortunately, Abbey and Daniel spot me, and Daniel starts packing up his stuff. "Hey, Lexi, sit here next to Abs."

I shake my head. "No, it's all good. You stay there. I'm off to the library." I turn and walk out the door, ignoring Abbey's frown.

I'm a coward, I know. Abbey is going to know something is wrong with me, and the way I just brushed her and Daniel off most likely hurt her feelings. She's done nothing wrong. It's my fucked up head that is all wrong, and she's better off if I'm not around her when I'm like this.

The library becomes my sanctuary for the first two periods. I decide that going to PE class is way beyond what I can deal with, so I convince Miss Tate, the librarian, to mark my attendance for period two as well. Normally she'd refuse such a request. I've seen many students try to convince her to let them hide away in here before. I'm not sure why she lets me, but I'm taking it as another small win in my otherwise crappy day.

I hide in the back corner of the library where it's a little darker and quieter, lounging on the beanbag that I moved up here from the silent reading area a couple of years ago. I have no idea why it's never been moved back, but I'm happy it's still here for me.

Relaxing back, I start to read *The Hate You Give* by Angie Thomas.

Immersing myself in a story about someone else's life helps to get me out of my screwed-up head. I'm an over-thinker, more so now than ever. It's exhausting. Reading typically helps me calm my thoughts and brings my mental state to somewhere closer to normal. At least to any onlookers, I appear normal, so hopefully, this will help me get through the rest of the day.

At recess, I avoid the newly relocated canteen, aka the cooking rooms, and head straight to where we hang out. I push down the guilt about the canteen, since I'm not sure if I'm even involved in the vandalism, and decide that worrying won't help.

My group of friends occupy a courtyard near the school hall. The girls typically sit on the retaining wall sheltered by trees, and the boys sit on the picnic tables out in the open. When we have sunny days like today, we usually spread out over the grass to soak up the sun and warm our skin from the winter chill. The courtyard is bustling with activity and conversation, and it puts me at ease. No one appears to be whispering or talking about me or my part in vandalising the school, so hopefully, that means I'm not involved, or the truth isn't out yet.

Our large group of friends comprises of people who are polar opposites. A mix of sporty, musical, artsy, and genius makes up our group, and although we are all different, we mostly mix well and look out for each other, Tasha being the exception. There never seems to be a dull moment. To me, this is as close to home as I get. Despite some of the girls being real bitches, I ignore the dumb shit they say and pull them up on the serious crap. It's nothing I can't handle. A few of the boys have been my friends since we were bratty kids, and I tend to get along with them better than the bitchy girls.

I spot Abbey and Daniel sitting at one of the picnic tables with Maddie and Kyle in one of their little love bubbles. It immediately turns me sour. I'm being replaced not just by Daniel but by another couple too. I see it right before my eyes, and I can feel a shift in the disposition of our group.

I don't want to be here.

"Jesus, you think they could at least wait until the end of the day before doing the whole couple hang out thing." I look up to see Simon, one of the boys from our group, standing next to me. He's glaring at Abbey and Daniel sitting across the courtyard.

I scoff, "Yeah, right, as if they'd do that."

Simon chuckles and looks down at me from his tall height, his ash blonde hair falling over his eyes before he Bieber whips the hair away. "You know, Lexi, you and I could be a couple and totally join them."

I roll my eyes, but he throws his arm around me anyway, leading me to the picnic tables where the boys are sitting. I don't fight him off. I secretly like the human contact.

"Like my new wifey?" Simon wags his brows suggestively at his mates, who look from me to him and laugh.

My smile is real, and it feels nice, getting caught up in the fun banter these boys have. "Wouldn't I have to agree to be your wife, Simon?"

"Oh, come on, of course, you agree. How could you not want all this," he gestures to himself, "as your man?"

Shaking my head, I try to stifle a stupid girly giggle. "Nice try, but this chick is happily single." I'm such a liar.

Feeling the intense stare of eyes on me again, I automatically search for the source.

It's him again. The newbie, who is grinning at the banter between Simon and me.

I nearly forget to breathe. That damn smile. It looks genuine and friendly, so unless he's a trained actor, I get the impression that I don't repulse him. Maybe he doesn't know my secret, or at least the secret I think happened over the weekend.

No one knows about my other secret, not even Abbey.

"You're delusional, Hastings. Lexi only has eyes for me." Shaun teases before blowing me a kiss.

"You wish, Bossi. Lexi knows you're a walking STD." Simon digs back, causing all the boys to chant an "ooooh".

I love this. Well, not being the centre of their conversation, but I love how they rib each other and can still laugh about it. It's the opposite of how the girls talk together. I laugh with the guys, finally feeling the smallest bit of happiness.

Allison eventually calls me away, and I reluctantly leave Simon's side, trying hard to ignore the new "couples" table where my best friend is. Joining the girls, I take a seat on the ledge, disappointed that the only sun I now feel is the small rays dotting through the tree's leaves overhead.

I'm quiet, keeping myself busy by scrolling through my SnapChats while I listen to the girls talk about their weekend shenanigans and how incredibly hot the new guy is. Every time they mention him, I can't help but look to where he is, and every time I do that, he is already looking at me. It makes me feel uncomfortable, but at the same time, I can't help but like his attention. I can feel the curiosity in his gaze, and I'm hoping it's not because he can see the secrets I keep.

The bell rings for the end of recess, drawing my awareness away from the attention I'm getting from the new guy, as does the text message that pops up on my phone. I stop breathing when I see Mike's name on the screen. My heart sinks and anxiety churns in my chest.

Like not being able to look away from a car accident, I just have to open the message even while knowing that nothing good ever comes from Mike texting me.

Mike (Shithead brother)
So it turns out that dad knows nothing about
the locks Ali.
Nice try bitch!

I re-read the text over and over, ignoring Mike's nickname for me as panic sets in.

Shit, shit, shit!

This isn't good.

Why did he talk to dad about the locks?

Why does he have to do this to me?

The small reprieve that recess and being surrounded by my friends had given me comes to a crashing halt because, with that one single message from Mike, I'm knocked back down. Drowning. Suffocating. Heavy.

Five

I'm late to class again. Mike's text message has thrown me, messing up my ability to function and keep my facade in place. I can feel the cracks in my armour getting bigger and bigger.

I hate him!

I have a double Maths class now, and because I'm late, there is only one seat left, and guess who it's with.

The new guy.

Seriously, who the hell did I piss off to be getting this kind of Karma?

With a huff, I walk through the bright classroom to the table at the back that I usually have to myself.

"Lexi, is everything okay?" Miss Dice is another of the good ones. I've found myself on more than one occasion opening up to her about my mum. She knows more about my troubles than any other teacher here, but what she knows doesn't even scratch the surface.

She has a warm, friendly face, heart-shaped and olive in tone, that ties in perfectly with her straight dark brown bob cut. Her deep brown eyes never have a speck of mascara framing them, her dark lashes needing no help to stand out. She wears the cutest clothes that can only be found in the city since I haven't come across a local store with such style. Cashmere sweaters and lace-trimmed blouses top the finest pencil skirts with intricate stitch detail. And then there's the shoes. I'm not really a shoe person, but I can tell Miss Dice is. I bet she has a room in her house dedicated to her shoe collection.

Turning back to Miss Dice, I smile and nod, appeasing her while taking the last few steps to my seat. She informs me to continue with the modules in my book as I sit, trying to ignore the grin on the new guy's face.

"Wow, you really don't want to sit next to me, do you?"

I'm not entirely sure what I thought his voice would sound like, but its gravelly tone sends a warm flush over my skin.

Sighing, I turn to him, hoping the flush on my cheeks isn't visible. "I'm sorry. I've been rude today. It's not you."

"Really?" He smirks. "You're giving me the 'it's not you, it's me' speech?"

I consider that and nod. "I guess I am."

"So you don't think I have cooties, then?" he asks, still grinning.

I'd like to know what he finds so damn amusing. Raking my eyes lower, I give him an obvious once over, trying to make him feel uncomfortable, but it has the opposite effect. He sits taller and I think he even puffs out his chest, not shying away from having my eyes on him.

"Nope, I think you're cootie free." I announce, and he chuckles.

Dear god, he chuckles, and I swear I can feel heat in places I'm not meant to. I can't control it, nor the grin that tugs at my lips. Turning away quickly, I pretend to read my Maths work, but he's not giving up that easily, thrusting his hand in my line of vision.

"I'm Ayden." He introduces himself, keeping his hand held out, waiting for me to take it.

My gaze locks on to his hand, all strong and manly, and like I have no control over my body, my hand slips into his warm palm.

Clearing my throat, I pry my eyes from where we are connected and glance up to meet his piercing blue gaze as I speak. "Lexi."

My voice is quiet, and husky, and Ayden smiles that same smile from earlier, hypnotising me. I feel my body betray me again, my cheeks flushing hot, and I reluctantly pull my hand away and turn back to focus on my work. His quiet chuckle floats over me before he does the same, shifting in his chair to focus on his own work.

When I say I focus on my work, what I mean is that I stare blankly at the page, not taking anything in, not seeing anything, and only thinking about how nice it felt to have my hand in his. It was a real struggle to remove my hand from his grip, not because he was holding too tight, but because I found it hard to want to let go.

The distraction of Ayden only lasts a few minutes before a new unwelcome distraction takes its place. My phone, which is face-up on the table above my workbook, vibrates with an incoming text message, and Mike's name pops up on the screen. I instantly feel sick, my empty tummy rolling over.

I don't want to read his message. Not now. Not ever. There won't be anything good in it, and I can't take the risk of prying eyes. I can't let anyone see the vile things he says to me.

The murky cloud I've been trying so hard to fend off all day hovers over me like a sinking sky, and my emotions are at war, battling to spill out through the cracks.

Miss Dice appears at my table then, squatting in front of me, to duck her head into my line of vision.

"Lexi, what's wrong?" she asks quietly.

Shit, I've failed to hide my emotions.

This isn't good.

I shake my head, letting her know I can't talk about it, and in understanding, she nods.

"Is it your mum?" The concern in her voice extracts a single tear from my right eye, and I brush it away quickly, shaking my head again. Miss Dice sighs, giving me a sympathetic look. "Do you need to go home?"

I shake my head fiercely.

Home is not where I need to be, but I can't tell her that. I can't tell anyone that.

Miss Dice frowns, and I'm worried she sees what I've been trying so hard to hide.

"It's just a bad day, and I'm struggling to concentrate, that's all. I'll be okay."

Lies, lies, lies!

She nods in understanding. "You can listen to your music if you want, Lexi. Zone out for a while. Just make sure you get the modules done before the next class."

"Thanks." I nod in relief, happy that she's a decent enough teacher not to be a dick about it, but also that she mustn't know what's really going on.

Smiling, she returns to her desk at the front of the classroom, and I search my blazer for my earphones but can't find them.

"Shit." I must have lost them.

An earbud appears in front of me then, and I turn to look at Ayden in question.

"It's clean," he states. "I'll share my music with you if it helps. I'll even let you choose a few songs." He winks.

I'm not familiar with accepting help, but thankful for the gesture, and unable to refuse him when he winks like that, I give him a small smile and nod.

Taking the earbud, I pop it in my left ear, and a smile instantly lifts my lips when I hear the familiar sound of *We As Human*.

"Take the bullets away. Nice."

A crease forms in between Ayden's brows. "You know this?"

I nod, and he raises a questioning brow. Grabbing my phone, I flash my Spotify screen to show him I'd been listening to the same song earlier. He looks surprised and then grabs my phone, trying to unlock it but gets blocked by my passcode.

He shoves it back to me. "Unlock it for me?" He smiles, trying to appear sweet. "Please."

Rolling my eyes at his pathetic attempt, I unlock it but make sure the text from Mike isn't visible before opening the Spotify app and handing my phone back to him.

I watch nervously as he scrolls through my playlist.

"Wow."

"What?" My self-conscious monster whispers insecurities in my ear. Is he about to give me his opinion on the dark music I listen to?

"Your playlist is nearly identical to mine." He sounds pleased, and I can't help but smile.

"Why is your playlist called Heavy?" he asks, looking back up to me, and my gut drops.

I quickly snatch my phone back, realising I shouldn't have let him look at my playlist. As weird as it sounds, that shit is personal.

"I just thought it was an appropriate name for it, okay?" I snap, shoving my phone back into my blazer pocket.

"Hey." He taps my hand to get me to look at him again. "Sorry, I didn't mean to pry."

Damn it. Why do I have to be such a fucking freak?

Why do I always assume that people will use the information they learn about me against me?

And why do I always feel like everyone is out to get me?

Shame fills me again, knowing the cracks are getting bigger, and my emotions are getting the better of me. Shaking my head, I try to look sincere.

"No, I'm the one that should be sorry. Your first encounter with me, and I'm having a stupid headcase day."

He chuckles, "A headcase day, hey? Haven't heard a bad day called that before, but it works."

And just like that, he's lightened my mood again.

We both turn our attention back to our work. Ayden stumbles his way through fractions while I doodle pictures along the white margins of my textbook as we listen to his playlist with most of the songs that I would have chosen myself.

Every now and then, I peek at Ayden as he works. Sometimes he catches me, and other times he doesn't. When he catches me, he gives me a smile or a wink, and the other times, I witness the most adorable look of concentration on his face as he works his way through the equations.

After class, Ayden walks with me to my locker before heading to his. Our conversation is light and involves which songs we think are better than others. It's refreshing to talk to someone who has the same taste in music as me. While I like all music, having a very eclectic taste, Abbey is a straight-up pop girl and doesn't understand my music preferences. She hates talking about the songs or artists I like, just as much as she hates listening to them.

There's just something about punk and heavy rock that speaks to my soul. Some say that type of music is too dark and violent. To me, it's calming, and I often feel like it understands me more than I understand myself. Maybe I am all sorts of screwed up, but knowing Ayden has the same taste in music helps me not care so much. Maybe I should just embrace my fucked up side.

The sun is high, warming up the courtyard during lunch, well as much as a seventeen-degree winter day can. Abbey, Daniel, Maddie, and Kyle have coupled together again on the far picnic table, making me feel like I've completely lost my best friend. Even though I'd prefer to hang with the boys, I sit with Tasha, Allison, Amanda and Sophie on the courtyard grass, listening to them babble about a party coming up in a few weeks. No one notices that I don't have food, but when Amanda offers some of her lunch platter to everyone, I don't refuse and try not to pounce on it like a starved animal. The two pieces of cubed cheese and three sticks of carrot are all I've eaten since the fruit last night. To say I'm hungry is an understatement.

Halfway through lunch, I lay back on the grass side by side with Amanda, enjoying the calm the sun brings me even though the air is still cold. Leave it to Simon to burst my peaceful bubble when his voice floats over from the table the boys are at, about how he would love to have my legs wrapped around him.

"I can hear you, Simon," I say loud enough to get momentary silence from the table before they burst out laughing.

"Oh, come on, Lexi. Don't knock it until you try it, baby."

The girls make gagging sounds and laugh at Simon before a shadow blocks the precious sun. At first, I think it's Simon coming over to stir the pot, but then earphones dangle in front of me, and I sit up, turning to Ayden, who is now on his haunches next me.

"Here are your earphones. You left them behind in Maths."

I'm about to say no, I didn't, knowing that the blue corded earphones are not mine, but then he whispers, "Just take them."

A small smile tugs at the corner of my mouth, and I silently do as he asks before he stands and returns to the picnic table with the rest of the guys.

The silence that greets me from the girls tells me that, if I look at them, I would probably see them all gaping at me. I ignore them, though, lying back down with the music now blaring through the earphones and blocking out the world. Papa Roach fills my ears with Last Resort, and I listen contently while scrolling through my Heavy playlist.

A Facebook notification pops up on my phone screen interrupting my scrolling, and I tap it open to find a new friend request from Ayden Mitchell.

My heart flutters, my cheeks warm, and my body tingles.

I'm such a girl.

I'm seriously swooning simply because I received a friend request from the new guy. If I were a stronger person, I'd ignore the friend request and give myself a stern talking to for being so easy. Since I'm not that person, I don't hesitate to accept it, and moments later, a message pops up from him.

Ayden Mitchell
I thought you might like to block out that dickhead's crude remarks by listening to your music. I hope you didn't mind me doing that?

Smiling, I reply.

Lexi West
I'm thankful. I'll return them when lunch ends.

Ayden Mitchell
No, you keep them. I have another set at home.

Lexi West
I can't just keep them, Ayden. I will at least pay you for them. Otherwise, you're taking them back.

Ayden Mitchell
Nope, not happening!

Lexi West
Ayden!

Ayden Mitchell
Lexi!

I laugh, getting unwanted attention from Tasha as she pops her head up from where she is laying to look at me, but I ignore her.

Lexi West
You can't just give me your earphones.

Ayden Mitchell
Think of them as a gift.

Lexi West
A gift? What for? It's not my birthday.

Ayden Mitchell
A thank you gift.

Lexi West
What on earth do you need to thank me for?
Being a rude bitch to you?

Ayden Mitchell
Talking to me. ☺

Jesus, now I'm giddy.

Lexi West
You don't have to thank me for that!
I should thank you for tolerating my bitchy
mood.

Ayden Mitchell
Yes, I do have to thank you for that.
I get the impression you don't talk to just
anyone.
I feel privileged, bitchy mood, and all.

I snort.

"Who are you texting, Lexi?" Tasha pries, now standing over me.

Shit. I didn't even notice that she'd stood up.

"Simon." I lie, laughing.

Ayden snorts then, and all eyes turn to him. I can barely contain my giggles, but I try hard since I'm enjoying keeping Tasha and her minions out of my happy bubble. Simon looks all kinds of confused as he glances at his phone screen to see if there is a message from me.

Ayden Mitchell
You're going to get us busted.

Lexi West
Probably.

Ayden Mitchell
You don't care?

I consider his question.

Lexi West
Actually, I do care.

Ayden Mitchell
I thought so.

The bell rings then, spoiling the small bit of fun I'm having in a day filled with dread. While everyone gets up with enthusiasm, I sigh, slowly dragging myself up off the grass. My next class is English, which I have to admit is my favourite, so it's not so bad, but it means that the school day is nearly over, and I will have to go back home before too long.

Thinking about going home reminds me that Mike sent me another text message during Maths, so I decide it's now or never and read it as I dilly-dally to my locker.

Mike (Shithead brother)
You are so fucked!

Okay, so I shouldn't have read it, because now, concentrating on English will be impossible.

Six

It's just after 7pm when I sneak in through my bedroom window. Avoiding my return home, I spent hours at the park around the corner doing my homework. Even after the night sky darkened, I couldn't bring myself to go home, and it wasn't until my phone battery was nearly dead that I put my big girl knickers on and forced myself to get it over and done with.

Mike's car sits in the carport, and loud music blares from inside the house. Given that the music is that loud, I have to assume my mum is passed out drunk, high, or is out getting another fix. Either way, Mike is inside, and that isn't a good scenario for me. That's why I choose to sneak in through my window.

Safely back in my room, I'm relieved to find my door still securely locked. After Mike's text messages earlier, I'd been afraid I would come home to a busted lock and a ransacked room. With my phone now on the charger, I change out of my school uniform and throw on my grey trackies and my favourite Metallica t-shirt before slipping my Slipknot hoodie over the top. Finally,

I feel comfortable in my own skin. I tug out my pristine school regulation ponytail, gathering up my blonde waves, and with a few twists of my hair elastic, I pile my hair into a messy bun on top of my head. Now I feel like myself.

Loud voices float up from downstairs, both male and female. Mike usually behaves himself when he has female company, so for now, I should be safe. Knowing this, I sneak out from the security of my room, locking it up behind me and letting the chain fall back around my neck to hide under my hoodie. First, I use the toilet before sneaking downstairs to the kitchen.

Eight people crowd around my kitchen table. A dirty green bong sits in the middle, and its woodsy smoke already hovers in the air, and along the other side of the table are several white lines of powder on top of my hand mirror that I keep in the upstairs bathroom. I hold in my curse when I see this. The fuckers are using my damn mirror to snort their filthy drugs off. The urge to snatch my mirror up and smash it over Mike's ugly face flits through my mind. If only I had that sort of courage. It would be so fucking satisfying.

As I walk past the table, I watch one of the girls bend over and snort a line of the white powder up her nose.

"Oh, who do we have here?" A sleazy male voice alerts everyone to my presence.

Trying to ignore them, I glance at my mum's closed bedroom door, wondering if she's home as I move deeper into the kitchen. Finding several pizza boxes on the kitchen bench, I flip one open, and my stomach rejoices as the smell of melted cheese and pizza sauce teases me. My mouth waters with want, and knowing it won't be long before Mike starts his shit with me, I grab a plate and fill it with four slices of Hawaiian pizza. Moving to the fridge, I grab out a can of Pepsi Max and a water bottle, and with my hands now full, I make my way out of the kitchen.

Mike has other ideas, though, and bolts up from his seat to block my path.

"Where are you going, sis?" His foul breath engulfs my face, and I have to fight back the urge to gag.

Trying to look unfazed by him, I raise a brow.

"You have a sister?" One of the girls squeaks, clapping her hands.

Really? She's clapping because Mr Dickhead has a sister? Jesus, they must be damn good drugs she's snorting up her nose.

"Yep, she's a little whore too." In response to Mike's statement, the males in the room hoot, but the girls go quiet.

"That's not nice, Mike." A girl with bright red hair scolds coming to stand by him.

Mike looks from me to her, "You're right, baby, that's not nice." He returns his gaze to me.

"Sorry little sis. Forgive me?" The girl beams, misunderstanding his sarcasm for sincerity.

"Sure, whatever," I move to step around him, and much to my surprise, he lets me.

Not one to second guess the situation, I take off quickly, going upstairs, two steps at a time before I remember my deal with Travis.

Shit. I have to get a bag of weed off Mike for him.

There's just one problem.

I can't ask Mike for it. Even if I had the money to buy the weed off him, Mike would still use it against me, and it could escalate an already out of hand situation. I glance at Mike's bedroom door, which is slightly ajar, and make a hasty decision. Returning to my room briefly to put down my one meal for the day, I hurry back out and creep down the hall to Mike's bedroom.

It's filthy and stinks like dirty socks. Screwing up my nose in distaste, I rummage through his cupboard and chest of drawers, coming up empty-handed. I'm about to give up when I notice his bedside table is out of place. Turning on the bedside lamp, I look behind the mahogany drawers to see the wall has a jagged cut in the plaster, which is slightly protruding. *Nice hiding spot, Mike!*

Making haste, I ease the drawers out of the way and pry open the plaster.

Bingo! Stacked neatly in the wall cavity is what I assume are bags of weed on one side, and on the other side is whatever the white powdery substance is that they are happily snorting up their noses downstairs.

Without thinking twice, I snatch a bag of weed, shoving it into my hoodie pocket, and then return everything to their original positions. I look back over Mike's room before leaving, making sure nothing looks out of place. Satisfied, I beeline back to my room, desperate to avoid another run-in with Mike, especially while I'm carrying a bag of his weed.

Once I'm inside my room again with the door locked behind me, I cry for the second time in as many nights. I let the tears fall silently for a few minutes, giving way to the emotions that have plagued me all day. It's been an arse-fuck of a day. Most of the time, my emotions were running scared, but there were some moments where I felt the little flickers of what happiness used to feel like. Most of that happiness came from the new guy, Ayden, but Simon and the other guys also had a hand in making me smile.

When I feel some of my control return, I pull myself together to eat the now cold pizza. The thing about pizza is that it's still yummy cold. There's a very real chance that I would eat anything cold right now despite how nice it tastes. Once my tummy is full for the first time in days, I remember I'm carrying a bag of weed in my pocket.

It's not safe to have it on me or even in my room. I need to hide it somewhere, so I rummage through my closet and find a small wooden box that I made in year seven woodwork. It's the perfect size to keep the weed protected.

With the weed inside the box, I quietly climb out my window again and sneak into my backyard. Since the back corner has good coverage, I head there and hide the wooden box underneath the shrubs. The last thing

I need is Mike breaking into my room and finding his missing weed. That definitely wouldn't end well for me.

Happy that it won't be found, I move back through the backyard and climb back onto the roof.

"Did you have some fruit tonight?" A whisper yell comes from behind me, and I turn to see Valarie, my twelve-year-old neighbour, poking her head out her bedroom window.

Raising my finger to my mouth, I shoosh her and shake my head. "Not tonight," I whisper back.

"Have you been out with your friends?" Valarie asks in the same loud whisper.

"Ah, yeah. Sure." I can't exactly tell her what I was really doing, so the lie will have to do, which she accepts and waves before closing her window. Weird kid.

Ducking back through my window, I'm just in time to hear my phone ring. Nathan's name flashes across the screen, and I hesitate for a moment before answering.

"Hello."

The line is silent for a moment before I hear Nathan's voice.

"Uh- hi, it's Nathan."

I grin at his awkwardness. Over the past four years, I don't think I've ever spoken to him on the phone. A few brief texts and some very basic small talk is all we'd shared when we were together.

"Hey." I try to sound casual, but silence greets me, and I sigh. Why is this so hard for him?

"Did you call me for a reason?" The annoyance in my voice is unmistakable.

"Ah, yeah."

Jesus, do I have to do all the work? I'm struggling to know what I ever saw in him.

"And that reason is?" I ask, trying to prompt him to find the courage to have a bloody conversation.

"There's a party," he exclaims, "tomorrow night at Paul's house over on Soloman. You want to go?"

"With you?" I need to confirm what exactly he is asking. For all I know, he could just be spreading the word that there's a party.

"Ah-yeah. Well, can you maybe meet me there?" Nathan is out of his comfort zone right now. It's kind of funny, and I hope like hell that he can't hear the humour in my voice.

I'm already going to the party to meet Travis to exchange drugs for information, but Nathan doesn't need to know that.

"I guess I can try to get there at some point."

"Good," Nathan sounds relieved. "That would be good."

"Okay, text me what number Paul's house is on Soloman. I'll text you when I get there tomorrow night." My phone vibrates, and I hold it away from my ear to check the screen. There's a Facebook message from Ayden. My heart flutters and then sinks, and for a moment, I'm unsure why. Then, I realise I feel bad because I'm kind of talking to two boys at the same time. The thing is, I don't really want to talk to Nathan, so I know I need to make sure I let him know we are over for good when I see him tomorrow night. As for Ayden, well, I'm pretty happy talking to him.

"Yep, okay. Sounds good," Nathan says.

"Okay, gotta go." I'm more eager to read Ayden's message than continue this awkward conversation with my ex-boyfriend.

"Yep, okay. Bye."

I hang up as soon as Nathan says the words. I know it's rude of me, but I'm finding it harder to control the bitch in me these days. The dejection spreading through my soul is turning me into a heartless, empty shell, and I'm not sure how to stop it. Or if I even want to. Being a bitch isn't so bad. Maybe people will leave me the hell alone if I show them that part of me. My bitch version would much rather deal with daily life instead of the fake prim and proper version who smiles like a bimbo.

Pushing the dark thoughts aside, I fall back on my bed, getting tangled in the charger cord before opening Ayden's message.

Ayden Mitchell
What are you doing?

Lexi West
Nosey much?

Ayden Mitchell
Yep! Now spill!

Lexi West
Oh, you know, just avoiding a house full of druggos doing lines on my kitchen table. You?

Ayden Mitchell
It's like that, is it? Okay then, I'll play along! I'm at a strip club getting a lap dance. ☺

I laugh! Of course he doesn't think I'm being honest, which is why I said it. No one knows about the crude acts that happen under this roof. Not even Abbey. Thinking of Abbey is just a brutal reminder of how I haven't heard from her much today. It feels like she doesn't care, and it hurts. I miss her, and I need her.

Desperate for the distraction, I focus on Ayden because he's the one happy to take time out of his day to chat with me.

Lexi West
I'd like photo evidence of this so-called lap dance, please?

Ayden Mitchell
Okay! BRB.

I shake my head, my smile genuine. I can't wait to see what he comes back with. Waiting patiently, I fill the time by scrolling through Instagram and see that Abbey is with Daniel, or so her post shows. Pictures of the two of them hugging and kissing fill my screen before Ayden's message pops up.

Ayden Mitchell
Here you go!

There's a video attached, so I hit play, and hysterics immediately take over. He went to the trouble of cutting out a picture of a half-naked woman, probably from a dirty magazine he hides under his bed. He's holding the picture over his lap and moving it around to make it look like it's dancing, and then he says, *"See, lap dance,"* and then he winks.

His voice! That wink! I turn to mush, and I'm so thankful he can't see the heat in my cheeks right now. I save the video because I know I will want to watch it over and over like an obsessive moron.

My happiness dies a quick death when a loud bang rattles my bedroom door.

"Alexis, you little whore, open the door!" Mike slurs. Shit, he's wasted.

I'm frozen, watching the handle jiggle violently before more banging shakes the door. With my phone clutched in my hand, I stand from my bed, ready to make a run for my window.

"Mike, baby. Leave her alone and come worship my body." The soft voice of the redheaded girl from earlier filters through the door. Then, the rustle of movement tells me that Mike is doing what the girl asked before his bedroom door slams shut. I feel both relief and dread. I'm relieved that he is away from me, but that poor girl doesn't know what she's in for, and part of me feels like I should warn her. I take a few moments to calm down, trying to slow my racing heart when my phone vibrates in my hand.

Looking down, I see that I have a few new messages from Ayden.

Ayden Mitchell
Realistic, hey!

Ayden Mitchell
Okay, so I'm a liar. I'm at home in my bedroom, bored.

Ayden Mitchell

*Have I lost you already? Are you not a fan of
my humour?*

His messages squeeze a small smile from me, but the reality of my situation has me on edge, and I just wish I could escape it.

Lexi West

*Sorry. My brother interrupted me.
Your video evidence was interesting. I hope
you enjoyed the lap dance!!
As to your humour, as much as I would like
to tell you that it sucks, honestly, I am in
hysterics.* ☺

Well, I was in hysterics until Mike fucked with my happy vibe.

Ayden Mitchell

You have no idea how happy that makes me.
☺

His words, although simple, do all sorts of strange butterfly flip things to my insides. There's something about this guy. Something that has me almost hooked. Not only is he blissfully easy on the eyes, but he really seems like a decent person. I'm incredibly drawn to him, which scares me a little. I know I long to have what Abbey and Daniel have, but I just don't know if I'm made of the right stuff to make something like that work. My dad is an absent arsehole. My mum is a self-absorbed addict. And my brother is bordering on being a predator. I carry secrets that, if revealed, would repulse people. I don't think I'm cut from the relationship cloth. But man, I want to be. I want to be so damn much.

As much as I know without a doubt that I'm attracted to Ayden, I can't be sure if he feels the same towards me. I have no idea if he is flirting with me or just needs a friend because he's new. I'm not sure what this is between us, but I do know that when I go to the party tomorrow night, I will only go to do the exchange with Travis and then come right back home. My time with Nathan is over for good. I'm more certain of this than anything else. Well, I'm also confident that Ayden Mitchell is hot as hell, and he is spending his time chatting with me right now, so I'm not going to ignore that.

Lexi West
I'm kind of jealous. Your stripper visit looks much more fun than my crack house.

Ayden Mitchell

You could always have your own male stripper cut out. I'd love to see that video!!

Lexi West

Unlike you, Ayden, I don't have any porn magazines hidden in my room.

Ayden Mitchell

I can see how that would be a problem. But I'm not convinced about your crack house. Evidence, please!!!

I contemplate his demand for evidence. I could get some talc powder and make lines on my dresser, or I could just send him proof of the real thing. He would probably still think it's a setup. But what if he doesn't? Do I want to be that honest with him? Even Abbey doesn't know what happens in this house, and although this is just one of the many bad things that occurs, do I want to let him get a glimpse? Unsure if this is too risky, but wanting to win the convincing game we are playing, I decide to send him the real thing.

Lexi West
BRB.

Jumping up from my bed, I put my ear to the door, listening for sound beyond. There's still music playing faintly somewhere, but I can't hear any voices, so I take a deep breath and leave the safety of my room.

Grunts and moans immediately meet my ears, coming from the direction of Mike's bedroom. An uncontrollable shudder sweeps over my body, and I try to push away any thoughts those noises bring. Moving quickly down the stairs, I stop at the bottom to listen again. The radio is still playing in the kitchen, and I can also hear the faint murmur of my mum's TV in her bedroom, but no other voices.

Darting down the hall to the kitchen, I find that Mike is just as predictable as I thought. He and his so-called mates left all the evidence out, spread across the kitchen table and part of the kitchen bench. I would laugh at his audacity if the situation weren't so serious. Shaking my head, I hold up my phone to record myself.

"Welcome to the West Crack House." I give the screen a wink, just the way Ayden did, and then turn the screen around to film the table. Zooming in, I record the specs of white powder which are left behind from the snorted lines, and the two lines that remain untouched, ready for the taking. I include the ugly green bong with remnants of burnt weed sitting in the bowl for good measure.

Before I second guess my actions, I send the video to Ayden, and a few moments later, my phone starts beeping with a messenger call from Ayden.

Oh shit!

What have I done?

I'm such an idiot!

Regret slams into me, knowing I should never have sent the video. Of course, it doesn't look like a setup. He can tell it's real.

Panic fills me as the call stops and a message comes through.

Ayden Mitchell

Lex. Pick up my call.

My phone beeps again with his incoming call, and I flick the silence button on and message him back quickly.

Lexi West

What's wrong? Not realistic enough? Lol.

Shit! Shit! Shit! I'm screwed!

Ayden Mitchell

That was 100% realistic, Lexi. Please pick up my call!

Fuck!

Lexi West

I can't talk right now, Ayden. My mum needs me.

I hope he believes my lie.

Ayden Mitchell

When can you talk?

Lexi West

Umm... Never?

Ayden Mitchell

Lexi!

Lexi West

Ayden!

Ayden Mitchell

Are you safe?

I want to tell him the truth, but what can he do with that information? Tell the teachers at school? Then Child Services will get involved, and I will end up in a foster home somewhere on the other side of the state. Not to mention that everyone will know my secrets. Everyone will know I come from nothing but trash. I don't want that. I just need to hold out a bit longer until I finish school. Shame tugs at me like a heavy anchor trying to drag me under.

Lexi West
Yes.

Ayden Mitchell
I need to hear your voice.

Well, if that's not a loaded statement, then I don't know what is. I met him today, for fuck's sake. This is ridiculous. He is acting like we have known each other for ages, but it's only been a few damn hours.

Even as I think this, there's a part of me that feels like I can trust him, and I'm torn because I kind of want to give him what he wants. But I can't.

Lexi West
Tomorrow. GTG.

And just like that, I've ruined a good thing. A really good thing. Tears pool in my eyes and my shoulders drop in defeat. Fed up with my reality and the heavy weight I carry, the overwhelming impulse to walk out my front door and never look back plagues me. I don't know where I'd go, but I just want to be gone.

Knowing another emotional breakdown isn't far away, I shove my phone in my pocket and pop my head in to check on mum while I'm downstairs. She's in her usual position, sitting up asleep, mouth open, with faint snores escaping.

I wish I had a different mum. I'm sure just thinking that makes me a bad person, but there you have it. Lexi West is not worth the air she breathes.

These destructive thoughts hurt, but so does the wish to have a mum who wants me. A mum who fights for me, who has time for me. One who can see what her stepson is doing to me.

Tears fall, and I don't fight them. I don't make any noise as I cry silently, standing just inside the door of my mum's room. The same room that should have my dad in it, but as usual, he's nowhere to be seen. Absent as always.

I retreat quietly, pulling the door closed and turning back to the kitchen area, only to scream.

Mere feet from me Mike is lurking, wearing only a pair of jocks, barely covering his prominent swell still lingering from his session with the red-haired girl. At least that's the reason I insist on telling myself about his current state.

His cold dark eyes roam over my body, and even though I'm covered with my baggy trackies and hoodie, he still licks his lips.

Sick fucker!

Cheeks still wet from tears, my crying is replaced with crippling fear. Mike remains in front of me, not saying a word, his penetrating glare looking sinister. I try to step to the right, but he follows, stepping in my path. I try for the left, and he moves with me.

"What do you want?" I spit.

He grins, "Oh little sis, I think you know what I want."

I shake my head, refusing to play his games.

"I have homework to do. Go play with your little redhead." I try to step around him again, but he matches my move.

"I've already played with her. Now it's your turn." He lunges for me, and I hurry in the other direction, running, but I'm not fast enough.

Mike fists my hair, pulling me back, inflicting burning pain that momentarily paralyses me. I scream again as I'm hurled across the room to land forcefully on the edge of one of the dining chairs. The corner of my eye slams into the kitchen table, and pain slices through me before my vision wavers.

"Mike!" I hear a female scream.

I scramble to get up, my feet slipping on the tile floor.

"Fuck off. This is family business!" Mike hisses at the red-haired girl.

I take that moment while he's distracted to push myself up, the room swaying slightly. I ignore the dizziness and don't think twice as I bolt for the back patio door, needing to escape. Frantically, I fumble with the latch before getting it unlocked and reef the glass door open, determination fuelling me as I run out into the lonely cold night.

Seven

It's 2am before I sneak back into my house, climbing through my bedroom window after hearing Mike's car speed off. I'd taken refuge in Valarie's backyard after running from my brother. The cushioned grass in Valarie's orchard is soft enough to lie on and I passed the time by reading back over Ayden's messages and replaying the video he sent me over and over until my phone battery finally died.

After that, I watched the angry clouds sweep across the dark sky, catching brief glimpses of the stars, reminding me that there's still beauty in the world, despite the ugliness it shows me more often than not.

Once I'm back in my bed, sleep evades me for most of the night. I fight off tears, not wanting to cry anymore and wishing I was someone else, living a different life. There has to be some reason why I'm forced to keep suffering at the hands of my brother. What have I done to deserve such menace? I doubt I'll ever know the answer to that. Perhaps just being born was the mistake I made.

A small reprieve is gifted to me when Mike doesn't return before I leave for school in the morning. My attempt to reduce my puffy eyes and the bruising just above my cheekbone with a bag of frozen peas doesn't help. Today, concealer is my friend.

I stew over the idea of staying home. It's risky going to school and having someone possibly seeing what Mike did to my face. The need to hide away also niggles at me, knowing there's a possibility of someone seeing the giant cracks forming in my composure. The problem with staying home is that it will most certainly guarantee another run-in with Mike.

No fucking thanks!

Exhaustion gnaws at me, a reminder of my lack of sleep, while sadness twists my heart in defeat. I'm so over this life I live. I just want out of it. I don't know how to achieve that or what it means exactly. Do I want to run away? Do I just desperately wish I was living a different life, like I think about so often? Or am I over my whole existence? Jesus, do I want to die? Is that what my brain is trying to tell me?

No. No! I want to live... I think.

Digging deep, I drag my sorry arse to school. I message Abbey, telling her I'm running late and I'll meet up with her later. I can't deal with her happy love bubble right now, and I hate myself for being so selfish. Abbey deserves to be happy, so being around me today will only bring her down.

I stroll when I should be walking briskly, taking the back streets and laneways, paranoia controlling me.

Every car I hear approaching has me nearly fleeing with worry that it's Mike. I'm so jumpy, and I hate Mike even more for having this effect on me.

I deliberately arrive late to school after homeroom has already started, wanting to avoid the typical morning ritual of throwing on a fake smile and pretending my life is just as good as everyone else's. Not today, I just can't.

I walk carelessly through the school corridors, done pretending to be okay. My usual fake smile is gone, and by the looks on the faces of the few students left still roaming the halls, it hasn't gone unnoticed.

Abbey finally replies to my text message. An apology, of sorts. Apparently, Daniel picked her up for school, and she forgot to tell me.

Wow! Just wow! I have officially been replaced with a person who has a dick between their legs. This pisses me off, probably more than it should, but I can't help it. Abbey forgetting to let me know her change of plans is just another kick to my gut while I'm down. *Fuck this shit!*

Shoving my phone in my blazer pocket, I ignore the messages Ayden sent. He's better off forgetting about me and making friends with... Well, anyone but me. He seems like a sweet guy, and all I'll do is taint his happy existence.

Skipping homeroom, I go straight to science, taking my usual seat. The empty room allows me to have a quiet moment to myself and try and pull my shit together. I use the opportunity to rest my head on my hands and close my eyes, briefly giving in to the exhaustion. I'm jolted out of my brief slumber when the period one bell shrieks loud through the classroom speaker, sending my heart racing.

My quiet place turns to chaos as students file in, taking their seats. Tasha, who is the last person I'll be able to tolerate today, tries to sit next to me. I glare at her and tell her, in a not so polite way, that the seat is taken. I hear the word "bitch" fall from her lips when she sneers back at me and moves to another table towards the front of the room. Unfortunately, I have to do the same with Allison and Ayden, although I avoid looking them in the eye when I speak. They get the message and take a seat somewhere else.

Mr Parsons is discussing something about atoms. Fucking atoms. When the hell will I ever in my future life need to know about atoms? Since I have no desire to become a damn scientist, I decide that sleep is a better option, and I return my head to the surface of the desk, closing my eyes.

"Miss West!" The deep rumble of Mr Parsons' voice jolts me from my much-needed shut-eye. I look up sleepily to see him frowning down at me.

"Sleep is what you are supposed to do at home. Try putting your damn phone away at night and sleep instead of staying up to chat with your friends."

Well. Isn't he just a treat?

I have no control over the dagger I throw his way, and he flinches back a little, probably shocked since I'm usually Miss Goody Two Shoes. Standing, I gather my books and give him a sour smile.

"Sure, Mr Parsons. I'll do that in future." I head towards the door.

"Where do you think you're going?" he demands.

I shrug. "Anywhere but here." I walk out of the classroom, hearing the whispered murmurs of the other students. I should care about the rumours that will spread, or even care about how rudely I spoke to Mr Parsons, but right now, in this moment, I don't.

A normal kid would wag school and go home, but since I'm not normal, I head to the library instead. I ignore Miss Tate, the librarian, when she asks me for my library pass. With my eyes cast down and a scowl on my face, I go to my spot in the back corner. Turning into the last aisle, I'm met with the wide eyes of two year nine girls taking up the space that I so desperately need.

"Move." I hiss, and they scramble quickly, gathering up their books to rush past me.

I fall to the beanbag in exhaustion, with hunger gnawing at me and the burn of tears in my eyes. Wishing them away, I settle into the beanbag and close my eyes, letting sleep drag me under.

Sometime later, I'm eased awake by the voice of my teacher, Miss Dice.

"Is she okay?"

"She will be." The second voice is male, and it takes me a few moments to recognise that it belongs to Ayden.

"Should I call her parents?" Miss Dice asks, her voice filled with concern.

"No, if she wanted to go home, she would have already gone. I think she had a rough night and just needs some sleep." Ayden sounds pretty convincing. For someone who doesn't know what's going on with me, he sure as shit gets pretty close to the truth.

"You really shouldn't be skipping classes, Ayden," Miss Dice says, concerned.

"I'm all caught up, don't worry. I've been doing my work while Lex has been sleeping."

He called me Lex. For the second time.

With darkness weaving a web inside me, dragging me into an abyss I fear I'll never find my way out of, Ayden's voice, his words seem to give off little sparks of light. Sparks of hope.

"Okay then, Ayden. Please make sure you let me know if Lexi needs help. Her behaviour today is so out of character. I'm worried about her." Miss Dice's sincerity induces a stray tear to escape from my closed eye, and I hope like hell they can't see it.

"I will, thanks Miss Dice."

Silence greets me as the sound of footsteps retreat. A moment later, the beanbag dips slightly before a gentle finger wipes the salty drop off the side of my face. My eyes flutter open, and Ayden's concerned blue eyes fill my vision.

"I'm okay," I lie.

He's quiet for a bit, his piercing eyes roaming my face like he's trying to see into my soul.

"I know you want me to think you're okay, Lex, but I can see that you're not."

"Because I was in a bad mood in Science?" He shakes his head at my question and looks at the corner of my eye, his expression pained.

"Because your tears have removed the camouflage, and I can see the evidence."

I sit up abruptly, slapping my hand over my eye to cover the bruise, but Ayden grabs my hand away and holds it in his gentle grip.

"I slipped." It's not a total lie. I did slip at one stage last night, right after my face slammed into the table.

Ayden shakes his head, looking down at our hands still entwined. I don't know what to say. I can see the disappointment on his face, and guilt builds in my chest.

"You should go to class, Ayden," I whisper.

He shakes his head, letting go of my hand, and moves back to sit against the wall.

"Nope. This is much more entertaining." He smiles at me, but I can tell it's forced. He's trying to lighten the mood, so I try to go with it.

"Watching me sleep is entertaining?"

He nods. "Yep. Especially the part when you started snoring."

I sit forward in the beanbag. "I did not."

He nods. "Yep, you sure did. But that wasn't my favourite part." He teases, and I raise a brow and wait for him to continue. "My favourite part was when the drooling began." He immediately laughs at my expression.

"I did not drool!" I whisper yell, "Did I?"

Ayden is laughing hard now, struggling to keep quiet and when he nods, heat reddens my cheeks, and I bury my head in my hands.

Ayden stops laughing.

"Don't do that."

I spread my fingers to peek at him. "What?"

"Don't cover up your blush. I love that about you."

Okay, well, I'm officially on fire. If he thought I was blushing before, he's now being gifted with the mother of all blushes.

Cue self-combustion!

His chuckles fill the aisle, and I remove my hands from my flaming face.

"I'm glad my embarrassment amuses you."

He says nothing and instead tries to calm himself before shooting me a wink. I shake my head at his audacity, trying once again to hide the heat he ignites when he does that.

We stay quiet for a while. Ayden draws something in his book, and I pretend to mess around on my phone while secretly snapping a few pictures of him. It will give me something to look at later when I can't play his video. This friendship between us, if you can call it that, confuses me. I've tried to push him away, but he's either dumb and doesn't understand my hints, or he's a stubborn shit who won't give up.

"It's probably in your best interest to stay away from me." Breaking the silence, my statement surprises him, causing his handsome face to contort into a frown.

"Let me guess. You think the baggage and drama in your life is too much to burden me with?"

Jesus, can he read my thoughts? I nod warily.

"Well, you're wrong." He returns his eyes to his sketching.

I frown. "And you're an expert, are you?"

"Yep," he glances at me through his dark lashes. "Been there, done that. It's self-destructive behaviour, and I won't let you do it."

I narrow my eyes at him. "Isn't it up to me to choose who I want in my life?"

He smiles, radiating confidence. "You can try to fight it, Lex, but you're wasting your energy. I'm meant to be in your life."

Part of me melts, but the bitch in me speaks.

"I'm good at fighting the people in my life, Ayden. You're the one who should stop wasting your energy." My tone is clipped, and he frowns, sighing.

"And just like that, she's back."

"She?" I ask.

"Heavy Lexi."

"I hope you don't mean my weight." I snap, even though I know that's not what he means. He's referring to my playlist's name, the one filled with dark music that speaks to my soul.

"As if. There's nothing of you."

I don't respond because he's right. My weight has dropped since Mike moved home, and even though I just met Ayden yesterday, I know he's noticed my lack of eating.

As if reading my mind, he pulls out a ham sandwich from his bag and shoves it at me.

"Eat."

"So bossy," I respond, but take the sandwich and pick at it.

"What do you mean when you say you've been there and done that? Have you been self-destructive?"

Ayden drops his gaze from mine and focuses on the book in his lap. He's silent for so long that I don't think he's going to answer, so I'm surprised when he speaks.

"Yes, I have been self-destructive in the past." He glances back up to me, and his eyes swim with emotions I recognise in myself—sadness, desperation, secrets.

Ayden shifts nervously from my analysing gaze. This conversation is making him extremely uncomfortable, and I almost want to change the subject just to save him. But I don't, because a part of me needs to connect with someone who understands.

"You don't seem self-destructive now. How did you change that?" I want to ask him more, like what made him that way or who hurt him so badly. I'm curious about this guy with dreamy eyes who's giving me his time, but we don't know each other, and I have no right to ask such invasive questions.

"I accepted help and support from the people who care about me. It wasn't easy, but it also wasn't as hard as I thought it would be." Ayden shrugs, giving me one last glance at his vulnerability before his wall of confidence slams back in place. "You were pretty hungry." He tilts his head, gesturing to my lap where nothing but crumbs remain. A look of smug satisfaction changes his expression, and I know that our brief conversation about him is over. For now, at least.

We spend the entire school day there in the back corner of the library. It's nice. I feel safe and less uncomfortable with Ayden than I thought I would. For someone that I only met yesterday, Ayden Mitchell has successfully worked his way under my skin, and not in a bad way.

When the bell rings to signal the end of the day, my face drops in dread, and Ayden doesn't miss it.

"Why don't you come over to my house? Maybe stay for dinner?"

Go to his house and stay for dinner? Holy shit, I really want to say yes. I'm not ready to continue my day without him by my side, attempting to make me smile and laugh. I can't go to his house, though, and I shake my head, knowing I have to get the weed to Travis at the party tonight. The unwelcome reminder fills me with shame. If only Ayden knew what low life measures I'm capable of, he would surely curl his lip in disgust and walk the other way.

Standing from the beanbag, I gather up my books. "I have to go home."

Ayden looks disappointed but doesn't push the subject. We walk in silence to my locker, and he waits patiently in deep thought while I get my books and bag.

"Lex," I look up at him, his eyes dark with concern. "Please don't push me away. Reach out to me if you need to. Let me be in your life."

I nod shyly... As if I'm even shy. Christ, what is this guy doing to me?

"Talk later?" Ayden holds up his phone, taking a few steps backward until I nod, and then he flashes me a small smile before turning and walking away.

Eight

Something has to be said about the Fox Pines High School parties. How on earth they aren't shut down by the police is beyond me, especially being on a Tuesday night. By the sounds of it, most of the party is inside, but there are a few groups scattered in the front yard. I witness one group undertaking a very obvious drug deal in plain sight of the street. Normally I would turn my nose up to such a thing, but I can't really judge because I'm basically here to do the same thing.

Hiding in the shadows across the street, I wait anxiously for Travis to show. I'd sent him a text when I wasn't far from the party asking him to meet me out the front so I can avoid going in. Now the arsehole is making me wait. Making me sweat. The bag of weed I stole from Mike is practically burning a hole in my pocket. If the cops come, I'm screwed.

The unease I've felt over the last few days is increasing. A few weeks ago, the anxiety would only rear its ugly head during certain situations. Now, however, it's rooted itself into my life every single waking minute. When I returned home from school this afternoon, even though Mike was nowhere to be seen, I couldn't shut off the dread gripping me. I should've been able to relax knowing he wasn't there, but that saving grace never came. I'm on edge constantly, always needing to be alert, ready to flee the moment the monsters come out.

My mum was the only one home after school. I overheard her arguing on the phone with my dad, which isn't anything new. She was begging him to come home, and by the sounds of her angry tone, he refused. The crying that came afterwards tugged at my heart, and when I went to see if she was okay, she told me to get out of her room.

I internally kicked myself for showing the slightest bit of sympathy towards her, and I slammed my invisible walls back up, deciding to focus on the bullshit I had to do tonight rather than worrying about a mother who doesn't worry about me.

"Here she is in the flesh. Sexy Lexi." Travis' voice induces a shudder from me.

"Douche," I respond, making him chuckle as he steps into the shadows with me. He's not as tall as most of the guys I know, although he still towers over me. I swear he's wearing the same pale blue t-shirt he had on Sunday morning at Tasha's. It looks well worn and adds to his all-over messy look. His mop of dirty blonde hair sweeps to one side, and the sides are nothing but the smooth skin of his scalp. He should get his money back from whoever did that haircut on him.

"You got my weed?"

I flash him the bag and duck it quickly behind my back when he tries to grab it.

"Nope, you don't get this until you tell me what happened Saturday night."

He sighs, "You're killing me, girl!" I give him an unimpressed brow raise, so he continues. "Okay, okay. I was out the front of Tasha's lighting up a joint, and you came out looking up at the stars as if they were magical or some shit. You spotted me and asked me for a drag of my joint, so I gave it to you, and you smoked the whole fucking thing."

"Shit." What the hell was wrong with me?

"Shit's right! I had to steal that joint off my brother, and you fucking sucked the life out of it. When I told you that, you brushed it off and walked off on your own. Me being the gentleman I am, couldn't let you wander off by yourself, so I went with you, to you know... keep you safe and shit."

I grunt, and Travis smirks.

"We went past your uppity school, and you started climbing the fence, so I joined you. Before I knew it, we were breaking into the classrooms and throwing chairs through the windows." He looks down at my hand. "You even punched one of the windows. Scared the absolute shit out of me at first. Had me thinking you cut an artery or something. But it turned out that the cuts weren't too bad."

"Fuck."

Travis laughs. "I haven't even got to the good part yet."

"Stop torturing me and tell me already." I nearly stomp my foot like a two-year-old having a tantrum.

"Well, we got hungry, you know, because of the munchies and shit. Anyway, you threw a chair through the canteen doors. And let me tell you, it was so fucking hot, Lexi. I just had to kiss you."

I groan, covering my face.

"I'm pretty sure you liked the kiss. I am, after all, a fucking awesome kisser." Travis insists.

"Unlikely."

He laughs. "So that's it. We grabbed some snacks and went back to Tasha's."

I'm such a fuckup. How could I do something like that?

Guilt, shame, and disgust sit like a heavy weight on my chest, darkness trying to creep its way in to destroy me. I have the overpowering urge to scream or punch something.

"Weed, please?" Travis puts his hand out expectantly. I'm so pissed that I toss it at his face, but the smug prick catches it quickly, and he tuts. Fucking tuts at me!

"You're looking a little uptight there, Lexi. Come in for a bit, have a joint with me. It'll help you forget your worries for a while." When I hesitate, Travis adds, "Nathan is waiting inside for you. You should at least go and see him. He's been walking around telling everyone his hot catholic side piece is coming to see him tonight."

Damn it. I need to make Nathan understand that we are over for good this time. I don't want him telling everyone the opposite of what I feel. This is why I nod and follow Travis into the party, hoping I can get this over and done with quickly.

That was a mistake.

From the moment I walked into the party, I got swarmed by Travis and Nathan's friends. A drink ended up in my hand, and before I knew it, I was laughing and dancing with some random Fox Pines High girls who apparently have an infatuation with me. Why? I have no idea.

The biggest mistake of all, though, was the moment I accepted a joint off Nathan. Why the hell did I think it was a good idea? Nothing good has come from me smoking weed. Yes, I may have only done it the one time last weekend, but it was a mindfuck of a night that I don't want to repeat. Apparently, my brain went on a fucking vacation, though.

A familiar feeling drags me out of sleep early the next morning. A dry mouth, smokey taste, and pounding head remind me of waking up at Tasha's on Sunday. This time, however, everything feels weird because I'm not laying down, and my chest seems to be rising and falling with someone else's pressed against it.

Shit!

Cracking my eyes open, the tip of a shoulder draws my attention, and I realise that it's my pillow.

Someone's shoulder is my bloody pillow!

I'm straddling someone!

Oh my fucking god. What have I done?

Hoping like hell that I don't wake whoever is under me, I slowly push myself back. Relief washes over me when I see Nathan's sleeping face resting back on the recliner that we occupy. The relief only lasts a minute, though, because why in the fuck am I straddling Nathan in some stranger's living room? I'm a pure fuckup. There is no other word for it, and let me tell you, the truth fucking hurts.

How did I end up here? I know the answer, but I hate admitting it, even to myself. I've done it again. I smoked weed. I did what I said I wouldn't do again and lost what little common sense I had. And just like last time, I have no memory, which is scary as fuck. The possibility that I did something last night that I know I will regret sits heavily on my shoulders.

Easing back a little further from Nathan's chest, I see I left behind a patch of drool on his red t-shirt. Which thank fuck he's wearing.

Glancing down at our bodies, relief sweeps over me when I see we are both fully clothed. If we had both been naked, even partially, then I'm fairly certain I would have died from shame alone. Just because we are dressed now doesn't mean we didn't get up to no good through the night, though.

Fuckety fuck!

I need to get out of here and try to get my head right. Fuck Travis for inviting me inside last night. My emotions are all over the place, and even though the devil lives under the same roof as I do, I need to get home.

Lifting myself off Nathan, I look down at his relaxed face and the way his dark mullet spikes up in disarray. I've never really seen him like this, so quiet and vulnerable. It doesn't change the way I feel about him, though. Our time together is over. I just hope like hell I didn't portray the opposite last night. Given I woke up on his lap, though, says I probably did.

A sea of teenage bodies are passed out on every surface in the living room. Looking at their faces, I only recognise a few. These are not my people. How stupid can I be? Going to a party with no friends to watch my back is the most foolish thing I have ever done. Well, except for maybe getting high and breaking into my school to vandalise it.

What was I thinking? I have so much hate for myself right now. Self-loathing chills my heart, a heart that is nearly as black as the darkness that threatens to drag me into its abyss.

Needing to escape, I pat down my body, relieved to find my phone is safe in the back pocket of my jeans.

Shit, it's 5:53am!

I don't waste another second and move quickly, sneaking out the front door.

Making the long walk home, I retrace the path I took last night to get to the party. As I walk, I busy myself by reading through text messages I hadn't responded to last night.

Abbey's messages fill me in with details on her love life with Daniel and how she thinks I'm rude by not responding to her. I respond by asking her to meet me before school. Hopefully, that appeases her until I can fill her in on what a fuckup her best friend is.

Ayden tried to get my attention by sending a stream of witty messages, and when that didn't work, he sent a concerned text saying that he hopes I'm safe. God, I wish so fucking much that I had walked away from the party last night and instead spent the night chatting with him. I'm so pathetic. He has no idea what a trashy bitch I am. I should just leave him alone. He deserves to have genuine decent people in his life that don't have fucked up secrets. I'm weak and selfish, though, so I send him a response saying that I didn't have my phone last night, but that I was okay.

Pathetic liar, Lexi!

Dad's message tells me he'll ring me tomorrow night around 8pm for our weekly catch up. That is tonight now, I guess. He calls me every Wednesday night, and even though it bugs me because he hasn't been home in so long, I still look forward to talking to him. It's as if my mind thinks that one day the man speaking down the line will be the dad who used to laugh and joke with me, and not the moody, neglectful shell of a man I know now. He rarely has much to say these days. It tends to be pretty brief.

How are your grades?

Are you getting your work in on time?

Are you behaving for your mother?

Tonight, though, I think I need to tell him about Mike. Each encounter I have with my brother is getting worse. I'm actually worried about how far he might go.

Speaking of Mike, he has graced me with a message as well.

Oh, joy!

His message is simple.

"You are fucked, Ali!"

It's almost laughable at how different each of the messages are from each person. The only one who seemed concerned about me was Ayden. I've known this guy for a whole twenty-four hours, and already I feel like he knows me better than anyone else.

After I finally arrive home and sneak through my bedroom window into my silent sleeping house, I plug my phone in to charge and quietly unlock my bedroom door. I need a shower, so I go to my mum's room since Mike won't be able to hear me in there. She is sound asleep, so I send her a text to tell her what I'm doing in case she wakes up wondering who the hell is in her bathroom.

I end my shower with cold water, hoping it will help my hungover eyes. It doesn't. Regret kicks my arse once again when I wipe the steam off the mirror and take in my appearance. Dark circles sit under my eyes, blending in with the slight green bruise still healing in the corner. Knowing I need to be quick in order to avoid Mike, I decide to air dry my hair today, leaving it out before rushing to get dressed.

I need shares in concealer. Honestly, I'm probably concealer's best customer right now. That thought alone is all kinds of fucked up. The only thing a seventeen-year-old should be using concealer for is pimples.

Sighing, I dab the concealer under my eyes and over the bruise, hoping it helps me appear somewhat normal.

Safely back in my room, I check my phone. Abbey sent a message asking me to meet her at our usual spot, and I send her a thumbs-up emoji. I hurry to finish getting ready and leave only minutes later, needing to be far from this house.

Using Ayden's blue corded earphones, I soak up the rawness of my Heavy playlist as I walk to wait for Abbey. When she appears in front of me, the sight of her breaks my strength, and I throw myself into her arms, crying. I can hear her asking me what's wrong, but I can't speak. I just need her hug, and she squeezes me tight, letting me know she's there for me.

When I'm finally able to pull myself together, we pull back, and Abbey sweeps my hair off my face.

"What have I missed?"

I think about telling her the truth, but I just can't bring myself to say the words. I just can't. How do I tell her about Mike? About the way he looks at me, or the things he says? How do I tell her about the things he does? It's bad enough having to deal with my brother, but now I'm doing shit that I wouldn't normally do. I feel like I'm spiralling.

I shake my head.

"What happened yesterday? Tasha called me last night and said you went crazy in class."

Of course, Tasha would call my actions crazy. *Bitch!*

"I couldn't find you at lunchtime yesterday, but Allison said she thought you went home."

I sigh, defeated, "I fucked up Abs. Not just once, but twice."

Abbey frowns. "What do you mean?"

I sit back on the fence, and Abbey stays standing in front of me, waiting for me to respond.

"Last Saturday at Tasha's party, apparently, I smoked Travis' joint and then went on a bloody walkabout. He told me he went with me so I wouldn't be alone. And then," I put my face in my hands, "It was me, Abbey! I was the one who vandalised the school!"

Abbey frowns in confusion, but then, as if a light bulb switches, her face morphs into understanding.

"Your hand, it was cut. That was from glass, and not a rosebush?"

I nod.

"Fuck me," Abbey curses.

"I know. It's bad. I'm bad!" I cry again.

Abbey hugs me, rubbing my back until I calm down.

"I hate to ask Lexi, but you said you fucked up twice. When was the second time?"

"Last night," I wipe the tears from my face. "I went to that party, but not to see Nathan. I needed to know what happened on Saturday night, and Travis would only tell me if I took him a bag of weed from Mike's stash, so I stole the weed and met Travis at the party."

"What!" Abbey yells, "You stole drugs? From your brother?"

I nod."That's not all." I hang my head in shame.

"Oh my god, what else, Lex?" Abbey sounds hysterical. Maybe telling her wasn't such a good idea. I'm in too deep now, though, so I may as well tell her the rest about the party. Not about Mike, though. I don't think I'll ever be able to tell her about that secret.

"Well, I was feeling down, and reckless, and Travis convinced me to go into the party, and all I really remember is smoking another joint, with Nathan this time. Then I woke up this morning, straddling Nathan's lap in an armchair."

"What!" Abbey screeches again. She's going to lose her voice at this rate.

"I was fully clothed, and so was Nathan, but I can't remember anything. What if I kissed him and led him on? Fucking hell, it was only a couple of days ago that I kissed Travis. I'm a slut!"

"You're not a slut. Besides, if you can't remember it, then it never happened." Abbey grins, trying to make me feel better.

I smile briefly, but it falls quickly from my face.

"Abbey, I really can't remember anything. What if I did something else, something more? What if I..." I trail off, waiting for Abbey to understand.

She considers my words for a moment. "Do you feel different? You know... down there?" Abbey points to her pelvic region.

I shake my head. "No, it all feels the same."

Abbey nods, "Good. Then you're most likely still a virgin. You would be able to feel it. It stings and burns for a bit."

My mouth drops open in shock. "Oh my god, Abbey Delany. You lost your virginity!"

"Shh." Abbey hisses, slapping her palm over my mouth.

I rip her hand away, pushing her back as I jump down from the fence.

"You had sex?" I whisper yell, gripping her shoulders.

She bites her lip, smiling, and nods.

"Holy shit!" We jump around, hugging each other like idiots, and my troubles are briefly forgotten.

I stop jumping and pull back to see Abbey's face.

"When?" I ask.

"Yesterday after school. Daniel's family was out for a few hours, and, well, one thing led to another."

"Wow," I whisper, happy for her and, dare I say, a little jealous, too.

"So, how was it?" I eagerly ask for details.

"Um, well, at first things were feeling so amazing before we... you know, had sex. Then it hurt, mainly at the start. It stung and burnt, and I wasn't sure if I could keep going, but Daniel was caring, and we figured it out, and the second time felt better than the first."

I gasp. "You did it more than once?"

"Three times." Abbey's grin is from ear to ear.

"Wow," I say again.

Abbey nods. "I have lots of details to fill you in with because a lot has changed this week, but Lexi," Abbey's smile disappears, "I've been a terrible friend. You're going through something, and I've been too caught up with Daniel."

My eyes glass over, feeling happy that she's still my friend because I had honestly thought Daniel was taking my place. I don't want to tell Abbey that, though, so I keep it to myself, just like all of my other secrets.

"Lexi, I need you to promise me something." Abbey looks so serious now, and it almost scares me, but I nod, waiting for her to continue. "I need you to stay away from drugs. Please." She pleads.

I nod again. "I will. I'm sure of it." I put my head down in shame. "Am I a bad person, Abs?"

"No, Lexi, a few bad choices doesn't equal a bad person."

I smile at the words I'm sure she stole from her mother.

"Come on, let's go to school."

On our walk, Abbey gives me more intimate details of her first experience with Daniel. Hearing it makes me even more curious, and I'm shocked when my thoughts automatically turn to Ayden. At this point, I'm nearly sure I have lost my marbles. I don't even know the guy. Why would I think of him when I think of that?

As Abbey and I part ways when we get to school, I get a message from Ayden, and my heart flutters even though I keep telling myself that he's better off not being my friend.

Ayden Mitchell

*I'm so glad you're okay. It worried me not
hearing back from you last night.
Did you sleep okay?*

Lexi West

*Sorry, I didn't mean to worry you. I slept like
a log.*

More like I was passed out like a log, but he doesn't
need to know that.

Ayden Mitchell

I'm glad you slept well. ☺
*I won't be at school today. I'm heading to my
dad's to spend the day with him.
I'll be back later tonight, though, so maybe
we can catch up then?*

I'm pathetic. Knowing Ayden won't be here today
makes me want to cry again.
Get a hold of yourself, Lexi!

Lexi West

*Have a great day with your dad! We will
definitely catch up tonight.* ☺

Ayden Mitchell
☺

I struggle through the morning with little enthusiasm. The darkness I felt earlier this morning has faded a little. I'd hate to admit it, but I'm pretty sure that sitting in class re-reading Ayden's messages is proving to be good for my soul.

Recess is uneventful, and I keep to myself even though my friends surround me. I automatically seek out Ayden, even though I know he isn't here. Marcus spots me and gives me a friendly smile that I now realise is very similar to Ayden's. I smile back briefly before blocking out the world with my music and trying to ignore the sting I feel of being left behind by Abbey again as she spends her time at the new couples' table.

If I thought my day would continue to be boring and eventless, then I should get my head checked because by the time lunch rolls around, I'm back to being thrown into the bottomless pit of hell when I get a call from my mum.

Nine

"Lexi, call the police!" My mum screams down the phone, which has me instantly jumping to my feet.

"What? Why?" Without even thinking, I'm rushing to my locker to get my bag. If my mum needs the police, then I need to go home.

She screams again, which is followed by Mike's raging temper.

"Lexi, if you call the fucking police, I will kill her!"

The line disconnects, and I freeze for a second, looking at the screen. Then I run.

I run the twenty-minute walk in ten minutes, skidding to a brief stop across from my house, my lungs on fire, air struggling to get in. An ambulance is sitting in my driveway.

"No," I whisper before running into my house.

"Mum!" I scream, "Mum!"

There's glass everywhere. Furniture is upturned, and some nasty-looking holes dent the walls in the hall.

"In here." An unfamiliar male voice calls, and I follow it without hesitation.

Entering the back living area, I see two paramedics securing my mum to a gurney.

"Mum!" Running to her side, I reach to grab her hand but think better of it when I see all the blood. Her face is smeared with the thick metallic liquid, which trails down her forehead and cheek from a large gash near her hairline.

"I'm okay, Lexi. I'll be okay." She's crying, but her words are strong.

"The police are searching the neighbourhood for the intruders. Your mum is very brave." I pay no attention to the paramedic who spoke, keeping my eyes on my mum.

"Intruders?"

"Yes, Lexi, intruders." Her tone and pointed glare tell me not to question her lie, and my shoulders drop.

Why is she lying about this? Why is she protecting Mike?

"Sweetie, I'll be in the hospital. Perhaps because intruders are running around, you should go stay with your friends?"

I nod, understanding the meaning behind my mum's suggestion. I need to get out of here before Mike gets back.

The paramedics load my mum into their ambulance before driving off to leave me alone in the house. I don't hesitate for another minute, making quick work of getting the hell out of here. Grabbing a backpack up in my room, I shove in some clothes, makeup, toothbrush, and phone charger before storming into

Mike's bedroom. He has a stash of money in his bedside drawer, so I steal $100 and leave the place that has been feeling less and less like my home every day.

Walking the back streets of Fox Pines, I head to the train station, deciding to go to my dad in the city. He will know what to do. I try calling him from the train, but it goes to voicemail, so I leave a brief message about what Mike did to mum as the train pulls out of the station.

My phone blows up with SnapChat messages, so I indulge in them to keep me distracted during the train ride.

Abbey-Delany
Girl where you at? Tasha said you ran off somewhere.

Lexi-West
Mum called. She's not well. Had to go to the hospital. I'm heading to the city to see my dad.

I can't tell Abbey the whole truth since I've kept her in the dark for so long about the situation at home. She doesn't need to know about Mike. Not yet, anyway.

Abbey-Delany

*Oh no. I hope your mum will be okay, Lex.
Say hi to your dad for me. It's been months
since I've seen him.*

It's been months since I've seen my dad, too. I wish
I could say that I'm looking forward to seeing him, but
I'm not. He never seems happy to see me either these
days, so I guess the feeling will be mutual.

Lexi-West

I will. ☺

Abbey-Delany

*GTG. Daniel keeps running his hand up my
leg under the table. Mr Todd is going to catch
us!! Lol.*

I roll my eyes. I hope they do get caught. I hope her
parents get called and they make her kneel and beg
God for forgiveness in front of that weird arse alter
thing they have in their living room.

Wait. No, I don't. I don't want that to happen at all. I
just really want Abbey to sound like she at least gives a
shit about what's going on with me. Maybe I'm being
selfish? I shoot Abbey a "talk later" message before
moving on to the next one, from Marcus.

Marcus-Grady

Hey Lexi. Is everything okay? I saw you run out of school earlier.

Lexi-West

Hi Marcus. All g. My mum's not well and had to go to hospital, but it's nothing serious.

Marcus-Grady

Are you sure? Going to hospital sounds pretty serious. Do you need anything? I can come and sit with you.

What is Marcus up to? Yes, we were close friends growing up, but we haven't been close for a few years now. His attention has come out of nowhere. Shit, has Ayden been telling him about me? Did he show Marcus the video of my crack house? Did he tell him about the bruise on my eye?

Lexi-West

It's fine, Marcus. I'm going to the city to see my dad, so don't worry. ☺

My lies are so convincing that even I'm starting to believe them.

More messages come in from the boys' group chat as well as the girls'. I spend less than a minute reading over Tasha's rant about some girl called Rhys deliberately tripping her in the hall in front of a group of year twelve guys. I really want to write "Go Rhys", but since I shouldn't, I keep that opinion to myself and move on to the boys' chat.

Shaun is laughing about Tasha getting tripped, and he sends a video through that is already going viral around school. I shouldn't watch it, but I do. I also shouldn't laugh, but I do. Tasha can be a real bitch, so maybe Karma is paying her a visit.

I leave the conversation when Simon starts talking about Tasha's rack and Garrett, Jared and Marcus start weighing in. Maybe I should have reminded them that I can see what they are writing. Then again, they know damn well I'm part of their group chat.

I jump back into the girls' chat to see if they know about the video of Tasha, and I almost wish I hadn't. Now Tasha is talking about a rumour going around. Apparently, there is a witness to the school vandalism, and the cops have been notified.

Shit! I really hope it's nothing more than a rumour, because if there is a witness, then I am screwed. Shit! Shit! Shit!

I debate reaching out to Travis, but think better of it. Bringing that up in a message could backfire and so far the only thing Travis and I discussed in our messages was getting weed off Mike. I'd be thankful if the police find out about that and bust my brother.

My heart is beating against my chest, and dread is crawling up my spine. I've fucked up so bad. Once people find out it was me that trashed the school, not only will I lose my friends and probably get kicked out of school, but I'll be nothing more than a low life criminal.

Seriously, fuck my life!

A little over an hour later, I disembark at Flinders Street Station and weave through the thick city crowds to my dad's apartment building on Queen Street. I try calling him a couple of times on the walk, but all I get is his voicemail again, so I leave a pissed off "call me dad" right before arriving at his building. It's the first time I've been to his apartment in the city, which now that I think about it, kind of seems strange. Why haven't I visited him before? He's never asked me to come here, so I guess that's why.

The foyer on the ground floor is small but chic. I ignore the security guard sitting behind the tall marble desk and move to the tenant panel on the wall, pushing the buzzer for Mr M West, Room 1123. There's no answer. No surprises there.

"Can I help you?" The deep voice of the security guard draws my attention, and I move to his desk.

"I'm here to see my dad. Mr West. Maxwell West."

"Your name?" The overweight redheaded security guard frowns at me and checks something on his computer.

"Alexis West."

The security guard frowns again and shakes his head.

"I'm sorry, I don't have any record of an Alexis West on file."

"Oh, try Lexi West." Dad probably used the name I go by.

He frowns again, looking at his screen, only to shake his head.

"No, I'm sorry, Miss West."

"He's my dad. Can you just call up to his apartment and see if he's there?"

"Mr West is out right now."

"Look, I'm his daughter. Can you just let me into his apartment so I can wait until he gets back? I have nowhere else to go." I force my eyes to tear up a little, hoping the lost puppy look will sway the security guard. It doesn't.

"If you're not on the list for Mr West, then I cannot grant you access. You are welcome to sit and wait for him to return." The annoying security guard points to a sofa by the window, and I glare at him before claiming a seat on it to wait. And wait. And wait.

I pass the time by falling asleep, re-watching Ayden's video, and re-reading his messages. Three hours pass, making me angrier by the minute, but then I remember my dad said he would call me at 8 o'clock tonight. He never misses these calls, so I'll just have to wait to tell him I'm here then.

A couple of hours after the sun has set on the bustling city, my eyes are drawn to a silver car pulling up outside the building—a car which looks a hell of a lot like my dad's. I sit up in relief when my dad steps out, and I stand gathering up my backpack and phone.

It's been a couple of months since I've been face-to-face with him, and even though he can be a moody hard arse, I realise now how much I've missed him.

Making his way around the car, I watch as my dad opens the passenger door holding his hand out, and a tall brunette in a fitted red dress steps out. Handing his keys to the valet, my dad then turns to cup the brunette's face and kisses her passionately.

What the actual fuck!

Ten

Time freezes. My breathing stops. My already fucked up world crashes down around me. I can't believe what I'm seeing, so I blink profusely, hoping I'm looking at someone else. Unfortunately, the tall man with hair the same shade of blonde as mine and the same blue eyes that match the ones he passed on to me is very much my dad. The woman he is with, however, is very much not my mum, and when the car pulls away, I witness my dad, hand in hand with this other woman, as they cross the street and disappear into an Italian restaurant.

Blood pumps profusely through my veins as shock and anger grip me.

This can't be happening. My dad can't be having an affair.

As much as I wish it weren't true, I can't ignore what I just saw.

I look at my phone. It's 7:55pm. He'll be ringing soon, he said as much in his text message this morning. Surely he won't call me while he's with another woman.

Right?

I see red! Fury takes over, and I storm out of the foyer and into the busy city street, barely looking to see if cars are coming as I stalk across the road. Watching them through the glass door, my dad and the brunette sit at a table in the centre of the restaurant while a waiter fills their glasses with red wine.

For fuck's sake, they aren't even trying to hide their relationship!

I think over everything I know about my parents, and things start to fall into place and begin to make sense. While I thought my dad was too busy working or possibly staying away because of my mum and her addiction, he, in fact, has really been too busy for us because he has found a new life. A life that includes a leggy brunette, apparently. He lives here in his bubble while my mum's lonely heart is numbed with substances, leaving me with no one to care for me or protect me from his deranged love child.

After clinking their glasses together and taking a sip, my dad stands looking at his watch and excuses himself from the table, but not before he leans down to kiss his mistress.

Fucking prick!

As he disappears somewhere towards the back of the restaurant, I take the opportunity to walk inside.

"Can I help you?" The hostess steps in my path, preventing me from making my way deeper into the restaurant, eyeing my school uniform. I guess a school uniform doesn't meet their clientele dress code.

"Oh no, it's okay. I'm here to see my dad, Mr West, and my new step-mum." I internally high five myself because I sound convincing as hell right now.

"Oh, of course." The hostess steps aside, and I give her a nice big fake smile as I brush by.

With my eyes locked on my target, I walk straight up to my dad's table and take his seat, lifting his wineglass to my lips, guzzling a long sip.

"Excuse me. Can I help you?" the brunette snaps, her large brown eyes widening.

I hold my finger up to hold her off while I take another sip. I'm going to need the confidence the smooth, rich liquid will bring. Putting the glass down, I use my dad's napkin to dab each side of my mouth before giving the brunette a big, cheesy smile.

"Nope, I'm just waiting for my dad."

The brunette frowns, "Well, as you can see, your dad, whoever he is, is not here."

"Oh no, he'll be calling any minute now." My smile is big and smug as I place my phone on the table, watching as 7:59 ticks over to 8pm. Then my phone rings.

"Oh, look, right on time," I answer it on loudspeaker, watching the frown deepen on the pretty brunette.

"Hi, Daddy," I say sweetly.

"Hi Princess, how are you?" His tone throws me a little, and I realise he hasn't listened to his voicemails and has no idea about mum and Mike. Otherwise, he would sound more concerned.

"I'm super." I give the brunette another toothy smile. "I'm just wondering when you're coming home. Mum misses you."

The brunette huffs, crossing her arms over her chest while looking around the restaurant, probably searching for a waiter to help her remove me from the table.

"Princess, you know I'm busy working. I can't come home yet. Maybe in a few weeks."

The more my dad talks, the more the brunette frowns, and I see the moment recognition flits across her face.

"That's a shame," I say to dad, "I'm actually in a super cool restaurant right now. Very fancy."

"Really? Lucky you," he says.

"Yeah. I'm just drinking wine with my future step-mum. She has killer curves. Gorgeous brown eyes and hair. Oh, and she looks super yummy in the red dress she's wearing."

My dad goes silent for a few moments.

"What did you just say, Alexis?"

Ha! Got you, arsehole!

The brunette looks confused.

"Say hi to my dad, Max West." I direct my words to the brunette.

"Max?" she asks although I don't know if she's speaking to me or the phone.

The line goes dead.

I pick up my phone and down some more of my dad's wine while I wait for the bastard to appear.

And there he is storming across the restaurant, his face red in anger.

"Oh, here he is," I say to the brunette as he reaches the table.

"Alexis, stand up and come with me," he hisses under his breath, and his tone reminds me so much of Mike, that I flinch.

"Max, what's going on?" the brunette asks as if she hasn't already worked it out.

I continue to drink the wine with a smirk on my face, which I just can't seem to wipe off. That is, until my dad's strong hand grabs my upper arm and pulls me forcefully out of the seat.

"Outside, Alexis," he growls.

I can't remember the last time he used my full name so much. Wow, I guess I'm in trouble. My dad's grip tightens when I try to sit back down, and the strength behind it makes me cry out in pain.

"Max, stop! You're hurting her!" At his mistress' distress and the growing audience of the restaurant's diners, he lets go of my arm. Trying to fight back tears and appear unaffected, I shove my hand out to the brunette.

"Hi, I'm Alexis West. Max's daughter."

Dazed, the brunette takes my hand and gently shakes it, looking between my dad and me dumbfounded, her mouth opening and closing like she's a fish out of water.

"Max? Is this true? Is this your daughter?" she asks, tears filling her eyes. For a moment, I feel bad for her, but only for a moment.

Hanging his head and gripping the back of his neck, my dad tries to massage out the tension.

"Oh, Daddy," I lace my voice with sarcasm, "You didn't tell your mistress about me? What about your wife, Ruth? Did you tell her you're married?"

A sob escapes the brunette as she picks up her purse off the table, and my father, now furious, seethes. "Hardly married, Alexis!"

I grit my teeth, livid. "You're a fucking coward!" I scream before grabbing up the brunette's wineglass and hurl it at my dad, which slams into his chest, red wine spilling down the front of his pristine Calvin Klein shirt. "While you play with your mistress, we're at home suffering. Mum is in the hospital because Mike attacked her today! I had to put locks on my doors to stop him from doing crude things to me! All while you fuck your secretary." I have no idea if the brunette is his secretary, nor do I care. I take one last look at both of them and then turn, running out of the restaurant.

I hate him!

I HATE HIM!

Tears stream down my face as I sprint towards the station, needing to get far away from my dad. The shout of my name is a deep bellow from behind me. My dad's voice is filled with a rage that scares me, so I push my burning legs harder to escape him. Footsteps pound the pavement not far behind, and I drive my legs harder, faster, desperate to flee from the man I no longer consider my dad.

Pulling my transport card out of my blazer pocket, I scan it and jump up and down with frantic impatience, waiting for the gate to open. When it does, I bolt towards platform three, hoping I'm not too late to get the train home, back to Fox Pines.

"Alexis!" The roar of my dad's voice comes right before his strong hand grips my wrist hauling me backward. The move jolts me, sending pain up my arm.

"No!" I scream, pulling myself in the other direction, trying desperately to get to the train. My scream captures the attention of bystanders, so I scream some more in the hopes someone will help, "Let go of me!"

I kick my legs towards his shins and flail my arms, trying to shake my dad off. The fury I see in his eyes terrifies me. It's almost like I'm looking into the eyes of a stranger, one who's possessed by evil. Right when I'm sure I'm about to lose this battle, a Protective Services Officer that patrols the train station appears behind my dad and grabs him, causing his grip on me to falter.

I don't think twice. I turn and bolt toward the train doors that are now closing.

"No, wait!" my dad yells, "She's my daughter!"

I make it onto the train just in time and spin to face my dad as he's manhandled by two PSOs on the platform.

"I AM NOT YOUR DAUGHTER!" I scream right before the doors seal shut.

The silence of the carriage meets me. Sobs jump out of my throat, and tears spill in a rush to the train floor below. As the train pulls off, I watch the man I used to consider my dad get dragged away.

Whispers dance around me, curious passengers packed into the tight space, witnessing the drama I brought so abruptly into their lives. All I want to do right now is hide.

My phone vibrates in my pocket, and I grab it out, hoping the distraction will help me stop crying in front of the audience.

It's a message from Ayden.

Ayden Mitchell
Lex, look to your left.

Confused at first, I re-read his simple message. What? Using my sleeve to wipe my eyes so I can see clearer, I slowly turn my head to the left. The train carriage is filled to the brim with bodies standing and sitting in each other's personal space, many of whom have their eyes on me.

That's when I see familiar piercing blue eyes that remind me of a summer sky.

Ayden.

"Come here." He mouths, and I choke on a loud sob and start weaving through the sea of bodies to get to him. When I reach him, his protective arm pulls me in tight, and I bury my face in his chest. Ayden's heat envelops me, his firm hold a cocoon of safety as we sway with the motion of the train. If it weren't for his strong body or the way he steadies us with the handgrip above, I would've fallen to the floor.

In his arms, I fall apart. Any chance at resembling the strong, smiling girl from school is long gone. From the moment Ayden laid eyes on me, I haven't been able to hide from him. He saw right through my charade, saw more than even my best friend had, more than anyone had.

"You know each other?" The concerned voice of a lady speaking to Ayden distracts me, and I feel a response rumble through his chest as he whispers to the lady.

"Yes, we go to school together."

"It seems like she's had a rough night. Please make sure she gets home safely."

"I will," Ayden assures her, and his hand leaves my back for a moment. "Thank you, she'll need these." Ayden gently nudges a small pack of tissues into my hand, and I have to pry my grip from his hoodie to accept them.

I use my close vicinity to Ayden to breathe in his scent, taking comfort in the way he gently rubs my back, the soft friction soothing me.

Why is he here? How is this even possible? I want to ask him, but I can't stop crying. Instead, I grip him tighter, never ever wanting to let go.

Some time passes, and my sobs turn into an occasional shudder as the sea of passengers thin out stop after stop.

"Lex, let's sit down." Ayden's gentle voice warms my ear, and I nod, not willing to let go of him. He manoeuvres us until we are seated, but the change in position means I have to let go of his chest. The thought of that suddenly seems terrifying to me, but before I freak out and make a fool of myself, Ayden settles me against him with my face turned into the crook of his neck.

I take in deep breaths, inhaling his scent again, which is even stronger from this vantage point. It calms me immediately, and I'm sure my new quest in life will be to figure out how to get his scent into a bottle so I can spray it on everything I own.

Ayden switches from stroking my arm to my head and then back to my arm. It's almost as if he can't control his need to touch me. Not that I'm complaining. Hell no. I'm not going to look a gift horse in the mouth, and this is one gift I'll gladly take. His touch is so soothing that my eyes flutter shut, and I fall asleep. It's a light and brief nap, but when I wake, the train is at a stop two towns away from Fox Pines for a 10-minute break.

The carriage lights are bright, and I become self-conscious of how I must look. I quickly excuse myself and dash to the nearby toilet, ducking my head in the hopes of hiding my snot covered red nose from Ayden's view.

The light in the toilet cabin is dull, making my pale skin almost appear green in the graffiti-covered mirror. Lifeless bloodshot eyes look back at me with not a speck of makeup living on my face anymore, the most colour in my face comes from the fading bruise courtesy of Mike.

I hardly recognise this stranger looking back at me. Who is she exactly? Is she like Mike and destined to be a violent abuser? Is she like my dad, willing to lie and cheat? Or is she like my mum, falling dependant on substances? And if she isn't like any of them, then who is she exactly?

Another pesky tear slips from my eye as I look at myself. I'm not really sure who I am, but I'm sure I don't want to be like any of my family members. Come to think of it, I'm not really sure who the man is that I've called my dad for the last seventeen years. He's a complete stranger to me. No, he's worse than a stranger. He's a deceiving bastard!

I grip my chest right over my heart, where pain stabs me. It's like a hand is reaching into my chest and wrapping a fist around the organ that gives me life. I curl my lip at my reflection in disgust. I hate this weak bitch that looks back at me. She's pathetic. No wonder my family treats me like the scum on their shoes.

STOP!

I grip the sides of my head, wanting to scream at the vile, toxic thoughts bouncing around in my head. I can't let them win. I can't let them consume me. I need to remember that just outside this filthy cubicle is a boy who has shown me more care than my parents have in years. He has taken the time to show me compassion. He has offered me friendship. I need to focus on that because having him come into my life must mean something, right? Is he the light in my world filled with darkness?

The need to be back by Ayden's side is all-consuming, so I attempt to freshen my appearance and splash water on my face. It doesn't really do much for me, other than make me feel fresher, rather than look it. It will have to do.

I'm nervous as I approach him, and I know he can tell as his eyes follow me. With my head hanging low, I avoid those ocean eyes and take a seat next to him, leaving a little space between us. Embarrassment and humiliation urge me to flee like a coward. I don't give in to the urge, though, selfishly needing him near to feel like I matter to at least one person in this shitful world.

Keeping my eyes downcast, they dance wearily between his masculine hands, which are resting in his lap, and to my jittery hands that I don't seem to know what to do with. Ayden reaches out and gently places his hand over mine, and I close my eyes, enjoying the contact.

"Talk to me, Lex."

I look up to meet his eyes, trying to figure out where to start. What do I tell him? What don't I tell him? He already knows the situation isn't good, so not telling him anything would be useless. He's not going to believe that.

"I don't know where to start." My voice is hoarse, and it hurts to speak.

Ayden chews on his bottom lip, considering something before asking, "How about I ask some questions, and maybe we can go from there?"

I nod, still keeping my head low.

"Was that your dad at the station tonight?"

When I nod, he continues, his thumb stroking over the back of my hand, "Why were you running from him?"

I clear my throat, trying to dislodge the lump that threatens to suffocate me. How do I even explain this? I can't imagine what it would have looked like to him or any of the passengers who witnessed it.

"I-I caught him with another woman," I choke out.

His eyes go wide in shock. "Shit, Lex, I'm so sorry."

"I made a scene at the restaurant he was at with her. I pissed him off, and instead of feeling guilty about cheating on my mum, he seemed more concerned that his mistress found out."

"Jesus." Ayden seems genuinely annoyed by this. He reaches out and strokes some stray strands of my hair behind my ear, and I automatically lean into his touch.

"Why were you there? Did you know he would be with another woman?"

I shake my head.

"No, I didn't know. I went there because I had to get away from..." Shit, do I tell him about Mike? That will just raise more questions. I can't tell him *that*.

"Lex, please talk to me," he quietly begs when I hesitate, lifting my chin, so I have no choice but to meet his concerned blue eyes.

It's a little unnerving the effect this guy has on me. I feel like I could tell him anything, even though I don't really know him. Sure, he's hot, but so was Ted Bundy, and he was a serial killer. Ayden has also been more caring and more thoughtful than... well, just about anyone I know, but that doesn't mean I know him well enough to divulge all of my secrets. Right?

I peer up into his eyes, which darken with more concern as he takes in my reactions. He must be able to see the torment I struggle with, and I kind of hate that it causes him distress. All I want to do is make his eyes glint with happiness again.

It's tough to refuse him, so I deflect. "How are you even here right now? There are millions of people in this city. How did we end up in the same cabin on the same train at the same time?"

The abrupt change in conversation takes him by surprise, and he sits back a little, the movement causing his hand to fall away from mine.

Damn it, Lexi!

Even though I'm mourning the loss of his touch, I am stumped as to how I managed to run into the guy that gives me neverending butterflies in a city filled with millions of people.

"Well, I spent the day with my dad in the city, and now I'm catching the train back to my mum's. I guess it was a pure fluke that we ended up in the same place. I'm glad we did, though." Ayden's smile is small, his concern still dominating his expression.

"So, your mum is in Fox Pines?" I ask the obvious, needing to confirm I understood correctly, and he gives me a small, no teeth smile and a nod.

Unlike me, Ayden is in casual clothes, the dark blue of his hoodie turning his eyes a deeper shade that resembles a rich sapphire. His dark hair peeks out from under a red and navy Red Dragon cap, curling up slightly at the ends, which just makes him even more adorable if that's even possible.

His usual shadow of facial hair looks a little darker today, making him look too old to be a year eleven student. I want to ask him about his age since I'm almost sure he's older than me and my friends, but now isn't the right time, so I shelve that for later.

He certainly looks good out of the uptight uniform we have to wear to school. Well, to be honest, he looks good when he's wearing the uptight school uniform as well.

"Nice deflection to my questioning, Lex." He gives me a knowing wink and returns his hand to mine. "Now, please talk to me. What did you have to get away from?"

His lips are a distraction, too. Their fullness keeps drawing my attention, and I wonder what it would be like to kiss them.

"Lex?" If Ayden has noticed my lusty ogling, he isn't letting on. I really should answer his question since he's been nothing but kind and patient towards me.

"My half brother Mike." I look back up to Ayden's serious gaze. "He beat up mum this afternoon and did a runner."

"Fuck, Lex."

I nod in agreement. It's a bad fucked up situation.

"By the time I ran home from school, my mum was in the care of paramedics. She told them there was an intruder," I shake my head at my mum's pathetic lie, "and knowing Mike would come back…" Nausea turns my tummy at the thought of what Mike would do if he got his hands on me, "I had to leave, I'm not safe there with him. That's why I came to the city to see my dad. I stupidly thought I could stay with him."

Ayden's jaw pops, his anger clear before he's able to hide it. For not knowing him very well, I feel so in tune with him. It's hard to explain how drawn to him I am. Maybe I'm just needy. Perhaps without realising it, I'm looking for a knight in shining armour to come and save me. Am I that pathetic? *Just like my mum!*

Ayden takes a few deep breaths, staring at our entwined hands.

"Is your brother the one that had all the drugs in your house?" His voice is strained and comes out raspy.

I nod.

"Is he the one that did that?" He lifts his hand to my eye and gently strokes his thumb over the discoloured green skin. I give another small nod, not wanting his hand to fall away.

Returning his gaze to our hands, Ayden is quiet for a moment, and he shakes his head before his eyes flick back to mine, fury and determination in them.

"You can't go home." It's a statement, not a question, and I nod.

"I know."

Eleven

Ayden's aunt's house is a cute, pale blue, two-story weatherboard. From the white picket fence to the matching white front porch railings, this house has all the makings of a Gilmore Girls film set. Even in the dark, it feels warm and inviting, and I remember it being that way when I was little and used to come over to play Lego with Marcus.

I want to go inside with Ayden, yet my brain is screaming at me to turn and run. How do we explain this to his mum and aunt? What if they call the police, or worse, my dad? I don't want them to know. I don't want anyone to know.

Ayden convinced me to come here with him when Abbey didn't answer the three calls I made to her phone. Given the proximity to midnight, I'm not that surprised she didn't answer. Abbey loves her sleep, and once she's out, she's out.

I tried to convince Ayden that I'd be okay sleeping in the park near my house. It wouldn't be the first time I've used the park as my refuge for the night. He wasn't having a bar of that, though, and with his hand in mine, he led me here, to the place he calls home.

Nerves flutter my heart and I dig my heels in, refusing to move when Ayden tugs on my hand to lead me up the driveway. Turning back to me, I can't gauge his expression because his face is masked in the shadows.

"Lex, what's wrong?"

"I can't go in there," I whisper, not wanting to disturb the peaceful neighbourhood. "They will have questions, Ayden. I can't tell them. I can't tell anyone."

Shifting closer, Ayden's face comes into better view and I'm able to make out the grin that spreads across his face.

"Am I amusing you?" I ask, and his grin grows wider.

"I'm sorry, Lex. I shouldn't laugh, given the seriousness of the situation, but..."

"But?" I snap, although it holds no venom.

"But you have nothing to worry about, and you need to trust me." His thumb strokes across the back of my hand. "You're also very cute when you frown like that."

Ugh! He's infuriating. But oh, how he melts the iceberg that is my heart when he says things like that.

It takes me a long moment before I internally shake off his hypnotising ways and remember why we are here.

"You don't understand, Ayden..." I lose all concentration as my breath catches when he slips his hand around my neck, cupping my nape. My breath stays trapped in my lungs, my feet cemented to the ground as he leans down, and his whisper warms my ear.

"Trust me, Lexi."

What were we talking about again?

All I can do is nod, losing the ability to speak, and my mind becomes nothing but mush.

Before I even realise it, my feet are moving as Ayden leads me quietly down the rose lined driveway that runs along the side of the house. The rose bushes have grown since the last time I was here. I remember Marcus' mum trying to plant them while we rode our bikes in the driveway, being nothing but pests.

Thinking we're about to turn the corner towards the backdoor, my body slams into Ayden's broad back when he takes a different path towards the stand-alone double story garage at the end of the driveway.

"Shit, sorry." My whisper meets his chuckles, and even in the dark, I see the flash of his white teeth as he glances over his shoulder at me.

"This way." His voice is low and quiet, tugging me deeper into the yard to the side of the garage.

Stepping through a door, Ayden uses his phone torch to light our path through the garage and up a staircase. At the top, he opens a door and flicks a light on, illuminating a small loft.

"So I'll take the couch tonight. You can take my bed."

Standing just inside the door, I take in the loft, which is decked out like a small apartment. Before me is a cosy living area with mismatched furniture. The blue couch looks like it could tell a thousand tales with tattered velvet that has been mended by hand in several places. On the far wall is a small kitchenette that looks more like a bar with a strip of blue lights that frames the mirror-lined shelving on the wall. Off to the other side of the loft is a partially opened door showing a hint of a white tiled floor and a bathroom beyond.

Glancing to the back of the loft, I take in the makeshift bedroom divided off by an old screen and a home-made curtain. From what I can see of the bed, it looks like a rose amongst the thorns compared to the rest of the furniture in here.

"You live here? Is this your room?" I ask, loving how it smells like him in here. I wonder if Ayden would think me creepy if I start sniffing stuff?

"Yep," he tugs me further into the room, "my older cousin moved out a few years ago, so this used to be Brayden's room. When he was younger, he and Marcus used to share the room Marcus is in now, and when Brayden was in high school, he convinced my uncle to let him use this space as his room. Rachel's room is empty too, but it's way too girly for me, so my aunt let me move in here."

Nodding, I look back over the space, wishing I could have something like this. Something private that has everything I need to just live on my own.

"And your mum, where does she stay?" I ask, wondering if I'm likely to bump into her.

"Mum stays in the main house with my aunt and uncle. She took their guest room, which has a little bathroom in it." Leading me towards the back of the loft, Ayden tugs me through the open curtain into the bedroom, before turning to me.

"You'll sleep here. That way I can hide you better from my mum if she makes a random visit when she gets home from her shift in the morning."

"Her shift?" I ask, and Ayden's eyes roam my face, studying me and making me squirm.

"She's a nurse. She works a lot of night shifts because the pay is better." I nod in understanding, my face heating under his curious gaze.

"And you'll sleep on the couch?" My voice cracks as I speak and my cheeks heat so much that I know he can see it.

Dear god, how much more can one embarrass themselves?

The smirk Ayden tries to hide tells me he can see how flustered I am, confirming my horror.

"Yes." He nods, his voice cracking too, but unlike me, I can tell it has more to do with how amusing I am to him.

"Okay." I clear my throat. "Good."

Jesus why am I so damn awkward around this guy?

We stand there for a few moments, the awkward silence meeting us as we stare at each other, yet neither of us breaks eye contact. His gaze searches mine, like he's deep in thought. What is he thinking? Is he secretly wishing he hadn't gotten involved in my drama? Perhaps he regrets bringing me back to his house.

Once again I let my insecurities consume me, my emotions swirling inside my head and my heart. There's a real possibility I'm going to fall apart in front of him again. I don't want to do that. I need to get some space between us.

"Bathroom," I squeak, and he jumps a little in surprise as my voice breaks the silence.

"Over there." His head gestures in the direction of the open door off to the side which I already gathered was the bathroom. "Why don't you have a hot shower and warm up? I'll go inside and grab some food. You must be hungry."

Food hasn't been on my radar, but my tummy rumbles loudly on cue, and Ayden chuckles.

"Food it is." He smiles before leaning in and placing a soft kiss to my forehead.

Instinctively, my lids flutter shut and I lean into it a little, loving the gentleness of his touch, but the spell is broken the moment he pulls back and leaves me in his room alone.

It takes me a moment to move after he walks out. His kiss was so unexpected but caring, something I'm not used to. His affection is throwing me a little. Is he just being kind, like a friend would be? I don't even know him, so I have no idea if this is the way he is with his friends. I trust him, though, more than I've ever trusted anyone, and the thought scares me, because maybe I'm looking for someone to save me, when really I should be saving myself.

Deciding a steaming hot shower would be great, I grab my backpack and shut myself in Ayden's small bathroom. The simple white space is styled with fluffy, teal green towels, and, like his bedroom, the bathroom smells like him too. It's a hint of spice and maybe vanilla. Whatever it is, it's intoxicating.

Closing my eyes, I inhale deeply, finding his scent calming. It wraps itself around me like a fluffy blanket that I never want to unravel.

My behaviour is ridiculous. Thinking these things and acting this way after what has happened today surely means there's a high chance I'm a head case destined to be institutionalised. My thoughts are all over the place, bouncing between what happened at home with Mike and my mum, to the shit show with my dad, and then my needy cravings for Ayden.

The poor guy is probably just trying to offer a helping hand, and I'm getting lost in my head from the smell of him.

Seriously, Lexi. Get a grip!

Stepping into the shower, a groan escapes when the stream of hot water hits my body. Oh man, I hope Ayden isn't outside the door hearing this. What would he think? I can't remember the last time a shower felt so good and so easy. The last few months having Mike back home has made it hard for me to relax. It's a relief not having to watch the door while I shower like I do at home, waiting for the moment Mike will barge in and sit and watch me. It's happened once, but that's all it took for me to realise I'm in real danger while he's around.

I shower longer than planned, the scalding water rendering me useless, and for the briefest time, I feel utterly relaxed and safe. I feel free.

There's no lock on Ayden's bathroom door, so technically, he can walk in at any moment. As much as that would be awkward, the idea doesn't make me want to vomit as it does at the thought of Mike walking through it. I know Ayden wouldn't do that, so for now, I'm safe.

With my hair secured in a top knot, it stays mostly dry as I wash. The temptation is strong to pull it loose and drench the strands in Ayden's shampoo, which I may or may not have smelt. As good as the shower is, the heat brings my attention to my right arm and wrist. Reddish blue bruises mark my skin, parts of which look distinctly like handprints. My dad, or at least the man I used to call my dad, had grabbed me hard in both places, and now I wear his mark.

I involuntarily gag. Sickness abruptly wracks my body as the memory of my dad's anger hits me. Taking deep breaths, I bend to support myself against the tiled wall as the water rains down over me. I gag again, but since there is nothing in my stomach, I'm able to force down the urge as I slide to the shower floor and cry.

I hate him. I hate Mike. They are both the cruellest, most disgusting people who roam this earth. I hate that I'm related to them. I hate that I carry the same last name as them. Mostly, though, I hate that I was so naïve with my dad. How could I have been so stupid as to not know what he was up to?

Not wanting to punish myself anymore, I push myself up and turn off the shower. Once dry, I rummage through my backpack, pulling out my hoodie and jeans, but damn it, in my haste to flee my house earlier, I failed to pack my oversized Metallica t-shirt that I usually wear to bed.

Great.

To add to my shitty night, I'll have to sleep in my jeans and hoodie. Either that or my school uniform, which is a definite no.

My mood now sour, I slide into my jeans and my black hoodie before heading back into Ayden's room.

The smell of delicious, mouth-watering food slams into my senses, and I nearly transform into a starved lion. Hearing me exit the bathroom, Ayden turns from his relaxed position on the couch to look at me, a smile tugging at his lips.

"Hungry?"

"That obvious?" Heat rises to my cheeks, embarrassed once again that he reads me so easily.

Chuckling, Ayden pats the spot next to him on the small blue two-seater couch, and there's no hesitation on my part. Food is a massive weakness of mine, and my eyes lock on the plate of roast lamb covered in gravy with steaming hot potatoes, carrots, and beans.

"Is that for me?" My butt makes contact with Ayden's couch as drool practically falls from my mouth.

"It is." His simple response is all I need.

Reaching forward, I snatch up the plate, sitting it on my lap, ready to dig in before I hesitate, remembering that I'm in Ayden's company.

"Is something wrong?" He dips his head to catch my attention, and I give it to him momentarily.

"Look, I'm just going to apologise right now because what you're about to witness will not be pretty."

My face is serious, and Ayden's is, too. He studies me for a long beat, before he bursts out laughing.

Falling off the couch, he clutches his middle, nearly hitting his head on the old brown coffee table. While he's busy laughing at my expense, I waste no time digging in, my taste buds having a party of their own.

Ayden eventually calms down and stops laughing, and I remain focused on cleaning every crumb of food off the plate.

The only time I ever get to eat food like this is when I go to Abbey's for dinner. My mum has never cooked for me. On the rare occasions that dad—or should I say the man that used to be my dad—would come home from the city, he would cook for me. Come to think of it, more than a year has passed since that's happened.

Putting the plate down on the coffee table when I'm done, I use my sleeve to wipe my mouth in a most unladylike manner.

"Good?" Ayden's lips quirk up at the corners.

He's been watching me the entire time. I should feel self-conscious, but it's amazing what a full tummy can do for a girl's mood and confidence, so I smile back, and nod.

Lounging back in the corner of the couch, Ayden's arm is resting along the back, and he has one leg propped up on his other knee.

Dear god. He looks like a well fucked rockstar. Not that I'd know what that looks like, but it's the first thing that comes to mind with how relaxed he is, like he's sitting on a throne.

He looks super yummy, and I have the strange urge to lick him.

"You okay?"

His deep voice shakes me out of my stupor, and I suck in a deep breath, hoping a good dose of oxygen will clear my head a little.

Now, what did he say?

Oh yeah. He asked if I'm okay.

Is he asking if I'm okay after my embarrassing feeding frenzy? Or is he asking if I'm okay after the day I've had?

I study him for a moment, trying to gauge the situation. When his face turns serious, I figure it's the latter.

"I guess." I shrug, unsure how to explain how I feel.

Numb is a good word to describe it, or maybe pissed off is even better. Exhausted is definitely one of the feelings overwhelming me right now.

As if my brain goes with that notion, I yawn.

"Bed?" Ayden asks, standing up from the couch, and I nod, suddenly feeling heavy with the pull of sleep.

Following him through the curtains into his bedroom, I stop at the foot of his bed, watching as he goes to his dresser and pulls out a couple of items, placing them on top. When he pulls his hoodie off, I worry that perhaps I wasn't meant to follow him in here, and my feet shuffle nervously on the spot as my eyes act like a peeping tom, ogling the way his body moves as the hoodie comes off. When his t-shirt underneath rides up with the hoodie, I'm rewarded with a glimpse of smooth sunkissed skin on his back and the edge of an intricate tattoo.

"How do you have a tattoo? Aren't you too young?"

The words rush from me before I'm able to stop them, and Ayden turns, eyeing me smugly as he slips into a new hoodie. This one is green. He looks good in every colour, it seems, and can make the simplest clothing item look freaking hot.

"I'm eighteen," he responds, walking back to me with the hoodie he just removed.

I knew he was older than me, but eighteen in year eleven is unusual.

"I thought you might like to wear it to bed." He holds out the hoodie he took off, and my eyes fall to it between us. "It's thicker than the one you have on, and a lot longer, so you don't have to wear your jeans."

Hesitantly, I take his hoodie offer and hold it to my chest, knowing very well that he didn't answer my question properly with his vague answer. Or maybe it's that his answer only asks more questions.

"You didn't have to take off the one you had on. I could have worn a different one." I point out, and he shrugs, waiting for me to put it on.

Ayden doesn't know I only have a bra on under my hoodie, so I step away from him and turn to face the wall. Without hesitation, I slide my hoodie off, dropping it by my feet, and the air's chill hits my bare skin, causing small goosebumps to form, before I hear Ayden inhale sharply.

At first, my stupid brain thinks he's ogling me the same way I was ogling him and likes what he sees. Perhaps my pale skin doesn't look so bad in this light? Yet when I feel a gentle hand on my shoulder and the strain in his voice, I can tell he wasn't standing there ogling me as I did him.

"Lex, your arm."

My eyes fall shut as his warm, gentle hands turn me slowly to face him. I keep them closed as he lifts my arm with such care as if I were made of glass and could shatter at any moment.

"Lex," Ayden whispers, and I peel my lids open to see his blue gaze looking almost broken.

"It'll fade, just like my eye will." I try to sound strong and confident, but my voice betrays me, and he shakes his head in disbelief.

"This is from your dad?"

He knows it is, but I can see he's struggling to accept that a parent can inflict this on their child.

"He was trying to stop me from running off. I guess he grabbed me a little too hard."

"A little," Ayden hisses. "Lex, what else has he done to you?"

I get it. He thinks my dad is abusive, and I probably would, too, if I were in his position. If my dad were an abusive father, this whole situation would be easier to handle, but he has never shown such aggression in my presence before. Never behaved so selfishly as he did tonight. That's what makes this so much harder.

"My dad has never hurt me."

"Until today?" Ayden's nostrils flare in anger. "The same day your brother hits your mum, and your dad gets sprung with his mistress?"

My eyes glass over at his harsh comment, even though I know it's the truth. It's a bitter pill to swallow. The bite in his tone sounds like he's having a dig at me, and I don't like how that makes me feel.

My face must give my emotions away, because Ayden curses, tugging me gently into his arms.

I blink away the pesky tears, not letting them win this time, and I wrap one arm around his firm waist and hug him close, needing the care he's offering.

I should probably be a little more self conscious of the fact he's now embracing me while I clutch his hoodie to my bra covered chest. The strange thing is, I don't. I don't feel exposed when I'm with him. The warmth of his embrace is welcoming, and I'd be happy to stay like this with him all night.

Ayden eventually loosens his hold on me and moves back a little, gently gliding his thumb over the bruise by my eye. He doesn't speak as he takes his hoodie from my grip and slips it over my head, helping me slide my arms in. I've never been handled with such care. Never known how loved it can make me feel.

Not that Ayden loves me. He likes me... as a friend. Maybe more. Maybe not.

"You look good in my hoodie." He smiles with pride, and my cheeks redden like a twelve-year-old girl in the schoolyard. "I think you should keep it."

"I can't keep your hoodie, Ayden." I shake my head, although I want to keep it. It smells like him. I'd be forever happy walking the earth in his hoodie, wrapped in his scent.

"It's yours. I want to know you have it. That you're wearing it to bed," he insists, his eyes roaming my face in that concerned, caring way again, not at all bothered about how forward his comment is.

"Why?" I ask.

Ayden shrugs. "Honestly. I don't know. I just like the thought of it."

I smile because I like the thought of it too.

Twelve

I can't breathe. My lungs ache and struggle to do their job as my chest heaves. Exhaustion burns my legs as they push hard to run. It's so dark, almost black. I'm not sure what I'm running from or running to, but terror grips me like a vise. Is someone chasing me? I think someone is, but I can't tell because it's too dark. Then I hear it—his voice. Terror turns me to see my dad's face, but when he speaks, it's Mike's voice I hear. "You're going to die, you little bitch!"

A scream rips from my throat, and uninvited hands are on me. My name is called over and over, but I can't focus enough to hear it, my fear too consuming. I blink rapidly, trying to see through the thick darkness, and as the haze clears, my eyes slowly take in my surroundings.

There's a bed and a chest of drawers, both of which I don't recognise, and my fear turns into terror when I see the dark silhouette of someone hovering over me.

"Lexi, wake up." A deep voice rumbles.

I swing my arms, trying to fight. "NO! STAY AWAY FROM ME!" My hand connects with a face, and I scramble off the bed, huddling in the corner of the room.

"Shit, Lexi, it's me, Ayden."

Light suddenly fills the room from a bedside lamp, illuminating the man standing by it. I blink again, trying to focus as he holds his hands up as a show of surrender.

Ayden.

Oh. My. God.

I'm a freak!

Tears stream down my face, and my body quakes with fear. Ayden's concerned blue eyes remind me that I'm safe, but my body is having a little trouble catching up to my brain. Wave after wave of trembling shakes me. Ayden, still with his arms outstretched, takes a few cautious steps towards me.

"Shh, Lex, it's okay."

A sob escapes when I try to speak. "A-Ayden?"

Upon hearing his name, Ayden closes the distance between us, kneeling to meet me as he cautiously takes my trembling hand.

"It was just a dream. I'm sorry I scared you."

"I-I'm sorry. I swear I'm not normally such a freak." He must think I'm a madwoman. I hate how pathetic and out of control I am.

"Lexi, don't say that." He scolds, frowning. Not happy with me.

He must regret letting me stay here and is probably trying to figure out how to get rid of me.

Not able to bear to see his distaste for me, I look away from his intense gaze, annoyed at myself. Why can't I just be someone else? Someone normal?

"Hey." Ayden's warm fingers caress my chin, gently lifting my head, causing my eyes to find his again. "You're not a freak, Lexi. You've been through an ordeal, and I'm guessing you've been through a lot more than you let on. You had a bad dream, one that terrified you. Don't apologise for things that are out of your control, and please don't apologise for how you need to handle the things done to you by people you should be able to trust. You need to cut yourself some slack."

I don't know where this guy came from and why it took so long for our paths to cross, but I sure as shit am glad they did. I know I shouldn't want someone to save me or protect me, and I don't think I've ever wanted anyone to do that until the day Ayden Mitchell walked into my life. Why he gives a shit about me is beyond me. He's taken an interest in me for some strange reason. Whatever his reasons for pursuing this friendship, I'm so grateful.

His concerned eyes roam my face as if trying to read my thoughts. Knowing I need affection, he pulls me slowly to his chest and wraps his strong arms around me. I instantly relax into his embrace, wrapping my arms around him and holding tight.

I need this. Caring arms. A place to feel safe. I wonder if he realises just how much he is saving me right now?

We sit in the hug for a few minutes before Ayden runs a hand soothingly over my back and places a soft kiss to the top of my head.

"Let's get you back to bed."

I move with him, letting him gently tug me towards the bed. Climbing back into its warmth, I get comfortable, and Ayden turns off the bedside lamp. I think he's going to leave and return to the couch where he'd been sleeping earlier, but he doesn't. Instead, the bed shifts behind me, and Ayden slips under the blankets, laying down.

Looking over my shoulder to see what he's doing, the faint light that filters in through the window is enough for me to catch the small smile tugging at his lips before he reaches across my body and pulls my back against his front.

Holy shit. Is he... spooning me?

Oh my fucking god, he is.

And I LIKE IT!

My heart races with anything but fear when all it should be doing is calming down for sleep. I can't stop it, though. I've never been spooned by a guy before. The fact that it's Ayden hugging me close in this position sends me into a spin, and my body responds in a way that leaves me needing something more.

I don't understand what's going on between us, and right now, I don't want to overthink it.

"Just try to relax. I won't let anything happen to you." The warm breath of his whisper dances over my ear, and I have to fight off a shiver.

I try to convince myself that he's just a friendly person who genuinely cares for the people in his life, and that's all that's going on here. In this very moment, I can't let myself think it's anything more, otherwise, there's no way I'm going to relax in his arms.

With that in mind, I try to focus on how warm I feel in his embrace. How comforting it is to hear his breathing next to my ear.

Shifting his arm, Ayden's hand finds mine, linking our fingers together, and that's how I fall asleep again. In Ayden's bed, being spooned, holding his hand.

No more bad dreams come for me. I sleep so heavily that I don't even notice when he moves out of the bed at some point, returning to the couch.

When I wake next, the soft glow of morning filters over the top of the screen and curtain that divides Ayden's bedroom from his living area. I'm about to let out a big loud yawn when I hear voices, and I stiffen, trying to remain quiet.

"You fall asleep on the couch again?" It's a lady's voice, and she sounds amused.

"Uh- yeah. Must've fallen asleep watching TV again, I guess." Ayden is quiet for a moment before continuing. "How was your shift?"

"Good. Busy. There was a big car accident out on the freeway about an hour into my shift. It went crazy after that."

"Shit, is everyone okay?" Ayden's concern is real, and I'm reminded again that he's genuinely a caring person.

The lady, his mum, I assume, sighs, "Language Ayden."

"Sorry," he chuckles, and it makes me smile that he's eighteen and getting told off for swearing.

"Everyone is alive, if that's what you're asking. But no, for one man, things don't look good. If he pulls through, then he's going to have a long, hard road ahead of him." His mum's voice sounds exhausted and holds the same care in it that I've become familiar with from her son.

"I'm sorry, mum. Are you okay?"

"Yeah. I'm exhausted, though. Do you mind if I skip breakfast with you this morning? I want to fall into bed and sleep for a week."

"Of course. You go to sleep."

I hear a kiss and imagine his mum kissing the top of his head, just like he did to me last night.

When a door closes, I hear movement right before Ayden walks through the curtain.

"Hey." His smile instantly warms me as he sits on the edge of the bed.

"Hey." I try to clear my hoarse throat, "Was that your mum?"

Ayden nods, "Yep. She looked exhausted."

"She sounds nice. Caring, like you."

Ayden's brows lift at my compliment, and he ducks his head, trying to hide a smirk. I see it, though.

"Did I say something funny?"

He shakes his head, "Nope. I guess I'm not so good at accepting compliments." His bright blue eyes glance up at me through dark thick lashes, and I don't miss the flush on his face.

Oh wow. I think I just made him blush. Ten points to me.

I can hardly contain my smug smile.

I made Ayden Mitchell blush!

"Stop gloating," Ayden shakes his head, a grin tugging at the corner of his mouth.

"What? I'm not gloating." *I totally am.*

He shakes his head and changes the conversation. "How are you feeling?"

I consider his question. I feel well-rested, which is different, but my arm is sore, as is my throat. I feel safe, which trumps all the other feelings.

"I feel okay. Thank you, Ayden."

"For what?" He looks confused.

"Making me feel safe." Feeling self-conscious, I focus on my fidgeting fingers in my lap. "I can't even begin to explain how nice it feels."

Ayden picks up my hand, and I glance up, meeting his intense ocean eyes, swimming with concern. The care he shows brings tears to my eyes, having the power to unravel my control, and the gentle squeeze of his hand offers unspoken support.

"I'm okay."

I'm not sure if I'm trying to convince him or myself.

Cupping the side of my face with his warm hand, Ayden strokes his thumb gently over my cheek. "You will be okay, Lex. I won't let anything happen to you." His words promise something I'm not sure he can deliver, but my heart wants nothing more than to believe him. A lone tear escapes, travelling down the side of my cheek, and he wipes it away before pulling me to his chest.

I hold back any more tears even though they want to burst free.

In this moment, I don't feel anger. I just feel sadness, like a part of my heart has broken away. The man I've looked up to since I was a little girl has betrayed me and betrayed my mum. I feel like the man I knew has died. I'm not even sure if I ever really knew him. Maybe he's always been like this and I was too naïve to see him for what he really is.

A monster.

I know people change, but do they change into a completely different person?

My mum comes to mind then. She's been sad for so long. I'd figured she was lonely, and that's why she turned to drugs and alcohol, but maybe it's more than that. Perhaps it's been that way for longer than I can remember. There must have been a time when she was happy being sober. A time when loving life was drug enough.

Eventually, Ayden breaks our hug and gifts me with one of his adorable grins before insisting I use the bathroom first to get ready for school.

School.

It's the last thing I want to think about, let alone do, but I don't need to draw attention to myself, and if I'm absent from school, my parents will be notified. That scenario will just make things worse for me.

While Ayden goes into the house to get us something to eat for breakfast, I use his bathroom to get ready. The process is quick and simple with a dab of concealer to hide the bruise by my eye, some mascara to wake up my eyes, and a little lip gloss for no other reason than wanting to draw Ayden's attention to my lips.

That's exactly what it does, too. I feel all sorts of powerful when I catch him darting his gaze to my lips after he returns with a croissant and a banana. Trying not to smile at my secret success is hard as hell when his eyes keep flicking to my lips, even to watch me eat.

Oh man, what have I done?

A laugh threatens to burst free, and the last thing I want to do now is to draw attention to my evil trickery, so I duck my head, pretending to scroll through Instagram on my phone. This works, breaking his attention, and he excuses himself to take a shower before school.

Alexis Amity West! If you aren't willing to follow through, then you shouldn't play with fire!

I definitely think I've lost my marbles.

One moment I'm crying in his arms, feeling broken about my family, and the next moment I'm trying to lure the guy, who has shown me nothing but kindness, to my lips.

For what? A kiss?

Do I want him to kiss me?

Well duh!

My thoughts, and probably my pink cheeks, are quickly swept away when the entrance door to Ayden's loft swings open, and Marcus steps in, stopping in place when he sees me.

"Lexi? What are you doing here?"

Shit. I open my mouth to speak, but the bathroom door swings open and a towel-clad, dripping wet Ayden steps into the room.

"Hey," he says to Marcus calmly and gives me a wink when he turns his head away from his cousin.

Holy hell, Lucifer, I praise you! I will spend a lifetime in your realm as a result of the sins rolling through my mind at the sight of Ayden Mitchell dripping with water and only wearing a towel.

Someone get me a damn fire extinguisher!

"Hey." Marcus is still standing in the same position, stunned, and Ayden ignores him, walking through the curtain into his bedroom.

With a clear look of confusion contorting his face, Marcus looks from me to where Ayden just disappeared and then moves to follow him.

Relief washes over me as I watch Marcus disappear through the curtain. I don't know what excuse to give Marcus about why I'm here. He probably doesn't even know that Ayden and I are friends.

"Dude, why is Lexi here?" Marcus asks his cousin quietly, and I strain my ears to wait for Ayden's response.

"She dropped off some work that I missed yesterday. I asked her to wait so I could walk with her to school." The fact that Ayden sounds so convincing annoys me a little. The lie comes so easily.

"Oh, cool." Marcus seems happy with the answer.

Thank god.

I glue my eyes to my phone, once again using the device to pretend I'm preoccupied when Marcus steps out from Ayden's bedroom and drops next to me on the couch, taking out his phone to do the same thing.

A text message pops up on my phone from Nathan, and I glance up quickly, hoping Marcus didn't see it, before opening the message.

Nathan

Hey Lexi. Thanks for coming to the party the other night. You really let loose. I haven't seen you like that before. ☺

Anyway, about what you said about things being over for good. Are you sure you meant that? Because the way you danced with me kind of said otherwise, and the way you cuddled me on the chair... I know you

I am going to hell. It's official. I'm a slut. Or a tease. Probably both by the sound of Nathan's message. I don't even know how to respond to it, so I don't. Maybe he'll get the hint if I ghost him.

"You going to Casey's party this weekend, Lex?" Marcus doesn't look up from his phone as he speaks, dragging me from my internal conflict. He hasn't mentioned my mum, which I'm glad about. Hopefully, he'll forget all about me running off yesterday.

"Not sure," I shrug answering him, knowing I have no idea what I'm doing tonight, let alone on the weekend. I would normally stay at Abbey's, but she might be going away with Daniel's family.

"How about you, Ayds? Are you going to come to Casey's party? It's going to be a ripper."

Ayden walks back into the room, looking all kinds of yummy dressed in his school uniform. "Maybe. Who's Casey again?"

Marcus chuckles. "I'll point her out again today."

"K," Ayden sits on the edge of the coffee table to put his shoes on and winks at me again when Marcus isn't looking. He's done that two times in the last five minutes. What does this batting of his lashes mean exactly? Is it a *'Marcus believed my bullshit lie'* type of wink, or is it a '*hi I'm Ayden and think you're cute*' type of wink?

The thought has my face heating again, and of course, Ayden notices. His gaze is almost intimidating as he stands, never taking his eyes off mine.

"Let's go," he announces, and Marcus stands, picking up his backpack by the door.

I step forward to do the same, and while Marcus' attention isn't on us, Ayden steps up to me, leaning in close to whisper in my ear.

"I don't know what you were just thinking about, Lex, but whatever it was that made my girl blush like that, means we will be having a chat about it later."

Heat flares from the tips of my toes to the top of my head. If I thought I was blushing before, then I'm as bright as Ronald McDonald's hair right now.

Ayden notices and grins with satisfaction as he turns and heads towards the door Marcus just disappeared through.

My girl? Did he just call me his girl?

"You coming, Lex?" Ayden calls.

I dip my head, embarrassed, and walk towards him, ignoring his pleased chuckle as I rush by.

What is this guy doing to me?

I'm usually so full of confidence and quick comebacks around the opposite sex. Boys are meant to get nervous around me, not the other way around. I can tell Ayden knows how he's affecting me, and I'm not sure I'm happy about being so transparent.

As the three of us walk towards my meet up spot with Abbey on our way to school, Ayden and Marcus talk about footy, PE class, and this weekend's meaningless party. Well, it's mostly Marcus talking, but Ayden listens to his cousin's babble, and I zone out since it doesn't hold any importance to me anymore.

A few months ago, I would have been all over that conversation, but now it seems insignificant.

My thoughts flutter between Ayden and the effect he is having on me, to my parents. Mum was taken to the hospital yesterday. I should probably call her and see if she's okay. She could be back home by now for all I know. What do I say when I see her? Do I tell her about dad?

"Lex!" The sound of my name snaps me back to reality, and I see Abbey up ahead with Daniel.

My smile is forced, but I wave and hope no one notices my inability to be genuinely happy.

"Hey girl, how are you?" Abbey draws me into a hug and whispers in my ear, "Why are you with Marcus and Ayden?"

I guess it's odd that I'm with these guys. A few years ago, it would've been typical for Marcus to be with me since we grew up and did everything together, but it all changed at some point, although I don't really know why.

When Abbey pulls back from our hug, I grin and shrug, knowing she will want answers as soon as we're alone, given the curious glint in her eyes.

As we walk, chatter starts up again about Casey's party this weekend. Walking next to me, Ayden takes the chance, while the others are distracted, to lightly brush his hand against mine, linking our fingers briefly while no one can see.

The action fills me with butterflies and draws my attention up to his face, and he mouths, "Are you okay?"

I shrug again, not knowing if I'm okay or not. When I'm with him, I feel like I could forget all of my worries. Well, almost all of my worries.

A car horn blares beside us on the road, making all of us jump in fright. The sudden outburst snaps our attention to the silver BMW that has pulled up.

"Lex, isn't that your dad?" Abbey asks, and my heart nearly flies out of my throat.

The silver car's tinted window slides down, and my dad leans across the seat.

"Alexis, get in the car." He sounds calm, but firm, like an authoritative dad. There's no way I'm getting into that car with him, though.

"Hi, Mr West." Abbey chirps with a big smile on her face, unaware of the hell that went down last night, "long time no see."

"Alexis, in the car now!" My dad growls harshly, ignoring Abbey.

Warm fingers link with mine again and gently tug me backward. "Don't go with him, Lex," Ayden whispers in my ear, and I relax a little, knowing he's there. It's what helps me summon up the courage to speak.

"Dad, I have to get to school. I'll see you tonight."

I won't, though, and he knows it. There is no way in hell I'll go back home. Not while things are the way they are.

"Alexis, get in the car now!"

Abbey finally picks up that there's a situation she doesn't know about, and in her true best friend style, she steps in to help.

"Mr West, we have a Maths test this morning during first period. Lexi can't miss it."

Oh, I love her!

"Abbey, this has nothing to do with you, and test or no test," my dad looks from Abbey to me, "Alexis, you will get in this car now!" he roars.

Angry tears form in my eyes, and my reckless fury takes over. Dropping my bag to the path, I rip off my school blazer, throwing it on the ground with force before I scream, "I will not go with you! I will never get in a car with someone who would do this to me!"

Gasps come from Abbey, Daniel, and Marcus when they witness the handprint bruises that mar my upper arm and wrist. My dad's face pales, and his head jerks like I've slapped him. Pain and remorse flash over his face briefly before it's replaced with anger, and saying nothing else, he slams his foot on the accelerator and speeds off, leaving me a trembling mess on the footpath with a group of confused friends behind me.

I'm shaking when Abbey steps up to me with tears of her own, pulling me into a hug. That's when I break.

Thirteen

The rest of the walk to school is quiet and awkward with the boys around. Daniel manages to pry himself away from Abbey to walk with Ayden and Marcus, giving us some well-needed girl time.

Like I did with Ayden, I leave a few details out when I share the crazy shit that happened over the past twenty-four hours with Abbey. I'm sure Ayden knows more than she does at this point. She still doesn't know about Mike hitting me and turning our home into a crack house. She only knows that I don't get along with him, and I'm sure she thinks it's just a sibling rivalry thing.

"You can't go back there tonight," Abbey states the obvious, which gains the boys' attention, and they stop walking, turning to us.

"She's right," Marcus' voice is filled with concern, and the look he gives me almost makes me break again, and I realise they must have overheard me telling Abbey what happened.

Nodding, I look to my feet, feeling overwhelmed with the attention on me before Abbey speaks.

"Wait, where did you stay last night?"

Damn it, Abbey!

I was hoping she wouldn't think about that.

"With me." Ayden doesn't hesitate with the truth, and my eyes shoot to his as he regards me with care.

"Dude." Marcus drawls at the same time that Abbey blurts. "You slept with Ayden? I-I mean, you slept *at* Ayden's?" Abbey's fumbled words don't go unnoticed by the boys, and Marcus snickers like an immature idiot. Daniel chuckles too, turning his attention to the street behind us in guilt when Abbey shoots him a death glare.

"Yes, I slept *at* Ayden's. He took the couch," I explain, watching Abbey's face as my words sink in, and thankfully she buys it.

"Oh man," Abbey grabs her phone out of her blazer pocket. "All the missed calls from you. I'm so sorry, Lex." Only now she realises I'd needed her. I wonder if she'd heard my calls and just ignored them because she was busy with Daniel or something.

It doesn't matter now.

"It's okay, Abs. Ayden was there to help."

"Good," Abbey nods. "I'm glad you didn't sleep in the park again."

My eyes widen at her comment and I stiffen.

Jesus Abbey. Let everyone in on the bullshit that is my life, why don't you.

"What?" Ayden snaps, looking a mixture of concerned and angry.

I let my head fall forward and sigh, hearing Abbey whisper, "Sorry."

"You weren't kidding about that?" Ayden steps closer, his fierce gaze locked on me. "You've slept in the park instead of going home before?"

My eyes plead with Ayden to drop it. This information doesn't need to be broadcast to everyone.

"We need to get to school." I insist, hoping to shift our huddled group back into walking, and try to move forward, but Ayden's strong arm stops me.

"Lex, we need a plan for tonight. You can't go home."

I look up at him, seeing the fear in his eyes.

"Ayden's right, Lex. You can't go home. I'll talk with my parents and see if they're happy for you to stay for a while. Maybe they can help?" Abbey sounds hopeful, but I'm not so sure. Her parents have always been nice enough to me, but I still get the impression they think I'm a bad influence on her. Their religious beliefs have been an issue over the years, and they have frowned upon some of the things I do, like my edgy taste in music. I can't play the music I like in their house.

Abbey may be right, though, and they may help. I have a terrible feeling that my current situation won't sit well with them, though.

"Okay, thanks Abs." I have to try at least, so I agree.

Ayden links his fingers with mine, no longer caring who sees, and we finish walking to school. The entire time I try to avoid Abbey's wagging eyebrows and pointed smirks. The moment we're alone, I just know she's going to hound me about what's going on with Ayden.

I'm not exactly sure what Ayden and I are. I met him three days ago, and in that short time, he's managed to insert himself into my life and take root. It should annoy me, but it doesn't. Having him around has been a blessing. I'm pretty sure he's interested in more than friendship with me. His flirting melts me like butter, rendering me senseless at times. But he also hasn't done anything more than kiss the top of my head or hold my hand. He did spoon me, which is more than a friend thing, right?

Shit, maybe he was just trying to comfort me, and that's all there is to it.

Whether Ayden's interest in me is in friendship or more, part of me feels like I should tell him to back off and not get too close. I worry that my tainted life will burn him and bring him down. He has such a kind heart. I'd hate myself profusely if I were the one to destroy that part of him. I have no idea what's going to happen in my life now.

Will my dad divorce my mum?

Should I even tell my mum about what her husband has been up to?

Will Mike ever leave me alone?

As my thoughts grow darker, I convince myself that Ayden will let go of my hand when we arrive at school. He isn't going to want anyone to know that he's associated with the kind of screwed up I am. As the little self-loathing devil sits on my shoulder, whispering every insecurity I can imagine, I'm proven wrong when Ayden squeezes my hand even tighter. Our arrival at school doesn't make him pull away, and his tightening grip feels almost as if he's afraid to let go.

Whispers start-up as we make our way through the yard. I don't care that they see Ayden's hand in mine, and I draw strength from his unwavering support. However, I do care that I'm the focus of the attention as we make our way to our lockers. I hate all the eyes on me, and I just want to fade into the background and disappear.

The first part of the day is easy. Ayden and I have the first two classes together, Maths and History, so we sit together like it's second nature. Anytime I start to get lost in my thoughts, Ayden puts his hand on my knee, pulling me back to the present and keeping me grounded.

At recess, we sit together and share a bucket of hot chips. I don't miss the fact Ayden makes me eat most of the chips while he keeps the conversation light and away from the intense events of my last twenty-four hours.

Tasha spends most of recess glaring at me like I've grown two heads. I don't know why exactly, but I'm willing to bet she's pissed that she didn't get the chance to dig her fake claws into Ayden. I try to ignore her, but her bitchy scowl is her not-so-subtle way of letting me know she has an issue with me. I'm sure before the day is through, Tasha will pounce and bare her teeth to me.

Bring it bitch!

After recess, I have Art, and I enter the same classroom I trashed only days earlier. Guilt is a bitch that doesn't give up, leaving me in a hot sweat throughout the lesson. I barely do any of my work getting sidetracked by the bright yellow tape which hasn't been removed from the newly installed windows.

I did that.

I'm a horrible person.

When Art is over, I can't get out of the classroom fast enough to head to my Pastoral Care class. Not because I like Pastoral Care, but because I can't stand another second in the room I trashed. Pastoral Care is a bullshit class made up so teachers can pry into our lives. They insist it's for guidance, but not once have I received any good advice from it. What makes it worse is it's another class I don't have with Ayden. I miss him already. He'd been reluctant to leave me after recess, but we had no choice, and he's now on the other side of the school in Woodwork.

"Excuse me, Lexi West?" Mrs Monaghan, the Pastoral Care teacher, calls from the front of the room.

I glance up to see the school secretary at the front of the room with the teacher, looking at me expectantly.

"Grab your things, please, and go to the office with Margaret."

I frown at Mrs Monaghan's words, "Why?"

"Just do as you're asked, please," she snaps back, and I huff in annoyance. My annoyance is quickly replaced with panic. Shit, do they know I'm the one who vandalised the school? It's unusual for a student to be collected from class, so of course, all eyes are on me. If I'm about to go down for the vandalism, then I'm about to be the talk of the school.

I reluctantly do as I'm asked and follow the secretary out of the classroom. The need to message Ayden is overwhelming, but I'm so ashamed to admit what I've done, so I keep my phone in my pocket. I can't bear to see the disappointment he'll wear on his face when he finds out who I really am and what I'm capable of.

"You need to grab your bag from your locker first." Margaret insists as we walk.

"What? Why?"

Oh my god. I'm so fucked!

"Like Mrs Monaghan said before, Miss West, just do as you are asked, please."

Her words are firm, almost scolding as if I'm in trouble. I probably am. I'm probably about to get kicked out of school. Maybe even arrested. When my dad finds out, things are definitely going to be bad for me.

When I follow the secretary into the Principal's office a few minutes after getting my bag, I freeze on the spot for a moment in shock before my instincts scream at me to turn and run. As if sensing where my head is at, Margaret hastily shuts the door in my face, and I reluctantly turn back to look at the man who has caused me so much pain in the last twenty-four hours.

My dad stands next to Mr Ryland's desk, his dark grey suit looking out of place amongst the Principal's chaotic mess.

"Please sit, Miss West." Principal Ryland's voice is stern, but it has nothing on the one my dad directed toward me earlier from his car.

I shake my head in refusal.

"Sit down, Alexis."

And there it is. Deep and fierce, his tone even makes my Principal flinch.

Squaring my shoulders and lifting my chin, I glare at my dad, allowing him to see the hate I have for him. Mr Ryland looks taken aback by my reaction but keeps his mouth shut.

"Alexis, I won't ask you again. SIT!"

The venom in his growl makes me obey unwillingly, and I sit, my chest visibly heaving in frustration and anger. My dad steps forward, holding a small cup of water out for me.

"Have a drink of water and take a moment to calm down."

I frown but take the water and drink it, trying to look compliant. If this is about the vandalism, then I need to be on my best behaviour.

"Miss West, your father has updated me on your..." he hesitates, looking sympathetic, "Condition."

My brows shoot up. "Condition?"

"Yes. I'm sorry to hear that you've been having such a tough time coping with things, but I agree with your dad. School is not as important as your wellbeing, and it's time for you to accept the help your family is offering."

"Help? What help?" I snap, directing my question to the Principal but glaring at my dad, my anger evident. This has nothing to do with the vandalism and everything to do with my dad's need to control me.

"Miss West, I ask that you remain calm while on the school grounds. I don't want to call security, but I will if you don't cooperate."

That gets my attention.

Shooting up from the chair, my body vibrates with alarm, and my eyes widen as I recognise *what* this situation actually is—an ambush. As I think this, the room starts to sway, and I frown, a feeling of lightness settling into my head.

My gaze darts to the empty cup I left abandoned on the chair and then back to my dad. A look of smug satisfaction is on his face, and it's then that I know I'm truly fucked.

What has he done?

I need to get to Ayden.

I need someone to help me.

"What help?" The slur in my voice is mild, but I notice it, and so does my dad. I hate that he gets to hear it. I can't tell where this conversation is going, but I know nothing good will come of it, especially since I'm pretty sure my dad gave me a spiked cup of water.

Surely Principal Ryland will notice and help me?

"Go home with your father, Miss West. Take the time you need to deal with your condition. When you are well again, we will welcome you back with open arms."

"My condition? What condition?" With a raised voice that has a more evident slur this time, I move to put more distance between my so-called dad and me, stepping behind the chair I'd been sitting in. My legs feel heavy and weak, like they might give out at any second.

"There is nothing to be ashamed of, Miss West. Many people suffer from mental health issues."

"What!" I screech, and Principal Ryland flinches. My dad, however, remains calm, which is almost scarier than him ranting and raving.

"Please, Mr Ryland," I beg weakly. "I can't go home with him. I'm not safe with him."

Principal Ryland sighs, turning to my dad, "you were right."

My dad gives Mr Ryland a fake sombre nod.

What the hell is he talking about? What was my dad right about?

"Alexis, your father filled me in on your situation, and he was afraid you would say that. Self-harming for attention is not healthy. You need to accept that you have a problem and go with your father."

"Self-harming?" I choke out, tears stinging my eyes.

Principal Ryland looks at me knowingly. "Your arm, Alexis. You've caused harm to your arm by bruising yourself. That's not normal. You need to accept help."

"No! He did that." I point to my dad as I try to back towards the door, needing to flee, but my legs nearly give out.

"I'm sorry, Mr Ryland. I'd hoped we could avoid doing this the hard way, but it can no longer be avoided." My dad uses his professional business tone with my Principal, still the epitome of calm, while I'm anything but.

"Yes, Mr West, I understand. Do what you need to do." Mr Ryland gestures to what exactly, I don't know, before moving around his desk, passing by me to leave the room.

Fuck this, I'm not sticking around to find out what my dad is going to do next. Turning on my heel, the room spins and my legs give out, sending me tumbling to the floor. I try to call out for help, but my words come out as gibberish.

Looking up, I see a security guard in the room with us, blocking the door.

My only escape.

"Don't make a scene, Alexis. It's for your own good." My dad's words are the last thing I hear before my world plunges into darkness.

Fourteen

"Pops, the little bitch is waking up."

Mike's revolting voice drags me abruptly out of the haze that has engulfed my body.

"Here, drink this." Standing before me, holding out a glass of water, is the man I used to consider as my dad.

"Fuck you!" I spit, scattering as far back into the corner of the couch as I can.

"Suit yourself." Sounding as if he couldn't care less, my dad puts the glass of water on the coffee table.

Being in the familiar living room should relax me since this is the home I grew up in, but with the two monsters lurking before me, this place is nothing like home. Looking around quickly, I see that yesterday's trashed mess is now clean. The only sign of Mike's attack on my mum are the holes that remain in the walls.

My eyes fall on Mike. His sick smirk sends chills down my spine as he leans against the wall across the room with cruelty in his eyes.

I gag.

"You feel sick?" Dad looks almost concerned.

I nod, hoping I can still reach the loving dad who once doted on his daughter. If I can do that, then I might be able to escape to the safety of my room.

Instinctively, I reach for the chain that hangs around my neck, holding the key to my bedroom. Only, I don't find it. It's gone.

Mike snickers, noticing my reaction, but stops the moment my dad glares at him.

"Alexis, I wish you hadn't put me in this position. If you had just stayed with me last night, or come with me this morning, then we could have avoided all of this."

Tears threaten again, and I try hard to hold them back, not wanting them to see the effect they have on me.

"Where's mum?" Mike scoffs at my question, and dad sighs.

"Your mother is being taken care of. No need to worry about her." My dad's answer is vague, and I can only hope she's still safe in hospital.

"Is she still in hospital?" I ask, wanting to speak to her to find out what happened yesterday with Mike. I guess I also need to tell her what her husband has been doing. It'll break her heart, but she needs to know.

"She's in the city now." My dad answers, his tone flat like he doesn't care. "I pulled some strings and got her into the new Lady Anne's Women's Hospital."

Lady Anne's isn't a typical hospital. It's a psychiatric hospital. That much, I know.

My mum has been in hospitals like this before due to her drug use and instability. It means she'll be under strict supervision and maybe even put through detox. If that's the case, they won't allow her phone calls because her mental stability will be at risk.

The fact that my dad said he pulled some strings to get mum into the facility in Melbourne concerns me. Has he done to my mum what he just did to me? Did he convince her doctors that she's mentally unstable like he convinced my Principal I was?

I don't want to believe it, but it feels possible, now that I can see my dad for the monster he is.

That thought is a reminder that I'm not safe here. I need to get away from both my dad and Mike.

"Where's my key?" I ask, hating how my voice wavers a little.

"Oh, you mean this key?" Mike's smug tone gets on my nerves as he dangles the key in question from his fat sausage fingers.

"Give it back!"

"Alexis, the key is useless now." My dad butts in. "I've removed your bedroom door, along with the toilet and bathroom doors upstairs. Until you can prove you are mentally stable, you'll have no privacy. We can't take the risk of you harming yourself, therefore, you will be monitored at all times."

No.

Did my dad just say that the doors are gone?

Surely I heard wrong?

"W-what?" I stutter as my anger boils to the surface. "That makes no sense, Dad. I am mentally stable!"

Sighing, he runs his hand through his hair in frustration. "No, Alexis, you're not. First, you make up some nonsense about Mike attacking your mother when it was actually an aggravated burglary. Then you accuse me of having an affair when I was having a business dinner. Not to mention how you ran off and slept god knows where last night. Let's not forget about the ridiculous lies you told your friends and your Principal, blaming me for the harm you caused to your own arm."

What the actual fuck!

Red hot tears tumble free as each accusation slices through my heart.

Why is my dad saying these things? He knows I'm telling the truth, so why would he say such lies about me?

"But—"

"NO!" My dad roars, "Just stop, Alexis! Shut your mouth and do as you're told for once!"

I flinch, his harsh tone catching me off guard. I hug my arms around my body, unable to control my whimpering, making me feel like a helpless child.

"Stop crying, damn it!" He lurches for me with his hand raised.

I recoil, crying out in fear as I see the rage on my dad's face. Mike, the arsehole, laughs, egging dad on in the background, which thankfully causes my dad to hesitate and not follow through.

Who the fuck are these people?

"God damn it!" My dad bellows right before the glass of water he offered me earlier is hurled across the room, shattering against the wall.

In all of my seventeen years, I've never once seen such a temper in my dad.

I don't take my eyes off him as he stomps across the room, speaking quietly to Mike. I try to hear past the pounding pulse in my ears, but I can't make out what he is saying. When he's done, he returns his attention back to me.

"Here's what's going to happen, Alexis. You will stay in this house until I return on Monday after I've tied up some loose ends in the city. Mike will watch you until then. We have taken your laptop and phone, so you can't contact your friends or your mother. You are grounded until you can prove obedience."

"What?" My heart momentarily stops. "No! Dad, no!" I beg, knowing I can't stay here with Mike. "Please take me with you. I'll be good, I promise. Please don't leave me here!"

My pleading falls on deaf ears as I watch him turn and walk away.

"Mike, keep her in check. I'll see you on Monday." With those final words, my dad picks up a bag near the door and walks out.

I scream!

I use the loudest version of my voice, begging him to take me with him, but he doesn't respond, even when I run across the room to catch up with him. I grip his arm in desperation, but he shakes it off in disgust as if I carry a contagious disease. The move pushes me backward, causing me to fall into Mike, and he wraps his filthy arms around my waist before carrying me kicking and screaming up the stairs.

I flail, kicking wildly, my feet hitting the walls as he climbs but he's too strong. My struggles are useless.

"Stop, would you!" Mike hisses, but I don't stop. *Never!*

Reaching my room, Mike throws me onto my bed, the force causing me to roll off the other side, and I slam into my dresser. Searing pain shoots through my back and ribs, wrenching a scream from my lungs.

"Fucking stay here and keep quiet, bitch. I'll be back soon to check on you."

When I hear Mike's retreating footsteps, I push past the pain and scramble to my window for an escape.

It's no use.

Disappointment seizes my throat like a strong hand wrapping around it when I see my window has been fitted with a lock. My god, my dad has thought of everything. He means to keep me a prisoner.

The panic that thought brings pushes me to keep trying, so I tug at the lock, trying to open it without success.

Reality, the bitch that it is, sends me to the floor in a distraught heap. My mind races. I need to find a way out of this. Maybe when Mike's asleep tonight, I can sneak downstairs and escape out the front or back door. Where will I go then? Abbey's? Ayden's? What if their parents don't believe me?

Desperation and angst squeeze my chest painfully, and I struggle to breathe as the reality of my situation slams into me.

I don't know how long I stay like that on the floor. The crying, the screaming, the numbness. It's all too consuming.

It's not until I hear Mike's footsteps coming up the stairs that I notice the sky outside is now dark.

Shit. He's coming back.

Fear kicks me in motion, and I scramble up in time to see my brother standing in the doorway.

"You stink bitch, take your clothes off." He sneers, curling his lip in disgust at me.

"W-what?"

"You heard me."

I shake my head. "No."

"When are you going to realise that your life will be a nightmare until you submit? Now get your fucking clothes off and get in that bathroom. You need to shower."

"I-I can d-do that myself. Y-you don't need to be here for t-that."

Mike chuckles, "Nice try, Princess. As if I'm going to miss watching you shower."

Oh my god, this can't be happening. I need to get out of here. I need Ayden.

The thought slices my heart open.

I was so close to happiness. So close to having something normal again. I finally found someone who cared enough to take time out of their day for me. Now, I'll never have that. I'll never have him.

I choke on a sob, and Mike huffs in frustration before stepping into my room. I back away frantically, trying to figure out how I can dodge him, but as I try to bolt, he grabs my arms, wrenching me back before slamming my face against the wall.

"Looks like you'll be learning the hard way." When I feel the gravel of his wet tongue run up the side of my face, I gag, not able to control the reaction. For that, Mike spins me to face him, and I'm hit with a stinging slap across the side of my face.

"If you throw up, I will make you lick it up, you filthy whore!"

My cheek is on fire from the force of Mike's hand, but it's quickly forgotten when he grabs a fistful of my hair and starts dragging me. My hands automatically wrap around his wrists, trying to release his painful grip while my legs kick out frantically, trying to pull myself up without victory.

He doesn't silence my screaming and seems to revel in it, laughing like a madman. As Mike drags me by my hair down the hall and into the bathroom, excruciating pain tears at my scalp before I sense warm moisture trickle over my head. Drops of red spill over my eyelid, thick blood oozing down my cheek.

My face forcefully meets the cold tiles of the bathroom floor as Mike finally releases me. I try to scramble away, but he quickly drags me up by my arms, pushing me against the tiled wall.

"Get your fucking clothes off!" His spittle flies onto my face, and his vile breath hits me, nearly making me gag again. I hold my breath, trying to control it, knowing he will make good on his previous threat.

It's then that I notice for the first time that my dad hadn't been kidding. There's no bathroom door to give me any privacy.

Jesus. Fuck. This can't be happening.

"C-can you p-please wait in the h-hall while I shower?" I whimper, forcing the words out, and Mike chuckles.

"As if I'm going to miss this, Princess. Now hurry the fuck up and get naked."

"P-please, Mike. Just wait in the ha—"

Mike's fist cuts me off as it slams into my cheek.

Never in my life have I felt such pain. My vision wavers, going black briefly as little lights dance before my eyes.

"Get your fucking clothes off, Ali!"

My fearful cries bounce off the bathroom walls, physical and emotional pain rendering me useless. He's too strong for me. I can't fight him off. He won't even listen to my pleas. There's no way I'm getting out of this, at least not brutally beaten or maybe even dead.

I have no choice.

I have to do as he says.

Keeping my eyes closed, I slide my blazer off, letting it fall to my feet. My shirt and skirt follow, and I ignore Mike's perverted ogling when I'm left standing in nothing but my bra and knickers.

"Keep going, Ali. Everything off."

Fifteen

My body trembles as I squeeze my eyes tight and try to control my breathing before I reach behind to unclasp my bra. My ribs instantly protest the action, and I bite the inside of my cheek, working hard to hold in my whimper. Breathing through the pain, I get it undone, and my bra joins the rest of my clothes by my feet.

"Ahh fuck, not bad at all, little sis." Mike visibly adjusts himself in his pants, and I cover my chest with my arms, but the sick fucker shakes his head.

"Uh-uh, you're not finished yet." He points down to my knickers.

In this moment, I'm thankful for my tears, since the blur distorts my ability to see the look on my brother's face while I continue to obey. Keeping one arm over my breasts, I use the other to pull down my knickers, stepping out of them, but my vision isn't blurry enough to miss Mike rubbing his hand over his tented pants.

"Fuuuck, this is gold."

I fight back a gag.

Needing to distract his perversion, I bolt for the shower, reaching in to turn on the water. I don't wait for the water to heat, stepping straight under the icy stream, feeling my flesh prickle as goosebumps travel over my skin. I reach to pull the frosted glass door closed, but Mike stops my attempt with his hand and shakes his head.

"Nope, this stays open."

If I thought I hated my dad before, then I was wrong, because right in this moment, knowing he willingly put me in this situation, fills me with more hate, more fury than I ever thought I could feel.

I try hard not to lose the little control I have and turn my back to the person who is meant to be my big brother. Meant to be my protector.

Even though the water is now hot, it does nothing to warm my skin. Nothing but my brother's death is ever going to be able to warm my flesh again.

Mike snaps orders at me as I wash, and I follow them, wanting this to be over quickly. I just need to get through this until he falls asleep later. Then I'll run and never look back.

"Wash those sexy legs, Ali."

I move to turn, so when I bend, I don't have to bare my arse to him, but he has other ideas.

"Stay right fucking there and do it. Don't you move unless I tell you to."

I fight back tears of humiliation as I bend and wash my legs, knowing that he's getting an intimate view that a brother should never see.

"Turn around now and wash your hair."

I do as he says, quickly massaging shampoo into my hair. As I rub the suds over my scalp, my fingers brush over a weeping graze on the crown of my head, and it causes a biting sting. I cringe from the pain and decide to cut the hair wash short and rinse it out. I don't even bother with conditioner. I'd much rather get this over and done with than to bother with having silky hair.

"Now wash in between those dirty legs, Ali. Let me see you wash that sweet pussy."

A sob leaps from my mouth.

I'm going to kill him.

Somehow, someway, I am going to fucking kill my brother, even if I have to die trying. I won't stop until it's done. Not until I've watched him take his last fucking breath.

Gritting my teeth, I use the sponge to do as he asks. I try to avoid looking at him, but I need to know where he is so I can be ready in case he comes for me. I don't want to be caught unaware.

"Now wash those perky little tits. Wash them nice and slow." The drawl in his voice forces me to look at him this time, and that's when I see his jeans are around his ankles and his hand is now stroking himself.

I lose all of my control.

I gag three times until vomit comes up, and I can no longer stop it. I retch and retch, thankful that I'm in the shower, so the rushing water quickly washes it away.

I expect Mike to scold me for doing something so vile in front of him, but the groans from his lips are in pleasure as he finishes himself off, watching me vomit in the shower.

He's fucking sick in the head!

I can't stop crying. I'm a sobbing mess. Never have I experienced something so vile. In this very moment, I wish I was dead. I don't want to be here and encounter another moment of this. I want out of this life now.

As soon as I have that thought, Ayden's face flashes through my mind.

Ayden.

I want to see him again. I want to be in his life, even if I don't deserve to be. I want to hold his hand again and breathe in his scent. I want to feel more of the care he offers.

I may currently be enduring the most heinous act I could ever imagine, but the thought of being able to see Ayden again is more than enough to remind me that I need to get through this somehow.

"Get out." Mike pulls his jeans up, leaving them half-zipped. "Now that you're nice and clean for me, I can have my fun with you."

No. This can't be happening.

I don't get the chance to speak, scream, or protest because Mike turns off the water and yanks me from the shower by my hair again. The pain intensifies, more hair ripping out as he drags me, dripping with water from the shower and out into the hall.

"No! No! No!" I scream over and over, finding my voice.

Having enough of my protests, Mike uses his fist again to silence me, the impact rattling my brain before darkness engulfs me.

For a brief time, everything is peaceful. A plain space of nothingness surrounds me. There's no pain here. No heartache. Just a calm peace that calls to me.

When my eyes blink open again, a thick fog contorts my perception. Pain in my head is the first thing to register before my vision comes into focus to see Mike looming over me.

As he starts to unzip his fly, I try to look around, but my head feels so heavy, making the move sluggish. My bedroom slowly comes into focus, and I realise I'm starfished on my bed, completely naked.

Panic seizes me, and I try to think of a way out of this because I'm one hundred percent sure my brother is about to rape me and take my virginity.

Fight Lexi!

I have to fight until either he's dead, or I am.

Before I can do anything to try and save myself, Mike's head snaps to look over his shoulder as if he can hear something, and I force my ears to work harder. That's when I hear it—the doorbell.

"Fuck." He whines with disappointment, and my lips part to release a scream, but the side of my face gets another rendezvous with Mike's fist, and I see stars.

"Keep your fucking mouth shut, or I'll send my mates up here to have their way with you, too. Stay right fucking there, and do NOT get dressed."

I whimper and try to nod. It's hard to tell if the movement works due to the pain I'm in.

Mike storms off down the stairs, and moments later, I hear a multitude of voices. It's his so-called mates—the ones who are nothing but a bunch of drug-addicted losers who use him for his endless supply of drugs.

Listening, I can tell they are moving to the kitchen at the back of the house. I need to flee, but how do I get out of this? If I get caught, I could find myself in an even worse situation with not just Mike but his druggo friends, too.

Sitting up, I wrap my fleece throw blanket around me. My hair is still dripping wet, and a watery trail of blood runs down my chest from my hair. My face feels weird, both painful and numb at the same time, and I can feel that my left eye is swollen and won't open.

Easing up off my bed, I stumble to my dresser mirror. Holy shit! I don't even recognise the left side of my face. If my right side weren't in better condition, I'd think it was someone else looking back at me.

The music from downstairs gets louder, the sound not helping my thumping skull, and it causes me to stumble as my legs give out. My head swims, balancing on the edge of consciousness as little lights flicker across my eyes. I'm going to pass out. I can feel it rise through my body like a numb, hot wave. I can't let myself faint. If I'm not conscious, then I can't fight.

The sound of a creak on the staircase makes me freeze.

Shit, someone is coming.

I listen, trying to hear past the music to see if I imagined it, but then I hear it again.

It could be Mike.

No, if it were him, he'd just charge up the stairs like he always does.

My heart races with even more panic as I realise it must be one of his friends. That could be a good thing or a bad thing, but it's more likely to be a bad thing. I've met his mates before. They are all just as fucked in the head as he is.

Even though Mike told me to stay on the bed, I can't bring myself to return to it and obey. Adrenaline hums through my veins, fueling my blood, and I try to move but my legs won't work sending me to the floor.

No! Work, you fucking useless things!

I need to hide, or better yet, get away, but my body isn't cooperating, and as if to remind me of the imminent danger I'm in, the creak on the stairs sounds again.

Shit! Shit! Shit!

My fear spikes, causing me to tremble, making any attempt at standing nearly impossible. Digging deep to find physical strength, I manage to slide myself across the carpeted floor towards my wardrobe. Tugging the door open, I push my way through the hanging clothes and huddle in the back corner as I tremble in fear. After I pull the door silently closed, my shaking hands making it more difficult than it should be, I wrap the blanket tight around me and bite down on it, hoping to stop any noise that my stupid ragged breathing and weak tears will bring.

Hiding in the wardrobe is so cliché. It's the first place the killers look in all the movies. What am I thinking? I should have stayed out on my bed and saved them the trouble.

As if to prove my point, the floor creaks just outside my wardrobe door.

Someone is in my room.

I hold my breath, struggling to hear much else but the erratic pounding of my heart, which feels like it's about to beat its way out of my chest.

"Lexi?" a familiar deep voice whisper yells. "Lexi, where are you?"

Is that... Ayden?

The wardrobe door slowly opens, and I try to scramble backward, but there's nowhere else to go.

"Holy shit." A different deep voice whispers, which I know is definitely not Ayden and a whimper escapes me.

I need to fight. I can't let them touch me.

"Lex, it's me, Ayden." The familiar, caring tone that can only belong to one person manages to break through my panic, and I try to pry my eyes open as wide as I can to see if he's real, and luckily, the dark hue of the closet isn't nearly enough to hide those piercing blue familiar eyes.

"Ayden?" His name is a soft whimper on my lips, and I can only just make out that there's someone else with him.

"Shit, man, she's hurt bad."

I know that voice. It's Marcus. Ayden's here with his cousin. My friend.

"Find a bag, Marcus. Throw some of her clothes in it." Ayden whispers over his shoulder and then looks back to me, his eyes pained. "We have to get you out of here, Lex. We don't have much time."

Nodding, desperate to escape, I try to stand, but my legs still won't cooperate, the move causing the blanket to fall past my shoulders, revealing that I'm naked underneath.

"Christ, we need to get her dressed." Marcus looks away quickly, pretending he didn't just see part of my bare flesh, and Ayden rushes to help right the blanket on me.

"No time," Ayden hisses and moves to help me stand, but I still can't make my legs work.

"Got as many clothes as I can fit." Marcus holds up my duffel bag, and Ayden nods, but doesn't take his eyes off me.

"Lex, we snuck through the front door. Marcus' sister called some mates to come and keep your brother busy, but we have to get out of here before he gets suss." His words are encouraging, and I nod in understanding. "I'm going to carry you, okay?"

Ayden's unwavering kindness ignites my waterworks again, and he leans down quickly, lifting me into his strong arms to cradle me against his chest. I keep the blanket hugged tight to my body and rest my head in the crook of his neck as he walks silently, following Marcus out of my room.

We descend the stairs quietly, and although I feel safe in Ayden's arms, I can't fight back my fear knowing somebody could catch us at any moment. Reaching the bottom step, I tense in Ayden's arms, but he tugs me close, looking around the corner down the hall to the kitchen where the music and laughter flow from.

"It's okay, beautiful," Ayden whispers. "I've got you."

Those words do something to me. They make me feel safer even though we're still in danger. They make me feel cared for even though I hardly know him. And they give me hope, where I've struggled to find an ounce of it recently.

We haven't even known each other for a week, and it feels like I've known him for so much longer. The way he knows just what to say, or can see my internal struggles when no one else does, just makes me that much more drawn to him.

"All clear," Marcus whispers before Ayden moves again, rushing for the open front door.

I hold on to his neck for dear life as he rushes with me in his arms. Cold air hits me once we are outside, and the music fades away as my body bounces in Ayden's arms while he runs from my home and away from my hell.

Squeezing my eyes shut, I hope like hell we don't get caught as I hold my breath, listening to the heavy feet pound the pavement as Marcus follows behind. I'm unsure where we're running to, but as long as it's far away from Mike, then I don't care.

"Oh, my god! Is she okay?" A female voice that I don't recognise comes from nearby, and I hear Marcus say something to the girl that I can't make out.

"Lex," Ayden whispers, "I'm going to put you in the car, okay?" I nod reluctantly because not being in his arms sounds terrifying.

"Door," Ayden snaps to someone, and I hear a car door creak open before Ayden lowers me into a cold seat.

Releasing my hold on his neck, I try to keep the blanket in place as he kneels in the open door, his gaze roaming my face with concern. His beautiful blue eyes glaze over with unshed tears, showing me the unwavering care he has in his heart.

"I'm so sorry, Lex. I should've been there to stop this from happening."

I've never really seen a guy cry before, but as a tear finally pops free and rolls down Ayden's cheek, my heart aches simply because it's him, and he deserves smiles, not tears.

Shaking my head at his words, I try to speak, but my throat feels like a thousand razor blades are lodged inside.

"Shh, don't speak." He whispers as his thumb rubs soothing circles over my blanket covered shoulder.

"Ayden, we should go to the cops." The girl steps forward, and I see her looming in the shadows next to Marcus.

I immediately shake my head and croak, "No cops."

The three of them frown, but they don't understand. As soon as the cops talk to my dad, they are likely to believe whatever tale he spins, and if they don't, they'll ask questions I just can't bring myself to answer or admit out loud. Then they'll want evidence and want to do tests. I just... can't handle that right now.

"Honey, I think you should go to the police. Your brother can't get away with this." Moving out of the shadows a little, I notice the girl has the same eye and hair colour as Marcus. Is this his older sister, Rachel? She looks familiar and could very well be his big sister, who I idolised when I was little.

Shaking my head, I glance back at Ayden, my eyes pleading with him to understand. His intense gaze studies mine for a long drawn out moment before he sighs, dropping his head to look at the ground, deep in thought. When he glances back up, my shoulders drop in relief as I see acceptance and resolve settle on his face.

"Rach, Marcus." He speaks louder to his cousins while keeping his eyes trained on me. "Can you cover for me with my mum? You can tell her I've gone to dad's in the city. Just don't tell her I drove."

"Yeah, sure, we can do that. But you owe us, Ayden. This is serious shit." The girl, who is definitely Rachel, doesn't seem happy.

Standing, Ayden turns to them. "I know. I wouldn't lie to my mum if I didn't have to. Once Lexi is safe and away from here, I'll explain everything to her. I'll pay you back for petrol, too. You know I'm good for it."

"Don't worry about that." Rachel waves a dismissive hand in the air. "Just look after her. And make sure you look after yourself, too. Don't slip up." Rachel gives him a pointed look, and I don't miss that there's some sort of hidden meaning in her comment.

"I won't." Ayden grunts as if he's unhappy she made the comment, and as curious as I am, I know it's none of my business.

They say nothing more before Ayden steps forward and hugs Rachel and then Marcus which ends with a slap on each other's backs before he turns towards me. Picking up the bag Marcus packed for me from the grassy ground, Ayden pops it on the back seat and then kneels before me again in the open door.

"Lex, do I have your permission to take you to my dad's place in the city? You'll be safe there. We can stay with him until we figure out what to do." He rakes a hand through his dark hair, making the ends stick up as his eyes fall to my trembling body. "If you want to get changed, we can stop down the road, and you can change in the car. I just want to get you away from here as fast as I can. I don't want to risk your brother coming to look for you."

"Y-you will stay with me?" I ask, hating how vulnerable I sound.

"Yes," he nods, "I'm not leaving you alone again. Ever."

Ever?

I try to smile at his declaration, but the movement stings my face, and I cringe, which also hurts.

He shoots me a sad smile and goes to stand, but I stop him. "Wait."

With his brows raised, he kneels back down, his big blue eyes swimming with concern as he waits for me to continue.

"You're driving?" I ask, wanting confirmation that it will just be him and me.

I don't trust anyone else.

He nods, "I'm eighteen remember? I have my licence. I haven't been driving because I made a deal with my parents that I wouldn't." He waves a dismissive hand. "It doesn't matter right now but I can fill you in about that later."

When I nod, Ayden gives me a sad smile with one of his signature winks before he stands and shuts the car door, closing me in the cabin.

Shit. This all feels so surreal. I really hope like hell that I'm not hallucinating right now, because if I am, then I'm not in this car about to be whisked away with Ayden, and I'm really still inside that house of horrors at the hands of the devil.

Sixteen

The car pulling to a stop wakes me from sleep. With my fleece throw blanket still wrapped around my nakedness and my lack of memory of the car ride, I realise I must have passed out or fallen asleep not long after leaving Marcus and his sister by the side of the road.

"Hey, sleeping beauty." Ayden's warm voice draws my attention.

The smile he wears isn't fooling me. I can see past the small dimple and upward turn of his mouth.

His eyes tell me the truth.

He's worried.

"What's wrong?" The hoarseness of my voice sounds like I'm a pack-a-day smoker, and its scratchiness feels like I've swallowed razor blades.

The ordinarily confident exterior of Ayden Mitchell looks anything but right now, with the way his shoulders slump and his eyes dance away from the left side of my battered face.

"I'm worried about you, Lex. I don't know if I should've let you fall asleep. You probably have a concussion given how bad…" He shakes his head, unable to finish.

"I'm okay now that I'm with you." My attempt at comforting him makes him smile, almost as if he'd needed to hear me say those words.

I stiffen as a man appears outside the car on Ayden's side, and I gasp, not able to hold back the reaction. Quickly turning to spot the man, Ayden's shoulders relax.

"It's okay, Lex. It's my dad." Reaching out, Ayden gives my hand a gentle squeeze. "Be right back."

He slips out of the car as I tighten the blanket around me, watching as Ayden talks quietly with his dad. The seriousness in their expressions worries me as they discuss something before Ayden walks around the car to open my door.

Leaning in, he gives me one of his winks again before lifting me in his arms, while his dad grabs my bag from the back seat.

"I can walk, you know?" My attempt to protest comes out more like a question than a statement. I actually have no clue if I can walk on my own because only a few hours ago, I couldn't.

"I know, but I need to do something to help."

What does he mean? He's already helped so much. Doesn't he know that? I should make a big deal about it, except I know this isn't the time or place, so I relax against his chest and just let it happen.

We walk through a relatively empty underground parking garage. The few cars that are here scream wealth. I haven't had a chance to get a good look at Ayden's dad yet, but what I did see of him wasn't enough to tell me he comes from the type of wealth to match the cars parked in here.

Taking the lift, we are all silent in the small space as we start to ascend. The awkward silence reminds me I'm putting an awful lot of trust in a guy I only met days earlier. Ayden has driven me somewhere. He said he was taking me to the city, to his dad's, but I have no memory of the trip, and all I've seen so far is the concrete walls of a parking garage. Now, I'm travelling in an elevator with *two* men I don't know while wrapped in a blanket without a single stitch of clothing underneath.

It's entirely possible I'm the dumbest person to walk this earth.

Jesus fucking Christ, Lexi, you could very well have traded one monster for another for all you know.

A chill from my sheer stupidity makes me stiffen in Ayden's arms, causing him to glance down at me in question.

What if Ayden and his dad are sick rapist serial killers?

"What's wrong?" Ayden's deep rasp is quiet in the small space, and I avoid his gaze, both loving and hating the way he looks at me.

Why does my body react like that around him?

Why does it trust him when it should be trying to protect itself?

Luckily for me, I'm able to avoid his question as the lift reaches its destination with a ding, and the doors glide open revealing a foyer that leads into an apartment.

"We need to have a chat and then get her cleaned up." The deep voice of Ayden's dad makes me stiffen as he steps past us, carrying my bag.

"Shh, it's okay. You're safe now, Lex." Ayden murmurs in response to my reaction to his dad's words, and I curl into his chest even as my mind screams at me to not be so trusting.

The vulnerability of my situation has my heart rate picking up as panic rises close to the surface, and as if he's noticed that reaction too, Ayden clutches me closer while he walks us through the foyer and down a hall into a luxurious living area.

My eyes dart around the room, taking in the modern and cosy space. The end wall is lined with rustic timber cabinets featuring a built-in fireplace encased in polished concrete. A huge TV sinks into the cabinetry above the fireplace, and an Aussie Rules Football game plays muted on the screen.

For some reason, seeing the familiar landscape of Melbourne's city lights through the floor to ceiling windows manages to slow my heart rate.

Okay, this is good. So far, Ayden hasn't lied.

An inviting grey cushioned couch sits before the fireplace, and when Ayden leans down to put me on it,

I tense, tightening my hold around his neck. Suddenly, the thought of not being in the safety of his arms seems terrifying.

"Hey," Ayden croons, "it's okay, Lex. You're safe here."

Looking up into his eyes, I plead with them for the truth.

Am I really safe here?

His blue ocean eyes are so sincere that I instantly hate myself for doubting him.

"I'll be right here with you, okay?" He offers, and I nod slightly before he moves to put me down again.

I shift nervously on the couch, trying to make sure the blanket covers all of my skin, before I peer up at the two men before me.

Their resemblance is unmistakable. They are very much father and son, having similar features with the same dark hair, blue eyes, and chiselled jawline.

Finally, I start to relax.

Clearing his throat, Ayden's dad places my bag down to the lush carpet by his feet before addressing me.

"Lexi, is it?"

I nod.

"I'm Peter, Ayden's dad. He uh... filled me in a little about what's been going on."

Confused when he was able to fill his dad in, I glance at Ayden, and he shrugs, "I called dad on the drive here while you were asleep."

Nodding again, I try not to be rude as I drag my gaze away from Ayden, to his dad. "I'm not sure what Ayden told you, and I appreciate the help, but I don't want to talk about it."

Peter nods as if he expected me to respond that way, but his face holds a determination that tells me he's not giving up so easily.

"I understand you've been through a very traumatic experience, but I'm afraid we need to have a quick chat about it."

"Dad." Ayden's face reddens, turning to his dad in anger.

"No, Ayden." Peter shakes his head, his expression serious as he speaks to his son. "I realise you're trying to protect your friend, but my job, as your father *and* an adult, is to make sure we do the right thing."

Dread claws at me, my chest squeezing in a tight, invisible grip. He's going to call my dad and believe his lies and be like all the other adults in my life that turn a blind eye. I can't let that happen.

"I don't mean to be rude or ungrateful, Mr Mitchell." I force my voice not to quiver, gaining the attention of both the Mitchell men. "But so far, all the adults in my life have done me wrong, so forgive me if I don't feel like adding another to the list."

Peter sighs, raking his hand through his thick dark hair, the movement reminding me of his son.

"Look, I hear what you're saying, so let me make this promise to you. I will help Ayden keep you safe. I won't let your father or your brother take you away. I will fight for you, Lexi, but in order to do that, I need to know everything."

For some reason I believe him. Maybe it's because he's so much like Ayden, or perhaps it's the other way around, but I trust his words. What renders me speechless for a few long beats though, is the last words he spoke.

"Everything?" I whisper as my lower lip starts to quiver and tears fill my eyes.

Peter nods and turns to Ayden. "Buddy, perhaps you should go to the kitchen. Give me some time alone with Lexi. It might be easier for her to talk about things if you're not here."

"What?! No, Dad. I'm not leaving her. I promised Lexi I wouldn't leave her." Ayden's fists tighten by his sides, struggling to rein in his anger as he squares off against his dad, ready to fight for me.

"That's not up to you, buddy. It's Lexi's decision. If she needs you to leave so she can talk freely, then you have to respect her wishes." Peter means business, his face showing a mature sternness that demands his son's obedience.

I watch conflicting emotions flit across Ayden's face as he looks between me and his dad, his Adam's apple bobbing as he swallows.

"I can't tell you everything." My shameful whisper is directed at both Ayden and Peter. When Ayden's pained expression meets mine, tears spring from my sore eyes.

"I need you to try so we can help you, Lexi." Peter directs his stern tone to me now, but it's not as demanding as it was with Ayden.

I take a long moment to study Peter, needing to believe his promises. When I'm sure I can, I nod before glancing at Ayden. He's so nervous. I can tell he wants to stay with me and know all of my vile truths. There's a part of me that doesn't want him to know, doesn't want him to see who I really am. There's also a part of me that is exhausted from hiding and hopes Ayden won't be repulsed when he learns the truth.

With my mind made up, I reach out to him and watch the relief fall over his face. He doesn't hesitate to take my hand, and he joins me on the couch, keeping my hand in his.

"Uh… can I get dressed first?" I ask Peter, who is dragging a brown ottoman across the room to sit on.

"Let's chat first? Then I'll leave you be for the night."

I sigh nervously, not wanting to do this and not sure where to start. As perceptive as his son, Peter prompts me.

"Tell me about your brother."

Swallowing hard, I try not to cry again, and instead, I focus on the hate I have toward Mike.

"Mike is my half brother. My dad had him before he married my mum. He only used to come and stay with us for holidays when we were kids, but that stopped a few years ago. I guess he got too old and didn't want to come and visit anymore, but a few months ago, he turned up and hasn't left since." Taking a deep breath, I try to shake off the tightness constricting my chest again. "He has always been different. Mean, inappropriate, irrational. But now, he's…" It takes me three attempts to swallow the lump in my throat. "He's a monster."

Ayden's thumb strokes over the back of my hand in support, and his touch, I realise, is keeping me grounded.

"Ayden said that you had a run-in with your father last night here in the city, and then he approached you on the way to school this morning, wanting you to go with him. How did you end up back with him after you went to school?"

I take a deep breath, not wanting to relive my dad's deceit. "He went to the Principal. Told him I'm suffering from a mental illness and that I'm self-harming. He convinced Principal Ryland that he was there to collect me from school to get me help. He gave me a cup of water to drink when I walked in. I didn't think anything of it, and I stupidly drank it. The water must have been spiked or something because not long after, I started feeling weird, and my words started slurring. I tried to get away, but my legs wouldn't work, and I fell. I blacked out and the next thing I knew, I was waking up at home with my dad and Mike there." I clear my throat as the memory of being in that house alone with Mike is almost too much to bear. "As punishment for being disobedient, my dad took the doors off the rooms upstairs and took away my phone and laptop before leaving me there with Mike."

I don't miss the way Ayden's grip tightens on my hand, or the disapproving frown that tugs in Peter's dark brows.

"Did your brother do that to you?" Peter gestures to the left side of my beaten face, and I nod. "Are you hurt anywhere else?"

I nod again. "My back and ribs. H-he threw me around a bit. I hit the wall and some furniture."

Ayden tenses beside me, not able to hold back a growl, causing Peter to shoot him a warning glare.

"My scalp hurts." I admit, redirecting both their attention to me. "I think he ripped out some of my hair when he dragged me."

Ayden flies out of his seat, no longer able to hold in his rage. "I'm gonna fucking kill him!"

Peter stands quickly, moving to his son. "Ayden, stop. This is why I was concerned about you being here. Your reaction won't help Lexi."

"Dad, are you shitting me right now? He fucking dragged her by her hair!" Ayden points in my direction, his face turning almost purple as his anger radiates from him in waves.

"Ayden, if you can't handle this, then leave the room!" Peter's boom causes me to flinch back and whimper, drawing Ayden's attention.

Fighting to calm himself, Ayden rakes his hand through his hair, just like his dad did earlier.

"No, I don't need to leave the room. I'm okay." He turns to me, "Sorry, Lex."

I don't respond, too busy biting the inside of my cheek to control my urge to run. Maybe this isn't such a good idea. I should just leave and deal with this on my own. Dragging other people, good people, into my shit show of a life isn't fair to them.

Before I can flee, Ayden returns to sit beside me on the couch and takes my hand in his again. His touch does something to me. Makes me dissolve with relief and I find myself exhaling, releasing my teeth from digging a hole in my cheek and soaking up the calming feel of his touch.

Sitting again, Peter drags his focus away from his son and back to me. "Let's get this chat finished. Do you hurt anywhere else, Lexi?"

"My arm. He grabbed me in the same place my dad did the night before. And my face hurts, too, obviously."

Strangely, I think that's what I hate the most about the bruises Mike left on me. I can cover my arm with clothes. I can cover my scalp by styling my hair a certain way. But my face... well, if it were just a bruise without all the swelling, I could use makeup to conceal it. But I can feel how puffy it is. How my eye barely opens. I can't hide that from anyone.

Peter nods at my words, "Anywhere else?"

I shake my head. "No, I think that's it."

"Are you sure, Lexi? Your brother didn't hurt you anywhere else?"

Frowning at Peter's repetitive questions, it takes me a moment to realise what he's trying to ask.

"Are you asking me if he raped me?" My voice is husky as I ask the question he is so clearly having trouble asking, and Ayden tenses, his breath hitching.

Thinking back over everything, I have no doubt that my brother would've raped me if Ayden hadn't come when he did.

Sighing, Peter nods. "Yes, I guess I am."

I hate that this is even a consideration, but the simple fact is, it was so close to happening. Too close.

I can't bear to look at Ayden or his dad in this moment, the shame of what I experienced almost crippling. The whole situation is just too sick and twisted to share with anyone, but I know I have to summon up all the courage I can in order to continue speaking.

Keeping my eyes downcast, I focus on the seam of the throw blanket that has become my second skin. "No, that never happened. Some visitors came to our house and interrupted him, so he never got that far."

Ayden lets out the breath he was holding and drops his head into his hands as he rests his elbows on his knees, perched on the edge of the couch.

My heart sinks.

He looks so depleted. I hate that I've affected him like this.

"Buddy," Peter moves to Ayden's other side. "She's okay, Ayden."

Shit. Is Ayden crying?

"I'm sorry," I whisper the words to Ayden as my eyes glass over, feeling bad that I've caused him such distress.

He turns to me then, his eyes red and glassy, just like mine.

"Can I please hug you?" His whisper is a plea, and I nod without hesitation.

The simple bob of my head is all he needs before he sweeps me up and cradles me in his arms on his lap. He holds me in such a way as if letting me go is too painful, and I feel it all the way to the thick layer of ice surrounding my heart.

Closing my eyes, I take the care he offers, and I hold him just as tightly, not wanting to ever let go. The addictive scent that is Ayden Mitchell envelops me, and the calm it brings makes me want to burrow under his skin.

I could happily stay like this all night in Ayden's embrace, but the sound of Peter clearing his throat breaks our bubble, and Ayden slowly pulls back, his tortured gaze roaming my face, bruises, swelling, and all.

"I won't let anyone hurt you again." He whispers so only I can hear, just as his dad speaks again.

"Sorry, Lexi. Just a few more questions."

Slowly, I nod, and Peter continues while Ayden pulls me to his side back on the couch.

"Ayden said you were soaking wet and wrapped in just the blanket when he found you. Can I ask why?"

My stomach churns with panic, and I can't speak. I don't want to say it.

"I'm sorry. I know this is hard, but every bit of information you can provide will help." Peter explains and I know he's right, but it doesn't make it any easier. I focus on the blanket's seam again, not wanting to look them in the eye when I admit this next part.

"Mike insisted that I... shower," I choke on a sob, "i-in front of him." As my tears fall, my mind goes back to a time I'd rather forget. "T-that's why I got so beat up because I wouldn't do what he asked. But then, I-I thought he might k-kill me, so I did it."

I don't look up. The silence blanketing the room is all I need to know.

They think I'm disgusting.

"Did he touch you? Inappropriately, I mean, or did he do anything else inappropriate?" Peter asks, and Ayden flies from his seat.

"What do you mean, dad? The whole fucking thing is inappropriate!"

Ignoring Ayden, Peter urges, "Lexi?"

I shake my head, and with tears streaming down my face, I whisper, "I can't say it."

Ayden stops pacing, his feet now pointing in my direction in front of the couch. I can't help but look up into the pained gaze of the boy who broke down my walls and became my lifeline.

"He didn't touch me." I tell Ayden, needing him to know that truth. There are so many disgusting things about this whole situation, but I need him to at least know that I fought hard to keep Mike from touching me in such an intimate way.

"But he did something else inappropriate?" Peter urges and reluctantly, I nod in answer. "Was it something sexual?"

When my mind conjures up the image of my brother standing mere feet from the open shower door with his pants around his ankles, and his hard dick in his hand, I gag.

My eyes widen in panic as I feel the warning of losing the contents of my stomach, and I stand in a rush, clapping my hand over my mouth.

Seventeen

I heave over the toilet and empty what little food I had in my stomach. The vileness of this act feels unusually good as I imagine it expelling the filthy taint that runs thick in my blood with each retch. Each sick act inflicted by my brother, and each deception delivered by my dad gets dragged out.

When my body is finally drained, I give myself a few minutes to recover before I force it to do it again, needing to exorcise the perversion.

When the horrid act is over, and I'm feeling spent, I continue to cry silently and lay the unharmed side of my face on the cold tiled floor and curl into myself.

I want this nightmare to end. I want to run away and forget it ever happened. I want to pretend I'm someone else who's never had to endure such vulgarness in their life.

Even as I think this, I know I'll never be able to forget what Mike did. What my dad did.

There's no escaping it. I'll carry this heaviness with me for the rest of my life, and somehow, I'll have to learn how to live in that world from now on.

A knock sounds at the door dragging me out of my dark thoughts, and I know it's Ayden. He's probably worried out of his mind. The look on his face when he realised that something more happened besides being beaten by my brother will haunt me forever. I never want to see his caring face with that expression on it again.

The knock sounds again, and I try to move, but I'm too tired to stand, so I pull the blanket over me, ensuring I'm covered before speaking. "It's open."

The door cracks open slowly, and Ayden peers down at me on the floor. I try my best at a reassuring smile. His small one, in return, tells me I failed, but he appreciated it anyway.

"No more questions tonight. We should clean you up and get you to bed."

Bed. Sleep sounds like heaven, so I nod eagerly, and Ayden leans down to help me stand.

"Are you okay to walk?" Ayden accepts my nod and puts his arm around me, leading me through his dad's apartment.

Peter is nowhere in sight, and I'm thankful. He seems like a nice man, but I don't want to talk about this fucked up stuff anymore. I can't bear it.

Ayden leads me down a hallway into a bedroom. His bedroom. I can tell because it smells like him, just like the loft at Marcus' house. The smell is instantly calming and I'm pretty sure I'll never want to leave this room ever again.

Sitting my bag on his bed, Ayden gestures to a door to the side.

"The bathroom is through that door. Do you, um, need me to help you?"

I feel the slightest smile tug at the corner of my lips. He's sweet. I can see how uncomfortable he is asking that question, but I can also see that he wants to help me if I need it.

I shake my head in answer. "I should be able to manage on my own, but can I borrow your phone?"

His brows shoot up in surprise, but he nods, "Yes, of course. Call whoever you need to."

I nod, but I won't be calling anyone. Not now anyway.

Since my dad took my phone, I need to use Ayden's to take some photos. I need to record the evidence on my body while it is still raw and bloody.

Handing me his phone, Ayden goes to leave the room, but I stop him.

"Wait."

He stops moving, turning back to me in surprise, and I shake my head annoyed that I sounded so panicked.

"I'm sorry to ask this, but can you please stay in your room while I shower?" I hate that my voice gives away how needy and vulnerable I am, but the thought of being alone right now is terrifying.

Ayden smiles warmly, "Of course."

"Thank you." I sigh, my shoulders dropping in relief.

I don't know how I'll ever be able to thank him enough for everything he's done. I will, though, somehow, I will find a way.

Taking my bag into the bathroom, I'm surprised at how big it is and how different it is from his loft in Fox Pines. Where that one is small and basic, this one is large with warm timber imitation tiles on the floor and a rustic timber vanity with white stone benchtops that tie in with the white toilet and bath. The walls are lined with white subway tiles and above the toilet are two black canvases, one with a bronze image of a Sherrin football and the other a bronze football player taking a mark.

This room is much more Ayden than the one at Fox Pines. He must miss living here with his dad. I'm guessing his parents must be divorced or something, which is sad. Both of his parents seem so nice.

Knowing I have to get this over and done with, I drop my bag to the floor and approach the large mirror to take in my appearance.

Shit.

I cringe.

The swelling around my left eye is worse than I thought, and my skin blends into shades of blue, black, green, and red. There are patches of dry blood too, and when I try to open my eye as much as the swelling will allow, I can just make out that the white of my eye is now blood red.

I drop the blanket that has been my second skin in shock. The bruising runs down my neck with several trails of blood following its path down to my chest. My arm looks worse than it did after dad had his way with it, and there's hideous purple and green bruising on my left ribs wrapping around to my back. Looking down at my legs, I see they came out the least scathed, only marked with a few scratches.

It's overwhelming to see myself like this, but I remind myself that it could have been worse. So much worse. I could be in hospital getting tested with a rape kit, or worse. Dead. I want to cry, but I don't. I'm safe now, and I know I'm going to do everything I can to make sure this doesn't happen again.

Picking up Ayden's phone, I start snapping pictures of my face, neck, arms, and head. I manage to get a couple of pictures of the side of my ribs, but I can't seem to get a good shot of my back, given the angle.

I sigh, knowing I'm going to need help.

Grabbing the blanket and wrapping it around myself again, I crack the door open to peer back into Ayden's bedroom.

My eyes fall to Ayden lying on his bed, his face creased in a frown as he stares at the ceiling. He's deep in thought, and by the look of it, the thoughts aren't good, and again, I feel guilty that I've brought my chaos into his life.

Clearing my throat, I gain his attention, his frown falling away as he turns his head to look at me.

"You okay, Lex?"

I open the door a little more. "Can you please give me a hand with something?"

"Yeah, of course," he sits up quickly, standing from his bed and is over to me in an instant.

"I ahh... was trying to get pictures of the bruising, but I can't get a good one of my back."

Leaning against the door frame, Ayden lifts his hand and grazes the backs of his fingers gently over the uninjured side of my face.

"I can take the picture for you, Lex." His voice is so soft and warm, and I don't even realise that my lids flutter closed and I lean into his touch.

When I feel the warmth of his lips on my temple, I sigh before prying my eyes open to stare up into his intense blue gaze.

If Ayden Mitchell were a drug, then I'm addicted!

Ayden's gaze is warm, yet still swims with concern, so I distract him and pull him towards the mirror, handing him his phone. He's quiet as he scrolls through the pictures I already took. He looks anguished, and I can tell he's blaming himself for not stopping it. It's not his fault, though, and I'll make sure he knows that when we talk more about things, but not right now. Now I need to focus on the task at hand to get cleaned up so I can go to bed.

Taking a deep breath, I carefully let the blanket drop down my back while clutching it to my chest.

Ayden hisses. "Fuck."

His pained eyes meet mine in the mirror and I shake my head.

"Don't think about it, Ayden. Just take the picture. Pretend it isn't real."

"But it is real." His whisper is laced with the same pain that his eyes reveal.

My eyes fill with uncontrollable tears that I try to ward off, but one escapes, rolling down my cheek.

"Please just take the picture." I manage to whisper, and Ayden nods, lining up the shot, and takes a few pictures, holding the phone up to show me when he's done.

"Thank you," I nod, pleased that he was able to get the shot I couldn't. My back looks bad. I couldn't see the full extent of it in the mirror, but the pictures show me everything. It could have been worse, though. Bones could have been broken, so I'm thankful it's just surface bruising.

Turning, I take the phone from his grip and email them to myself and Abbey from Ayden's email account. Abbey is going to freak, so I add a note that I'm okay and safe now and that I will call her tomorrow, asking her not to tell anyone that I'm with Ayden.

After hitting send, I hand Ayden's phone back to him. "Thank you."

"You don't need to keep thanking me."

"Yes, I do, Ayden. I'm so thankful. I don't know how I'll ever repay you for saving me from..." I can't finish the sentence, but he understands what I'm trying to say.

Pulling me to his chest, Ayden gathers up the blanket which had fallen to reveal my back, being the gentleman he is. Who knew they still existed?

We stand and hug each other for a long time. A few times, he loosens his grip to break it, but I squeeze tighter, silently telling him I'm not ready to let go yet. When I finally do let him go, he returns to his room, and

I do the excruciating task of showering and washing my battered body.

The water tints red as I wash away the blood, the evidence swirling on the shower floor before disappearing down the drain. I cry as I wash, mostly from the pain of the wound on my head where some of my hair has been torn from my scalp. I watch strands of my hair slide down my body and pool over the drain. At first, there are only a few, but more join them, and my scalp stings unbearably from the raw patch left in their place.

When I can't take the pain any longer, I turn off the shower and bend to pick up the clump of hair that used to be on my head. I'm going to need to take another picture of my head now that the dried blood is gone, but that can wait for tomorrow. Right now, I just want to go to bed.

Returning to Ayden's room after showering and changing, I find him hunched over, sitting on the side of the bed. The room is so quiet, and he's so still that I wonder if he's asleep like that. With his elbows on his knees and his hands entwined in his hair, he doesn't hear me approach. It's only when my feet stop in front of him that he looks up at me, and his anguished expression softens when his eyes meet mine, and a small smile tugs at his lips.

"Hey."

"Hey." I smile back, knowing part of my face resembles a monster, just like the man who made it that way.

Taking my hand in his, he pulls me to him, wrapping his arms gently around my waist and resting his head right over my chest. I still for a moment, mostly because I'm waiting for something to hurt, but when it doesn't, I relax and run my fingers through his silky dark hair.

I've never run my hands through a guy's hair before. It's something I never did with Nathan. Now that I think about it, there was never any real affection or passion with Nathan. Ayden, however, is a different story. This guy makes me want to reveal all of my secrets and let down all of my walls.

It seems strange in a way that we are so drawn to each other. Whatever this relationship is between us seems more like two people who have known each other for years rather than a few days. I don't even know what this is between us, but I know it's more than a friendship, and the pull Ayden has on me is real.

"Will you sleep with me?" I stiffen at his quiet question, and he tilts his head back to peer up at me through his dark lashes, smirking. "I should probably rephrase that."

I can't hide my amusement and raise my right brow in question.

"Will you sleep in my bed with me? Just sleep. Nothing more. I just..." he hesitates, contemplating his words. "I just really need to hold you and know you're safe."

I smile. "Well, how can a girl refuse that?"

Eighteen

Just like last time, Ayden spoons me close, holding my hand throughout the night. I'd been apprehensive that thoughts of the day would stop me from being able to sleep, but I was wrong. In Ayden's arms, I sleep all night. No dreams, good or bad, just simple nothingness, which is a welcome respite for my brain.

I want to stay asleep in his arms until the end of time, but voices slowly drag me awake and back to reality. Keeping my eyes closed, I listen to the quiet voices that come from somewhere in the room. Voices that don't belong to Ayden, who I can feel still embracing me in his warmth.

"Peter, I understand he cares for this girl, and I feel for what she's been through, but this level of stress could send him over the edge again. He could relapse."

Relapse? What?

"He's been fine, Andrea. He handled everything pretty well and didn't do anything rash."

"You don't call this situation rash? Taking his cousin's car even though he promised us he wouldn't drive is rash, Peter. Not to mention running off to the city with a girl who has experienced violence. It's not normal behaviour."

"Calm down, Andrea."

"Don't tell me to calm down," she whisper yells. "I moved him away to avoid things like this. I haven't even unpacked properly yet, and he's already gotten himself in over his head."

I hear Peter sigh at the same moment I feel Ayden's thumb stroking the back of my hand. He's awake too.

"Look, the situation isn't ideal, but I'm proud of him. He could've run off and gone into hiding with the girl and not reached out for help. But he did reach out. He came straight to me and asked for my help. The old Ayden would never have done that."

"I guess you're right. I just worry about him, Peter."

"I don't suppose you could go and worry somewhere else?" Ayden's voice cuts through his parents' conversation, and my eyes shoot open in surprise. I hear Peter curse, and Ayden shifts behind me in the bed, but he doesn't let go. He pulls me closer, snuggling his face into my neck.

The bed shifts in front of me, and I stare up into the face of Ayden's mum. I try to smile, but it hurts, causing me to wince and Andrea hisses in sympathy.

"Oh my goodness," she reaches out to lower the blanket from my chin, her eyes instantly glassing over. "I'm so sorry this happened to you, Alexis."

"It's Lexi." Ayden corrects, and she nods.

"Oh, okay, sorry." Reaching over, she lifts strands of my unruly hair off my face, assessing the damage. "We should get ice on this, sweetheart."

I nod, feeling a little taken aback by her empathy. A minute ago, she wasn't happy about Ayden helping me, but now she looks genuinely concerned and wants to help.

"How old are you, Lexi?" she asks and my brows shoot up at her abrupt question.

"Does it matter, mum?" Ayden props himself up on his arm behind me to look at her, and I instantly miss the feel of his breath on my neck.

"Well... yes, it does, Ayden. You're in bed with a girl."

"Are you serious right now? I'm eighteen." Ayden snaps, and his mum nods.

"Yes, but Lexi looks a lot younger than eighteen."

"I'm seventeen." I butt in, my voice still hoarse, and I try to clear my throat. "I can see if my ID is in my bag."

"No, no, it's fine, Lexi. I'm sorry, I'm just a big worrywart."

Ayden scoffs, "That's an understatement."

"Ayden." Peter growls in warning from across the room, and Ayden mutters an apology to his mum.

Moving off the bed, Andrea stands to look down at us. "I understand that you've been through a lot, Lexi, and that you spoke to Peter about it last night, but if it's okay, I'd like to look over your injuries and make sure we don't need to take you to hospital."

"Okay," I nod slowly.

"Later, mum. Give Lex some time to wake up properly first, please?"

Andrea nods and smiles lovingly at her son. "Yes, of course. I'll be in the kitchen when you're ready."

Ayden's mum walks to the door, and I watch Peter reach out and cup her face before he leans in, kissing her. When they leave the room, closing the door behind them, I slowly roll over to face Ayden, trying to ignore the way my whole body aches.

"I'm confused." I admit, and Ayden frowns.

"About what?" Lifting his hand from under the covers, he strokes a stray hair off my face.

"Your parents don't act like they're divorced or separated." I state and he grins.

"That's because they aren't."

"Now, I'm even more confused." Why would Ayden's parents live apart if they weren't separated or divorced?

Ayden chuckles at my frown. "They're still happily married."

"Then why did your mum move to Fox Pines?"

Ayden's smile drops away and he falls quiet for a beat. His ocean eyes roam my face, studying my bruises before he speaks. "Mum moved *me* there."

He's vague, and it annoys me. I know it isn't any of my business, but I have this pesky need to want to know everything about him.

"Why did she move you there?"

Again, he's quiet. Maybe I've overstepped, and I'm being too nosey.

"They thought it would be better for me to live somewhere where I was less likely to get into trouble, so mum lined up a new job in the Fox Pines District Hospital and told me I was moving there with her."

This time I study his face and I can tell he's hiding something from me. Who am I to judge, though, given the secrets I've kept for so long? He certainly knows a hell of a lot more about me than anyone else, but there are still things he doesn't know, and I'm not sure I want him to.

"What sort of trouble is she worried about you getting into?"

"Oh, you know. Just normal boy stuff."

No, I don't really know what normal boy stuff is, and he's still being annoyingly vague. Something his mum said earlier is bothering me, though, and if I'm going to trust him, I'm going to need to know who he is. I still can't be sure that I'm not in the bed of a serial killer.

"What did your mum mean when she said she's worried about you relapsing?"

"You caught that, huh?" He doesn't seem annoyed by my question, but I can tell he hoped I didn't pick up on what his mum said.

"I also caught that she thinks I may send you over the edge. What did she mean by that? Can you explain it to me?" My words are quiet as I stare at him hopefully, but when he screws his nose up, my heart sinks.

"Not really."

I can't help it, I glare at him. "Really?"

"Yeah." He shrugs, his expression impassive.

Wow. Okay.

His response pisses me off. I guess it's none of my business, but the fact that he pushed his way into my *fucked up* life and knows personal things about me, yet won't reveal any secrets about himself, just makes me want to slam my walls back up and flee.

Loneliness slithers its way back into my chest even though I'm not alone, still with Ayden in his bed. It's confusing to feel lonely when he's right here with me, but doubts begin to whisper in my ear, and I'm suddenly unsure if Ayden is someone I *can* or *should* have trusted with my darkest secrets.

The burn of angry tears forces me to look away from his blue gaze, and I nod, letting him know that I've accepted his response as I slip out of his bed.

Last night, Ayden insisted I wear his hoodie again, and I didn't refuse. Now, however, I feel like it's suffocating me and I need to get it off. I need to get out of here.

I disregard the fact I only have my knickers and bra on underneath the hoodie and turn my back to him, slipping his hoodie off before dropping it to the floor beside the bed. Ignoring Ayden's sharp intake of breath, I force my aching body to move faster as I open my bag to find something to wear. I really hope Marcus used his brain when he packed for me.

"What are you doing?" I see Ayden sit up in his bed in my peripheral vision, but I'm too exasperated to answer him right now.

"Lex?"

Jesus Marcus, what did you pack?

Nothing matches. It's going to be impossible to pull a decent outfit together with the random clothes he threw in. I guess I should be thankful that I have anything, so I continue to rummage until I find a pair of skinny blue jeans and an old Slipknot t-shirt that's probably too small for me now.

The rustling of blankets alerts me to Ayden moving out of the bed before his body heat warms my back, sending anxiety to stiffen my spine. "Lex, what's going on?"

"I'll be out of your hair in a few minutes."

"What? No." Ayden gently snags my hand as I try to put my foot in the leg of my jeans, almost causing me to tumble over.

"Yes!" I snap, instantly regretting it when I see the hurt on his face. *Shit!*

"No, Lexi. What's going on? Talk to me, please." Leaning down, he pulls the jeans out of my grip, tossing them on the bed behind him, leaving me standing in front of him with barely a scrap of fabric to cover my body.

I didn't think this through, did I?

"Please, Lexi, talk to me."

I want to yell at him, but I also want to kiss him, which is confusing as fuck, and I struggle to understand how I can refuse him? His face is creased with worry and confusion, but damn him, he still looks adorable with messy bed hair and the way his grey t-shirt hugs his sculpted body. I'm so screwed when it comes to

Ayden Mitchell. I feel like I may just give him anything he wants, repercussions be damned.

"You don't trust me." My words are a whisper, but he hears them, a frown creasing his brow.

"What do you mean? Of course, I trust you."

"No, you don't, Ayden. If you did, you would tell me what your mum was referring to, and the real reason why you moved to Fox Pines. I have trusted you with the darkest part of my life, and I kind of thought it would be reciprocated."

He sighs, looking a little helpless. "Lex, it's not that I don't trust you. It's more because…" I can see the internal battle he's struggling with written across his expression.

Taking his hand in mine, I stroke my thumb over the back of his hand just like he's done to mine so many times, while I wait for him to continue.

"I'm ashamed." He admits, hanging his head to avoid my eyes.

I can see the shame he speaks of, twisting his expression. It's a feeling I know all too well.

"What are you ashamed of?" I ask, hoping he'll open up to me, and I wait a beat for him to respond. When I'm just about to give up, he glances up, revealing the torment swimming in his eyes.

"My past, Lex. If I tell you, then you'll think differently about me, and I don't think I can bear that."

His past?

I step up to him then, no longer caring about my mostly naked body, and I cup his face. The skin on his jaw is a combination of soft and scratchy, with the short stubble looking a little longer than it was yesterday. I've never touched a guy's face like this. At first, I feel like I should drop my hold, but when he leans into my hand, I know I'm a goner, and I never want to let go.

"I won't think differently about you, Ayden. We all have a past. I know you know how hard it's been for me to open up about the burdens I bear. There are still things you don't know about me, too, things that aren't good, but I hope that if you ever find out about them, you won't hate me or judge me too harshly. I carry so much shame for the vile secrets I've been keeping, so I get it. I really do. I'd still like to know you, though. All of you. The good and the bad."

His gaze is so intense, peering deeply into mine while he takes in my words. Finally his lips quirk up at the corners turning into one of his adorable grins before he places his hand over the one I have cupping his face and licks his lips taking a deep breath.

"Lexi, I'm having a little trouble concentrating right now." I frown in confusion at his words before he continues. "You do know you are practically naked, right?"

I can't control the laugh that escapes, and when I go to pull away from him in embarrassment, he holds me in place.

"Uh-uh. If I have to tell you about my past, then you have to stay just like that." His words are light and teasing, but his eyes are dark and determined, sending a shiver up my spine.

"Cold?" He knows I'm not, and I could wipe that stupid grin off his face by putting clothes on, but I don't.

I have a brief moment where I feel a flicker of fear at Ayden's demand, reminding me of the way Mike ordered me around in the shower. It's not Mike here with me though, it's Ayden. So, I swallow the dread down, working hard to push anything related to that arsehole to the deep, dark depths of my mind, not wanting to allow him to taint my life any further.

I want Ayden to tell me about his past, which is what I tell myself is the reason I continue to stand nearly naked in front of him, and that it has nothing to do with how much I like his eyes on me even though I'm battered and bruised.

"Fine." I sigh like it's a big deal. "I'm not getting dressed, so you'd better spill, Ayden Mitchell."

He laughs at me playfully. "You drive a hard bargain, Lexi West."

I shrug, trying to smile past my split lip and my increasingly painful cheek.

Stepping back to the bed, Ayden tugs me along with him, sitting on the edge so we can face each other. He's quiet for a few moments, his eyes trained on where our fingers are linked. Just as I'd seen last night, this version of Ayden lacks the usual cocky confidence he typically shows the world. It's hard to see him like this, and even though part of me wants to tell him not to worry about telling me, I don't because I feel that even though he won't admit it, he needs to tell me his truth too.

Exhaling, Ayden clears his throat and begins.

"Back when I was in year ten, I got involved with this girl..." His eyes flick up at me briefly before returning to our hands. "Her name was Daniella. She was wild and fun, and every guy wanted to be with her, but she chose me. I thought I was the luckiest guy. Special somehow. She introduced me to a whole new world that I didn't even know existed. In the beginning, I thought it was the shit, you know. Dani had endless connections. There were parties nearly every night of the week, and the people I met through her were, well... let's just say I was star-struck."

Taking a few moments stuck in his own head, Ayden's eyes go distant, and I don't interrupt, knowing he's remembering a past he's tried to forget.

"We'd been together for nearly a year when it happened. We'd gone out to yet another party, but I left early because we kinda got into a fight. It was a stupid fight. I was jealous of the attention she'd been getting from this older guy. The right thing to do would've been to stay and keep an eye on her, especially since she'd started taking her partying to the next level. It was the Coke she was using..." he sucks in a slow breath, "or I should say, we were using."

Ayden's intense blue eyes flick up through his dark lashes again, seeking my reaction, but when he sees my unchanged expression, he continues.

"Long story short, she died that night of an overdose. She'd been with the guy who I'd been jealous of, and now he still walks this earth while she's gone from it forever."

Clearing his throat, Ayden takes a deep breath, struggling to control his emotions. I don't miss the way his hand trembles slightly in mine, and I feel bad for asking him to tell me about his heartbreaking past. All I can do is squeeze his hand to offer some comfort.

"Ayden, you don't need to tell me any more details. I'm sorry for prying. It's none of my business."

His eyes shoot up to mine, glassy from unshed tears, and my heart breaks a little more in that moment.

"No, I do need to tell you, Lex. I want you to know, I do. I can't explain why I need that, but I just do." Sounding about as confused as I am, I give his hand another gentle squeeze to let him know I'm here for him. If telling me is what he wants, I won't stop him, even though I feel like I forced him to speak up.

"It filled me with so much anger after Dani died. I stopped turning up to school and spent my days with some mates I met through her. I was high 24/7 and only went home to wash and sleep every few days. My parents didn't know what to do with me and weren't able to control me, but everything changed a few months later when I ran into the guy who was with Dani when she overdosed. And I saw red."

Not able to continue, Ayden turns his gaze to the window above his bed, his face contorting into an angry frown, his nostrils flaring.

"I put him in hospital, Lex." His eyes find mine again filled with regret. "He nearly died from his injuries. Injuries that I inflicted."

My eyes soften, watching him battle with his internal pain, and I can't hold myself back from touching him. Reaching up, I cup his face, wanting him to know that despite what he'd just told me, I still care for him.

Leaning into my hand, Ayden shuts his eyes, taking a few deep breaths. We sit like this for a few minutes, me stroking the pad of my thumb over his stubble while he leans into my hand like it's a lifeline, and when his eyes flutter open again, he appears to have pushed away his pain, the blue in his eyes looking a little brighter.

"I ended up going to Juvi for six weeks and then to rehab. My parents struck a deal with the guy's brother and got my charges reduced. They were there for me the entire time, giving me the support I didn't think I deserved. When I left rehab, I went back home and helped dad in the studio for the rest of the school year because mum was too afraid to send me back to my old school. She knew if I saw the friends I made through Dani, I would end up back in the party scene and all screwed up again. That's when she came up with the plan to move to my aunty's place. She quit her job in the city when she got a job at the hospital in Fox Pines, and my parents rent out our Prahran house, and dad moved into this apartment because it's in the same building as his recording studio. Their plan is to get me through high school and then see where to go after that. So here I am, repeating year eleven. Trying to start over."

Remorse fills me for dragging him into my drama. He doesn't need this shit. He doesn't need to worry about a helpless girl with a fucked up family when he should be trying to heal himself. Like so many times over the last few days, my eyes glass over with hot tears before I have time to stop them.

"Hey, what's wrong, beautiful?" Ayden encloses my face between his hands, cupping it gently, concern splashed across his face.

"I'm sorry," I whisper.

"What for?"

"Your mum is right. You don't need my drama in your life. You don't deserve to be dragged into my bullshit."

He shakes his head, his thumb gently stroking my cheeks, taking care where the bruising is.

"Lexi, don't be silly. This isn't the same situation, and you didn't drag me, remember? I didn't really give you any other option."

"Can you do me a favour, please?" I push past the lump that has formed in my throat, commanding my inner strength to bury my pain and appear like I have my shit together. When Ayden nods, I continue, "If at any stage, my drama gets to be too much, I want you to tell me. I won't hold it against you. I will understand, and I will give you space."

"Lex, that's not going to be a problem."

"Promise me." I practically beg.

He shakes his head. "No, Lex, I don't need to. I will never ask you to give me space."

"Damn it, Ayden, I need you to promise me, please!"

He's silent as he studies me, his eyes searching mine. I can see he wants to refuse me again, but then his face softens.

"Fine, I promise."

Nineteen

Ayden's mum, Andrea, spends the rest of the morning fussing over me. After making sure I'd eaten, she took me into her room, and we talked. I reluctantly told her the same information I'd given to Peter the night before and managed not to hurl this time. She then checked over my body, and knowing she's a nurse, I felt comfortable enough letting her examine the damage my brother inflicted.

"Lexi, I think we should get some photos of this bruising, just in case you need them for legal reasons down the track."

"Uh- yeah. I already got some pictures last night on Ayden's phone." I explain, hoping she doesn't insist on taking more. I don't think I can handle going through that process again.

"Oh, good thinking. Do you mind if I ask Ayden to send me copies? I won't use them without your permission, I promise. I think it would be a good idea for me to have them as well just to be safe so I can help you if you need me to." Andrea sounds sincere, so

I agree and nod. I don't bother telling her I sent copies to Abbey as well. I trust them both.

Clearing her throat, Andrea looks a little uneasy as she sits next to me on her bed. "Look, Lexi. I need to tell you something."

Nervous by her statement, I wait patiently, sitting on the edge of the bed for her to continue. "I called one of my co-workers at the Fox Pines Hospital so I could get an update on your mum. Unfortunately, she couldn't tell me much as your mum has been transferred to a hospital here in the city. The records say she should have arrived at the Lady Anne's Hospital yesterday, however, they have no record of her arriving."

I frown. That doesn't make sense.

"My co-worker said your mum's injuries weren't very bad, so it's strange that she's been transferred to a hospital in Melbourne. Do you have any idea why she would have been moved?"

It's a common confusion with my mum, as her drug and alcohol use is a well-kept secret. She would rather the few friends she has think she is having some sort of cosmetic surgery than admitting to her addiction.

I blow out a frustrated breath, wishing for the millionth time that my life was more simple.

"My mum has trouble with drugs and alcohol. Dad told me once that she's depressed, and while I'm sure that's probably true and would explain why she uses substances, I'm beginning to think there may be more to it. She's been in rehab a few times. I don't ask her any questions about it, and she's happy not telling me anything."

"So maybe she's been taken to a rehab facility in the city instead? Do you remember the names of the facilities she's been at previously?"

I guess this is where I should have been a better daughter. I should have been taking notice of her hospital stays over the years, but I gave up when my parents continually danced around the truth.

My mum has rarely been present for me. Even when she was physically there, her mind was far away. I usually feel angry when I think of this, but now I'm just worried. Why isn't she at the hospital listed on her record? My dad said he pulled some strings to get her transferred to Lady Anne's, so why isn't she there?

"I'm sorry. I should know some of the names, shouldn't I?" I frown in frustration.

"It's okay, Lexi." Andrea gently pulls me in for a hug, being careful not to hurt my bruised body. "I'll see if I can get a hold of the ambulance transporter who drove your mum, and we'll soon find out where she is."

"Thank you so much." The support that Ayden and his parents are giving me is so overwhelming. I've never known such generosity, especially when they don't expect anything in return. Reluctantly, I let go of her hug as she pulls away.

"I'd better let you get back to Ayden before he barges in here like a possessive caveman." Her amused tone makes me smile as I walk out of her room and back to the living area where I left Ayden earlier.

Seeing me enter the room, he moves immediately to my side, taking my hand and leading me to the cosy living room we were in last night.

"Are you okay?" Concern is evident in his tone, and he pulls me down to the couch, keeping me close to his side as his eyes stay glued on my face.

Biting back a grin, I nod, enjoying the instant calm his nearness brings.

"That's a stupid thing to ask, sorry." He frowns, shaking his head at himself. "Of course, you aren't okay. I guess I meant, are you coping okay, given the situation?"

This time I giggle, which sends a sharp pain to my ribs but also feels good all the same.

"What's so funny?" he asks, smirking back, his ocean blues dancing between mine.

"I'm sorry. I shouldn't laugh, but you are just so adorable." I admit, and his dark brows shoot up, even though his grin remains.

"Oh, I see," he says playfully. "You think my concern is adorable?"

"Well... yeah." I smile, and his smile widens as he shakes his head at me before leaning closer.

My heart rate picks up as his eyes remain locked on mine.

Is he going to kiss me?

I can't think straight as he draws closer, and instinctively my lids flutter shut as I stay as still as possible, anticipation spiking my pulse.

I wait for his lips to touch mine, unmoving, but instead of pressing to my lips, they gently kiss my temple, like he did last night. Even though I'm slightly disappointed that he didn't kiss my lips, his gentle touch and intoxicating scent turns me to mush, filling me with that familiar comfort that always comes from Ayden Mitchell being close.

When he pulls back, my lids flutter open to see our faces are mere inches apart. His blue gaze studies mine, not breaking the moment between us, and I can't seem to force myself to look away, lost in his gaze.

I'm not sure if it's normal to feel this intensely drawn to another person so much so that I struggle to hold myself back. It's a foreign feeling for me, having never been so taken by another person in my life. It's like he can see inside my soul. The idea of which would normally scare me, but right now, it doesn't. I want him to... no, it's more like I *need* him to see inside my soul, to know who Lexi West really is.

The irritating buzz of a phone ringing on silent breaks our bubble, and Ayden moves to pull his phone from his back pocket, glancing at the screen.

"I don't know this number." He doesn't show me the screen and answers the call instead.

I hear a panicked high pitch voice, practically yelling through the phone's speaker, and immediately know who it is.

Abbey.

Frowning, Ayden holds his phone out to me. "It's Abbey. She got my number from Marcus, apparently."

I smile, knowing Abbey would have broken into the school to steal Ayden's student file just to get the number if she had to. Taking the phone, I brace myself for a long conversation.

Once I'm able to calm Abbey down, I fill her in with the same information I told Ayden's parents. When I finish that painful task, I get nothing but silence down the line, and for a moment, I think our connection has been lost.

Then I hear her crying.

"It's okay, Abs. I'm alright." I try to reassure her.

"I know, but this could have been avoided, Lex. I tried to tell my parents about what happened with your family, but they rang your dad. He told them you're suffering from mental health issues and that you need medical help. And the idiots believed him." Abbey's distraught sobs pang my heart. "When rumours started spreading about you being taken from school by your dad... Ahh!" She growls, and I hear something crash in the background. "No, taken is the wrong word." She snaps. "More like kidnapped. Tony Anders told Simon, who told me that Tony saw your dad carrying you out of the school unconscious. I tried to get a hold of you when I found out, and then I tried to get the teachers to listen to me. The only one who seemed concerned was Miss Dice, and she gave me her mobile number to keep in contact with her about the situation."

"You can't tell her, Abbey." I cry as panic wraps its fist around my heart.

"She should know, Lexi. She can help."

"No. No one else needs to know anything. I don't want people knowing. I just want to forget about it and move on."

Abbey sighs. "Fine, but if things escalate, I'm telling her, Lexi. I know you don't want anyone to know, but that doesn't mean that they shouldn't know. This is serious stuff."

"Don't you think I know that, Abbey? Each cut and bruise on my body reminds me every time I try to move just how serious this is!"

"I'm so sorry, Lexi. What can I do to help you?" Abbey sobs, and guilt squeezes my heart, making me feel like shit for losing my patience with her.

"Nothing Abs. Just be here for me, okay? And please keep this information to yourself."

"Fine, but only if things don't get worse. If that happens, Lex, then all bets are off."

Sighing, I know I have to be happy with that answer since I know it's as good as I'm going to get from her.

"Fine," I agree.

"I love you, Lex." Her words bring me more of those pesky tears, and Ayden, having sat next to me the entire time listening to our conversation, pulls me closer to his side.

"I love you too, Abs," I whisper.

"I'm sorry. I made you cry. Please don't cry," she says even as *she* cries.

"Okay, I'll try," I say as I cry even more.

Abbey, knowing the secret ingredients to turn my sour mood happy, manages to make me stop crying with ridiculous sex jokes, and I eventually end up in a fit of laughter at a stupid story she tells me about an awkward moment between her and Daniel. I'm glad she found a nice guy, and I hate that I'd been jealous about him taking her away from me. Even if she spends some of her time with him and not me, we'll always be sisters from another mister.

By the time I end the call with Abbey, my mood is lighter than it's been in days, and Ayden quickly helps me settle in for a Friday of binge-watching Netflix. We spend the time in comfortable silence, in between my dramatic overreactions to comical scenes, making Ayden laugh harder at me than at the movie, and Ayden's need to keep asking me if I'm okay every other minute.

Andrea brings me ice packs throughout the day, while Peter serves us chicken salad rolls for lunch and a platter of cheese and crackers mid-afternoon. It's around this time that Ayden gets an incoming SnapChat call and he rolls his eyes, showing me the screen.

It's the boys' chat group. They must have added Ayden to it.

"You should answer it. As long as it's only a voice call." I state, not wanting the guys from school to see the damage Mike did, or even know what happened. Obviously, Marcus knows, but hopefully, he's kept that information to himself.

Ayden shoots me a small smile before answering the call, and Jared's concerned voice immediately fills the room.

"Is Lexi there with you?" He sounds pissed and demanding. Something I'm not used to hearing from Jared.

"I'm here, Jar." I roll my eyes, this time making Ayden smile.

"Lex," he sighs, sounding relieved, "What's going on? Tony Anders saw your dad carry you out of school yesterday, and Marcus fucking knows what's going on, but won't tell us anything."

"That's because it's none of your business," Marcus snaps.

"Marcus is right, man, it's none of your business." Ayden backs his cousin up, and I study his face, now red with anger. His eyes jump to mine, and I raise a questioning brow, but he doesn't falter.

"Fuck that! Who the fuck are you to come in and claim her? You've been here for five fucking minutes!" Jared hisses, and Ayden's eyes darken even more.

"That's enough." I snap before Ayden can get another word in. "What I don't need is my friends at each other's throats."

I glare at Ayden, hoping he gets the point and his face softens before an apology slips past his lips. Jared gives his own apology, but it's hardly convincing.

"Lex?" Garrett chimes in. "Can you please give us something? Anything? Like are you okay?"

I smile at the care in Garrett's tone. He's big for our age, but he's such a teddy bear. To me anyway.

"I'm okay," I respond. "Just some family drama going on. It's nothing to worry about."

Ayden's brows shoot up at my lie, and I shake my head, trying to silently tell him I'm not going to even hint as to what's really going on.

"That doesn't really explain why you were carried out of school unconscious Lex." Shaun, the normally over-energetic playboy of the group, sounds so serious. Shaun Bossier, aka Bossi, is never serious.

"Look, I've had a crazy week. Mum went to hospital on Wednesday, and I guess I didn't really eat properly and I must have fainted. I'm okay, though."

"You're sure? You'd tell us if something was going on, right?" Jared expresses his concern again.

"I'm sure. It's all good," I say, feeling anxious as Ayden watches the lies slip so easily from my lips. I wait for a frown or a look of disapproval, but instead, he gives me a sympathetic smile. He understands I don't want to share my vile truth with the guys.

"So tell me about school today. Any tea?" I steer the conversation in another direction, hoping they will follow, using the "in" word we use in place of gossip.

"Well Lexi, since you've run off with another man, I have had to let all the girls know I'm back on the market," Simon jokes, and everyone laughs except for Ayden.

If only Simon could see the daggers Ayden is shooting him through the phone. It's cute in a caveman kind of way.

"Yeah right, Hastings. The only girl who threw herself at you today was Beccy, and that's because she tripped on her laces," Shaun teases.

"Shut up Bossi. You're just jealous, bro." Simon bites back, and I try not to laugh when Ayden rolls his eyes at their immature banter. I love this about these guys. They help me forget my worries, even if it's for the briefest time.

"Hey, did you hear about Travis Watson?" Marcus says, "Cops picked him up earlier today for the vandalism at school."

"What?" I squeak before trying to school my features and hide the fact that this news affects me. Ayden notices though and frowns, mouthing, "Are you okay?"

I nod quickly.

"Yeah, I heard that too. Wasn't he at Tasha's party on the weekend? Her place isn't that far from school." Garrett adds and my heart sinks.

I'm so fucked.

"I heard Allison hooked up with Travis at the party. Maybe she was the other person who trashed the place with him," Jared says.

"What do you mean, other person?" I ask, trying to sound not as concerned as I feel.

"The witness said there were two of them who did it. I can't see a girl doing something like that, though." Jared answers me, and I frown. If only they knew that not only could a girl do the crime, but that the girl in question is me.

"If it was a girl, it was probably one of the FP High chicks. Those bitches are cut from a different cloth than the classy girls at FP Catholic."

Oh, Simon. If you only knew.

"I don't know about that." Shaun disagrees. "The chick that tripped Tasha at school can be pretty brutal. Just thinking about what she did makes my dick hard."

"And on that note, we have to go." Ayden picks the phone up from the couch where he placed it between us.

They all protest, but Ayden gets his way, and the call is ended before they can all say their goodbyes. I immediately miss their voices. Those guys have the ability to make me feel lighter without even knowing they're doing it.

"They are... A lot." Ayden's face creases into a cringe, and I laugh. Well, I pretend to laugh, because really, I'm freaking the fuck out. I need to speak with Travis, but I don't have my phone. Can I even speak to him? If the cops have arrested him, then maybe he's in jail. Do sixteen-year-old kids even go to jail? Shit, I don't know.

"You okay, Lex?" Ayden's voice reminds me that he's sitting in front of me, watching my every move.

I clear my throat. "Yep. Wanna watch another movie?"

Ayden's brows pull together and his blue gaze searches mine, looking for answers, but I hold strong.

Until the police come to take me away for the vandalism, I'm going to pretend it never happened.

Ayden caves and nods, bringing up the Netflix screen again so we can choose something else to watch, and we settle in to watch another action movie.

After movie number three, and a brief nana nap on my part, Ayden slips out of the room to speak with his dad while I take a much-needed toilet break.

When I step out of the toilet, Ayden is leaning against his bedroom door, looking all sorts of yummy in his grey sweatpants and chest hugging navy t-shirt. I suddenly feel self-conscious about my appearance. Besides the fact that one eye is partially closed over, taking on the look of a pufferfish with shaded dark purple bruising, my blonde hair is an unruly mess, the waves having a mind of their own adding more volume than I'd like. I feel and look terrible, and without a second thought, I nervously run my hand over my messy hair, hoping to tame it and cover up the wound where my hair has been torn from the roots.

"Don't do that." Ayden crosses his arms over his chest looking all sexy with his dark hair a little messed, and his lip spreading wide as if he's trying to hide a smirk.

Jesus, that look should be illegal.

"Do what?" I rasp out, my voice a little husky from my visceral reaction to him.

Pushing off his door frame, he steps closer, lifting his hand before his gentle fingers sear a path down my temple, tucking some of my blonde hair behind my ear. His blue gaze, somehow more penetrating than normal, dances between mine, before his lips part to respond.

"Don't for a minute think you aren't beautiful right now."

Oh fuck me. How does he know just the right things to say to make me squirm?

I scoff, trying to reject his compliment, but it comes out more like a squeak. "I think you need your eyes tested."

His grin quirks up, drawing my eyes to his mouth in time to see the tip of his tongue pop out to lick his lips.

"Nope." He shakes his head, but my gaze never leaves his lips. "My eyesight is perfect. I can even see that pretty pink flush that just crept over your face."

Fucking holy hell. He's killing me.

"There it is again." He chuckles as my cheeks burn even more.

Smart arse!

"Would you stop it?" I hiss playfully, barging past him in the doorway, but I don't get far inside his room when Ayden's hand latches on to mine, turning me back to face him.

"I'm sorry." He offers, even as he fights back a smirk, contradicting what he just said.

"You don't seem sorry." I bite the inside of my cheek, trying to hide my own smirk, and he shrugs.

"You're right. I'm not really." His grin is wide as he admits that, and he reaches up again, retracing the path his fingers took out in the hall, re-tucking my hair back behind my ear before he speaks again. "I was speaking the truth when I said you're still beautiful, Lex, and I love seeing you blush. Please stop trying to hide it from me."

I can't respond. What do I even say to that? Maybe I could have thought of a fun, witty response if I wasn't silently begging for him to kiss me. I guess I could always make the first move and kiss him. But if I'm being honest, I'm too scared to do that, partly because I'm a chicken and partly because even though I think I'm reading his signals right, there's a part of me that doubts I even have a chance with him.

We stand motionless, staring at each other in his doorway, and after a few long beats, Ayden breaks the connection.

"Do you feel like getting out of here for a bit?" he asks, and my brows shoot up at the sudden conversation change.

"Uh... I don't really want anyone to see me like this." I admit.

It's easy to forget how bad I look when Ayden looks at me the way he does. The painful swelling is a constant reminder, though, and the times I've summoned up the courage to look at myself in the mirror scares me to see the monster looking back. I can't imagine having other people see that too. It's hard enough knowing Ayden can see it.

"Well, I was thinking of heading down to my dad's recording studio on the tenth floor. No one is there now, and dad gave me the key. We will have the place to ourselves. You won't have to see anyone but me."

Liking the sound of that, I smile and nod. That does kind of sound interesting. I've never been to a recording studio before.

"Sure, why not?"

Ayden's smile instantly broadens at my response, and he takes my hand, leading me to the lifts in the foyer of his dad's skyrise apartment.

Travelling down from the twenty-fourth floor to the tenth doesn't take as long as I thought it would. The lift opens into a sleek foyer and reception area with a sign above the counter saying 'MitchWave Studios.'

The name is familiar, and it hadn't even clicked previously when Ayden said his dad did this for a living.

"Hold up," I say, lifting my hand in a stop motion as we step off the lift. "Your dad owns MitchWave?"

Ayden smiles. "You've heard of it?"

"Uh- yeah. Archer 9 recorded their most recent album here. It's their sickest one yet." I try, and fail, to contain my excitement, and I can tell it's hard for Ayden to hide his smirk at my reaction.

"Yep, that's right. They recorded in this studio." Ayden gestures to the room, saying 'Studio two' on the door.

"No, shit?" My voice is high pitched with my excitement, and I eagerly walk up to the door, easing it open.

The room lights up when Ayden flicks a switch and I stand in awe. Deep red walls encase the room with grey carpet underfoot, both colours providing regal warmth.

"This is the live room where they catch full bands and do live sessions." Ayden steps into the room with me before moving to the ebony grand piano and takes a seat. I follow, running my finger along the glossy surface of the piano, noticing that there isn't a speck of dust on it.

"Have you watched recordings being done in this room?" I ask, my tone still lit with excitement and he nods.

"Yep, I've sat in on a few. Not Archer 9, though."

Wow.

Just wow.

I never want to leave this place.

The smooth timbre of the piano snaps me out of my trance, and my gaze falls to Ayden's talented hands gliding over the keys.

Is there nothing this beautiful being can't do?

Resting my chin in my hands, I lean on the lid of the piano and stare, transfixed on Ayden's face, lit with peaceful concentration. It doesn't take me long to recognise the piece he is playing.

"Foo Fighters?"

He nods at my guess. "Yep, Everlong."

I smile. It's probably a ridiculous, dorky smile too, but I don't care. I've officially found my new happy place.

"Come sit next to me." Even though Ayden looks up at me as he speaks, the musical flow of Everlong doesn't get interrupted.

I do as he asks while he continues to play, and I watch, captivated, as his fingers create the music filling the room. His hands look strong, like they could easily break bones, yet are always so gentle when they touch me. I don't think I've ever taken notice of someone's hands before, but Ayden's draw me in, and I silently wish they were holding mine, touching my face, or stroking my hair, just as he's done so many times over the last few days.

As the song winds down, Ayden turns his head to stare at me, giving me a toothy smile that lights up his whole face before his hands fall to his lap.

"What were you just thinking about?" he asks.

"Um, nothing?" It's meant to be an answer, but comes out like a question.

His right brow lifts. "Really?"

I nod, not trusting my voice.

Lifting his hand to my face, he grazes the backs of his fingers along my un-bruised cheek.

"Lexi, Lexi, Lexi. When are you going to learn that your pretty pink blush keeps giving you away?"

My face instantly heats again, and his small smirk tells me he can see yet another red flush sweep across my face. I would usually duck my head and try to hide it, but this time I don't. For some reason, I don't feel so embarrassed to let him see what he does to me, and I like that he can see my flaming cheeks.

"So beautiful." His words are barely a whisper, and I feel the heat of his breath across my cheek as he leans in. I'm lost, aching to have him kiss me, my eyes fluttering closed in anticipation.

This time, his lips brush my cheek where his fingers touched only moments before, and I can feel the heat of his breath dance across my skin, coming closer to my mouth. I wait, the anticipation of finally feeling his lips on mine nearly too much, but something I refuse to deny myself in this moment.

I wait, and wait, and wait, expecting to feel his lips press against mine at any moment. But it never comes.

My eyes snap open to see him sitting back again, smiling down at me.

Oh my god. Was he watching me looking desperate waiting for him to kiss me?

"You want to play the piano?" His question is playful, and throws me off a little.

"I-ah…" Shit. I need to focus, but it's hard knowing he obviously doesn't want to kiss me. "I don't know how to play."

Why doesn't he want to kiss me? He calls me beautiful, touches me like I'm the most precious thing in the world, and yet he still doesn't kiss me the way I so desperately want him to.

"I'll teach you the basics." He smiles back, warmly.

And just like that, as if the moment we just shared didn't even happen, he's teaching me to play the piano.

Twenty

We spend hours in the studio. Ayden teaches me how to play *Mary had a little lamb* on the piano before moving to the drum kit, bashing out all of our frustrations. It's so much fun that I temporarily forget how Ayden didn't kiss me, and by the end of it, I try to convince Ayden that I'm going to be the next drumming sensation.

Ayden's dad cooks a roast for dinner, and to say it's delicious is an understatement. I try not to scoff the food in front of Ayden's parents, but it's hard to control myself.

"You like the roast, hey, Lexi?" Peter asks with a smirk, and I feel my cheeks heat in embarrassment even as I nod.

"It's delicious. Thank you so much."

"Does your family have roast dinners often, Lexi?" Andrea asks, and I try to hide my cringe by clearing my throat.

"Ah... no. The last time I had a roast was at Abbey's house last year when we had leftovers from

Christmas." I admit, and then instantly regret telling them.

The pity on their faces is almost suffocating, and it makes me squirm with the need to leave the room. I also feel bad for lying to them because the last time I had roast was a couple of days ago when Ayden hid me away in his loft and snuck food to me.

"What does your family usually do for dinners? Do you sit together for meals?" Andrea asks, her expression not hiding her concern, and I feel like it's the beginning of an interrogation.

Instantly, my need to protect myself is almost overwhelming.

"Mum, stop with the questions." Ayden snaps, obviously picking up on my discomfort.

Looking away from me, Andrea glances at her son, shrugging, "What? I'm just asking."

"No you're not! You're interrogating her!" He stands abruptly from the table, his chair scraping loudly across the tiled floor.

Shit.

I don't want this.

I don't want to come between Ayden and his parents, who have so generously helped me.

"It's okay." I reach out to cover Ayden's hand with my own, trying to let him know I don't mind, even though I do.

His eyes fall to our hands and then lift to my face before he slowly lowers himself back to his seat.

Scooting his chair closer to mine, Ayden locks our fingers together, not caring that his parents can see his affection towards me, and I gotta admit, he's confusing the hell out of me.

Is his affection that of a friend, or more?

To move past the awkwardness filling the room, I answer Andrea's question.

"No, Andrea," I smile warmly towards her. "We haven't had a family dinner together for years. I usually have to cook something for mum and me. Dad is never home, and Mike only moved in a few months back. Mostly, I just fend for myself."

The room is uncomfortably silent while they digest what I've just said. There's still pity written across their faces, and now I wish I'd just lied to them. Made up some bullshit story so they can sleep better at night.

"I'm so sorry, Lexi. That must be hard." Andrea's eyes hold regret as she breaks the awkward silence, and I shake my head.

"It's not that hard when it's all I know."

"Well, I want you to know you will always have a seat at our table, Lexi. Here or at my sister's table in Fox Pines."

Her generosity is, once again, overwhelming, and I have to fight to control my emotions as I feel the warning of tears prick my eyes.

"Thank you, Andrea, that's so kind of you."

The gentle squeeze of Ayden's hand reminds me he's still here for me too, and I'm thankful when the conversation turns a little lighter, with Andrea and Peter discussing something about her sister's family.

After dinner, I try to help with the dishes, but Andrea and Peter insist on doing them and shoo us away. I'm left feeling exhausted even though it's still early in the evening, and Ayden picks up on that, insisting we have an early night, which I don't protest.

I shower, trying to ease the pain, which is a stiffening ache all over my body and has become increasingly worse as the day went on. The heat helps a little with the soreness and calms my chaotic mind.

When I finally return to Ayden's room, he has paracetamol ready for me. I didn't even have to ask. He knew anyway, reading me like an open book.

"Thank you for this." I swallow down the two tablets and turn to Ayden to see him studying my every move from his desk chair. His gaze is darker than usual, and the intensity of it makes me shift nervously.

"What?" I ask, feeling self-conscious.

He gives me that devilish grin of his. "What?"

I raise my brows at him asking the same thing back. Well, I try to raise my brows at him. Only one lifts, the other one is frozen in its horrid purple, puffy swell.

Ayden chuckles and walks over to me.

"I like you wearing my hoodie." He admits as I crane my neck to look up at him. "I think you should wear it all the time."

Reaching out, he strokes a stray hair off my face, being careful to avoid the bruising and as usual, I feel the way my cheeks heat as my body reacts to his touch.

"What is it with you wanting me to wear your hoodie?" I ask, feeling a little breathless as his blue eyes roam my face, taking their slow, torturous time before stopping on my lips.

Is this it? The moment he'll finally kiss me? How many times does a girl have to hope for a damn kiss?

"Lexi," he whispers.

"Yes?"

"Do you have any objections if I sleep in the same bed with you again?"

I take a moment to comprehend his words, my heart in my throat as my mind tries to play catch up, only to feel disappointment when he takes a small step back.

Ugh! I could scream!

I desperately want him to kiss me, but he won't make the first move, and it's driving me crazy. I'm so close to losing my mind and climbing him like a damn tree, just to feel his lips on mine.

"I thought you might like a bit of space since you've been stuck with me so much lately." His eyes drop to his feet briefly as if he's unsure, but then the two blue pools return to mine with the smallest grin tugging at his lips, "But Lex, I selfishly don't want to give you space. I can't seem to get enough of you..." He hesitates and shakes his head. "I'm a prick, I know. But if you tell me to, I'll back off and give you some room to breathe. The last thing I want to do is suffocate you."

Air slowly seeps back into my lungs as I process what he just said. I was so sure he was going to kiss me with the way his eyes drank me in, but then he bloody backed off, only to tell me he wants to sleep in the same bed as me again and that he can't get enough of me.

I'm so confused. Am I misinterpreting things? Am I delusional thinking that Ayden Mitchell could ever want me the way I want him?

"No." My head is all messed up, and emotions that I don't want to feel are strangling me again. Feelings of not being good enough, of not being the person people expect me to be, are clawing their way into my brain.

"No?" Ayden asks, "As in, no, you don't want me to sleep in the same bed with you?"

"What?" My confusion is making me more confused, if that's even possible. I take a moment to process his words again. "Oh, wait. I mean, no, I don't want you to back off. I'd rather not be alone." Sucking in my bottom lip, I chew on it as nerves unsettle me for being so frank.

Ayden grins, "So I can sleep with you? In the same bed, I mean."

I grin back because his awkward words are now making *him* squirm. "Yes."

He nods, "Okay. I'll uh… go take a quick shower."

I nod, but he doesn't see it since he's already turned to flee into the bathroom.

Shaking my head, the stupid grin on my face probably resembles a twelve-year-old girl who just opened her first valentine's card. If I could just stop acting like a love-struck idiot, then maybe Ayden wouldn't be so standoffish. I'm almost sure he feels the same way about me as I do him, but I don't understand why he's holding back. It has to be because I'm a weirdo or because of my heavy baggage. Perhaps it's because I look like a monster.

Deciding not to torture myself any further, I climb into Ayden's bed, lying down on the same side I slept last night. Ayden's intoxicating scent surrounds me, soaking into my pores, creating a relieving calm for my aching body. It's addictive and makes me crave his powerful arms around me, so I pull his blanket over me, tucking it around my body, and close my eyes to wait for him to join me in bed.

Sometime later, I wake up to Ayden slipping into the bed. I hadn't realised I was asleep, my body instantly finding its peace where it feels safe.

Reaching out, Ayden pulls me close, this time with my head tucked into the crook of his neck. Sliding my hand over his chest without thinking twice, we shuffle closer and he instinctively pulls my leg up over his hip.

And now I'm wide awake.

With our close proximity, and the way I'm pressed against his firm body, I'm in both heaven and hell right now. The urge to moan—yes, moan—is almost overwhelming because I'm so obsessively drawn to his touch. The need for more is like dangling a lollipop in front of a three-year-old. It's impossible to resist and I'm hyper-aware of every part of my body that touches his. I'm sure it's going to drive me mad with a level of lust I've never experienced.

It takes an extremely long time to simmer down the heat pulsing through my body, but eventually, I'm able to calm myself before I make a real idiot out of myself and do something embarrassing like rub up against him like a wanton cat.

Ayden doesn't say a word, remaining quiet as we lay together in the dark. It helps me to relax, and eventually, sleep drags me under as I listen to the sound of his steady breathing.

I sleep soundly all night, which is another glorious reprieve for my exhausted mind and body. No dreams plague me, reminding me of the nightmare I've been living.

As I stir from sleep the next morning, I can't stop a smile from forming when my nose picks up the addictive scent of Ayden. His muscular body warms my back in a delicious spoon, and I almost moan from the comfort it brings.

I quickly become hyper-aware of the very prominent bulge pressing against my backside and am glad I held in my moan, because that would have been embarrassing.

"Sorry," Ayden whispers, startling me. I hadn't realised he was awake. "It'll go away soon."

I stifle a giggle at his lack of embarrassment. "Really?"

He pulls me closer, tighter against his body and the bulge becomes even more evident. "Probably not."

"I don't think pulling me closer is going to help." I point out, my smile is ridiculously big, which causes a stinging pinch on the bruised side of my face.

"Again, probably not." He shifts a little, and I can feel his warm breath on my ear.

Did he just smell me?

"Ah... Would it help if I get out of bed?" I ask.

Part of me likes how tightly he has me in his arms as if he needs me to breathe, but another part of me feels uncomfortable because of the intimacy. I've never had this level of intimacy before. Not even with Nathan.

"No, that won't help." He admits, giving me a little squeeze.

Silence fills the room for a few minutes as I lay as still as I can in his arms, trying to figure out how to handle this situation.

Like, does it even need handling?

I have no idea.

"I'm sorry, I'm probably making you uncomfortable." Ayden rasps close to my ear, like he's able to read my thoughts, and when he goes to move away from me, I grab his arm, stopping him.

"Don't go," my whisper stills him momentarily before he pulls me back against him again.

"Shit, Lex. I don't know how much longer I can handle having you close without mauling you." He tries to sound playful, but I can hear the underlying strain in his voice.

I want to tell him to maul away, but I'm also a big chicken. Ayden Mitchell is rapidly inducing feelings in me that I've never felt before, and I'm not just talking about my emotions.

Lucky for me, or maybe unluckily, a knock sounds at the door, interrupting us, and Ayden's dad, Peter, pops his head in.

"Good morning, guys. Breakfast will be ready in ten minutes." Peter's eyes rake over our cocooned forms in his son's bed before he continues, "Lexi, I believe Andrea has news on your mum."

I quickly sit up to acknowledge Peter. "Okay, thank you."

He smiles before backing up and closing the door behind him.

Ayden chuckles, "Saved by the bell."

I smile at him, and he looks at me with such care that it melts me like butter.

Shifting in the bed, Ayden quickly throws the blankets off him, leaping out of the bed, keeping his back to me.

"I need a shower. A *very cold* shower." He admits, and I try to hold in my laugh, but I fail.

Ayden's attempt at sending me a death glare over his shoulder, looks more adorable than annoyed or intimidating, and I can't hold back my shit-eating grin.

"Enjoy your shower." I tease, and he grunts, before locking himself in his bathroom.

I try my best not to think about him on the other side of the door, naked, in the shower, with the water running over his body.

I really do try.

Get your head out of the gutter, Lexi.

I move quickly to dress before Ayden returns from the bathroom, pulling on my blue skinny jeans again and my bra. Although I'm thankful for Marcus packing my bag, I'm a bit annoyed at his terrible effort, which has left me with little to wear.

Deciding to rummage through Ayden's drawers, I search for a top that might be suitable. Finding a hooded footy jersey, I slip into it before moving to close the drawer, but my eyes land on a black box hidden at the back, peeking out from under the clothes.

Unable to stop my curiosity, I pull the box out, realising it's actually an old lunch tin.

I know I shouldn't open it. I know I should put it back and walk away, but do I?

Nope. I let my curiosity get the better of me and open the damn tin, just in time for Ayden's return.

"Jesus Christ, woman, are you trying to kill me?"

I spin, shocked to see Ayden standing just outside the bathroom door in only a pair of grey sweatpants, which ride low on his hips.

I can't form words for a moment as my eyes latch on to a drop of water that has dripped from his hair, running a path down the centre of his chest and abdomen before soaking into the waistband of his pants.

"W-what do you mean?" I ask, shaking my head as I try to focus on Ayden's words.

Fuck. Now I'm stuttering.

I need to get a grip.

Ayden sighs. "As if you don't already look hot enough in my hoodie, but now you tempt me by wearing my jersey?"

Ahhhh... what?

He just called me hot, right?

Did I hear that correctly?

"You want me to take it off?" I ask, grabbing the hem of the jersey with my free hand before I start to lift it, revealing my bare tummy.

"No!" Ayden yells. "Leave it on."

"Leave it on?" I ask innocently, my hand stilling, showing off my abs and probably the bottom of my black bra.

Frowning, Ayden saunters over to me, his ocean eyes fixed on my face before dropping to my hand. The same hand still clasping the tin.

My eyes follow his, lowering to the now open tin and I freeze at what I see.

Holy shit. What have I done?

There in the tin lies a syringe, a long rubber type of band, a lighter, an old bent spoon, and a foil packet.

Reaching out, Ayden gently takes the end of the jersey from my hand and pulls it back in place, covering my bare skin, all while keeping his eyes locked on the contents of the tin.

"Ayden I—"

"You wanna tell me why you're holding something that doesn't belong to you?"

My heart races and my breathing picks up as his words, quiet, but almost lethal, sink in.

"I was looking for a jumper." I manage to admit as I take in the fire darkening his eyes as he glances up from the tin.

"You found a jumper, Lexi. So why do you have that?" He points to the tin, his expression hard with anger, something I haven't seen on him before.

The rise and fall of his chest matches mine, but we each struggle with our emotions for two entirely different reasons.

I'm scared. Not of him physically hurting me, but of him being so mad that he no longer wants to be associated with me.

Come to think of it. That would hurt more than any fist ever could.

As we stand there is silence, staring at each other, I can see Ayden trying hard to control his breathing. His chest is rising and falling in slow, long, deep breaths, and I can tell he is trying hard to stay in control.

"I-I..." Shit. I stumble over my words, feeling my cheeks flare with shame.

He hates me. I can see it in his eyes.

What the fuck have I done?

Why do I keep doing things to fuck up my already fucked up existence?

Raising his brows impatiently, Ayden waits for me to give him some sort of pathetic excuse. So I decide to go with honesty.

"I'm sorry. I saw it when I grabbed the jumper out, and my curiosity got the better of me. I should never have done that, Ayden. I'm so sorry."

He rolls his tongue in his closed mouth, trying to stay calm, and I wish I knew what he was thinking.

Does he hate me now?

Ayden's eyes dart between mine, looking for a lie, searching for the truth. He doesn't do anything else but glare at me, so I move to flip the lid back over to close it, but he stops me with his hand on my wrist.

"You don't want to know why I have that?" His voice cracks a little, and I glance back up to see his gaze locked on the tin.

"It's none of my business, Ayden. I'm sorry for snooping."

He releases my wrist.

"Don't do that." He shakes his head, those piercing eyes pinning me in place. "Don't give in so easily, Lex. Yeah, you shouldn't be snooping, but you did, and you found something you know I shouldn't have, given my history. You found it, so now you're involved. Hold me accountable and ask me what you really want to know."

I'm shaking, even more scared that he's going to tell me to leave, and get out of his life. Even if he does ask that of me, I still need to do what he asked and hold him accountable, so I force the words out.

"Why do you have this if you say you're no longer using?"

A breath whooshes from his parted lips as if he was holding it in for a long time, relieved that I finally asked.

"I have it to keep me strong." He admits, before clearing his throat. "The temptation is always there, especially when I'm having a bad day, but I keep it to prove to myself that I'm strong enough *not* to use it. It's a fucked up way of thinking, but it's worked so far." He shrugs before continuing. "It's also a reminder of what

310

I did when I put that guy in hospital. That's the potent shit I was shooting into my veins when I turned into a monster."

The tin rattles and we both look down to see my hands shaking. Ayden sighs and gently removes the tin from my hand, closing the lid and slipping it back into the drawer.

Licking his lips, he takes a steady breath before cupping my bruised cheek.

"It's looking less angry today."

"Does it?" My voice is shaky, and I feel like crying as he nods.

"It does." Dropping his hand, he gestures to the door. "We should go have breakfast."

What? That's it? I find his drug tin after snooping, and he doesn't yell at me?

"Ayden, I'm sorry." I tell him again, feeling tears prick my eyes.

My heart hurts just thinking about him being upset with me. I feel like I've stepped over an invisible line that I can never reverse, and somehow I manage to hold the tears back.

I'm so fucking sick of crying.

"It's okay Lex. It is what it is." He shrugs one shoulder and gives me a small, forced grin. "Come on, just forget about it and let's eat."

I nod warily, taking the lead to head to the dining room and I swear I can feel Ayden's fierce gaze boring into the back of my head as we go.

I find a thin veil of calm when we're greeted with a spread of cereals, pastries, and fruit covering the dining table.

"Good morning, Lexi. Did you sleep well?" Andrea asks, carrying a tray of muffins from the kitchen bench and placing them on the table.

"Yes, thanks." I force a smile, taking a seat next to Ayden.

Does he even want me sitting next to him?

"I slept great, thanks, mum." The sarcasm rolls off Ayden's tongue quickly as he lounges back in his chair before shooting me a wink.

My heart leaps at that simple action, hope blooming in my chest.

Is he really not angry with me anymore?

Andrea scoffs and rolls her eyes. "Don't be dramatic, Ayden. I was going to ask you next."

"Sure, you were." He teases and piles his plate with pastries.

Andrea's laughter fills the room as she takes a seat next to Peter, who's pouring everyone a glass of orange juice.

I watch with fascination as they fill their plates with freshly baked croissants and muffins like this sort of breakfast spread is normal. I've never seen anything like it. Even at Abbey's house, our breakfasts only consist of toast or cereal.

Ayden's warm hand squeezes my thigh under the table, gaining my attention, and I turn my head in his direction.

"You okay?"

I nod, still shaken from the tin incident and feeling a little silly as I watch Ayden's family dig into the food. Andrea and Peter look up at me, a frown creasing both of their brows before Andrea speaks.

"Are you feeling okay, sweetie?"

I nod again and clear my throat. "Is this normal?" I gesture to the food in front of us. "This sort of breakfast, I mean. Do you eat like this often?"

"Uh…" Andrea stalls, but then Ayden jumps in.

"No, Lex. Mum is giving you a long weekend breakfast."

"Long weekend breakfast?" I ask, confused. I've never heard of that.

"I'm sorry, Lexi. I just wanted to make sure you have a nutritious breakfast." Andrea puts down the blueberry muffin she's holding. "This is the breakfast we usually have on Mondays of long weekends." She grimaces a little but tries to hide it by re-focusing on the muffin in front of her.

"Oh. Well, this is great, thank you." I force another smile, pushing past my emotions, which are threatening to turn me into a blubbering mess. Her gesture to take care of me like this is overwhelming, yet welcome.

"You are welcome, honey. Always." Andrea smiles at my thanks before returning her attention to her food, and Ayden decides to take it upon himself to serve my breakfast, loading up my plate with so much food that I won't be able to eat it all.

"Eat," he gestures to the plate.

I try to shoot him an annoyed look, which only makes him grin, so I give up and start with a choc chip muffin.

"So, Lexi, I think I've found your mum at a psychiatric hospital on the other side of the city." Andrea looks pleased with herself. "I've reached out to an old colleague to see if she can get us on the permitted visitor's list so you can visit your mum."

A sense of relief washes over me at hearing this news. To be honest, I'm a little shocked that I feel anything at all given my mum's lack of interest in me, but she's still my mum, and she's been hurt by Mike as well.

"Thank you so much, Mrs Mitchell." I smile, embracing the relief I feel.

"Please call me Andrea. Mrs Mitchell is Peter's mum." She insists, and we all laugh and dig into the lavish breakfast.

As great as it is to hear that my mum has been found, my ease doesn't last long as my mind continually goes back to Ayden's room, and his expression when I found his drugs. I want to accept that he's no longer annoyed at me over it, but I can't stop my mind from worrying that I may have ruined whatever it is that Ayden and I have together, before it's really begun.

Twenty-One

We spend the morning back in the studio, messing about on the instruments and recording equipment. Ayden insists I practise *Mary had a little lamb* on the piano again before letting me bash the crap out of the drums. I humour him briefly. When I get my hands on the drumsticks again, I feel so free. Each hit expels pockets of anger that have been weighing me down, and in their place is a small bubble of happiness. I think I'm officially addicted to not just Ayden, but to the drums, too.

He doesn't mention the tin incident again and acts like it never happened. I still feel bad, but at the same time, I feel like I know him a little better and that he's allowed me to see more into the life he's trying to move on from.

It's a little after one in the afternoon when we venture back up to the apartment feeling light, and dare I say, happy. I'm an idiot to think happiness could possibly be part of my life, though. I should've known it would be short-lived.

Very short-lived.

Standing rigid in front of the TV, Andrea and Peter are watching a news broadcast. Curious about what's grabbed their attention, we step up beside them to see my worst nightmare.

There on the screen is my face, a close up picture of me from last year's school photos.

"Authorities from Fox Pines Police Department are looking for missing teen, Miss Alexis West, who is thought to be injured and possibly in danger. Alexis, who is known by her friends as Lexi, lives in the house behind me."

The camera pans out from the young news reporter zooming in on my house.

"From the outside, this house looks like all the other family homes in this neighbourhood. However, witnesses have confirmed that what goes on inside this house is something more from a horror movie.

Video evidence has been secured by the police, which is said to capture some of the horrors that were inflicted on young Alexis the night she disappeared."

I'm crying. Burning tears fall uncontrollably from my eyes. The news reporter is talking about me, broadcasting my face and name to millions of homes across the state, maybe even across Australia. My house, the one I grew up in, is now on show for the world to see.

> *"Police believe Alexis may have fled the scene with a friend and has gone into hiding. Authorities are extremely concerned for her welfare. If anyone knows the whereabouts of Alexis West, you are asked to contact the Fox Pines Police Department or Crime Stoppers on the numbers at the bottom of the screen. Authorities are also looking for Max West, Miss West's father, for questioning, and an arrest warrant has been issued for Mike West in relation to this matter."*

My sobs fill the room, and my knees buckle.

Strong arms wrap around me, sweeping me up before I hit the floor. Ayden's scent wraps around me, reminding me I'm not alone as he cradles me to his chest and carries me out of the room, and I can vaguely hear Andrea's and Peter's concerned voices fade into the background. My ears are ringing, and I can't seem to make myself focus on what Ayden's parents are saying. Ayden ignores them, continuing through his dad's apartment before lying me down with him on his bed, pulling me close while I cry.

The buzz of Ayden's phone goes off continuously, but he makes no move to answer it, keeping his hold on me tight and offering me the comfort I need.

"I'm so sorry, Lex. I know you didn't want anyone to know." His whisper soaks into my heart, filling me with his gentle compassion, making me cry even more.

The world knows now. There will be questions, so many questions. People will stare and whisper, spreading rumours that aren't true. I'll have no privacy. All I'll have is my heavy shame.

Mike is still out there somewhere. He could still find me and finish what he started. My dad will be beyond furious, and I hate to think what he'll do.

Uncontrollable trembles convulse my body as the reality of my future sinks in.

"Ayden, we need to talk with Lexi." Peter's voice is quiet but firm, but Ayden responds in a hiss.

"Later."

"It can't wait, buddy." Peter's voice brokers no argument, and I whisper into Ayden's chest.

"In a few minutes."

At hearing my request, Ayden shifts, and I imagine him craning his neck up to look at his dad.

"Okay. In a few minutes. Let me help Lexi calm down first." Ayden's lips press to my forehead then, and my death grip around his waist tightens.

My need for him is quickly becoming harder and harder to hide. The way he gets me. The way he reads me when I don't even speak. The way he shows affection. It's unravelling me. Breaking down all of my defences and in all honesty. It's scary as hell, because I know I'll never want to let him go, even though he deserves better than someone like me.

The click of the door closing is loud in the silent room as Peter retreats, and we both relax a fraction.

My hold on Ayden is still as tight as a vise. I don't think I could let go of him even if I wanted to. My body is clinging to life just by his touch, craving the strength he offers. I hate that I'm so needy in front of him. This is not the version of me I want him to see. I want him to see the confident Lexi. The fun Lexi that laughs and smiles and is playful. I have no idea why he hasn't run in the other direction, given the shit storm I have dragged into his life. He hasn't really met the fun version of me, only the broken version that carries heavy secrets.

I could spend my time overthinking it, but the selfish part of me wins, and I push the negative thoughts aside, deciding just to be thankful he is here, willing to comfort me and keep me safe.

Those are the thoughts that help to turn my sobs into silent tears, which eventually dry up. Unfortunately, my nose didn't get the memo, and I find myself in an embarrassing snotty mess.

"Tissue." I whimper, keeping my head tucked into Ayden's chest, and he moves to reach over my body before presenting me with a handful of tissues.

I give him a nasally thank you and clean myself up. When I sit up, I see his shirt didn't escape my snotty attack.

"I'm so sorry." I reach out with the pile of snotty tissues to clean it up, but he slides me back with one firm hand and rolls off the bed.

Given the circumstances, I shouldn't be taking such pleasure in watching him as he pulls his shirt over his head, tossing it in the hamper by his door. His muscles ripple as he moves, giving me a better look at the tattoo on his back. It's too late when I realise I sigh out loud, drawing his attention to my ogling. Stopping by his dresser, he raises a dark brow, a smug grin tugging at his lips, and just like that, heat flushes my face. Because of course, why would my body want to save me from more embarrassment?

"You know, Lex, you really should stop trying to hide what you feel and just admit that you think I have a rockin' body."

"Rockin' body? Really?" I scoff at his cockiness and roll off the bed, giving him my back while trying to compose myself a little more. His chuckle floats across the room, making me feel okay for a moment. Knowing Ayden, it's probably exactly why he made that comment. He always seems to know how to keep me grounded.

A strong hand appears in my line of sight, and I blink at his fingers briefly trying to figure out a way to avoid what has to happen now. I don't want to do this. He knows it, and I sure as fuck know it, but I know I can no longer run from this secret, because it's no longer a secret. The world knows now.

It's time to speak with his parents and get this over and done with, so I breathe in and hold the air in my lungs for a few long beats before releasing it and accept his hand.

His palm is warm as he links our fingers and tugs me up off the bed and I let him guide me out of his room to have a conversation I don't want to have.

In the dining room, his parents sit waiting at the table, and Andrea's warm gaze meets mine as she gestures to the empty seats.

"Okay, Lexi. We're going to get straight to the point and not dance around things." She starts, her tone kind.

As much as I don't want to talk about this subject, I know it has to be done, so in a way I'm glad she's not beating around the bush.

Ayden seats me next to him, keeping his fingers entwined with mine with a grip that tells me he's not going to let go anytime soon.

"We have to contact the police to let them know you're safe." Peter speaks this time, and he lets the sentence hang in the air for a few moments before continuing. "They will most likely need to speak with you, and we can give them the pictures showing the evidence of the attack."

I nod. I know this has to happen. I may not like it, but I know there's no way to avoid it now. I also worry that Travis may have dobbed me in for vandalising the school, and the moment the cops know where I am, they'll come and take me away. But I can't run from this situation any longer, so I guess I'll just have to deal with that if and when it happens.

"Lexi, if it's okay with you, I'd like to let the authorities know that you're welcome to stay with us either here or at my sister's back in Fox Pines." Andrea offers.

"Thank you." I choke out, the gravel in my voice is evidence of my recent tears, and I work hard to let my gratitude show on my face.

"Do you have any other family that may want you to stay with them?" she asks, and I shake my head.

"My aunt Liz passed away a few years ago. The only other relative I have, which kind of doesn't count as a relative, is Mike's mum. She lives in Queensland."

Andrea and Peter nod in unison, taking in my words.

"Well, as I said, you're welcome here, but if there's someone else you prefer to stay with, then that's okay, too. We can arrange to take you wherever you need to go."

Ayden's hand squeezes mine a little tighter at Andrea's offer. I'm not sure if he meant to do it or not. It's almost as if he doesn't like the idea of me going to stay with someone else. Glancing at him, his eyes are already locked on my face like he's been watching me the entire time. He looks worried. Am I misinterpreting his concern? Maybe he's not concerned about me leaving, and really he's hoping I'll leave. It is asking a lot of him and his family to keep being put out because of me.

"Is that okay?" I whisper to him, "I can go to a friend's place back home if you prefer me to."

Before I even finish speaking, his head shakes, and Ayden moves closer to me like he's trying to block out his parents. "I don't want you being with anyone else, Lex. The thought of not knowing if you're safe terrifies me."

I'm momentarily breathless.

The honesty and rawness in his words succeed in prying a couple of tears out of me, and I see it then as I stare into his intense blue eyes. He really is terrified, almost desperate to keep me safe. I can see that this friendship between us means more to him than I realised. He's avoided sharing *that* truth with me, and I get the impression it has nothing to do with being shy and everything to do with timing. I imagine it's kind of hard to start something romantic with someone who you know has been assaulted in a way that will leave internal scars for a long time after the external ones have healed.

"I'll stay with you." I tell him. "Until you ask me to leave." I let a small smile slip through, hoping it and my words will wipe the panic from his face and it works. His face transforms into a pleasing smile.

Peter stands from the table, breaking the little bubble I'm in with his son. "I'll go make some calls and keep you updated with what's happening."

I turn and nod a thank you at him as he leaves the table, leaving Andrea looking concerned. Her eyes flick to Ayden, and I get the distinct impression her concern isn't for me. When she notices me examining her, she softens her expression, trying to hide what it was.

"There are salad rolls in the fridge if you two feel like eating."

"Thanks, mum." Ayden speaks for the both of us standing from his seat. I have no choice but to go with him since he hasn't let go of my hand, forcing me to trail behind him as he collects the salad rolls and a couple of water bottles from the fridge before leading me back to his room.

We eat in comfortable silence on his bed. Well, he eats. I just take a few bites and then kind of pick at the roll before putting it aside on the bedside table. Looking around the room, which has become my sanctuary, I take in the modern décor splashed with grey and orange tones and white furnishings that hint at his father's wealth.

This room is a contradiction to the room he lives in above his aunty's garage at Fox Pines. The furniture there looks like miss-matched hand-me-downs passed around a few different family members over the years.

Ayden's bed there is probably the only thing that appears as if it came from the life he has here in the city. It's just as cosy and is dressed in the same quality sheets. I wonder if he secretly hates living in something less than he has here with his dad?

"Penny for your thoughts." Ayden's warm voice breaks my mulling, and I glance at him as he wipes the corners of his mouth with his thumb, having just finished eating.

"You don't have a penny."

He nods, grinning. "True. How about a kiss for your thoughts?"

I freeze, internally fighting to keep my face from reacting. If I tell him what I was thinking, will he really kiss me?

God, I'm acting like I've never been kissed before.

"Sorry, that was inappropriate, given the circumstances." His face falls, guilt washing over his features.

Shit. I want that kiss, damn it!

"I was just thinking how your bedroom here is so different from your bedroom at Fox Pines," I blurt out in a rush. "I wondered if you feel uncomfortable at your aunty's because it's not so..." I don't know how to finish the sentence without it sounding like a putdown.

"So?" he asks. "Snobby? Stuck up?"

"What? No." I squeak, shifting to my knees to face him, and his laughter abruptly fills the room.

"Your face," he croaks in between laughs, "priceless."

"You arsehole!" I smack him on the shoulder, which just seems to make him laugh even more. He can't seem to stop laughing, and I fight hard not to join him, but I have a one-track mind, and I'm determined to get what I want.

"Ayden, I told you my thoughts. Now pay up."

He slowly stops laughing, sucking air deep into his lungs, his ocean eyes roaming my face.

He's quiet then, studying me as if to see signs of me joking around, but I lift a challenging brow and sit back on my heels, waiting patiently. I'm dead serious, and it shows on my face. I see the exact moment he realises it, too, because those hypnotising blue pools of his soften, and almost appear drunk.

His breathing deepens. I see it in my peripheral, my eyes remaining locked on his as I watch his blue gaze flick back and forth from my eyes to my mouth.

Playing with fire, I purposely dart my tongue out and lick my upper lip, hoping he'll get the message.

He does.

Lurching forward, his fingers grip the hair at my nape tugging me back up on my knees before his lips slam into mine. Heat rushes over my body as we press our chests together and my lips part, accepting his deliciously soft lips.

As he tilts my head with his hand in my hair, deepening the kiss, my hands have a mind of their own, tangling in his dark hair, tugging him closer even though there's no more room to move.

The moment our tongues meet for the first time, brushing together, we both moan, the sound carrying through the room.

I've been kissed several times since becoming a hormonal teenager. Most of the kisses I wanted. But none were like this. Never have I felt this pull. I can't seem to get enough of Ayden, and even this kiss doesn't feel like it's enough. I have an overwhelming urge to crawl under his skin. The thought is both exciting and terrifying because who the hell thinks like that?

Ayden's other hand slides over my back, his fingers grazing my skin where the jersey has risen. I stop thinking, my lips just as hungry as his, and we somehow end up horizontal on his bed.

The way his body presses me into the mattress only makes me more frenzied, my body lighting on fire with a heat I've never felt before. Well, with someone else in the room, anyway.

"Ayden?" Peter's voice suddenly cracks through our lust-filled haze, and I'm hit with cold air as Ayden pushes away from me, quickly taking his delicious body heat with him.

I sit up just as fast, trying to look like I hadn't nearly been caught before the bedroom door opens, and Peter pops his head in.

"Ah, Lexi. I spoke with Officer Reynolds from the Fox Pines Police Department. He'll be here in a few hours with someone from Child Services."

"What!" I cry, leaping up off the bed as fear grips me at the thought of being taken away.

Peter's eyes widen at my reaction and he holds his hand up. "It's okay. They just need to speak with you about what happened at your home, and to make sure you are in good care here with us."

"They won't take her away, right?" Ayden snaps, sounding just as worried as I feel.

"No." Peter gives his head a shake. "They'll most likely ask if this is where Lexi wants to be, and probably want to make sure we aren't holding her against her will."

I know Peter is sure about what he's saying, but the adults in my life have always managed to let me down and just put me in more danger. The urge to run is making me twitchy, my heart hammering against my chest.

"Thanks, dad. Maybe Lex should have a rest before they get here." Ayden suggests and his dad glances between the two of us before nodding and leaving the room.

Frantically, my eyes dart around the room, trying to assess how quickly I can get out of here.

"Lex?"

I find my bag and start packing my stray clothes into it.

"Lex." Ayden gently grips my upper arm, pulling me up from where I'm now kneeling on the floor. "Stop."

I shake my head, not able to find words, my gaze dropping back down to the bag of clothes.

"I won't let them take you away from me." He states, his tone certain and I glance back up to see his eyes filled with determination.

"What if you can't stop them?" I whisper, my eyes flooding so fast that his blue pools turn blurry.

"The only way anyone is taking you away from me is if they kill me first. I'm not going to let it happen, so stop trying to figure out an escape plan and just let my family help you."

His words send the tears tumbling from my eyes, and my fear is trying to rule me right now and I don't know what to do.

"I- I'm not a fan of letting people help, Ayden." I admit quietly. "They usually end up letting me down."

Sorrow fills his eyes as he cups my face, his thumb wiping over my healing bruise. "I'm so sorry that's happened to you. It eats at me to know you've been treated that way. I want to kill every fucker that has ever wronged you." His other hand comes up to cup the other side of my face as he steps even closer. "But believe me please when I say we want to help you. And we *will* help you, Lex. I promise I'll never let you down."

"You can't promise that, Ayden." I try to step away from him, but he doesn't let go of me, and his grip on me tells me he doesn't intend to anytime soon.

"I *can*, and I *will* promise that." He breathes so close now, his ocean eyes dancing between mine. "Please don't push me away because you're scared. Instead, let me comfort you. Let me keep you safe." He releases one side of my face to brush back some unruly strands of my hair before adding. "Let me protect you."

I'm not sure how he might do all of that, but my heart sure wants to let him try. It's a risk, but where Ayden is concerned, I can't seem to see reason, so I nod in his palm.

Relief instantly washes over his features before I'm pulled to his chest in a hug that I could happily drown in.

If only his hug could take all of my problems away.

Twenty-Two

Officer Reynolds is a burly man with greying hair and a thickening waistline. His partner, Officer Zimora, is at least twenty years younger and looks like he spends every spare minute he has away from work, lifting weights at the gym. The woman with them is from the Department of Health and Human Services. This is the lady that acts in the best interest of children, apparently. She looks more like a hippy than a government worker.

I'm nervous with all the eyes on me, studying me. It's weird having these people filling the space in Peter's living room. It's also strange that I think that since this isn't even my home. I hadn't realised how comfortable I felt here with them until now.

The gentle squeeze of Ayden's hand in mine reminds me he has my back, and I swallow the lump in my throat before speaking, reluctantly re-telling the nightmare I'd rather bury deep and never speak of again.

When my emotions consume me, Ayden rubs my back, trying to soothe away the tears. I'm so grateful that I gave in to his attention towards me in the beginning, which seems like so long ago, yet a week hasn't even passed. If Ayden wasn't in my life, then I'm positive I'd be dead by now.

"May we see the photos of Alexis when she first came to you?" Claudia, the Child Services hippy, asks Andrea, who nods, placing her laptop in front of Claudia and the officers on the coffee table.

As they scroll through the pictures, my body heats with humiliation. I know we took the photos for this purpose, but now that I know they are being viewed, I feel so exposed. The officers' faces show no emotion while they look on, but Claudia doesn't seem to have a poker face, and what she sees affects her.

"Alexis, do you mind if we speak in private?" Claudia asks, and I shake my head before she even finishes.

"No need. Any questions you have can be asked in front of the Mitchells."

"Are you sure, sweetie? I need to ask you some fairly personal questions." Claudia glances between me and Ayden's parents, who are looking to me for direction.

"Yes," I nod. "I've already told them everything. There's nothing I need to hide from them."

Claudia nods and clears her throat. "Can I have your permission to arrange a rape test?"

"What? No!" I hiss, panic filling me, and I nearly leap from the damn couch but Ayden rubs my back again, keeping me calm enough not to flee... for now.

There's this strange pull between us. Like an invisible rope connecting us, and when he offers me comfort, my body responds, but I can feel there's a very fine line

I'm balancing on. At any moment I could tip, and if it's in the other direction I don't think even Ayden can stop me from falling.

"Alexis, if you were sexually assaulted then we need to do one." Claudia continues and my cheeks flare with the anger boiling up inside me.

"I told you everything already. What makes you think I need a rape test?" I sound like an ungrateful bitch, but my hackles are up, so I don't give a shit right now. I'm pissed off because this is just another adult who isn't listening to me.

"I thought perhaps you might have left some details out given the company in the room, which is why I asked to speak with you in private." Claudia sounds genuine in her answer, but it still pisses me off.

"I didn't leave anything out. I told you exactly what Mike did to me, what my dad did. While we are at it, how about what my Principal did? He turned a blind eye when my dad sprouted lies, saying I was mentally unstable. The Principal stood by and let my dad drug me and take me away against my will. I pleaded with him for help, but he didn't listen. What I need is for the adults in my life to stop doing wrong by me. Please tell me you aren't like them?" I snap, not willing to sit by and let this happen again.

"No, Miss West, I'm not like them. I'm so sorry you've experienced such disgusting behaviour from the people you should be able to trust. I'll certainly look into everything you have told me." Claudia's statement is strong and honest as far as I can tell, so I nod, letting her know I accept what she's saying.

"Miss West," Officer Reynolds gains my attention, "we still haven't been able to apprehend your brother Mike, but we have spoken with your father over the phone. Given the information you have told us, I think we have grounds to charge him as well." He turns to address Ayden's parents, "Mrs Mitchell, you said you've located Mrs West in a hospital in the city, is that correct?"

"Yes, that's right. Lexi's mum was transferred to the city from the Fox Pines Hospital. However, there must have been an error in her paperwork because she never ended up at the record's destination. I've since managed to locate her at Richmond Circle Psychiatric Hospital. Her records have a 'no visitors' rule on them. I've been trying to get Lexi approved to see her mum, but I keep getting the run-around. The whole thing seems a little odd to me."

"Given the fact she's a key witness, I'll be able to get in to see Mrs West and question her. We will see if we can get Alexis approved to visit with her mother." Officer Reynolds confirms and Andrea smiles warmly at him.

"Thank you," Andrea and I say at the same time, and she shoots me a small smile that warms the edges of my bitter heart.

"Alexis would like to stay with us," Ayden announces, drawing everyone's attention. It's weird to hear him call me by my actual name. I hate *that* name because of how my family uses it when they're inflicting their cruel, selfish, and twisted ways on me. However, Ayden says it with such warmth that I don't entirely hate the sound of it falling from his lips.

"Is that what you want to do, Alexis?" Officer Reynolds asks.

I nod, trying to focus on the conversation and not the way Ayden affects me. "Yes, please."

Claudia nods and looks at Ayden's parents. "Are you happy with this arrangement?"

"Yes," Peter says without a doubt. "If this is where Lexi would like to be, then we are more than happy to accommodate her and keep her safe. Given that her brother is still on the loose, we thought perhaps she should stay here in the city a little longer to lie low. Once it's no longer an issue, then Lexi is welcome to stay with my wife at her sister's in Fox Pines so she can return to school."

"That sounds great, although it may be a good idea for you to reach out to your teachers, Alexis. Perhaps they can send you work, so you don't fall behind?" Claudia recommends and I nod.

As much as school isn't a priority right now, I know I need to make it one so I don't fail the school year. Failing is the last thing I need if I ever want to get away from my parents and make a life of my own.

"Well, I think we can work with this information." Officer Reynolds stands from the couch, and the others follow.

"Can you please forward those pictures to this email address?" Officer Zimora speaks for the first time, handing Andrea a card.

"Yes, certainly," she nods.

"Wait!" I call as my mind goes back to the news report we saw on the TV earlier. "Where did you get the video footage of what happened?"

I have my suspicions, but I want to know for sure.

Officer Reynolds looks to Officer Zimora for the answer. "Oh, your neighbour, the young girl Valarie. It seems she's a bit of a sticky nose when it comes to you."

I nod, fighting a grin. I knew it—bloody Valarie. I should be thankful, I guess, but I'm not happy that my private hell has been broadcast on national television.

"You know her well?" Claudia asks.

"Kind of," I shrug. "Maybe not well, but she's been around when things weren't ideal. I guess she's my little guardian angel."

"Seems that way. She went to her mother for help. That's who called triple zero." Officer Zimora's deep voice is one that commands attention when he speaks, yet he carries a smile to melt the panties off all the girls. Especially in that uniform.

"Why would your neighbour have a video of what happened?" Ayden asks, confused, and I shrug.

"Young Valarie has quite the setup in her bedroom," Officer Zimora explains. "With her corner window, she has a good view over the street as well as your house, Alexis. It turns out she's been recording the comings and goings of your family as well as some of the other neighbours. But don't worry, we've spoken with her parents in regards to the seriousness of respecting the privacy of others. I guess in this case, we should be thankful, as the footage is so graphic and damning. There's no way your brother will be able to get out of the charges. He'll be going to prison for a long time when we catch up with him."

I hate that everyone knows now, but maybe the video footage is a good thing after all. If it helps keep Mike away from me, then I'm all for it.

Andrea and Peter usher the authorities out of the apartment while I remain standing in the living room, exhausted and numb.

"You're a perv." Ayden's warm breath whispers over my ear, snapping me back to reality.

"What?" Turning, I see a ridiculous shit-eating grin spread across his face.

"You think Officer Zimora is hot?" He wags his dark eyebrows.

"What? No!" Needing to avoid the truth and my embarrassing red face, I stalk off back towards the kitchen.

"Yes you do."

I roll my eyes even though he can't see it as I continue forward, weaving through the kitchen and towards his bedroom.

"You can't escape me." Ayden's playful tone gets closer, so I run knowing he's doing this to take my mind off the heavy crap going on in my life.

Heavy feet pound the carpeted floor behind me as I burst through his bedroom door with him on my heels. The door slams shut right before strong arms wrap around my waist, and I'm tackled onto the bed.

Tears run down my cheeks as laughter spills from me, a sound and feeling that's foreign lately.

Ayden's light chuckle matches mine, warming my heart, and in a tangle of arms and legs, I somehow end up pinned under the weight of his body with his face close to mine.

"Just admit it," Ayden chokes out between chuckles. "You think that cop is hot."

"Never. I won't admit it." I shake my head, trying to squirm underneath his heavy weight. The move causes more friction between our bodies, igniting a fire within me. Just as affected, Ayden's deep laughter stops, his smile turning serious as his ocean eyes turn dark, settling on my lips.

All thoughts of Officer, whatever his name is, vanish as we both stare at each other, breathing deeply, trying to keep our control. Hypnotised by lust and the need to show each other how we feel pushes us towards a line, that if we cross, will change what we have together.

I'm not sure if I'm ready for that. The searing heat pumping through my veins tells me my body is ready. My heart's desire to have his kisses and his touch is stronger than my need to breathe.

A memory suddenly bursts into my brain, of rough hands and crude acts.

"Looks like you'll be learning the hard way."
The gravel of his wet tongue runs up the side
of my face, and I gag, not able to control the
reaction. For that, his hand slaps across the
side of my face.

"Hurry the fuck up and get naked."
I beg him to stop but he responds with his
fist, slamming into my cheek.
"Get your fucking clothes off, Ali!"

"Wash those perky little tits. Wash them nice
and slow." His jeans are around his ankles
and his hand is stroking himself.

My heart races for all the wrong reasons, and I can no longer get air into my lungs. I try to breathe, but nothing happens, and my surroundings become fuzzy as panic sets in. The room becomes suffocating as if the walls, floor, and ceiling are all closing in on me.

The weight over my body disappears, and I'm pulled up to sit, my hands automatically swinging out, trying to push away.

"Shh, Lex, it's okay. Shh."

Ayden's voice is soothing. I try to focus on it instead of the images flashing through my mind.

Mike.

His face.

The feel and smell of his vile breath.

The way he used his hand on himself while he watched me, naked and vomiting.

Why is this happening now? Ayden and I kissed earlier today, and I was fine. Now I'm consumed by the burn of my lungs as they struggle to get air, while Mike's revolting face and parts of his body that I never wanted to see engulf my mind.

Warm hands cup my face, and I fight the urge to bat them away.

It's okay. I'm safe!

"Lexi, baby, calm down, please. Breathe for me."

I'm trying to breathe, but it's not working. The burn in my chest is a raging fire, and I feel like I'm going to choke.

"Lex, listen to my voice. Can you hear me?" He sounds so scared. His usually calm, confident tone has vanished. I don't like that. I don't want to hear his voice sounding so frightened. It hurts my heart almost worse than the burning in my lungs, so I focus on what he said. He told me to listen to his voice. He asked me if I can hear him.

I can, so I force my head to move and nod.

"Okay, good. Can you feel me, Lex? I'm touching your face. Can you feel that?"

I can. I can feel his warm hands. They are gentle and soft, and I don't want them to leave. He has caring hands that deliver magical currents over my skin. I love these hands, and I *need* these hands, so I nod again, still fighting to breathe.

"Can you see me, Lexi?"

Can I see him? Blinking my eyes, I urge them to focus, but they don't. I can't see anything. Why can't I see him?

"Blink your eyes more, baby. Clear away the tears. Try to see me."

I blink rapidly, focusing on his voice, which doesn't sound as scared as before. I continue to blink until my blurred vision begins to clear. The room slowly morphs into focus, and then my sight is dominated by the most caring face I've ever seen.

Ayden.

"Can you see me?"

Nodding, I feel the air slowly seep into my lungs, but it's not enough.

Ayden smiles, happy I can see him, his eyes showing overwhelming care, a sight I could easily get addicted to seeing.

"Lexi, use your nose now. Can you smell me? I probably smell like boy cooties, but can you smell it?"

His eyes dart between each of mine, an edge of desperation in his expression. I focus on him as I try to make my nose work, and when it does, the intoxicating scent of Ayden engulfs me.

"That's it. Can you smell me?"

I nod again, still cupped between his palms.

"Pretty yuck, hey?" His grin is adorable, the dimple on the left of his mouth caving in. I shake my head in disagreement. He smells good enough to eat.

It takes a moment to comprehend that I'm breathing again, my lungs filling with the air they so desperately need. As Ayden continues to study my face, reality creeps in, and I realise that I just had some fucked up version of a panic attack.

Shit.

My expression must change because Ayden's grip on my face tightens, and he ducks to get in my line of sight.

"It's okay, Lex."

"N-no, it's n-not." I can't hide the tremble in my voice, nor hide the fact that I sound like a chain smoker right now with the husky rasp it brings.

"Seriously, Lex. After what you've been through, what just happened is understandable. Please don't beat yourself up about this."

His compassion is overwhelming. I'm not used to anyone paying me so much attention, but here he is, giving me more than I deserve. Tears spill from my eyes, and he wipes them away with the pad of his thumbs.

"I don't deserve you," I whisper, believing the words.

"Jesus, Lexi. I'm the one who doesn't deserve you. You are so beautiful, so strong and fierce. I'm batting way above my average. I'm lucky to have someone like you give me your time."

Well, shit. How can I argue with that? Why would I want to? I'm a selfish person, and I want him in my life even if I'm not worthy.

"Kiss." It's all I can say.

"Kiss?" he asks, still holding my face in his hands, his brow furrowed in confusion.

"Kiss." I nod.

His brows rise before a grin lights up his face. "Ahhh, kiss." He nods knowingly before moving in to press his lips to mine.

Twenty-Three

♥

I'm tired—exhausted. I can't seem to get enough sleep. The more I sleep, the more I seem to need. Darkness weighs heavily on me like chains pulling me down to the bottom of the deepest, darkest ocean. I don't want to be here in this abyss, but I can't seem to find my way out. Deception, lies, and crude acts consume my thoughts, making me wish I wasn't me. Making me wish I didn't exist to endure such cruelty.

Everyone knows. All my friends from school. The teachers. The neighbours. They all know.

I never wanted anyone to know. Never believed it would get as bad as it did either. I'd hoped I could hold the facade of a carefree teenager long enough to get through school and then get the hell out of Fox Pines.

I should be thankful to Valarie for trying to help, but her attempt to help just means I have no choice but to be someone different.

Now my friends will look at me as the girl whose brother assaulted her and whose dad allowed it to happen. There's a chance my friends will be disgusted by me and will rid themselves of our friendship. After all, I'm as vile as all the other school outcasts that my friends regard as nothing more than trash.

That's who I am now.

I'm the freak no longer worthy of their time.

"I didn't last long on the motorbike with my dad. We got maybe one hundred metres before hitting a rock, and we both flew over the handlebars."

Ayden's been telling me stories from his childhood. We are in his bed, where I haven't moved since last night, while he holds me close, sharing stories with me, being the lifeline that is saving me from falling completely into the never ending darkness.

I haven't spoken. I can't seem to find my voice, but he continues to tell me stories, somehow knowing it's helping me.

"Mum completely lost her shit, running and screaming after us. She was pissed when she found us rolling around on the ground laughing, covered in mud. It was fun. That's when I knew I loved that sort of thing. Activities that have an element of danger."

He speaks more of the antics he got up to with his dad. It's nice to hear. Sometimes I manage to pull myself out of the pitch black hole of nothingness enough to focus on his stories, and other times, the darkness is too suffocating.

His parents pop in to check on me throughout the day. They offer to call a doctor to come and check on me, and my only response is a shake of my head.

I'm not entirely sure, but my guess is that I've completely lost my marbles as a result of having to retell my nightmare to the authorities yesterday.

The memories are too much.

The need to close my eyes and sleep is paralysing, and the times I submit to the demand, I'm not sure if I'll ever be able to force my way back to reality again.

That's how I spend my Sunday with Ayden.

Numb. Consumed by darkness.

Fortunately, when I wake early Monday morning, I'm relieved to find the black hole I was in has ebbed and is now just a lingering shadow, allowing a little light in.

The chill of the morning air fills Ayden's room, and all I can hear is his slow, steady breathing as he sleeps soundly next to me.

Shit. A girl could get used to this.

I'm used to mostly always being alone. Having to always have eyes in the back of my head to protect myself. Never feeling safe.

Being here with Ayden, knowing he's watching my back. Knowing he wants to protect me is... something else. Something I crave so much it nearly hurts.

Sitting up carefully so I don't wake him, I stare at his peaceful face, feeling something warm inside my chest when I study him. It's kind of overwhelming how my heart seems almost happy and sad at the same time. It both hurts and feels good, which is nothing short of confusing.

The need to pee stops me from ogling Ayden, so I carefully slide off the bed and lock myself in the bathroom. Showering feels fantastic, the heat soothing my healing body. What isn't fantastic is the time I have to think while showering.

Ugh. I hate my stupid brain right now.

Why can't I just switch it off? Why does it want to torture me all the time, especially when I shower?

I hate Mike for ruining showers for me!

I attempt to focus on something else, and my mind goes to the bits and pieces of stories Ayden told me yesterday, trying to imagine him as a kid running around, causing havoc with his dad.

I'm jealous. I never had what he has with his dad. I never will. Not even my mum has made the time to create fun memories with me. The most fun we ever had was when she came home smoking a joint after a night out with her friends last year, and that only lasted for an hour before she passed out and then forgot about the laughs we had when she woke the next day.

Sick of my thoughts, I finish up in the shower and try to make myself look presentable. Not for the first time, I curse the mirror for being so efficient at showing me my hideous reflection. Although the swelling has gone down, the still healing bruises on the side of my face are an ugly reminder of the hell I escaped.

I have no makeup with me to even attempt to cover the evidence Mike left on my face. Nor do I have my purse, so I can go shopping to buy some.

Ugh, everything just sucks dog's balls!

Knowing my mood won't improve if I continue to look at my reflection, I throw my hair up in a messy bun and get dressed in my black skinny jeans and Ayden's hoodie before slipping back into his room to find him still sound asleep.

My nose alerts me to the delicious smell of bacon, so I decide to let Ayden sleep and follow the smell into the kitchen.

In the kitchen, I find Andrea cooking some scrambled eggs to go with the bacon, which smells divine, nearly making me moan out loud.

"Good morning, Lexi." Her smile is warm as her eyes follow me. "Hungry?"

"Can you adopt me?" I ask and Andrea chuckles at my question, not realising how serious I am.

Well, maybe not, but hey, she's offering me bacon.

"You're pretty hungry, hey?"

Joining me at the table, Andrea hands me a plate of heaven, and we both tuck in like we're starved animals.

The silence is easy as we eat. I find I'm quite comfortable with her, and I'm not sure if it's because she reminds me so much of Ayden, or if I just trust her that much.

"Yesterday was a tough day." Andrea breaks the silence, going straight for the hard truth.

If there's one thing I've learnt about Ayden's mum, it's that she doesn't beat around the bush.

Nodding in response, I feel my face heat with embarrassment.

"I'll be honest Lexi, I was a little worried there for a while. Does that happen often?" She's referring to my comatose state.

I'm good at denial. I was going to play that card for the entire day, but Andrea isn't likely to let this drop, so there's no escaping her question.

"No," I shake my head and stare at my food, not wanting to read her thoughts in her expression. "Honestly, I don't think I've ever felt safe enough to let myself feel that much..." I struggle to finish the sentence.

"Pain?" Andrea understands with a nod.

She's quiet for a few moments, her eyes roaming my face as she thinks.

Is this what normal mums are like? Abbey's mum isn't like Andrea, though, so perhaps she's just something special.

"So if you had let yourself feel that level of pain in the past, you would've made yourself vulnerable to your brother?" Yep, she understands.

Nausea rolls the eggs I just ate, and my breathing deepens as I try to help it pass. Throwing up right now wouldn't be ideal. Also, wasting the delicious food that Andrea cooked should be considered illegal.

I give Andrea another nod, feeling the shame I wear like a glove these days. I don't want to talk about this stuff. Not now. Not ever.

Once again, all I want is to be out of this situation, and the urge to flee nudges my control.

Sighing, Andrea reaches across the table, taking my hand. "Lexi, I don't know if you need to hear this, but I'm so sorry all of this has happened to you. I'm sorry you haven't had parents that protect you the way you deserve." Her eyes glass over as if she may cry. "I am, however, glad you feel safe enough here with us to let go and feel what you need to feel. It may not seem like it, but you need to let yourself feel all the pain in order to heal."

Tears bead and fall from my eyes before I even realise.

"It hurts so much. I don't want to feel it," I whisper, and she gives my hand a gentle squeeze.

"I know you don't, and I know you don't want to talk about it either, but talking will help."

I nod again because, apparently, that's all I know how to do.

Peter enters the kitchen, humming to himself, so I wipe away my tears while he's busy drooling over the pan of bacon on the bench, and Andrea and I turn our attention back to our plates.

Someone once told me that we can't control the actions of others, but we can control how we react to their actions. At the time, I didn't know what those words meant, but now I do.

I can let the vulgar things Mike did control me, and turn me into a scared shell of myself, or I can stand tall and refuse to let it break me.

Sounds easy enough, right?

I wish I could find the strength to take my own advice right in this moment. Perhaps over time I will, but right now, I feel so raw and exposed, like all of my weaknesses are on display to the world.

Baby steps, Lexi.

How can I try to take back control of my life today?

I immediately think of how I can't stand to look at my reflection. Every time I see myself, I'm reminded of what Mike did. I'm sick of seeing it, and I want to feel less like a monster. In order to do that, though, I'm going to need a shit load of makeup. I know it's not a world changing step, but feeling a little more human in my own skin will help me feel like I have some sort of control.

I wouldn't exactly call myself vain, but I've never hated my looks and kind of think I'm pretty. Well, I *was* pretty until Mike turned my face into a swollen purple and green ogre.

I hate that fucker!

"Excuse me, Andrea?" I ask, clearing my throat as I summon up the courage to ask for help. "I don't suppose you have any foundation that might cover some of this bruising?"

I instantly feel self conscious for asking for help. I don't know why it's hard for me to do, but right now, I'm not foolish enough to think I can do this shit on my own.

Andrea shakes her head. "I'm sorry, sweetie. I left everything back in Fox Pines."

"We can go to the shops today, Lex." Ayden takes that moment to join us in the kitchen, popping down in the seat next to me.

I have to stop myself from leaning into him when his scent wraps around me. The pull he has on me is ridiculous.

Facing me with his knees on either side of my chair, he keeps his focus solely on studying my face. He's trying to read me, needing to check how I'm doing after being a depressed zombie yesterday.

I hate that I was too weak to fight it. I hate that he witnessed me at my lowest. No one wants to see that shit. Surely he's changed his mind about me and wants to bolt screaming in the other direction.

And there it is again. The self-loathing arsehole that sits on my shoulder, whispering its negativity in my mind, trying to pull me back down.

Take control, Lexi.

Attempting to take my own advice, I give Ayden a small smile, hoping he'll see I'm okay and not a complete nut job. I'm instantly rewarded with his smile, the damn thing having the power to make my face light up like a beacon once again. Naturally, I duck my head, not wanting to show the effect he has on me.

"I told you to stop trying to hide that from me." His whisper sends a shiver up my spine, his breath warm on the side of my face, making my cheeks heat even more.

"Stop it." I whisper playfully, slapping his knee, and feign ignorance at his flirting in front of his parents.

When I check to see if they saw, I find Andrea has moved over to the kitchen counter, talking to Peter in hushed tones.

Ayden's chuckle gains my attention again.

"No way. Not going to happen. The way you respond to me is just too beautiful."

God damn it, now I'm blushing even more. This guy is turning me into mush, and I'm helpless to stop it.

Worried I might self combust at any moment, I revert the conversation to what he said when he walked into the room.

"I don't have any money on me to buy makeup." I admit and he grins.

"Changing the subject, I see."

"Ayden, stop being weird," Andrea says, wiping the grin off Ayden's face. "Lexi, honey, I can give you some money."

"Oh no, I can't take money off you, but thank you for the offer."

"Bullshit, yes she can," Ayden huffs, standing from the chair and heading over to the kitchen counter to steal a slice of bacon off his dad's plate.

"Seriously, Ayden, do you have to swear?" Andrea scolds with her hands on her hips. Her serious expression is quickly replaced with a frustrated smile as Ayden gives her a toothy grin around the slice of bacon in his mouth. She shakes her head, turning her attention back to me.

"It's no problem at all, honey. If it makes you feel better, we can pretend it's a loan." Andrea gives me a wink, and Ayden looks over at me, smiling and nodding like he's proud of himself.

Adorable smug arsehole!

Knowing I won't win this argument, I thank Andrea when she passes me some folded fifty dollar notes, and I slide them into the back pocket of my jeans. After

Ayden has his fill of bacon and eggs, he gets ready quickly, and we walk the six blocks to the Melbourne Central Shopping Centre.

Ayden holds my hand as we walk, my fingers linked tightly in his, helping me feel safe and cared for. As we get deeper into the city, the crowds grow thicker, and he tugs me close while we weave our way through the hordes of people.

I'm still wearing his hoodie. It's too big for me, but the comfort it brings, outweighs my need to look fashionable right now. Not to mention, having his scent wrapped around me is calming for my jittery nerves.

Even though we are walking the streets of Melbourne, and not Fox Pines, I'm still anxious that I'm going to run into my dad or that my brother is going to jump out from around every corner.

Mike still hasn't been found by the police, and as far as I know, my dad is still in the city. The thought of seeing their faces again makes me feel sick to my stomach, so I try my best not to think about them and just enjoy my time with Ayden.

Reaching the shopping centre, I let Ayden continue to lead the way since he seems to be on a mission. Before I know it, we are standing outside a Sephora store, the same one Abbey and I snuck off to when we were at City camp last year.

"You know, it's kind of concerning that you know exactly where this shop is." I grin at Ayden and he gives me a wink.

"I'm not just a pretty face. Come on, let's go make you feel a little more human."

I can't contain my smile as we walk into the store. He always seems to know what I'm thinking or how to put a smile on my face.

Like the last time I was in this store, I'm overwhelmed with the number of options before me. We roam the aisles before I spot a brand I recognise from a YouTube tutorial I saw last month. That will do.

I test out the foundation on my skin and realise I'm going to need more than just a foundation to cover up the bruising. Ayden must notice my dilemma and moves away from me to speak to one of the store girls. A brief conversation and some colour testing later, and I have a little bag filled with foundation, concealer, and skincare goodies that Ayden insists on paying for, even though his mum gave me money.

The need to have people stop staring at my battered face consumes me, so Ayden waits patiently outside the restrooms with all the other boyfriends and husbands while I tend to my face.

I try my best to make myself appear somewhat normal with the makeup Ayden just bought me, and once I'm done, I have to admit, it's worked. It's a little hard to look completely normal with the slight swelling still there, and the healing cut on my cheek, but I figure it's better than nothing.

Feeling more human than I have in days helps me to hold my head a little higher by the time I get back to Ayden.

"Feel better?" He grins as I approach, and I won't lie. The way he watches me sends all sorts of girly butterflies fluttering through my tummy. It does wonders for my confidence, which has been on hiatus for a while now.

"Kinda." I shrug, smiling back.

Ayden steps into my personal space, leaning in to place a gentle kiss on my forehead before linking his fingers with mine. Even though I know I don't look great, Ayden has a way of making me feel like the most beautiful girl in the room. It's an unfamiliar feeling, but one I hope to experience again.

Our conversation is light as we wander through the shopping centre. I bring up some of the stories I can vaguely remember him telling me the night before, and he fills in the blanks, never once making me feel bad for shutting down yesterday.

For a short time, as we fill our day window shopping, I feel like a normal girl.

Walking past a communications store, I'm reminded that my dad took my phone. It was a calculated move on his part. A way to ensure I couldn't reach out for help. It's also a small form of torture to take a teenage girl's phone away from her. Does that man have a death wish?

Ayden has been letting me use his phone the few times I asked, and as much as I appreciate it, not having my own phone is just another reminder of the control I have lost, so I pull him towards the shop.

"Where are you taking me?" He asks through a chuckle, and I grin at him over my shoulder.

"I need to get a new phone." I stop in front of the shop window, eyeing the display of phones available.

"If you like, you can have my old phone. It's in my room at dad's place. It works fine, so we can just grab you a new sim card, and you can use that."

Dragging my gaze from the display, I frown up at Ayden. "If your old phone works fine, why did you get a new one?"

Ayden shrugs. "The new model came out, and I wanted it."

"Oh." I mutter, kind of annoyed.

I have no idea what it would be like just to get something because I want it. Most of the things I have or do are out of necessity. It's not even from lack of family money, just lack of my parents giving me any, instead keeping it for themselves.

Ayden ignores my frown and leads the way into the store. Taking charge, he organises the new sim card, and pre-purchases credit for me, once again not accepting the money his mum gave me, and instead, using his own.

"Ayden, you can't keep paying for things. Your mum gave me money." I pull the notes from my back pocket and shove them to his chest after we step out of the store, but he bats my hand away.

"Just hang on to it, Lex. You might need other things at some stage. At least then you'll have some cash and won't get all worried about having to ask my mum for more. Not that she'd care." He grabs my free hand and starts walking, effectively ending the conversation, and I roll my eyes and move with him, not in the mood to argue.

As we walk, I feel his eyes shift to me frequently, which eventually ignites the fire in my cheeks, causing him to chuckle. The smart arse is doing it on purpose. I would've slapped that grin off his adorable face, with love of course, if we weren't walking the streets of Melbourne.

I can't stop darting my gaze everywhere, waiting for something bad to happen, and Ayden notices, giving my shoulder a nudge with his, even as his linked fingers squeeze mine a little tighter.

"It makes you nervous walking around the city, doesn't it?" he asks, and I nod, feeling embarrassed that once again, I'm so easy to read. "You know I won't let anything happen to you, right?" Again he gives my hand a squeeze and I glance up at him as we walk, noticing how serious he is.

I believe *he* believes he can keep me safe.

"Yep," I give him a small smile, hoping it's convincing.

Ayden stops abruptly and spins me around, pulling me to his chest, and the move is so abrupt that a gasp flies from my parted lips.

"I will never let anyone hurt you again, Lex." His voice is low, husky, and serious as his warm hands cup either side of my face, and he gently brushes his thumb across my unharmed cheek.

The city-goers scurry around us, not paying us any attention, almost like we are nothing more than a post in the middle of a path, but I hardly notice them as Ayden's ocean eyes draw me in, and the fire in them holds me captive.

"I know," I whisper, "I'm sorry."

He frowns. "Babe, don't be sorry. I just want you to know without a doubt that I'll do anything to keep you safe."

Babe. Did he just call me babe? The endearment makes a grin tug at the corner of my mouth.

"Something amuse you?" His eyes give away that he already knows what caused my reaction.

"Babe?" I ask.

Smiling, he licks his lips and leans in, brushing mine briefly before he deepens the kiss. I clutch at his hoodie while the feel of his warm, soft lips heat me from the inside.

Honestly, we must look ridiculous standing in the middle of a city path, kissing while people rush around us.

I should care, right?

I don't, though. I can't seem to find a care in the world right in this moment.

Deepening the kiss again, Ayden's tongue invades my mouth, wringing a moan from me. Releasing my hold of his hoodie with one hand, I weave my fingers into his hair, desperate to pull him closer while on the tips of my toes, trying to stretch up and meet his height. I don't know how long we stand there in our own little bubble, exploring each other's mouths, building this undeniable heat between us, but it eventually gets too much for me to continue doing it in public, and I reluctantly break the kiss.

"Shit, sorry, Lex." Almost panting, Ayden still holds my head in his hands, and I can't help but smile.

"Never apologise for that." I advise and he grins knowing I've thrown his own words back at him.

"I didn't get too carried away then?" The concern etched across his face is adorable.

"No, you didn't, but I don't think it would have stayed legal had we kept kissing like that." I grin and his lips spread wide.

That smile. If I thought I'd seen him smile before, then I was wrong. This smile lights up his whole face. His slightly puffy, well-kissed lips extend up and out, showing his pearly white teeth and a dimple in each cheek.

"Jesus Ayden, that smile is lethal."

His dark brows shoot up before he throws his head back, laughing. "You are," he speaks between laughs, "fucking adorable."

"Oh, shut up." I smack him on the arm and spin, stalking off.

He catches up quickly, linking his fingers with mine again, still wearing a cheesy grin. "What? You don't like being adorable?"

"Would you?" I attempt to keep a straight face.

"Only if it's you thinking it." He's such a cocky dick, and I gotta admit. I love it.

Biting his lower lip as his blue gaze locks on to mine again, I feel a buzz of heat between my legs and have to fight the urge to rub my thighs together.

"Fuck, Lex. I could kiss you all day."

A whimper escapes me that I have no chance of stopping, and he takes my hand, leading us up the path in the direction of his dad's apartment with urgency. When his eyes meet mine again, the ocean blue has turned into a dark storm, and his voice is so deep and husky that I feel moisture pool between my legs.

"We need to get back before I really do something that will get us arrested."

I nod in agreement because the visceral reaction I'm having to him isn't something I've had before, and I'm almost scared of how far I'd let myself go. Even in public.

Twenty-Four

With the way I was almost self combusting on the walk back, I'd kind of thought we might hide away in Ayden's bedroom, but Ayden had other ideas, and after getting food he set us up in the cosy living area to watch more Netflix.

Am I disappointed? Yes, a little, but I really should stop being a hornbag.

I don't pay much attention to the movie on the screen, too busy setting up Ayden's hand-me-down phone and reloading all of my apps. As I go through logging into each social media account, a string of message notifications pop up, and unable to beat my curiosity, I start reading through them.

Not so sweet Catholic Girls Group

Tasha-Pritchard
Uh- Lexi. Did I really just see a news report about you? WTF is going on?

Allison-May

That was totally Lexi's house. Where are you, Lexi?

Sophie-Smig

My mum drove past, and the street is blocked off. Abbey, WTF is happening with Lexi?

Abbey-Delany

All you need to know is that Lexi is safe now.

Tasha-Pritchard

You knew about this and didn't say anything?

Abbey-Delany

It's not my story to tell, Tasha!

I always knew Tasha was a bitch. She'd be pissed off if I died suddenly and didn't let her know beforehand. I contemplate telling her what I think, but decide against it and just send a simple message.

Lexi-West
I'll be okay X

There are a few private messages from Marcus checking in with me, asking if I'm coping alright. I respond with the same message I sent the girls' group chat and move on to the boys' group chat. I don't know what I was expecting, but it wasn't this.

Jared-Crowley
Fuck you Grady, you've known all along what happened to Lexi, haven't you?

Marcus-Grady
It's none of your business, man. None of anyone's business.

Jared-Crowley
Like fuck, it's none of my business. Six has been living a fucking nightmare. I should have been there to help her.

Shaun-Bossier

Six?

Marcus-Grady

Six is the code name we called Lexi when we were kids. We did this stupid thing where we spelt our names backwards and used the first three letters as our code name. Alexis was Six. Jared was Der (lol Der!), Abbey's was Yeb, and mine was fucking Suc. Lex had the best code name.

Shaun-Bossier

Wow! You lot really were dorks when you were kids, weren't you? Lol Suc.

Jared-Crowley

Who cares about the code names? Is she okay? Like, what did that fucker do to her? I'm going to fucking kill him! Is that why she's with Ayden? And why Ayden? What does he have to do with any of this?

Ayden-Mitchell

She's with me because I'm looking after her. I got her out of town, and she is safe away from her brother while the cops hunt him down.

Jared-Crowley

So you and her are a thing now? Real fucking smooth jumping in and taking advantage of her while she's fucking vulnerable!

Ayden-Mitchell

I don't know who the fuck you think you are, but let me make one thing really fucking clear right now! I have not, and will not EVER take advantage of Lex.

Simon-Hastings

Ooooh, Lexi has a boyfriend!!!

Garrett-Cole

Dude, not the right time to be joking.

Simon-Hastings

Someone has to try and get these cavemen to calm down.

Lexi will read this shit, and then how do you think she will feel?

Garrett-Cole

I hate to say this, guys, but Hastings has a point.

Jared-Crowley

I'm sorry Lexi! I didn't mean to stir shit up. I just feel so helpless.

Please respond when you can. Call me anytime. X

Shaun-Bossier

Did you just send Lexi a kiss, Jar? XXX lol.

Jesus, man, I didn't know you lost your balls over her.

Jared-Crowley

You might want to shut your fucking mouth, Bossi, before I feed you my fist.
You're just jealous you don't have the history Marcus and I have with her.

Shaun-Bossier

You guys have a threesome or something?
Or a foursome including Abbey?
Man, that's hot! Please tell me you did that???

Ayden-Mitchell

I know you're trying to be funny Shaun, but have some fucking respect for Lexi!

Shaun-Bossier

She knows I'm joking around!
Right Lex? You know I'm just joking?
Fuck. I'm sorry.

Garrett-Cole

Ignore Bossi, Lexi. He doesn't know what self control is.
I know this sounds stupid given the situation, but I hope you're okay, Lex.

Shaun-Bossier

Same!

Marcus-Grady

Same!

Simon-Hastings

Same! I'll happily give you my balls, Lexi. XXXXXXXXXX

Ayden-Mitchell

Jesus Christ!

Wow. Everyone is freaking out. I didn't really think anyone would care. Jared's reference to my childhood code name warms my heart.

Six.

I can't remember when it was that we stopped using the silly code names we made up, but hearing it for the first time in years brings a rush of memories from a time in our lives when we really had few cares in the world.

I try to think of something special to write back to the boys. It's kind of weird that I want to send them a special message, but to the girls, I felt the opposite.

Girls are bitches. Well, Tasha Pritchard is anyway. The boys, though, they're different.

Yes, they flirt with me. Yes, they make innuendos and inappropriate comments, but I know they don't mean any harm by it.

Lexi-West

Guys, I'm okay. I'm sorry for not saying anything sooner. It's just a lot to wrap my head around right now. Please don't be angry with Marcus. It was a secret I'd hoped would never get out.

Ayden is right. I am safe with him. He's taking very good care of me and definitely not taking advantage of me. I'm grateful to him and his family for taking me in.

Jar, I haven't even thought about those silly code names in years. I really DO think mine is the best. Marcus, yours really does SUC! ☺
Lol sorry, I couldn't help it.

Sorry to burst your bubble Shaun, but there were no threesomes or foursomes. And yes,

I shake my head at how ridiculous all the messages are. Ridiculous, but good. There's a message from Nathan too which simply says, "Call me when you can," and one from Travis saying, "Sorry to hear about what happened at home, Lexi. I don't want you to worry about anything. It's all good."

Travis' message is cryptic, but I think I get what he's saying. I shouldn't worry about getting caught for the vandalism. It fills me with relief, but also guilt. Am I really going to let Travis take the fall for something I did, too? I shouldn't, and maybe I won't, but right now I have bigger things to worry about, like the Messenger message from Mike.

Mike West

You little slut! I don't know how you got away, but I will find you, and when I do, I'll make our last encounter seem like foreplay! You were never good at Hide and Seek, Ali. When you least expect it, I'll be there to catch you!

Air fails to expand my lungs for a moment, and when Ayden looks at me with concern, I try to quickly school my expression and force myself to breathe.

I should show him the message, but I don't. I can't bring myself to let Mike push his way into our bubble, so I delete it and pretend it never existed.

Andrea takes that moment to come into the room, dragging my attention away from my phone.

"Oh good, you're back. Did you get what you needed, Lexi?"

"Yes, thank you," I smile at Andrea and slip my new, hand-me-down phone into my hoodie pocket.

"That's good." Andrea continues, her face turning serious. "So I heard from Officer Zimora. They went to see your mum and, after examining the situation, have ordered her transfer to a different hospital to receive different care."

I frown. "Different, how?"

"I believe the current hospital had your mum so sedated that she was incoherent. After some discussions with the doctors, the officers determined that your mum's best interests weren't being met. In the new facility, she'll be put through detox this week, and once she's clear of mind, new doctors will determine her needs."

"I don't understand." I shift forward on the couch, keeping my focus on Andrea. "So she's at rehab?"

Pity flashes across Andrea's face. "Yes. It is a rehab facility. However, the officers seem to believe that perhaps your mum's addiction issues were being fed by her local doctor for some reason. The fact that she'd been taken to a different medical facility in the first place has raised red flags, and the officers believe that perhaps your dad was in cahoots with your mum's doctor. They suspect your dad has been keeping your mum medicated and addicted to alcohol to maintain her control."

"Fuck," Ayden curses, saying aloud what I'm thinking.

Dread sits heavy in my belly with the knowledge that what Andrea said could be true. How could my dad do that to my mum? And why?

As far-fetched as it sounds, it all makes so much sense. Having her dosed up on drugs or wasted on alcohol made it easier for him to go off and live his second life. I thought him having a mistress was a new revelation, but there's a big fat chance this has been going on for years.

That fucking prick. If he didn't want to be with her, then why didn't the arsehole just put her out of her misery and leave her so she could move on?

"When can I see her?"

"It will be in a couple more days. The withdrawal process can be brutal, so it's probably best you wait a little longer until the worst is over."

I nod in understanding. I'd seen it once when I was around twelve-years-old. My mum decided to try and do it herself. I didn't understand what was happening at the time, but I know now. She failed, of course, and then went on a bender that nearly killed her.

"I know none of this sounds good, Lexi, but at least something is happening about it now. If the officers are right, then you haven't been the only victim in your family."

My heart sinks.

She's right.

My mum has been manipulated too, drugged just like I was when dad came to take me from school. I never deserved that. And even though she's been a shitty mum, being spaced out all these years has probably been the main contributing factor. For all I know, my mum could be a nice person. Hell, she may even love me deep down.

Maybe.

Ayden slides his arm around my shoulders, and I lean into his side, accepting the support.

"So, in a few days, we will take Lex to see her mum?" he asks and Andrea nods.

"Thank you," I speak quietly, still reeling from this information.

Andrea reaches out and gives my shoulder a supportive squeeze matched with a small smile before leaving the room.

My brain is in overload.

What the actual fuck?

"You okay?" Turning me in his arms, Ayden runs worried eyes over my face.

"How much more fucked up is this going to get?" I whisper and he gives my shoulder a squeeze as he tugs me closer.

"I don't know, Lex. But just remember, we are going to be with you every step of the way."

His words warm my heart once again, and I feel the slightest glimmer of hope. Because that's all I have left.

Hope.

Twenty-Five

♥

The stars glitter above in the chilly night sky, and I wrap the fleece blanket around my shoulders, not wanting to give in to the cold and go back inside. The rooftop gardens at the height of Ayden's dad's apartment and studio building are tranquil, and if Ayden hadn't brought me up here, I would never have known it existed.

The setting is beautiful. The cabana loveseat we occupy is secluded from the garden centre in a private courtyard to look out over the city.

I breathe in the crisp air letting the fresh bite clear my mind, which has been fucked up to no end lately.

"Here you go, beautiful."

Accepting the mug of steamy hot chocolate off Ayden, my hands relish the warmth.

"Thank you." I smile back at Ayden as he sinks down beside me in the loveseat.

We sit in silence, sipping our drinks, lost in thought as the hot liquid warms us. We've been out here for a while now and should really go back inside, but I just can't bring myself to do it. It's less suffocating up here, high above the city. The open space and beautiful ambience of watching the sunset frees my mind from its regular turmoil. Of course, so does the nearness of Ayden as we curl up on the loveseat together.

What is it about sunsets and hope? It briefly scares all my worries away, making them seem insignificant as I watch the big flaming ball that heats our earth descend past the horizon, creating beautiful pinks and oranges to dance across the sky.

"I need to admit something to you."

Ayden's deep voice breaks my train of thought, instantly gaining my attention and I angle myself towards him. His hood is pulled up over his head, just the same as mine, and like me, he's wrapped in a fleece blanket while he clasps his warm mug with both hands. Just the sight of him makes my heart flutter.

"Oh, you do, do you?" I ask, intrigued to know what he had to admit to me, and he nods, taking another sip of his hot chocolate before putting me out of my misery.

"I knew who you were before my first day at school."

What? How is that possible?

Ayden chuckles at whatever expression he sees on my face. "Marcus kinda told me all about the who's who of Fox Pines Catholic College a few days before I started. You were someone he seemed to know a lot about."

"Why? Because we grew up together and are in the same friendship circle?"

Ayden grins, "Well yes, that, and the fact he's been crushing on you for a few years now."

"What!" I squeak, nearly spilling my hot drink, which just makes Ayden laugh again.

"Didn't know, huh?"

"Uh, no. He said nothing." I'm so confused. I think back to all the times at school and the parties we've been to together. I can't think of any times I got any '*I like you more than friends*' vibes off Marcus, although he has been more chatty over the last week.

"Yeah, he's a chickenshit. He was too scared you'd turn him down."

I'm genuinely shocked.

"Anyway," Ayden continues, "when he showed me your Instagram feed, I was immediately intrigued by you."

"Intrigued by me?" I'm grinning ear to ear now, and he smiles back.

"Yes. You intrigued me. Your beauty. The way you seemed so happy in the pictures. Your confidence."

I cringe. That doesn't sound like me at all. Not the real me, anyway. He saw the image I portrayed to fool everyone.

"I could see why Marcus had a thing for you. But then that first day at school, when I searched the crowds to find you, I couldn't see you at first because I was looking for that happy, carefree girl in the pictures. Marcus spotted you before I did and directed my attention behind the crowd, and that's when I saw it."

"Saw what?"

"I saw the damaged soul that matched my own." Ayden's gaze is piercing, locking me in place. It's like his eyes have the power to see directly into my soul.

Uncomfortable under his scrutiny, the need to run teases me again, and tears spring to my eyes, so I move to turn away, but Ayden stops me by cupping my face with his warm hand.

"Don't run from me." His whisper is pleading.

Hot droplets pop out of my eyes and roll down my cheeks. I tell myself to stay put. I don't want to run from him. However, I do want to run from the ugly truth I've been trying to hide from everyone.

"When I saw you that day, I was pretty confused. I asked Marcus if something bad had happened to you or if something had changed in your life, but he couldn't think of anything, so we re-stalked your Instagram account and noticed you hadn't posted anything for a few months. No more laughing selfies with Abbey, no more party pictures with you and the group. I berated Marcus for not noticing that something was up."

"You berated him?" I squeak again in shock, and Ayden grins, dropping his hand from my face.

"Yep, sure as shit did. Made him feel real bad, too, for not noticing something was wrong. That's when I knew I had to find out why your smiles didn't reach your eyes anymore and why you looked so defeated when you thought no one was looking."

I can't speak. I can cry apparently, but I can't find any words. I feel too exposed, yet relieved that someone noticed when most people didn't. It's just plain confusing.

Putting his mug down on the table next to the loveseat, Ayden takes mine, placing it next to his before he turns back and his warm fingers swipe away my tears until my cheeks no longer feel wet.

"I was just so drawn to you that day, Lexi," he whispers. "I could see your beauty, but that isn't what drove my need to know you. It was the pain I could see you working so hard to hide, and no one else seemed to notice it. I just really needed to help you. Protect you."

"Your need to protect me. Is that because of what happened with Dani?" I didn't want to ask, but I have to know. I'm worried I'm nothing more than a project for him to focus on. To fix.

Ayden is quiet for a moment, his blue eyes boring into mine.

"I'd like to say it has nothing to do with what happened with Dani and not being able to protect her, but I'd be lying. I don't want to lie to you, Lex. I care about you in a way that is hard to explain without sounding obsessed or over the top, especially since we only met a week ago. Honestly, I'd do anything to protect you and make you feel loved and safe." He takes a moment to think over his next words, his tongue darting out to wet his lips, and I have a hard time concentrating.

Why is that so hot?

"The thing that happened with Dani isn't the reason I pursued you, though. I'm not here with you trying to be a hero because I couldn't be one to Dani. I'm here with you because everything about you lures me in. Your smile, your humour, your backbone, your sassy mouth, your morals." He brushes the backs of his fingers down the side of my face. "The way those pretty cheeks turn pink for me." And then his thumb gently glides over my lower lip. "And these lips. Fuck, Lexi. Your lips are so soft and demanding. I don't have to worry about an addiction to illicit drugs anymore. Not when *you* are my drug."

Holy. Fucking. Hell.

I'm quiet for a few moments. Mainly because the lump in my throat prevents my voice from working, but also because I don't know what to say.

"Tell me what you're thinking, beautiful."

His endearment melts my heart, not just by the words he speaks, but by the love he says them with.

Well, maybe not love, but care. He *can't* love me. It's too soon.

"I don't really know what to say. Thank you, I guess." I smile, wanting to say more, but can't.

A warm, caring smile tugs at his lips before his ocean blues dance to my own. He wants to kiss me again. I can see it in the way his eyes turn almost drunk and by the way his breath quickens.

Unwavering need consumes me, silently begging for the kiss he wants to give. I dart out my tongue to wet my lips in an obvious invitation, and Ayden takes it, leaning in to brush his lips against mine.

Letting my emotional chaos slip away, I focus on the feel of his lips and the way he laps at mine in small nibbles. The need to be closer to him is overpowering, and without thinking twice, I drop my blanket and shift to straddle his lap and deepen the kiss.

This time it's Ayden who moans, and knowing I'm the cause of it makes me feel powerful.

His athletic body is flush against mine in an intoxicating embrace and I can feel his very prominent bulge between our bodies. Without thinking, I grind against him and our moans fill the air, his hold on me tightening around my waist. His hands almost hurt, pressing into my skin, but it's the good kind of hurt that has me craving more. The heat building inside me sends a flush over my skin from head to toe, and I'm lost. Our mouths are hungry, our hands roam of their own accord, and our bodies respond to each other like they were made to fit.

I hadn't meant for things to go further than kissing, but the drug that is Ayden Mitchell has released a beast within me, and I'm consumed by sheer need and desire.

Ayden's hands slide to my hips before they find their way under the hem of my hoodie. His magical fingers glide over the bare skin of my back, searing my flesh like a brand.

As if just realising he's touching my bare skin, he moves to pull his hand away and I growl.

Like actually growl like a damn animal!

His responding moan spears me on, and I grip his wrist, guiding his hand to the bare skin of my abs before slowly sliding it up my front to meet my wanting bra covered breasts.

"Lex." Ayden chokes out, his lips still pressed to mine. "We should stop."

"No, not yet. Please, Ayden." Yep, I just begged. My need for his touch feels more overwhelming than my need for air.

Pulling back from me, a mix of pleasure and pain twists his beautiful face.

"Lex, you've been through a lot. Now isn't the right time to be doing this. I don't need anything more from you."

Panting from the ache between my legs, I sit back to look at him properly. His lips are puffy and well kissed, his cheeks are flushed with heat, and his eyes look drunk with lust. This look, right here, I definitely need more of.

"I want more." My admission is a whisper, but I look him dead in the eyes, not shying away from my embarrassment at being so forward. I need him to see that I mean what I'm saying. "Can you give me more, Ayden? Because I want to give you more. It's the truest thing I know right now. I've never wanted this with anyone before, but I know I want it with you." My bold words die off as self doubt seeps its way in. "I mean, if you want to. I..."

My nerves get the better of me, and my confidence wanes. Maybe he isn't attracted to me in that way?

Perhaps he's a virgin and is saving himself for marriage?

No, that can't be it. I'm sure he would have had sex with Dani. Jesus, maybe it's just me he's not interested in. My beaten face must be a real turnoff.

Ayden's gentle fingers trace my jawline, shaking me out of my thoughts.

"Stop overthinking, Lex." Those plump lips of his curve up into a smile.

I don't say anything, but I return his touch, grazing my fingers over the short stubble along his jaw and up to his lips. As I slide my thumb over his bottom lip, his lids flutter closed before he darts his tongue out and draws my thumb into his mouth.

I won't lie. It's fucking hot. And when he moans, I shudder from the intense appetite throbbing between my legs.

"I want you, Ayden. All of you." His eyes snap open at my words, and I slowly draw my thumb from his warm mouth. Reaching down, I grab the hem of my hoodie and slowly lift it over my head, tossing it somewhere behind me. "Do you want me?"

"Fuck, Lex, you have no idea how much I want you." His chest rises and falls with deep breaths, and his eyes flick down to the black lace that covers my breasts.

An internal struggle contorts his expression, giving away a mix of emotions. I know he believes I'm fragile because of what happened with my brother, and that holding back is doing the right thing, but I need him to see that I'm okay with this.

"I need this, Ayden."

I slowly glide my hands up my thighs and watch as his gaze immediately follows. The way he watches me, his eyes almost black with desire, makes me feel powerful and in control. I'm the one causing his reaction. I'm the girl who he has his eyes transfixed on as my hands slide up and over my bare abdomen to the swell of my breasts.

Ayden's breathing is more rapid now, and I still my hands briefly before working up the courage and slowly cupping both my breasts. When his tongue darts out to wet his parted lips, I drag the tips of my fingers over each lace covered nipple.

"Fuck. You don't play fair, Lexi West."

I can't help but grin at his use of my full name. The prowess coursing through my veins is like a high I've never felt. It's heady and bold and delivers a rush of control that is both satisfying and leaves me yearning for more. Right now, in this situation with Ayden, I feel safe. I have no vulnerability, just pure desire for this guy in front of me, who I'm pretty sure has stolen my heart.

With Ayden's eyes still focused on my hands, I move them around my back and unclasp my bra. He sucks in a breath, holding on to it as I let each strap drop off my shoulders before releasing my hands and letting it slip down my arms to expose my hot, needy nipples to the cool night air.

"Lex," Ayden whispers, drawing his eyes back to my face.

"Touch me, please, Ayden." Yes, I'm back to begging, and I'm not ashamed, especially when I witness the moment his expression softens, and he caves to my request.

His eyes dart to my pebbled nipples, and he lifts one hand towards my breast and my back arches a little to push me closer to him. I feel like I'm going to die of anticipation at his slow perusal, and I almost growl in frustration.

All thoughts are lost when his warm fingers finally contact the underside of my left breast. I can't help but look down to watch his fingers as they graze a trail up the side of my plump needy skin, before his thumb finds its way to my nipple and circles it.

I'm the one to moan this time, and I glance back to his face, meeting his heated gaze and he bites his bottom lip.

"You're so fucking beautiful."

I don't say anything because I don't need to. My care for him is written all over my face, and as he slowly leans in, my nipples between his fingers, he claims my mouth in the hottest kiss yet.

My control snaps.

Grinding myself on him again in a fevered demand, I throw my head back as Ayden's lips travel to my ear to nip at the lobe.

"I'm such a goner over you, Lexi." His breath tickles my ear before he nips at it again and travels searing kisses down my neck, leaving a trail of molten desire as he roams down to my aching breasts.

I'm panting like a dog in heat, loving the way it feels to have his hands gripping the bare skin of my back like he might die if the connection is lost.

Jesus, I think *I* might die if the connection is lost!

Ayden's eyes flick up to catch mine a moment before his mouth claims a nipple, and oh my... Of their own accord, my hands fist in his hair, dragging him closer, pleasure building inside me each time his tongue flicks or his teeth graze.

This feels amazing.

"Fuck, Ayden." I can't control the way my body responds to him. My pelvis thrusts towards his, seeking more.

"That's so fucking hot." Ayden moves to my other breast, showing it the same attention.

"W-what is?" I can barely speak, and he releases my nipple to answer.

"When you say *fuck, Ayden*."

His words make me grin, and I take in the look of bliss on his face while he devours my nipple again.

"Fuck, Ayden." I moan again and get the desired reaction from him when he pulls my hips down over his hard length, trapped inside his jeans.

My desperate need for more forges my hips down in grinding thrusts, meeting his own frenzied need. Ayden skims his hand down my front, moving towards the ache that is begging for his touch. The moment his feverish hand slides over my denim covered mound between my legs, I cry out, nearly climaxing from that single caress.

I'm panting with uninhibited need as he rubs over my jean-clad core, quickly driving me over the edge, my cries of ecstasy floating into the city's night sky.

I can't stop kissing him. My tongue tangles with his, my lips meet his passionate kisses, and I know this moment between us has only just begun.

No longer able to control myself, I reach for the hard bulge in his pants, causing him to thrust under my touch.

He's big. Like really big. And hard.

It excites me, but it also has me hesitating for a brief moment. Ayden doesn't notice, thank fuck, but it has me pausing because how on earth is that going to fit? Even as I think it, more warmth pools between my legs, my body reminding me how much I want everything Ayden has to give. This is natural and normal. My body is made for this, right?

Ayden's gravelly moan pulls me out of my thoughts, and the sound reminds my body once again how much it's craving every inch of him. The need to feel the heat of his bare skin against mine urges me forward, and I reach for his hoodie, dragging it up. Ayden breaks our kiss to help me lift it over his head, and when it joins my hoodie in a pile somewhere behind us, I press my hands to his strong chest, running them over his pecs and stopping to roll his nipple between my fingers.

"Lex, you're so fucking perfect."

Dragging my eyes from his chest to his face to see where his attention is, I find it on my lips. He grins and licks his own.

"The way you're biting your lip while you look at me makes me feel so...."

"So?" I ask.

"So wanted." He finishes and then claims my lips again.

My hands roam his chest while his slide down my back to grip my butt, pulling me down on his arousal again.

"Pants off." I gasp between our parted lips and Ayden places one last searing kiss to my neck before lifting me off him and standing.

Dear god, this guy and his hotness should be illegal.

I watch as he flicks the button on his jeans and then slowly drags his fly down.

I stop breathing.

I should care about that, right? You know, because in order to live, I must breathe.

I could care less, though. All that matters is Ayden.

"Are you sure about this, Lexi? We can stop, you know. We don't have to do this."

"Look at me, Ayden. Do I look like I want to stop?" I raise a single brow and he chuckles and shakes his head.

"Nope. You're totally eye-fucking me right now."

"Damn straight, I am." I grin, fucking proud of that.

Chuckling again, he hooks his fingers in his jeans and drags them down, kicking them off, and leaving him in nothing but his black boxer briefs.

Holy hell, I want to eat that.

I moan, and he stalks forward with determination that makes my heart beat erratically. Leaning over me on the loveseat, he places his hands on either side of my body, urging me to fall back, and the sight of him hovering over me in his almost naked glory sends a hot flush through my aching core.

"You're beautiful." His sexy as sin grin caves in his dimples, and I have to fight the urge to lick them because that would be weird, right?

"My turn?" I can barely speak with my heart racing so fast.

He doesn't answer, but shows me by trailing kisses over my shoulder, down the side of my breast, and over my navel until he reaches the top of my jeans. Flicking his eyes up to mine, we keep our gazes locked as his hand slides up my thigh to just barely pass by the ache between my legs. Placing another kiss on my tummy, his hands make fast work of sliding my jeans off and freeing me from the annoying barrier.

Leaving my knickers on, Ayden stands back and takes me in. I expect the self-conscious bitch that sits inside my head to come out, but it doesn't, Ayden's heated gaze making me feel beautiful, bruises and all.

Bending, Ayden lifts my leg and trails kisses over the inside, from my ankle up to my knee. I never imagined having my ankle kissed would be worth thinking about, but damn, not only does it add to the heat building inside me, but it makes me feel adored.

He treats my other leg to the same gentle worshipping, and I'm powerless to stop my lids from fluttering closed, needing to just feel every small touch of his lips on my skin.

I don't expect what happens next, but oh wow, I'm not going to complain. My eyes fly open, and my mouth forms a silent O when his hot kisses travel up the inside of my thigh and find my heat through the thin barrier of my black cotton knickers.

My hands instantly dive into Ayden's hair, holding him in place while his lips continue their kissing assault over the fabric.

I can no longer hear the bustle of the city. Blood rushing through my veins soars loud in my ears. My skin is on fire, and my hips gyrate against Ayden's mouth as I desperately seek more. As if sensing my thirst, Ayden hooks his fingers in one side of my knickers and pulls them aside.

A whimper escapes me the instant his soft lips meet the bare flesh of my folds, and I'm gone, lost to him.

He kisses me there, his tongue lapping at me, before his fingers join in, grazing over my entrance teasingly. I arch up, seeking more, and he gives me exactly what I want, slowly easing them inside. I cry out as the stretch of his two fingers spiral me into an intense orgasm, but he doesn't stop, and a third finger joins the other two, causing a biting sting as they stretch me further than I've been stretched before.

I think I say his name. I can't be sure. He's managed to render me useless while I ride out another intense climax as he curls his fingers inside.

I'm panting uncontrollably. I'm pretty sure my hearing vanishes for a minute or so, but as he eases his fingers from my heat and flicks his tongue over my clit softly, the sounds of the city come whooshing back.

As my chest rises and falls, trying to get my breath back, Ayden kisses a trail up my body, stopping to take each nipple in his mouth before returning to my lips. I kiss him back through panting breaths, and when I taste myself on his lips, I moan as more arousal grips my core.

I'm never going to get enough of this guy.

I'm absolutely hooked.

Slapping my hands against his chest, I push him off me, and confusion contorts his flushed face as he sits back on his haunches. Grinning, I turn my focus to the firm bulge hidden by his boxers and reach out, gliding my hand down his stomach to the waistband of his boxers and tug them towards me a little. Ayden relaxes under my touch, now realising that I wasn't pushing him away, and his eyes follow my hand as I drag his boxers down to free his hard length.

I freeze for a moment, taking in the sight of him and knowing more than ever that what Ayden and I have is right. It's perfect.

Ayden shifts back off the loveseat and tugs his boxers right off, and I do the same, kicking my knickers off while I watch him. The need to touch him is an addiction I can no longer deny, so I shift forward to the edge of the seat, and run my fingers over the firm velvet of his erection, touching it for the first time.

Ayden sucks in a sharp breath at the contact, and I wonder if I should tell him it's the first time I've ever touched a dick before.

Now's probably not the right time to bring that up, so I focus on his face, and his lust drunk gaze as he watches me like he wants to devour me.

I like the way he makes me feel. Sexy. Worshipped. Strong and powerful.

Wanting to be the one who makes him lose control this time, I wrap my hand around his girth and slowly pump.

Ayden bucks under my touch. His fists flexed tight by his sides like he's fighting for control. The same control I want him to lose.

Is he trying to hold himself back from touching me? From letting go? No way am I letting him do that. I want all of him, damn it.

Nerves flutter through my body, but determination drives me, so I lean closer to his hard dick before flicking my tongue out and licking over his slit, tasting the salty drop beaded on the tip.

"Fuck, Lexi." He rasps, his tone husky, and fuck, I like the sound of him saying those words too. So much so that this time, I part my lips and take him deep into my mouth. Instantly his hands fist in my hair, and I know I've got him. I've broken his restraint.

Hoping I'm doing this right, using my hand, lips, tongue, and throat, I work him until his legs tremble, and I think he's going to cum in my mouth.

He doesn't, though, because, in the next instant, I find my mouth empty, and my back meets the loveseat as he pushes me down and rises over me.

"You little minx." He nips at my lips, and I wrap my legs around his hips, pulling him close to my heat.

We both groan as our arousals meet for the first time. Our kisses grow desperate, and Ayden's hand finds my breast, kneading it before rolling my nipple between his fingers, sending me almost fevered, ready to combust.

"More, please." I beg into his mouth.

"Are you sure?" He rasps in that fucking sexy husk again, against my lips.

I nod. "Yes, Ayden. I want this with you. Here. Now."

Breaking our kiss, Ayden shifts away, taking the heat of his body with him, and I feel my heart start to crack.

Is he refusing? Doesn't he want this too?

Propping up on my elbows with concern, I watch Ayden bend and toss our clothes around before he stands to his full height with relief washed over his face.

The moment his gaze locks on mine again, I know I was worrying about nothing. The heat in his eyes, the flush of his cheeks, and the way his dick looks harder than before, jutting out with want tells me he definitely wants this too.

That's when I see *why* he moved away from me.

The foil packet in his hands is quickly torn open, and Ayden pulls out a condom, pressing it to the tip of his hardness, before rolling it down his length.

"Shit Ayden, that's hot. Everything you do turns me on."

My admission is rewarded with a devilish grin, and Ayden returns to me, taking my mouth for another searing kiss. Our lips don't lose contact as he moves over me, pressing his hips to mine as he lines himself up at my entrance, and then presses forward.

The need to be filled is consuming as he eases himself in. I rise up to take more of him, hungry for his offering, only to tense the moment when he breaks through my barrier. There's an intense pinch that stings and burns, and Ayden looks down at me with concern when I go rigid under him.

"Don't stop," I whisper, hoping my eyes express that I'm okay even though they begin to water.

"Are you sure?" There's so much concern in his tone, and I do the only thing I can think of to assure him, and reach around to grab his bare arse, tugging him closer.

"You mean everything to me, Lex." He whispers before taking my lips in his again, and he shows me with his kiss just what his words mean.

One of his hands finds my nipple, rolling it which sends waves of pleasure to my centre, while his other hand links our fingers together by my head and he eases himself in further.

It burns and stretches, almost unbearably, and I wonder for a moment if I can really handle this.

Somehow knowing what I need, Ayden slides his hand between us and his fingers press to my clit, the sensitive bud reacting instantly to his touch, sending heat rushing through my veins.

There are so many sensations burning through my body and mind that the pain starts to vanish, and in its place is unbridled arousal.

Sinking all the way in, Ayden slowly starts to rock in and out, his fingers picking up pace as his lips claim mine like a brand. Pleasure builds inside me as he pumps his hips, and it's not long before mine matches his pace, my body responding to his like it's always known how to do this. It's as if our bodies are made for each other, moulding together perfectly, dancing a dance only recognisable by each other as if no one else could ever connect with either of us in the same way.

Our thrusts, moans, and kisses all intertwine as some sort of frenzy takes over sending us up, up, up, until it feels like electrical currents of pleasure explode across every inch of my skin and my insides start clamping around him.

My climax is like a detonation, and even though I can't hear anything, the one thing I do hear is Ayden's yelled grunt as our lips break apart, and he throws his head back, stiffening as he comes hard.

There's nothing else but us in this moment. Just him and me entwined and connected in a way that surpasses any other high this life can give.

We have no cares in the world right now on the rooftop of the apartment building. Our only need is each other and the pleasure we share in our little bubble of heaven. I have never felt this way before, so consumed by the need to ride this addicting high with another person.

No sick thoughts of my past invade the experience. No barriers hold me back. We spend hours on the roof exploring each other's bodies in the chilly night air that we somehow can't seem to feel.

This moment changes everything for me. Our relationship, which had been a flirting friendship not so long ago, is now so much more than I've ever had in my life. It also changes me as a person because up until now, I haven't ever fully trusted anyone like this. I've never let down my walls enough for someone to see the battered and bruised version of myself. Not even Abbey, who has been my best friend ever since I can remember, had seen the real me when it counted.

I trust Ayden, though. With every part of my being, I know that is true. My life may have turned into a fucked up hell of late, but I'm almost thankful that it did because if it didn't happen, then this, here tonight may never have happened. I may never have had the opportunity to get this close to Ayden. To the boy who owns my heart.

Twenty-Six

Over the next couple of days, we stay in our little bubble of happiness. I've ignored my phone because I just can't bring myself to face reality. I almost wish I could block Abbey from contacting me. She's had too many questions and is texting me too much "tea" about the rumours already spreading about me. It's like my pain has become gossip and everyone's new entertainment.

Ayden ended up calling Abbey and asking her to give it a rest and to pass the same message on to the other girls who've been just as inconsiderate. I hadn't asked him to, and I feel bad for making Abbey feel like crap, but I just couldn't handle it. I thought she understood how serious this is.

Now, as we drive through the city in Peter's car to visit my mum, I look at the last text Abbey sent me.

I'm so sorry, Lex. I didn't think.

My heart hurts knowing she's probably been beating herself up over it but probably hates me by now since I haven't replied yet.

Another reason why I regret getting the phone is because of the email I'm staring at right now. Sitting in my inbox is an email from my dad.

> *Alexis,*
>
> *I am appalled that you would let the police believe that your own brother could inflict such a heinous act on his own sister, and dragging me into it is not only disrespectful but utterly wrong.*
>
> *Mike is distraught that you would do this to him. He is lying low and will reach out to you when the time is right. Make sure you apologise to him. You'd better hope like hell he will be forgiving.*
>
> *As for me. Right now, I am ashamed to call myself your father. You have disgraced our family name with these lies and your self-destructive behaviour. Do you even understand how serious this is, and what you have done to my reputation and my career?*
>
> *Your mother may have been removed from the care she needed, but don't fool yourself into thinking that I can't get to her. If you do not tell the police that you are lying and the whole situation has been fabricated, then*

"Here we are," Peter announces as we pull into the parking garage of the new facility where my mum had been relocated. My heart is practically beating out of my chest from reading the email from my dad.

It's like he believes his own lies.

I'm not going to respond. He doesn't deserve my time.

Dragging my attention away from my phone, I reluctantly take in my surroundings, which makes my stomach rebel, nausea churning as my anxiety picks up. Not only do I hate hospitals, but I have no clue what version of my mum I'm going to visit today. Both issues tempt me to refuse to get out of the car, but knowing Ayden's parents have gone out of their way to bring me here, and the need to make sure my mum is okay after what I read in the email, I swallow down my worries and force myself to move.

Getting out of the car, Ayden rushes around to meet me, taking my hand in his, trying to be all gentlemanly. It's cute, and I try to hide my grin, but he notices and gives me his signature wink, and I'm thankful for the brief distraction. He has the power to make me feel at ease, and I just know he's a drug I'll never be able to give up.

Peter and Andrea take the lead, walking hand in hand, whispering ahead of us while Ayden and I follow, dragging our feet. Well, I'm dragging my feet. Ayden is just walking at my slow pace, trying to show his support.

He pulls me into his side, wrapping his arm around me as we walk, and kisses the top of my head. I lean in, circling my arms around his waist, breathing in his spicy scent, trying to reach the calm I usually get from smelling him.

Yes, I know it's creepy, but we all have our vices.

I should've worn his hoodie.

Why didn't I wear his hoodie?

Ugh! I'm an idiot.

I would've felt better if I had it on, but I didn't want my mum to see me wearing it and ask questions. She would've known immediately that it wasn't mine, and it belonged to a guy. I'd prefer to avoid that particular conversation with her for now.

The hospital is a tall white building showing signs of ageing, with its peeling paint and a few visible cracks in the render. The structure doesn't scream hospital, but once you step through the front doors, the clinical smell reminds you that it is.

Approaching the reception desk, a plump woman with short grey curly hair and black-framed glasses peers up from her paperwork raising a brow.

"Ah, hi. We're looking for Mrs West's room." Andrea shifts nervously under the lady's glare who pouts her mouth, eyeing us over the top of her glasses, before turning to her computer and keying something in.

She takes her sweet time while I stand close to Ayden's side, feeling more and more anxious by the second.

"Who, may I ask, is here to visit Mrs West?" Her voice is unusually low and gruff for a woman, and it makes me do a double-take to check if she's actually a woman.

"I have her daughter here," Andrea gestures to me, "Alexis West."

The lady behind the counter nods her head, looking me over.

"Alexis, you may go through to see your mother. However, visitors must be immediate family only. Unless the rest of you are immediate family, then you will have to stay out here."

My heart races with more damn anxiety knowing I'm going to be on my own. I'm nervous about seeing my mum, but I'm also not sure I want Ayden and his parents to see my mum, anyway. Not like this, in hospital when she'll be at her worst.

Maybe never meeting my mum is a better option.

"Sorry Lexi, will you be okay?" Andrea looks concerned, so I nod, not wanting her to worry. She's already given me so much support and I still struggle to accept her kindness without feeling guilty.

"I'll be fine, thanks. I can handle my mum." I attempt to make my voice sound confident, but I don't know if I pull it off.

Andrea gives me one of her sympathetic smiles before Ayden turns me to face him, leaning in close.

"We will be right out here." His voice is low, so only I can hear as he wraps me in a hug, and I squeeze him for a moment, trying to take as much calm from him as I can before I face this alone.

Reluctantly pulling away from the safety of his arms, I follow the plump woman who seems to become more impatient by the minute as she leads me through a blue door and stops in front of a bank of elevators.

"Floor three, room 302." She pushes the button, and the elevator doors spring open. Stepping in, I press the third-floor button while the plump lady gives me her back before walking away.

Well, isn't she a ray of sunshine?

She must really love her job.

As the lift rises, thoughts of my dad's email bombard me reminding me that this nightmare is nowhere near over, and by the time the brief trip to the third-floor ends, I struggle to keep my hands from trembling. The evil anxiety demon that sits on my shoulder is whispering scenarios to me of running into my dad here in the hospital, or worse, Mike. I'm sure they aren't on my mum's visitors list given the situation, but then again, who would've thought my dad would willingly let Mike do what he did?

I've learned the hard way that anything is possible.

"Hey there, honey, can I help you?" The friendly voice comes from a tall nurse wearing a deep purple uniform with long black braids in her hair. Her face holds a friendly expression, so I try to relax a little.

"Oh, um, I'm looking for my mum. Room 302."

The nurse studies me for a moment, tilting her head to the side, and then something like recognition flashes across her face.

"You're Alexis?" It isn't really a question, more like understanding. The fact that she knows my name makes me squirm, causing me to shift nervously on my feet and I glance over my shoulder to see if there are other people around.

"Oh, I'm sorry honey. I didn't mean to make you feel uncomfortable. I'm Erica, one of your mum's nurses. Her room is this way."

I examine the nurse again, looking for signs that she's out to do me wrong. However, all I see is a friendly demeanour, so I push my self-conscious thoughts aside and follow her down the hall.

"Your mum is having a bit of a hard time today. The effects of the drugs have worn off, but she's still in withdrawal, which is making her a Crabby Abbey."

"Great." I scoff, and Erica glances back, giving me a warm, sympathetic smile before stopping in front of the door for room 302.

"I'll be right over there at the nurse's station, honey. If you need anything, just give me a yell."

I nod and smile at Erica before taking a deep breath to calm my nerves. I can't go into the lion's den looking like a nervous child. My mum needs to see that I am strong, no matter what version of her I get today.

Any ideas I entertained of me having a warm welcoming reunion with my mum fly right out the door as it swings shut behind me.

"Jesus Christ, Alexis. What the fuck have you gone and done?"

And there she is.

My mum.

"What? Me?" Fury climbs onto the shoulders of my nerves and squashes it like a fly as I stare at my mum, looking more than dishevelled in the hospital bed. "What do you mean? What have I done?"

"You just have to cause so much fucking drama, don't you? Why couldn't you just do what the hell you are told, instead of setting off your dad and brother?"

What the hell? She surely isn't blaming me for all of this?

"Oh, I'm sorry mum, I should have just allowed Mike to keep fucking beating me and trying to rape me?!" My voice is loud and unrecognisable to my ears. It's kind of like a scream and yell all in one, and I can't control it.

"If you didn't walk around looking like a little whore all the time, then maybe you wouldn't have teased your brother to lose his control."

The air whooshes from my lungs at her words. They are like a cold slap to my face, while ripping out my heart. Before I can stop myself, I'm at her bedside with my hand raised, ready to hit her.

"Go ahead, behave like your father! You're just as bad as he is!"

I stop short at her words, stumbling back as if I was the one struck by an invisible hand. Tears blur my vision briefly before I see my mother's eyes doing the same.

"You did this to me," she whispers. Part of her looks like she's sorry, and part of her looks like she's angry at me.

"What did *I* do to *you* other than try to find where the hell you were? Do you even know that we couldn't find you because you were taken to a different hospital than what was on record?"

My mum is silent for a few moments while she takes in what I said, and then a calm washes over her features as she juts up her chin.

"Your actions mean the doctors here won't give me what I need, Alexis." She totally disregards my concerns about her.

"The drugs you mean?" I ask, well aware of her addiction, even if she's not willing to admit she has a problem.

Jesus, doesn't she know the drugs were keeping her from living?

My mum scoffs. "I'm talking about the medication I need to function, Alexis. Not only won't they give me anything, but I have to see a fucking Psychologist. Do you know how degrading that is for me?"

I study the woman who I'm sure was once happy to be my mum, as she sits up rigidly in the hospital bed.

She looks terrible, yet she has more colour in her skin than I've seen in years. Her brown hair is a tangled mess, and her hospital gown has come undone at the neck, falling off her right shoulder. On her lap, her hands are balled into fists matching my own, filled with anger, only for a completely different reason.

"You mean drugs, right? Not medication?" I snap. "Because I'm fairly certain doctors don't prescribe illicit drugs, mum. Why do you need them?"

She's quiet for a few long beats, her eyes darting around the room before landing on me, and she speaks quietly. "Because I'm unwell, Alexis."

"Unwell with what illness? What illness, besides addiction, requires illicit drugs?" My question annoys her. Her telltale nostril flare is in full force, and I bet if I look closely, I'd be able to see steam coming from her ears.

"I'm just unwell. The medication helps me feel better." Her voice is calmer now, and her fists have loosened.

"How do the *drugs* make you feel better?"

She scoffs, "Jesus, Alexis! They just make me feel more at peace, okay? Is that a good enough answer for you?"

I shake my head. "When did you first start taking drugs to make you feel better?"

My mum thinks about my question for a moment, her face showing that she has no idea.

"Do you know the cops think dad has been feeding your addiction? That he has been helping you stay under the influence for years so he can live his second life?"

I'm almost sure my questions are going to send my mum into a murderous rage, but instead, she's eerily calm.

"Why are you here, Alexis? Money? Is that what you want?"

"Maybe I wanted to make sure my mum is okay," I tell her honestly.

"Nope, that's not it. The doctors and police have set this up, haven't they? They want you to get me to say bad things about your father. Well, I won't." She sneers and crosses her arms over her chest in protest.

"Mum, I'm just here to make sure you're okay."

"Bullshit!" She turns in her bed to reach into the drawer of the side table. "Here, take the bank card, buy the shit you need. I'll use my other card and account for myself until your father can catch up with you and take care of things."

Catch up with me and take care of things? That doesn't sound good. My mum throws the bank card, which slaps against my chest, before falling to the floor.

"Have you spoken with dad? Is he looking for me?" My heart races again. What if this is a setup? A way to coax me out so he can take me again?

She waves me off. "Of course I haven't spoken to your father. These arseholes here have taken my phone and disconnected the room phone, so I can't call anyone. But I'm sure your father is looking for *you*, Alexis, and will catch up with you soon."

I bend to pick up the bank card and slide it into the back pocket of my jeans, knowing I'll need the money.

"You do know you're a victim here, right mum? Dad drugged you to control you so he could do what he wanted without your interference. He did that to me as well. Did you know that?" A frown twists her features, and I continue, "When he realised he couldn't control me, he sweet-talked my Principal and spiked my drink, which knocked me out so he could take me out of the school without making a scene. Then he left me with Mike, knowing exactly what his disturbed son would try to do to me. We are both victims here, mum, and I'm sorry I never saw what was going on with you."

I was hoping my words would show her how much I care and understand. Instead, it sets her into another rage.

"You fucking little bitch, you don't know what you are talking about! Your father works hard to give you the things you need, and this is how you thank him!"

A bowl of red jelly from her little table flies at my head, and I duck just in time to hear it crash against the wall behind me. She's screaming now, her words making no sense to me, so I turn and quickly bolt out of the room just in time to hear something else crash into the closed door.

Hot tears stream down my face, and I heave even as my chest feels like it's in a vise.

"Oh, honey, are you okay?" Erica, the nurse, appears before me holding a box of tissues, and I take her offering to dry up the flow of tears.

"I'm sorry, honey. Maybe today wasn't the best day for a visit."

"N-no d-day i-is." I'm a blubbering mess, still hearing the harsh words my mum hissed bouncing around in my head. I just don't understand what's so wrong with me that she doesn't love me? What's so bad about me that my dad thought punishment from Mike was the best course of action?

I've always tried hard in school, always done the right thing, well, mostly. I know I have a smart mouth on me, but am I just meant to sit back and take their verbal beatings and not fight back? Maybe I am, but I just can't be that person.

Anger blooms wildly in my chest, and I growl through my tears.

"Come with me, honey. I have just the place for you to take the moment you need." Erica's words are soft and knowing, so I let her lead me down the hall and through another set of doors.

"Go on in there, honey, and take a moment or two. Cry, scream, and yell if that's what you need. It will help."

I look at the door we are standing before and read the sign saying Chapel.

A giggle slips past my crying lips. "Are you trying to kill me?"

Erica rears back a little. "What? No, of course not, honey. Why?"

"Because if I go in there, I'm likely to burst into flames." I try to joke.

The laugh that rips from Erica's chest is loud and infectious, her head thrown back, and her hands clutch her middle.

"Oh, girl, trust me. If anyone was likely to burst into flames, it's me, and I go in this room daily to tell that SOB holier than all gods, that he's an arse."

It's my turn to laugh now, but it's brief as reality quickly sets back in.

Erica sighs, "You've been through a lot, especially for someone so young. Get all of those negative thoughts and feelings out. My preferred treatment is a big long scream. It's amazing how therapeutic it can be."

"I can't scream in there."

"Oh, yes you can. Trust me, no one will give it a second thought in this place, and I'll stand guard for you."

Erica's enthusiasm urges me forward, so I nod and enter the small Chapel, taking a steady breath. The makeshift Chapel has three rows of hard plastic chairs with a timber altar that looks like it's older than Erica, sitting at the front of the room. The dimly lit area is a little musty, and the smell immediately reminds me of my mum's hospital room.

I choke on a sob, replaying everything she said. My heart cracks wide open, aching inside my chest, and my knees meet the floor as a billowing scream rises from my lungs and bursts from my mouth. It's long and harsh and not enough, so I do it again, but this time it carries so much more pain.

My hands fist in my hair, pulling at the roots as I cry through each scream, letting each slice of my heart explode from me until I can't scream anymore. I cry then, like I've never cried before, allowing myself to feel all the pain and betrayal that my so-called family has delivered.

Anger and hate rattle my insides, poisoning my blood before overwhelming sadness takes over. I feel like I've missed out on something as vital as love growing up in the West family, the thought adding bitterness and resentment to join all the emotions swarming through me.

After an impossible amount of tears have fallen, a strange calm washes over me. My tears stop, the hate eases, and the sense of fear slips away. At first, the sensation is numbing. I conclude that I've finally cracked, my heart and body wanting to slam up the thickest walls to shield me from pain. But then, ocean eyes, dark hair, and a dimpled smile bounce through my mind.

Ayden.

My heart flutters at the mere thought of him—the boy who saved me in more ways than just physical. Peter and Andrea pop into my head, too. Their support has been just as unwavering as their son's.

I understand now. My mind isn't shutting down. It's showing me that I am cared about. Abbey, Marcus and the guys from school, and Valarie come to mind too, and I know without a doubt that not only do they care for me on some level, but I care for them as well. These people are important. I may not have a family in the traditional sense, but I have people who I trust and care about.

They are my family.

Resolve washes over me, and finding strength I didn't know I had, I stand slowly off the hard-tiled floor of the Chapel and leave the room with my head held high.

Twenty-Seven

After my so-called therapy session in the hospital Chapel, Erica took me to a bathroom so I could clean myself up before I went back to face Ayden and his parents again. I was grateful for her help and knew that even though my mum didn't deserve it, she would be in good hands with Erica around.

Ayden's parents say nothing about my lack of makeup when I return to them in the hospital's reception and Ayden looks at me with concern but keeps his mouth shut. He doesn't ask, and I don't tell, which is fine by me. At least for the moment.

We spend the rest of the day in the city with Ayden's parents. They treat us to a beautiful lunch in a restaurant overlooking the Yarra River, followed by a visit to the Gold Class cinemas at The Crown Complex. I've never been there before, and now that I've had the opportunity to indulge, I just know I'll be keen to do it again.

Ayden picks up on my excitement of sitting in reclining chairs in the cinema and teases me, saying I'm cute. I do kind of feel like a little girl at the circus for the first time, but I don't care. It's been a long time since I've had this much fun.

While we wait for the movie to start, I send a reply to Abbey's text message, but she doesn't respond. I guess she's shitty at me for not replying sooner, so I try calling her quickly while the trailers are on, but it goes to voicemail. The message I leave is a lengthy, heartfelt apology and hope it'll be enough for her to love me again.

After our day in the city, we return to Peter's apartment, only to have Ayden declare that he's taking me out for some more.

"Where are we going?" I grin, loving that this is a day of surprises of the good kind.

"Here, put this on." Ayden ignores my question before a heavy jumper lands on my head.

A laugh escapes me as I tug it off my head to see black and white vertical stripes.

"What is this?" I hold the jumper out with two fingers as if it were covered in mud and filth, screwing up my nose in disgust.

"My Pies jersey. Pop it on. You're going to need it."

I frown. "First, why will I need it? And second, ew." I let it fall from my fingers to the floor at my feet as I bite back a smirk.

"Hey!" Sweeping in to save his jumper, Ayden pulls it close to his chest as if it were the most precious thing in his life.

I laugh.

"I take it you don't like the Collingwood football club?" He grumbles, and I roll my tongue in my mouth to hold back another laugh.

"The fact that *you* do has me questioning if I'm even that attracted to you anymore." I cock my hip, placing my hand on it, and raise a brow to be convincing.

I fail.

Before I even know what's happening, Ayden sweeps me up and over his shoulder, giving my arse a good, hard slap.

"Ouch!" Screeching and squirming, I try to break the hold he has on me, but his strength outdoes mine tenfold. "Put me down, you big lug!"

From my perspective, I have an excellent upside-down view of his tight jean-clad arse, so I do what any girl would do and start slapping him back. He chuckles and wiggles his hips as he walks, showing me he loves what I'm doing, so I change tactics and pinch.

"Ahh!" His deep voice turns high pitched, and he tries to scoot forward out of my reach.

I'm laughing so hard that tears spring from my eyes, and for once, I'm thrilled they are happy tears and not because someone has done wrong by me again.

Loving his reaction to my pinching fingers, I do it again, with both hands this time and Ayden's knees buckle before my momentum is thrown off and his cute butt is no longer in reach.

"Girl, stop it!" He hisses and suddenly I find the world the right way up again, and I have to reach out for the wall to steady myself as the blood rushes away from my brain.

I'm still laughing and now seeing Ayden's face trying to be all serious just makes me laugh harder.

He smirks. "You don't play fair, Miss West."

"Miss West, is it?" I challenge him with the same raised brow as before, and all it does is turn his gaze lustful. The look he gives me should be illegal.

"You know all that sass turns me on, Lex. If we're going to get out of this apartment soon, I'd put that attitude away if I were you." He admits with no shame, his confidence making me nervous and at the same time, sending a flutter of anticipation to my core.

So naturally, I remedy that.

I'm on him before he even blinks, my lips crashing against his, the collar of his jumper clenched tight in my hands, pulling him down to my level. Strong hands grip my arse, and my feet meet air as he lifts me off the floor. My legs know what they want and wrap around his hips, gripping his backside and pulling him close to the ache between my legs. The wall outside Ayden's bedroom meets my back, sandwiching me between it and Ayden, causing more friction, and I nearly lose it right there and then.

That is, until a clearing throat douses us with an invisible bucket of water.

Whoops.

"Ah... yeah. Dad, sorry." Ayden slowly unwinds my legs and lowers me to the ground while I keep my face tucked against his chest, mortification turning it red hot.

Jesus Christ. His bloody dad just saw us grinding on each other like horny rabbits.

Kill me now!

"I've left some money on the kitchen bench for you. Enjoy your night out, and try not to have too much fun." Peter's voice is quiet but firm. I can't tell if he's angry or embarrassed. Probably both.

"Thanks, Dad. I'll see you later tonight when we get back in." If I were looking at Ayden's face now, I know it would be a glowing beacon like mine. I can hear the embarrassment in his tone, which lacks the confidence it had only minutes before.

I hear Peter walk away as Ayden tries to step back from me, but mortified me is glued to him, and I refuse to let go or lift my head. He chuckles.

"It's okay, Lex."

"Nope. Nope. Nope." I shake my head vigorously, which just makes him laugh even more.

Trying to grip my chin to lift it, he gives up and reaches for my wrists, unclasping my hands from his hoodie and pulling them out to our sides.

"Look at me." As if I could ever deny his demand. A demand that sends heat to my core. Reluctantly, I peek up at him from under my lashes. "There's my girl."

"Mortified." It's all I can manage to say, and he grins at me, letting go of my wrists and tilting my chin up.

"My dad is probably more embarrassed than we are." He gently strokes his thumb over my bottom lip, and I melt like butter.

"I doubt that."

The whisper has barely left my lips when he catches my mouth in another searing kiss. My body instantly reacts, and all I want to do is wrap my legs around him again. Unfortunately for both of us, common sense wins, and we both pull away reluctantly.

"So," Ayden is as breathless as I am, "the Collingwood jumper. Are you going to wear it?"

"Nope." I push past him, satisfied when he pops his lips into a pout. "I have better taste than that, Ayden."

He growls and slips the jumper on himself before catching up to me, entwining his fingers with mine.

The banter between us is carefree and fun as we walk to the MCG to watch the Pies clash against the Bulldogs. I don't really follow any particular AFL team, probably because my parents were never into sports, so the only footy I've watched is our local boys.

Ayden struggles to believe that I don't barrack for a particular team and makes it his mission to turn me into a Pies supporter. Teasing him with the threat that I might choose to follow the Bulldogs is all-night entertainment, and he even gets the other Collingwood supporters sitting around us to make cases to me during the game for reasons why the Pies are the better option.

The entire experience is hilarious and filled with heartfelt fun, something which I've never really had. I'm now a football fan, and I'm sure I wouldn't even care which teams were playing because I think I'll like them all. The atmosphere, the hilarious banter between fans, the entire experience is unforgettable.

Mostly, though, the time with Ayden where we aren't so weighed down with the darkness that has shadowed our brief time together is absolutely the best part. He's so easy to be with, and just looking at him turns my tummy into a million butterflies.

After leaving the MCG, we take our time strolling along the Yarra River back into the city and head to Federation Square. Sitting amongst the other Melburnians, we huddle close together, and people watch while we eat some Maccas fries. I never imagined I'd feel comfortable with a guy, just being alone together, enjoying each other's company.

Ayden steals kisses every now and then, and I keep myself tucked close to his side, only now realising that I haven't once worried about the possibility of running into my dad, or that Mike will jump out from around a corner.

We detour a little to walk along the Southbank waterfront where the nightlife is kicking up. Laughter flows out from the riverside restaurants and cafes, which adds to the ambience of romance in the little bubble we have together.

A street performer gains our interest as he beats on different sized and shaped containers, tubs, and tins to create an alluring drumming beat that has bystanders tapping their toes. I'm just as caught up in his act when I feel Ayden tense next to me.

Glancing up to his face, I see that he's no longer watching the street performer, but is glaring at something or someone across from us. Following his line of sight, I notice a group of guys wearing scary as fuck expressions returning his glare.

"Ayden," turning from them to get his attention, I tug on his arm, "do you know them?"

Ayden doesn't answer and I look back and focus on one of the guys, who resembles a gang banger that hasn't washed in days, as he pulls out his phone and starts talking into it, not taking his eyes off Ayden.

"Time to go." Without warning, Ayden spins, pulling me along with him, picking up the pace and heading in the opposite direction.

"What's going on?" I stumble a little, just trying to match his strides but he shakes his head and doesn't answer.

A look I've never seen him wear torments his face. It's a mixture of fear, anger, and something else, and it unsettles the shit out of me.

As he pulls me along, I quickly glance over my shoulder to see the group of guys following behind, their eyes trained on us looking like they are on a mission—a mission to kill.

"Ayden?" My heart is racing, and I'm reminded of the terror I experienced from what Mike inflicted on me.

I'm scared.

My voice must give that away because Ayden's gaze snaps to mine, and something like regret flashes in his eyes. I think he's going to say something. Maybe apologise, but he never gets the chance, because as we turn the corner, a car comes to a skidding stop a foot in front of us.

A scream rips from me as Ayden and I both jump back in unison to escape getting struck by the car. Ayden goes to turn, but it's too late. Behind us is a wall of scary fucking guys who don't look much older than we do, closing in on us.

The door of the dark blue car opens and a man looking more like he belongs to a biker gang than what the shiny blue car suggests, climbs out and tuts through his teeth, looking knowingly at Ayden.

"Aydo, Aydo, Aydo, where have you been? We've been missing you." The guy kicks the car door closed with the back of his foot and leans against it, crossing his heavily tattooed arms over his chest.

Ayden is as stiff as a board next to me. My normally confident, cocky guy is gone, which only fills me with more fear.

"Muz." Even though I know he's nervous, Ayden's voice doesn't come out any other way but sure and strong as he acknowledges the thug in front of us.

"Where have you been, buddy? Found another crew to roll with?" The Muz guy pops a cigarette in his mouth and lights it, sucking in deep before blowing the smoke up to the night sky.

"Nah, man. I told you I was out. Been lying low, keeping out of trouble." Ayden's grip around me is hurting my shoulder, but there's no way I want him to let go.

Muz chuckles and the guys behind us join in.

"You must be hungry then, hey? Want a little candy? Sugar?"

As naïve as I am, I know he isn't talking about actual candy or sugar. Ayden told me a little about his past, and I'm betting his old drug dealer is the guy standing before us now.

"Nah, thanks anyway, man. We have somewhere to be. Nice seeing you." Ayden moves to lead me away, but forceful hands grip our shoulders, and we both try to struggle free. That's when Muz, who's still dragging back on his smoke, not looking the least bit bothered, lifts his shirt to reveal a handgun sticking out of the waist of his baggy jeans.

We both freeze.

Muz turns his gaze on me then, "Mmm, you always knew how to find the juicy little pieces of meat to keep you busy, didn't you, Aydo?" Stepping up to me, Muz breathes his disgusting ashtray breath on me and grazes the back of his fingers down the side of my face over the fading bruises. "I see you know how to control her, too."

"Muz, man, leave her alone. She's not from around here. She doesn't know this world." Unfortunately, Ayden's words only make Muz even more interested, and he leans in close to my face as if he might put his slimy lips on me.

I arch back as far as I can until the back of my head meets the chest of the guy holding me in place. Thankfully, Muz pulls back and returns his attention to Ayden.

"You're coming with us." Not an invitation, but a statement said by Muz as he turns to open the car door.

"Ah, yeah, okay, sure. Let me just grab a cab for my girl so she can get home safe." I'm about to protest because there's no way in hell I'm leaving Ayden, and there's no way in hell he is leaving with this man.

Muz laughs. Not a single part of his laugh sounds humorous, though. It's downright scary.

"The bitch comes too, Aydo. If she doesn't know this world, then what sort of gentleman am I if I don't show her?"

Ayden growls and struggles against the guy holding him. Pulling free, he swings a punch, clocking one of the guys in the chin, making him stumble back. Meanwhile, vile ashtray breath engulfs my nose again, and I'm ripped forward by rough hands.

A whimper escapes me as Muz holds me back against his chest, digging his fingers into my arms, no doubt adding to the bruises left by my dad and Mike.

"Aydo, man, calm the fuck down and get in the car with your little bitch." Muz snakes his rough hands up the front of my body, cupping my breast before his fingers wrap around my throat. All while Ayden watches the whole thing, unable to stop it.

Twenty-Eight

♥

It's times like this that I wish I had some kind of superpower. Having superhuman strength would come in handy right about now. Hell, I'd even settle for telekinesis so I could use my mind to get our phones out from the glove compartment where Muz stashed them. Since I'm shit out of luck in the superpower department, I have no choice but to try and remain calm in the back of the car Muz forced us in.

Thankfully, Ayden is sitting in the middle of the back seat with me, so Muz, who's sitting on Ayden's other side, can't put his slimy hands on me. Ayden barely acknowledges Muz during the drive as he keeps me tucked close to his side. His warm breath flutters over my ear repeatedly as he whispers apologies over and over. When he's not whispering to me, he's pressing long kisses to the top of my head and temple.

The car fills with choking smoke as Muz and the thug driving both suck on cancer sticks, barely cracking the window to let the smoke out. As the city streets disappear and we drive through the suburbs, I try to keep track of street signs or shop names to help me get a sense of where we are. The twenty minute car ride takes us north of the city, and I'm sure we're somewhere near Brunswick, but I can't find anything else to confirm our location before we finally pull up outside a large house.

As soon as the car doors open, the loud thump of music greets us, rattling the windows of the house where people are spilling out.

"Lex, just go along with whatever happens and do as I say. As soon as I can, I'll get us out of this." Ayden's voice is quiet and rushed against my ear before the door next to me swings open, and Muz leans in, grabbing my arm in a biting pinch.

"Welcome to our world, pretty girl."

Pulling me forcefully from the car, Muz pins me with his heated gaze and once I'm out, I rip my arm from his grip and square off against him. "Stop fucking putting your hands on me without permission!"

Ayden curses behind me, and the other guys hoot and laugh. At first, I think Muz is going to shoot me down, so I jut out my chin in defiance, and he chuckles.

"Got yourself a real firecracker here, Aydo. I can see why you're interested. She must fuck like a bitch in heat."

I hiss, which only makes Muz laugh harder before he turns his gaze to Ayden.

"Grab your bitch and keep her under control."

Ayden hooks me under his arm, pulling me tight to his side. "Lex, please don't provoke him. Just do what I say, okay?" His quiet words piss me off, but I give him the nod I know he's expecting, and we follow Muz into the house, his entourage close behind us.

Looking at the dense crowd of people, I wonder how on earth we are ever going to get inside. Then, as if Muz is a god parting the sea, the crowd splits, clearing a path, letting us through with ease.

Well, shit, I guess he's some sort of big deal. A gang leader, maybe?

Whoever he is, I know we are well and truly in over our heads.

As he passes by the drunk and high teenagers, they all attempt to say hi or give him a nod in greeting. They all hold some misguided respect for the dickhead who leads us right into the heart of his lion's den.

The house is narrow but runs deep into the property, and after weaving through different rooms and down a hall, we enter a room filled with mismatched couches and coffee tables bathed in low amber light.

Piling into the room, a few girls join us, slipping through the doors before they close. They move straight to Muz and rub themselves up the side of their apparent leader like cats.

"Sit," Muz speaks, and everyone obeys without having to be told twice. Ayden and I remain standing, though, and when Muz raises a brow at our disobedience, Ayden gives in, leading me to sit on the couch next to the armchair holding their king.

"Candy honey, go get the treats." A sharp slap fills the room, and Candy giggles and retreats, rubbing her right arse cheek, which I'm sure is now marked with a pink handprint under her tight red skirt.

"Shit." Ayden curses quietly next to me, and I can feel the slight tremble that sweeps over his body. It's not obvious to everyone else in the room, but to me, I can feel the way his hand shakes on my shoulder and the way his knee jitters a little.

Glancing at him, I attempt to catch his gaze, but he avoids my eyes.

"Hey, it's okay," I whisper in his ear, and he shakes his head slightly before turning to me with a face filled with so much torment.

"I'm so fucking sorry, Lex." He looks broken. I squeeze his hand to provide reassurance. "I just want you to know that if shit goes bad, please believe that it isn't the real me."

What?

I'm confused.

I don't understand his underlying meaning, but before I get the chance to ask, the room erupts in cheers.

"Party fucking time!" One thug yells, and the others cheer as Candy walks back into the room carrying two trays.

"Candy has your sugar fellas." She shakes her hips in a little dance as she holds the trays up, pleased with the attention.

Handing one tray to the cheering thug, Candy places the other in front of Muz on the coffee table.

"Come have your fill, beautiful," Muz purrs to Candy, and she strolls around the coffee table as if she's giving everyone a show.

When she's in front of Muz, she lowers to her knees, seductively giving him her back before leaning over the tray holding white lines of powder. As she snorts one of the lines through a cut off straw, Muz sits forward and palms her arse before lifting her skirt and revealing her bare cheeks underneath.

I turn away as he strokes her skin, which results in her moaning loudly.

Suddenly my hands look interesting as I try to focus on anything but what Muz is doing to Candy, and Ayden's hand pops into view, rubbing his fingers over mine, probably finding our hands just as interesting as I do.

"You and your girl are up, Aydo."

I freeze as I comprehend the words Muz spoke.

He can't mean...

"Nah, man. We're okay. Thanks anyway." Ayden speaks for both of us, and I glance back over at Muz, who now has Candy straddling his waist, giving him a bad version of a lap dance.

Muz drags his tongue up Candy's neck before biting it hard, and she squeals and slaps a hand over the broken skin, now with noticeable indents from his teeth.

She looks mad and upset, but she doesn't dare tell him. Instead, she increases her grinding and unbuttons his shirt.

"I wasn't asking, Aydo. You know the drill." Muz sneers and I shrink back a little.

What the hell have we gotten involved in?

"I can't, man. Sorry. I don't mean any disrespect. I'm clean now." Ayden's nerves tremble in his voice, matching the ones shaking his entire body. The fact that he's reacting this way only tells me how fucked we are.

Muz reaches between his pelvis and Candy, and nausea rolls my gut.

Is he about to bring his cock out?

I realise that would have been the better option, as the black metal of his gun comes back out with his hand, and Muz points it at my head.

Squeezing my eyes shut, I cry out, and Ayden lifts me over his lap to sit me on his other side, trying to shield me.

"Hiding her won't protect either of you." Muz scoffs, giving his gun a little shake. "Once I put a bullet in your head, I'll put one in hers." His brows shoot up before he chuckles. "Scratch that. First I'll test out that tight little pussy of hers, and *then* I'll put a bullet between her eyes." Muz doesn't look like he is bluffing. I don't think I've ever seen someone look more convincing in my life. "There are a few lines there for the both of you. Have them, or eat lead brother."

Ayden's chest is rising and falling quickly, his heavy breathing filling the room. He's scared, and there's no way out.

"Okay, okay." I hold up a hand in a calming gesture. "I'll have some... um, sugar?"

Muz chuckles at my obvious lack of drug knowledge, but it doesn't deter me, and I move to stand to get it over and done with.

What's the worst that can happen?

I get high and stop feeling so scared?

Maybe I have fun?

Or perhaps it kills me.

If that's the case, I think I'd prefer to die from the drugs rather than the bullet Muz has in his gun for me.

"No!" Ayden's hand shoots out, pulling me back down. His shout quietens the room, and Muz raises his brows.

"No?"

"Leave her out of this man. She has a medical condition. This shit might kill her." Ayden's lie sounds convincing, but Muz doesn't give two shits. He takes a moment to consider Ayden's words.

"Either you both have two lines each, or you have all four yourself." Muz lifts a challenging brow at Ayden, and he stills, as they fall into a stare-off.

I pull at his sleeve. "Ayden, it's fine. I'll just do it."

He spins to glare at me, "Like fuck you will."

With that, Ayden stands, taking a few steps towards the coffee table before falling to his knees, his eyes trained on the white powder in front of him. I have no idea what's going through his head, but I know doing this will kill him on the inside. We haven't spoken much about the addiction he had before coming to Fox Pines, but I can see how torn he is right now, and my heart shatters into a million pieces for him.

I can't let him do this, so I stand abruptly. "Ayden, I'll have some too."

Ayden doesn't look at me but sucks a deep breath in.

With his eyes still locked on the white lines of whatever the hell it is on the tray, he shakes his head, his hands clasping tightly on to the sides of the coffee table, turning his knuckles white before he speaks.

"Butch, take my girl outside."

At first I don't think it's him speaking because the voice is in a tone that I don't recognise.

"What?" I whimper as disbelief rushes through me, and go to step towards Ayden but freeze when I see Muz turn the gun back on me.

"Uh-uh." Muz shakes his head as a big guy that looks like a bouncer steps up to me from the side of the room, glaring down at me, oozing all sorts of scary.

"Go with Butch, Lexi." Ayden's voice slices through my heart and I hate how flat and defeated it sounds.

The big guy, Butch, grabs my upper arm and leads me towards the doors. I try to pull away, but this guy is like a brick wall, and I can't budge free from his hold.

As he forcefully pulls me out the door, I turn back in time to see Ayden throw his head back, his eyes rolling into the back of his head in ecstasy and his beautiful nose coated in white powder.

Twenty-Nine

Rough hands push me through the back door into a large courtyard. When I turn to go back inside, a massive wall of scary arse Butch stands in my way, glaring at me with his arms folded over his chest.

Arsehole!

I want to cry and scream in panic and frustration. Why did Ayden do that? Why did he turn to ice and have me kicked out?

Okay, so I get it. He's trying to protect me, I know that, but it doesn't mean I'm not pissed at him for treating me like that.

Now I'm outside in the backyard of the house party, a party where I don't know another single soul, while he is in that room snorting drugs up his beautiful nose.

Four lines. Four fucking lines!

That's a lot, right?

Fuck. I don't know, but I'm almost positive it's too much.

FUCK!

I gag. This time, I know I'm going to be sick.

Turning, I rush towards the bushes by the back door, heaving uncontrollably as I throw up. A deep rumble comes from Butch as he says something like "disgusting bitch" before stepping back into the house and closing the door. There aren't many people back here, but there are enough to fill me with embarrassment as I try to control the horrendous act of throwing up in public.

No one comes to my aid, and when I finally finish, I make sure my mouth is clean by using the only thing I can.

My sleeve. *Ew!*

I need to get Ayden out of here. I need to find a way back inside so I can get to my guy.

Looking around, I notice the courtyard wraps around the east side of the house, so I follow the yard around to the unlit area to find an eight-foot brick wall lines this side of the yard, which joins on to the garage.

Shit. I can't jump that.

Squinting through the shadows, I make out a small access door at the back of the garage.

Bingo!

Rushing forward, I turn the handle and do a happy dance in my head when I find the door unlocked.

Moving quickly into the dark garage, I follow the light spilling from under another door, and with nothing but getting to Ayden in my mind, I hurry forward.

What if four lines *is* too much, and he overdoses and dies?

Fuck that! He's not leaving me, god damn it! Not when I just found him!

The door opens into a butler's pantry lined with shelves of alcohol, and I swipe a bottle of vodka on my way through to use as a weapon, or maybe just to blend in with the others partying inside. Entering the kitchen, I see Butch's broad shoulders over by the door he pushed me out of. He's talking with a few girls, one of whom is rubbing herself up against him like she's a damn cat.

Good work, catgirl, distract him for me.

Heading in the opposite direction of Butch, I end up in the party's eye. The music is too loud, and sweaty bodies jump and thrash on the makeshift dance floor as I try to push myself through the crowd. After getting nudged and elbowed repeatedly, I manage to weave my way through to the other side to peer around the corner that leads to the room I left Ayden in.

It's not going to be easy to get back in since there's another man standing guard by the door.

My heart sinks.

How am I ever going to get back in that room to Ayden?

I need help. I can't do this by myself.

Reaching for my back pocket, I find it empty and remember that Muz took my phone. The last time I saw it was in the glove compartment of his car. I need to get my phone. If I can get someone to come and help me, then Ayden should be okay. *Right?*

The need to get my phone drives me forward, and I push my way through the crowd towards the front door. Once I'm free, I run, still carrying the bottle of vodka in my hand, rushing across the road to the car we arrived in. I tug on the door handle, but it's locked.

Ugh! Of course it's fucking locked.

Panic and desperation have their claws deep in me now, so I don't give it a second thought when I throw the bottle of vodka hard at the side window of the car. The bottle shatters, splashing vodka everywhere over the shiny blue car, but unfortunately, the window holds strong, and a few people standing on the front lawn look over at me.

Shit, shit, shit.

I start crying, feeling helpless, my hands fisting in my hair, a frustrated scream silently lodged in my throat.

Think, Lexi, think!

The jagged edge of a rock protruding out of a nearby garden catches my eye and I hurry forward, stepping into the garden of a stranger's house. I quickly pull the rock out of the bark, testing its weight in my hand. It feels heavy enough. Heavier than the bottle of vodka I had, so satisfied that it will do some damage, I turn back to the car and throw it.

The loud sound of the smashing window surprises me, my mind briefly flicking back to the night I broke into the school with Travis. So much has happened between then and now. That night was nearly two weeks ago. Back then, it was just me fighting against the evil in my world, all alone. But my life changed from the day Ayden Mitchell walked into it, and I haven't been alone since.

The concerned voices of the onlookers remind me of my goal and I hurry forward, nicking my arm on the small shards of glass as I reach in through the window and open the glove compartment.

Yes, our phones are still there!

Taking both phones, I bolt over to the other side of the street to stand in the shadows just a few doors down from the party and call Peter. He answers after two rings.

"P-Peter!"

"Lexi? What's wrong?"

"These guys, they grabbed us. Took us to a party and forced Ayden to do drugs."

"Christ. Where are you?" Peter's tone of authority is reassuring, and I know I've done the right thing by calling him. Ayden will probably be angry that I called him, but I don't care. He can be mad all he wants because there's no way I'm letting him risk his life.

"I don't know exactly where we are. Somewhere near Brunswick, I think."

"Can you check your phone map for your location?"

"Oh, yes." I can't believe I didn't think of that. I pull my phone away and open the map app. "I'm going to text it through now. Hang on." I type in the location and hit send.

"Got it," Peter confirms a moment later, and then I hear him speaking to someone else in the background.

Andrea, most likely. "Okay, Lexi. Are you with Ayden now?"

"No," I cry again. "He's in the house where the party is, in a room in the back. They kicked me out." I can hear Peter moving as I speak. I hope he can get here quickly.

"Do you know any of the guys' names that took you?"

"Muz. He's the main one."

"Shit." Peter curses and then relays that to whoever is with him. "Do you know any other names?"

"Uh, a guy called Butch kicked me out. There's a chick called Candy. I don't know. I don't know any others!"

"Lexi, honey, it's Andrea. It will be okay. We are on our way. Peter is using my phone to call reinforcements. We will be there in about fifteen to twenty minutes."

Hearing Andrea's voice calms me. She isn't panicking. Why isn't she panicking? Her son is in a strange house, snorting drugs!

"You there, Lexi?" Andrea asks.

"Yes, sorry. I'm scared. I need to go back to Ayden, but I'm scared that Muz will shoot me."

"He has a gun?" Peter's angry voice comes down the line. I must be on the speaker.

"Yes. He had it pointed at my head. That's why Ayden snorted the drugs. There were too many lines, though. He wouldn't let me have any. That's why they kicked me out."

"For fuck's sake, I'm going to kill that fucking little bastard!"

"Mr Mitchell, it's not Ayden's fault." I protest.

Why is he angry at Ayden? I don't think I've ever heard someone as angry as Peter is in this moment. It's scary as hell.

I'll have to remember never to piss him off.

"I'm not angry at Ayden, Lexi," Peter growls.

"Peter, calm down. Ringo will make sure Muz pays for this."

Ringo? Who the hell is Andrea talking about now?

"Lexi, honey, how many lines of powder did Ayden have?" I realise that Andrea's calmness is probably because I'm talking to Nurse Andrea right now.

"There were four lines. Muz wanted us to have two each, but Ayden told him I couldn't have any, and Muz said that Ayden had to have all four if I didn't have my share." I choke on a sob, "That's like a lot, right? Too much?"

"Yeah, honey, it is a lot. Is there any chance you can go back and find him?"

"Andrea, no. You heard what she said. Muz had a gun pointed at her head. Her going back in could set him off."

"I need eyes on him, Peter. What if he's overdosing already?"

I'm moving before Andrea has even finished talking, knowing not only that she is right, and I need to be there with him to help him, but I also can't stand being away from him any longer.

"I have to go, Andrea. I'm going to find him. Once I'm with him, I'll call you back."

"Wait! No!"

I hang up on Andrea and storm up the steps of the house. Anger consumes me, taking over my fear and pushing me forward with determination.

Fuck this Muz guy and his gun! He will have to shoot me in the head if he wants to stop me from getting to Ayden.

I'm sick of arseholes trying to control me with violence. Trying to make me do things I don't want to do.

No fucking more!

People inside the party see me coming and scatter out of the way. I must look like a crazed bitch right now, but I don't care. I *am* a crazed bitch, and anyone who gets in my way is going to wish they hadn't.

Big thoughts from a small girl, Lexi.

The thought makes me smirk.

Yep, I've officially lost my mind.

No one is guarding the back room now, so I open the door and burst in. Two guys are lounging on chairs facing Ayden with a look of ecstasy spread across their faces, and Candy is on Ayden's lap, grinding her arse against him.

Bitch!

I see red. Lurching forward, I grab a fistful of her fake blonde hair and pull hard, ripping her off Ayden's lap with such force that she flies back and crashes into the two guys, sending them all to the floor.

"Stay the fuck away from him!" The roar of my voice is unrecognisable, and I love it. I feel confident power zapping through my veins, and the need to inflict pain on all of these arseholes is at the forefront of my mind.

It should scare me at how easily I could cause harm to them without feeling guilty about it. I'm not scared, though, because right now, I'm someone else. Someone dark and twisted and fearless.

My chest heaves and my heart is nearly beating through my ribcage, ready to rip free of my body. Strength and madness dominate me, so this Candy bitch better not try to come at me, or shit is going to go down.

"Ouch, you cow, that hurt!" Candy stands from the tangle of limbs she's in, rubbing at the back of her head.

"It wasn't meant to fucking tickle!" I hiss.

"Leexxxxi baabby." Ayden slurs, trying to sit forward, but he can't seem to lift his body. His slurred voice almost breaks the crazy bitch attitude I have going on right now.

My poor Ayden.

"I wasn't going to do anything," Candy cries. "I was just giving him a little dance, just like Muz told me to." She pleads her case, standing there unaware that her skirt has gathered up around her waist.

The guys are still on the floor and are now drooling over the view of her bare arse, which is basically in their faces.

"You can come sit on my cock, Candy," one idiot says, and they both chuckle like it's the best joke they've ever heard.

Dickheads!

"Fuck, Muz." I hiss. "Do you have to do everything that dick says?"

"Well, duh! Unless I want him to blow my head off with that gun of his, then yes, I do." Candy looks torn for a moment. Almost as if she wishes she didn't have to do what her leader demands. It doesn't last, though, because a moment later, she's opening her mouth and spewing venom again. "You should just go already. No one wants you here."

"I want herrr hereeee." I turn back to Ayden's slurred voice and take in his face.

His lids are mostly closed, his normally blue eyes now almost black, peeking through before they roll into the back of his head as he tries to pry them open. He's wearing a slight grin, if that's what you can call it, lifting one side of his mouth while the other side is slack. My heart hurts just seeing him like this.

"Commme sittt on my cockkkk."

I know it's the drugs talking, but Ayden's crude words bite, cracking my heart wide open.

I move to him, ignoring the snickers of the other two idiots, and grab his hand. It feels cold and clammy.

"Ayden, you need to stand up so we can leave."

"Bitch, you ain't going anywhere until that last line has been snorted up your nose or his." Candy points down to the tray that still has one line left on it.

"Fine," I shrug, walking over to the tray and Candy's eyes widened.

The dumb bitch thinks I'm going to snort it, so her reaction is priceless when I flip the tray over, kicking up a small cloud of white powder.

Candy gasps, and when I look at her, she resembles a fish, opening and closing her mouth repeatedly.

"Damn, girl, I would have had that line if I knew you were going to waste it," one idiot says, sitting up on the floor while his mate lays starfished, looking up at the ceiling.

"That's it!" Candy stomps her foot. Like actually stomps it. "I'm telling Muz." She spins with her lips pouting, and that stupid skirt still bunched around her waist.

If I were a better person, I'd fix her clothes for her, but I'm not, so she can go to hell and walk right out that door looking like the whore she is.

The moment she disappears out the door, I know I only have a minute or two to try to get Ayden out of here before Muz comes back to shoot me in the head.

"Ayden, come on, we have to go." I try to pull him up, but he's dead weight. "Ayden, try to stand, please."

"Nahhh. Stayyy hereee." He waves me off right before his head tips to the side and his lids seal shut.

"Ayden?"

Shit, shit, shit!

He's out like a light. Or dead. Fuck, I don't know.

Panicked and desperate, I slap his face, and I'm relieved when he groans quietly.

"Wake the fuck up, Ayden!" I yell in his face this time, becoming frantic as I take in my beautiful guy slumped back on the disgusting orange couch.

"Looks like you're shit out of luck, pretty girl."

A gasp escapes me as I spin, hearing Muz behind me. Candy is in the doorway looking like a smug bitch, and I'm tempted to go smack the look off her face, however, Muz catches my attention. The look in his eyes is all too familiar, and for a moment, I think it's Mike standing before me.

Predators, when they think they are winning, are so transparent, like they can no longer hide or control their restraint. The fact that I know this makes my tummy churn. I should never have been put in such situations to know this.

Now is not the time to feel sorry for myself, though.

Now is the time to fight.

Muz is right. I'm shit out of luck. Ayden is passed out, or worse, and I have no one here who is likely to go against Muz and his crew.

"Stay away." I hiss, jutting my chin up, feigning the crazed bitch I was minutes before.

I probably look ridiculous.

"Hmmm, no. I don't think I will." Muz smirks. "A pretty girl like you needs some breaking in, and I'm definitely in the mood to break you in."

He steps towards me, and I instinctively shoot forward, latching on to an empty beer bottle on the table and smash it against the edge.

"Back the fuck off!" I scream like a maniac wielding a sharp object.

"Whoa there, pretty girl. No need to get violent." Muz holds his hands up, his eyes dancing between the broken bottle pointed at him clutched in my hand, and to my eyes.

I have no delusions about this situation. I know damn well I'm not only outnumbered but also out-muscled. That doesn't mean I'm not going down without one hell of a fight.

Despite my threat, Muz steps forward.

"Back off!" My scream is piercing this time, and Candy flinches back.

Unfortunately Muz doesn't even bat an eyelid.

"You heard her, Muz, back off NOW!"

Everyone in the room flinches at the boom of the new deep voice joining the conversation. Candy is suddenly dragged out of the room while four large biker looking guys with tattooed bodies and long beards step in, looking all kinds of scary.

Butch has nothing on these guys.

My hand shakes still pointed out in front of me with the jagged glass still aimed towards Muz and I watch his face change from the menacing man threatening me, to something very close to a scared teenager.

In this moment, he doesn't quite seem as old as I thought he was. His Adam's apple bobs as he swallows, and I notice for the first time that he has his gun in his hand, and I watch him tuck it into the back of his pants as he turns to face the four men.

"Ringo," Muz says with a slight tremble in his voice.

"What the actual fuck, man? Do you know what I had to do to fucking keep you out of jail the last time? You were told, very fucking clearly, I might add, to stay the fuck away from Ayden Mitchell and his family!"

I'm not sure who this Ringo guy is, but I think I like him.

"Nah, Ringo, man. We were just fucking around. We didn't mean no harm."

Ringo stalks forward and clips Muz across the side of the head with a slap, sending him tumbling to the floor.

"Dad must be turning in his fucking grave at the waste of space you've turned out to be." He snarls down at Muz who moves to stand back up, but Ringo pushes him back to the floor with his heavy boot. "Stay the fuck there!"

The room falls eerily silent before Ringo turns to one of his biker looking mates

"Bring them in."

The guy nods at Ringo, turning to the door as tears stream from my eyes, contorting my vision as a blurred version of Peter and Andrea rush into the room with another guy carrying a medical bag.

They're here.

The broken glass bottle slips from my hand, smashing by my feet as Andrea sweeps me in for a quick hug.

"You did good, honey." Andrea says against my head as she rubs my back. "Once we get Ayden stable, we'll get you back home."

Home?

I don't even know where my home is.

The thought is temporarily crushing until my eyes find Ayden's unconscious face and I know, without a doubt, *he* is my home.

Thirty

The drive home is long and tortuous. Andrea and the other man with them work their medical magic on Ayden inside the house before a couple of the big bikers carry him out to Peter's car.

Andrea spends the trip trying to get Ayden conscious in the back seat while Peter drives like a madman.

I keep quiet. I don't want to burden them with stupid questions or added worry while their hearts are filled with fear for their son.

I also can't help feeling like the whole situation is my fault.

I mean, if I hadn't been so weak, needing a guy to sweep in and save me from my brother, then Ayden would never have whisked me away from Fox Pines, back to the place which held all of his own demons.

When we arrive back at Peter's, Andrea ushers me into Ayden's room so they can tend to their son without an audience, and I spend the rest of the night alone.

So many times through the night I contemplate going into the living room where they are looking after Ayden to offer help or just to say sorry. But I don't, knowing they didn't want me there in the first place. Even though Andrea didn't say it outright when she led me to Ayden's bedroom after getting home, I could tell she wanted me out of the way.

Eventually I cry myself to sleep at some stage only to be woken by the sounds of loud voices and rushing movement through the apartment. I can't hear what's happening, but I know by the clear sounds of desperation that things aren't good.

I cry once again, cursing my existence and the shame it's brought to this nice family. I cry so much that I eventually cry myself to sleep again.

This happens multiple times through the night before a long stretch of sleep keeps me under. When I wake again, the apartment is quiet, and the sun is filtering through the gaps around the blinds on Ayden's window.

His room is lonely without him. I hate the idea of him never being in here with me again. He has to be okay. I *need* him to be okay.

I'm a mess, both mentally and physically, so I shower quickly before working up enough courage to leave the safety of his room to find out if he's alright.

Padding into the kitchen, I find Andrea looking exhausted, sitting at the small kitchen table with a hot cup of coffee clasped between both hands. She looks up, noticing me.

"Hey, honey. Did you sleep, okay?"

"Where's Ayden?" I glance in the living room, but he isn't there.

Andrea sighs, "He's in my room, honey. He's not really up for seeing anyone right now."

"Oh." Disappointment floods me, but if he's not up for seeing anyone, then it must mean he's alright. "So, he's okay?"

Andrea chews on her bottom lip, looking towards her bedroom door across the apartment. "He's alive."

My heart sinks.

Maybe he isn't okay.

Andrea is being vague, and for the first time since coming here, I feel like an intruder.

I don't belong here.

"Is Peter with him?" I ask, my voice shaky as the reality of my situation sinks in.

I'm in the way.

Andrea takes a long sip of her coffee, staring into the cup as she swallows and shakes her head. "No, Peter had to go and do damage control."

"Damage control?" I frown, confused, fisting my hands together nervously.

"Lexi, honey, it might be best if you spend the day in Ayden's room. Maybe grab yourself something to eat and watch a few movies."

She makes it sound like a suggestion, but I can tell it's more of a gentle order. She still wants me out of the way. She has no interest in dealing with me right now, and I don't blame her.

Andrea isn't like my mum. She cares unconditionally for her son, more than the air she breathes. Right now, her focus is on him, and I'm so grateful that he has parents who fight so fiercely to keep him safe.

I say nothing as I go to the kitchen bench and grab an apple before returning to Ayden's room, where I hide for another hour. I try calling Abbey again, but she still doesn't answer, so I send her a private message through SnapChat.

My message to her is brief, but I tell her I've tried to call and text and that I'm sorry if I upset her, and finally, a few minutes after sending it, my phone rings, and Abbey's name flashes across the screen.

"Abs?"

"What do you mean you've been trying to ring me? I haven't had any missed calls from you, Lex."

"What? I've called so many times."

"Really? That's strange. Hang on a minute." I can hear Abbey doing something with her phone before I hear her curse in the background, "Motherfuckers."

Abbey doesn't swear much, not like I do anyway, so it's always weird to hear.

"What?"

"My parents, Lex. It has to be them."

"Your parents, what? I'm confused."

Abbey huffs down the line. "Your number has been blocked in my phone. My parents have been demanding that I hand over my phone every night before bed. The arseholes must have blocked your number."

"What? But why?"

Abbey sighs, "I'm sorry, Lex. They're on some god preaching mission at the moment. It's as if being your friend is going to make me rebel against them or something."

I'm at a loss for words.

Why would they think that?

I knew they were feeling uncomfortable with my family situation and didn't want to interfere, but how the hell does that mean I'm going to lead Abbey astray?

"Don't worry about them, Lex. You know they're nut jobs."

"I don't understand. What did I do wrong?" I whisper, tears wetting my eyes.

"Lexi, you know you didn't do anything wrong. They are weirdos. You know that."

"I guess." They are weird, but this feels a little extreme.

"Stuff them, Lexi. Tell me what's been going on."

"Oh, you know, just the usual getting drugged and kidnapped by my dad so my brother can beat me and try to molest me."

"Shit Lex. I'm sorry. That was an insensitive question."

"No, I'm sorry." I sigh. "I'm feeling a little bitter today."

"Rightfully so. Is everything okay with Ayden? You guys seem close."

My stomach sinks.

We *were* close. So close that he's taken a chunk of my heart, and now he's paying for that in some kind of hell across the other side of this apartment.

"Lex?"

"Uh, yeah. He's a good friend."

For some reason, I just can't tell her how close Ayden and I have gotten. I don't know why. A part of me wants to tell her about what happened last night, but a part of me knows it's not really my story to tell.

Last night links to Ayden's past. A past he was reluctant to tell me about, so there's no way I'm going to blab about it to anyone else.

"I bet he is a *really* good friend," insinuation fills Abbey's voice, and a small smile tugs at my lips. She knows me too well. "Shit, I have to go." Abbey rushes out and the line goes dead.

I look at my phone, confused, and replay our conversation over and over.

Her parents must have walked in or something for her to hang up like that. What the hell is going on?

A sob escapes me as utter loneliness seeps into my heart.

I don't understand why Abbey's parents feel the way they do. It has to be because my dad was spouting lies to them. I hate that son of a bitch.

The threat my dad made in the email comes to my mind, and I have an urgent need to speak with my mum. I need to know she is still safe, so I call the hospital, and they allow my call to go through to her room. I guess she has been given phone privileges again.

"Hello?" The sound of my mum's voice is surprisingly welcome.

"Mum, it's Lexi."

"Oh. Alexis. This is a surprise."

Actually, I think the surprise is the tone of her voice. She sounds calm.

"I just wanted to check in with you. See how you are doing?"

"That's nice of you. I guess I'm doing okay. The doctors here are tolerable." I can't remember my mum ever sounding this normal.

"That's great, mum. I'm glad they are helping you."

My mum sighs. "I'll admit they are helping a little. I don't see why I have to stay here, though. They won't let me contact your dad, and I can't understand why."

"Don't you remember what happened? With Mike? And what happened to me?"

"How could I forget Alexis? I'm going to need to change my damn name after I get out of here. Have you spoken with your father? Has he said anything about finding the file?"

What is she talking about?

"What file?" I ask, and she sighs.

"If Mike found it, then we are utterly screwed. He could have had it this whole time, for all we know."

"Mum, I'm not following. What does Mike have?"

"Then again, if Mike found it, he would've passed it on to your dad. I can only assume because the money is still in the accounts that they both haven't got their dirty hands on it."

What the fuck is she going on about?

"Mum? What file are you talking about? What's going on?"

"You sound good, Alexis. Strong." My mum's voice sounds peppy and pleased. "You've always been the strong one. The defiant one. As annoying as it was to try and parent your stubbornness and strong will, I know it's what will get you through this. Don't let them get to you. Don't let them get to *it*. When they think you're going to cower Alexis, show them your roar."

What? Am I really talking to my mum right now? Sure, her voice sounds like my mum, but her calmness and tone, and the words she uses sound nothing like the woman who was too wrapped up in substance abuse to raise me.

"Mum?" I ask, because that's all I can manage.

"I have to go now, Alexis. It's time for my therapy session. We'll speak soon."

"Uh... okay. Bye mum."

"Goodbye Alexis."

The line goes dead once again, and I'm left to my lonely thoughts. Who the fuck did I just talk to? Was that really my mum?

Lonely despair grips me, feeding my need to see Ayden. I know Andrea said to spend the day in his room, but I *have* to see him. I have to know he's okay.

I need to see his face and his eyes and hear his voice. I need to hold him and show him how much I care about him, just the way he did with me. I need to take care of him.

Never one to follow the rules, I quietly sneak out of Ayden's room and down the hall that passes the kitchen and leads to the other side of the apartment.

Sneaking past the living area, I see Andrea curled up asleep on the couch. There's still no sign of Peter, so he must be doing damage control still. Whatever the hell that means.

Moving quickly before I second guess myself, I reach Peter's bedroom and slowly open the door, trying to be quiet.

Ayden's form lies on the large bed facing the other direction. A big shop front type of window lines that side of the room, looking out over the city below. It's a great view that I'm sure I'd appreciate more under different circumstances.

I move slowly, trying to close the door quietly, but when it clicks loudly through the silence, Ayden turns to see me.

Whoops. Sprung.

My small smile drops when I notice the angry scowl Ayden shoots me before he turns back towards the window.

"Go away, Lexi." His heated words instantly rip my heart in two.

"Why?" I whisper, fighting back the urge to cry.

"Just go." His voice is level, calm, and void of emotion. Nothing like the Ayden I know.

I can't help it. My need to make sure he's okay urges me forward, and I move to the other side of the room by the window to see his face.

Bad idea.

"Fuck, Lexi!" Ayden bolts to sit up, fury contorting his normally friendly face. "Can't you just do what I ask and fucking go!?"

My lower lip trembles as the venom in his tone hits me like a freight train.

"I don't understand," I whisper, hating the way he glares at me. "I was worried about you. I just wanted to make sure you're okay."

He scoffs, shaking his head like he's disgusted. "Right well, what's the diagnosis then, hey? Do you think I'm okay?"

His bitter tone is a slap in the face and sounds nothing like the boy who only yesterday whispered his loving feelings in my ear. Tears I try to hold back spring from my eyes, showing my vulnerability and I dig deep to find those walls he managed to break down, needing them to slam back up in place.

"You asked me to tell you if I ever needed space," he hisses, curling his lip. "So listen carefully because I'm not going to repeat myself. I fucking want space, Lexi." He surges up off the bed, his face contorted in fury. "Get the fuck out!"

His roar wrenches a whimper from me, and the bedroom door flies open, smashing against the wall before rough hands drag me away so quickly that it takes me a few moments to realise it's Andrea's hands on me.

I'm shoved out in the hall before the door is slammed shut, separating me and Ayden, and Andrea's furious face fills my vision.

"God damn it, Lexi. I asked you to stay in Ayden's bedroom."

"I'm s-sorry. I just n-needed to s-see if he was o-okay." I'm a stuttering, sobbing mess once again. I hate this weakness and vulnerability that I had felt so safe revealing in this apartment only yesterday.

Now, it's not welcome.

Now *I'm* not welcome.

The sound of glass smashing comes from Peter's bedroom, and Andrea pushes me aside and rushes into the room with Ayden, slamming the door shut.

Ayden is yelling. He's in a rage. More things are breaking.

With my heart hammering in my chest, I turn and run to Ayden's bedroom, knowing the only thing I can do for him, for his parents, is to leave.

They have their own shit to deal with, and so do I.

As I throw my clothes in my bag, I think back over the last couple of weeks. Everything has spiralled since Tasha's party and my decision to smoke weed. I still can't believe I broke into the school and helped Travis trash it. Now he's being held by the police while I roam free.

Maybe I should have turned myself in on Tuesday night after Travis filled in the blanks for me. Then I could have stopped myself from acting like a slut and sending mixed messages to poor Nathan. Maybe I would have been locked up, and the other bad things with Mike would never have happened.

That's not right, though. Mike attacking my mum had nothing to do with me. I didn't cause that, he did. Maybe I went over the top when I sprung my dad with that whore in the restaurant. If I hadn't run off on him, if I had stayed and talked things out with him, would things have turned out differently?

They might have in the way that my dad probably wouldn't have gone to extreme measures to punish me, which still seems so over the top. Something more is going on with him, and I can't even begin to know what it is.

Mike. The stuff with Mike still would have happened. Maybe not the way it did and when it did, but it would have happened, eventually. He would have figured out a way to get the lock off my bedroom door. He would have found a way in.

My secret is out now. The whole of Australia knows about what I was dealing with at home. Everyone knows that my own brother assaulted me and tried to molest me. There's no point in hiding it. There's no point in hiding myself anymore.

I'm tainted. Stained. Damaged goods that are far from the perfect persona I tricked everyone with for so long. There's no point in hiding it now. Everyone will see the real me from now on, and if they don't like it, they can stay the fuck out of my way.

Taking off Ayden's hoodie, I lay it flat across the end of his bed and try to remain strong, but fail. For the briefest time, I thought I could be normal.

Have something normal. I honestly fooled myself into thinking what Ayden and I had was real.

I was wrong.

My sobs are loud, and I can't contain them. The pain in my heart is blinding, and I'm sure death would be less painful. I turn back to take in Ayden's bedroom one last time before I leave that sacred space and run through the apartment.

On my way out, I toss the cash on the table that Andrea had lent me, not wanting to owe her anything else. These people have suffered enough because of me. I will not repay them by bringing more pain into their lives.

I hear the agonised tenor of Ayden's voice as Andrea tries to help him while I make my way to the entrance, and with a broken heart, I walk out of the apartment that has been my refuge for nearly a week.

Each step I take distances me from the family who opened their hearts to me, and from the one boy who has stolen my heart and crushed it all at the same time.

I am now more alone than ever, and I don't know what I'm going to do.

My heavy heart bleeds painfully as if a knife is embedded in it, and there's no way to pull it free because it's just too deep.

Are you ready to find out what happens between Lexi & Ayden?
Check out Heavy Hearts book 2 – DEEP!
https://books2read.com/HeavyHeartsBook2

Sarah JDs Books

SERIES TWO

THE INSATIABLE SERIES
A DARK REVERSE HAREM HIGH SCHOOL ROMANCE

INSATIABLE KITTEN (Book 1):
https://books2read.com/KittenBookOne
TAINED KITTEN (Book 2):
https://books2read.com/Kitten2
VICIOUS KITTEN (Book 3):
https://books2read.com/KittenBookThree

SERIES THREE

BREAKING THE SILENCE
A DARK HIGH SCHOOL ROMANCE

SILENT HUSH (Book 1):
https://books2read.com/BTSbook1
SAVAGE SCREAM (Book 2):
https://books2read.com/BTSbook2

SERIES FOUR

THE SCANDALOUS SECRETS SERIES
A DARK TABOO/FORBIDDEN MF ROMANCE

Three book shared world dark taboo series with **B. Lybaek, Sarah JD, and TL Hodel**.
(Books can be read as standalones)

DANTES STORM (Book 1) by B/ Lybaek:
https://books2read.com/SS1zon
LILY'S ASH (Book 2) by Sarah JD:
https://books2read.com/LilysAshSSbook2
AVERY'S FALL (Book 3) by TL Hodel:
https://books2read.com/SS3zon

STANDALONE

SUBBING FOR SANTA
A DARK CHRISTMAS ROMANCE WITH
STALKER VIBES

SUBBING FOR SANTA:
https://books2read.com/SubbingForSanta

SERIES FIVE

THE CRUZ KINGS MC SERIES
A DARK ENEMIES-TO-LOVERS MC
ROMANCE
by B. Lybaek & Sarah JD

TEMPTED BY A KING (Book 1):
https://books2read.com/CruzKingsBook1
WANTED BY A KING (Book 2):
https://books2read.com/CruzKingsBook2
CLAIMED BY A KING (Book 3):
https://books2read.com/CruzKingsBook3

STAY CONNECTED

Want to find out all the Tea before everyone else?
Join my VIP readers list to hear more about Lexi and the gang, plus the other characters that join them along the way.

SIGN UP HERE!
https://sarahjaneduncan.com/newsletter/

Want to join the conversation about your fav characters?
Join my Facebook Readers Group
SARAH'S VICIOUS KITTENS

JOIN HERE!
https://www.facebook.com/groups/
sarahjaneduncanreadersgroup

For more information on books & book
signing events please visit:
sarahjaneduncan.com

STALK ME HERE:

Sarah JD

Sarah JD, also known as Sarah Jane Duncan, is a dark romance author living in Australia with Mr Duncan who stole her off the market back in high school.

Sarah can be found in her writing room plotting out her next smut filled romance filled with angst, violence, and themes so dark you should probably question why you love it so much.

Sarah writes about strong females who have to fight against the odds to find their power, their voice, and their truth. Her heroines possess the strength that only comes from being a survivor, and through their trauma, battles and struggles, they learn to trust again, and find love.

There's nothing easy about their stories. They are hard, gritty, and painfully heartbreaking at times. But what doesn't kill us makes us stronger, right? And when you throw in a swoon worthy guy, or an alphahole that you just want to slap, but also fall to your knees and obey, it's the recipe for a rollercoaster ride.

So buckle up. Read the warnings. And let yourself get lost in the dark stories Sarah creates.